RYAN'S ROBOT

Also By Brian Kacica

Jake & the Dragons of Asheville

"*Jake & the Dragons of Asheville* is original, and exciting. It is a fresh take on the well-explored dragon fantasy, and a twist at the end hints at additional adventures for Jake and his family."
- IndieReader -

"In *Jake & the Dragons of Asheville*, author Brian Kacica delivers a fun and memorable novel that both young readers and adults will enjoy."
- Selfpublishingreview.com -

"Kacica's writing is wonderfully descriptive, and the characters shine with originality and humor. He has a terrific ear for dialogue - especially for the play-ful, sometimes off-color banter of adolescents. Delightfully quirky, the book is a fun combination of the movie *Super 8*, with its smart teen cast and undertone of danger, and the Keystone Cops, with pratfalls by dull-witted characters. Readers may sense a hint of a sequel in the surprise ending."
- BlueInk Review -

"This is a finely wrought, well-crafted and meticulously edited story with wonderful humor and relatable characters of all ages. Even though it's clearly geared for a Young Adult audience, just about anyone can get easily wrapped up in Jake's improbable quest, which is skillfully rendered very believable by the author."
- Publishers Daily Reviews -

"A compelling, fast paced adventure about dragons, heritage and finding power within us."
- US Book Views -

RYAN'S ROBOT

BRIAN KACICA

Magic Penny Press

Ryan's Robot

For Ryan

1

Suspension

Ryan Westbrook stared at the postcard image of the quaint coastal getaway he was trapped in, with the small lighthouse at the end of the peninsula - travelers in clean, white summer wear, with gummy-soled Topsiders and flashy jewelry. He stood at the entrance to the gift shop near the pier on Smuggler's Cove, looking at the rack of swag, equally annoyed by the tourists with well-behaved kids as those with loud, bratty runts. There was a history of depression that ran in the family and Ryan was feeling it.

Just behind the gift shop, running north along the edge of the beach, was a row of dusty white cottages. The Westbrooks were staying in the fifth one up - the one with its shutters painted red. He could see his mother, Claire, drape her wet bathing suit over the porch railing and then turn to look for him. He saw the smile on her face when she noticed him. He didn't return it because she wasn't happy; it was a look of relief. He hated that look. He'd seen it a lot lately.

Ryan was fifteen, but he didn't feel fifteen. He was five feet seven inches, had rough skin, and felt like he was living in dog years. He saw himself as an old soul not meant to be living in this moment in time. These thoughts sprang from the internal machinations of the medication he was on; the pharmaceuticals that his parents demanded and the psychiatrist highly recommended after the last stunt he pulled.

It wasn't the front porch he rammed into at forty-five miles per hour on his skateboard that worried them, but the cars that regularly blew the stop sign at the heavily traveled intersection he had to pass. It was a black diamond vertical death trap and none of the kids in the neighborhood dared to skateboard down that hill. None but Ryan. He ran the calculations and timed it to perfection, then placed an old mattress against the front porch of the empty house at the bottom, leaving his top hat upside down. On the hat was "Zar", painted in gold. When Ryan pulled off these stunts, he was known as Zar the Magnificent, Zar the Great, or whatever he was feeling in the moment. The hat was for tips or wagers. Nothing was free.

Claire and Victor were terrified by Ryan's appetite for thrills. Out of fear, they could only see it as the actions of someone deeply disturbed, resulting from some sort of chemical imbalance; but to Ryan this was an ordinary stunt on an average day. It was Ryan feeling good about himself. It was a moment without depression. He knew he was afflicted, but it wasn't an imbalance that made him a thrill seeker. It was his lust for life and his drive to kill the demons of an ordinary existence.

~

Once things settled (which, to Victor, meant that his son was dulled-up on medication and complacent), he thought the family could use a vacation to cheer everyone up. That was Smuggler's Cove, Cape Cod. The Westbrooks had made the drive for years. It was where Ryan got his first thrills on a boogie board while Victor and Claire watched from the sand, toasting plastic wine cups - hoping Ryan's spirits would remain positive. It was a place of fond memories and better times. In Victor's mind, it was a short term fix for everything.

Victor was a slight man of average height. The one everyone quickly forgot at the party because he was excruciatingly normal at first glance. But Victor was special. Underneath the drab veneer, his brain was working overtime. He was doing calculations, running numbers and juggling formulas that would boggle the average person's mind. Even while he was in the bedroom of their cottage, looking at himself in the mirror and holding up two plain button-downs, he was thinking about the possibility of time travel and how he'd need to live at least three lifetimes to even come close to a plausible set of equations. He was leading the team at Wardlow Technologies, carving out new territory in advanced physics alongside their hallmark work with artificial intelligence, an obsession of his that wouldn't bear fruit for years to come.

The only thing that could shut down the constant processing of his mind was Claire. It was that look of distress he'd been seeing on her ever since the last stunt of Ryan's that caught his attention.

He turned from the mirror, jiggling the shirts in his hand, doing an unusual dance with his hips.

"Which one, Stilts?" Claire hadn't heard that nickname since they first met, but it didn't resonate. Victor gave her a moment to respond, then tried again.

"C'mon, you know you can't resist my signature moves."

Claire didn't bite. She was flipping through a magazine, unable to focus. The front page article read, *Coping With Mental Illness*. As she lay on the bed, her feet hung out nearly a foot over the edge. Victor was reminded of her volleyball days in college. Her height was something everyone noticed, especially Victor, who was several inches shorter.

Victor raised the muted green shirt in his right hand. "What do you think, split pea? Actually, I'm not even sure what color this is."

Claire didn't even look over her shoulder. "It doesn't matter. They're all the same."

Victor could hear the exhaustion in her voice. Determined to alter her mood, he tossed the shirts and hopped onto the mattress. He was lying next to her, looking her in the eyes. She was off somewhere, so he rolled onto his back and looked up at the ceiling.

"I know, I can't get him out of my mind, either. I'm glad we're here, though, away from the city where there's less chance for things to go wrong. It feels like a break, right?"

"It's just giving me more time to think."

"Shit, I never thought to look at it that way." For a moment, Victor felt it wasn't such a great idea to bring them to the Cape. The ocean make you feel small. "Why don't we go for a walk on the beach, or out to eat. Make a date out of it."

Claire rolled onto her side, hiding her appreciation. "You're starting to sound like Ryan."

Victor pulled her back toward him. "Huh?"

Claire had a smile on her face. It was the first real smile he'd seen in a while. "I'm kidding. That's actually a great idea. Now, if I could only get my ass out of this bed."

Claire noticed him taking a hard look at her. When their eyes met again, she was daring him to reach for her, but Victor was exhausted, too.

"We're doing the best we can, right?" Claire nodded her head, agreeing, as Victor continued, "It's tough with the launch date. Can you believe we're actually replacing meter maids with our droids? Damn Wardlow. It's everything until it's not, you know. Family first, then work. I have a feeling these AI might actually change the world for the better. Then I look at us, and I'm worried."

"I know. I see you trying to juggle it all."

"There's nothing more important than you and Ryan. I'm sorry I'm in the lab so much. You're really taking the brunt of all this. I promise I'll try and loosen up my hours at the lab."

Claire sat up. "Okay, okay, I'm ready to go out, now. But, before we do, will you help me with one sticky little thing?"

~

Ryan shook off his disdain for the tourists and looked down the dock, facing the ocean. Hanging off the end, out over the water, was a makeshift hoist with block and tackle for lifting loads from the small fishing boats that would drop fresh catch for the locals. Ryan stared at it for some time before slowly making his way toward their cottage. He had an idea.

It didn't take him any more than the steps to the porch to figure out the plan for his next stunt. But between him and his room, where he'd begin prepping, both his parents were waiting for him in the living room. Victor was holding a glass of water in one hand and the prescription bottle in the other.

Ryan looked at his father. He spoke with sarcasm. "Must be a special occasion." Upon seeing Victor's confused look, he clarified, "That pukey green shirt?"

Victor had a knot in his throat, so Claire started the conversation. "Sorry, honey, but I can't take another sleepless night."

Ryan just blinked and walked past them, disappearing into his room. He returned a moment later with a pair of handcuffs. "Hell, no. No more pills. They're killing me. Anything but those damn zombie-makers." He locked one of his wrists in the cuffs and slapped the other around the wooden armrest on the couch. "I won't go anywhere like this." He tugged on the cuff, showing how secure it was. "No one can escape Zar's cuffs. Not even Zar himself. Nothing to worry about here."

Claire shook her head. She wasn't in the mood. "That's not funny."

Ryan shook his head. "Where's the trust?"

Victor didn't know what to say, so he just repeated the last thing he could remember. "Ryan, your mother can't take another night without sleep."

Claire didn't like being portrayed as the only one affected. "Dammit, Victor, we're all having trouble with this."

Victor nodded, appreciating her honesty, then held out his hand. "I think your mother and I will feel better if you just take these. We're not asking much."

Ryan used his free hand to pick the lock. He stepped up to his father and smiled, placating the two of them, and grabbed the pills. He popped them in his mouth and washed them down with the glass of water. When he looked at his parents, he noticed that both of them had that of relief written across their faces. He almost reacted by shaking his head, but stopped himself from making them feel any worse. All things equal, he loved them.

Ryan walked into his bedroom and shut the door. He pushed the curtain aside, slid open the window, jammed two fingers down his throat, and spit up the pills along with the water he'd just swallowed.

The first couple of nights were easy for Ryan. It was the third that had him stirring and a bit annoyed not only from the side effects of the medication wearing away, but also the kid. The one his same age that got carried out to sea in a riptide, who stole his limelight. He was actually jealous, not insensitive, but jilted that he'd been upstaged by this kid who couldn't tread water for more than twenty minutes. He knew he'd be able to swim for hours if he had to, to stay alive. Hell, it was exactly what he was all about - doing the impossible. *Zar, The Ruler of the Ocean* - and that's exactly what he could be tomorrow when he pulled his stunt.

Ryan reached under the bed and slid out his black bag, the one with a collapsible top hat, and returned his cuffs, dropping them on top of a handgun. He was sweating. It wasn't just the August heat, it was also the chemicals. Three days in and it was all coming out.

He slipped out of his shirt and headed out of the cottage to the sounds of crickets in the moonlight. The cool breeze was a nice relief, giving him goosebumps before the moisture dissipated from his skin. Ryan looked back at the cottage. He watched the lights in his parents' room shut off. That was it. He was now Zar. *Hell, anything was better than being the misdiagnosed teenager, Ryan Westbrook.* He could feel the electricity in his blood as he walked down the pier. This is what he lived for. Just a little freedom and the excitement of a gig. And it would start with the small boat tied up at the very end of the dock.

Ryan dropped his black bag and climbed into it. He grabbed some rope, slung it up onto the deck, and climbed back up to attach the mooring line to the block and tackle. He checked the tide tables on his phone, wrote down the times, sat back, closed his eyes, and waited for the sun to rise.

~

Ryan was startled awake by the sound of someone rooting through his bag. When he opened his eyes, he was in the shadow of a teenage girl who wore an old flannel with the sleeves ripped off. Tattoos covered her arms and a trucker hat read, "Don't Mess".

The sun caught the edges of her hair. She'd dyed it *panic red*, giving the illusion of flames coming out of the side of the hat. She held up his pistol, aiming it directly at him, then cocked her head.

"What's with the tide tables?"

Ryan was dismissive. "It's only loaded with blanks."

She looked at the gun. "Oh."

Ryan rolled over and stood up. "The tide tables are for—"

There was a loud *CRACK* when she pulled the trigger.

When the gun went off, Ryan closed his eyes and imagined himself no longer a heap of flesh. He leaned against the handrail, smelled the ocean, and felt like floating in the breeze before hearing the last of the seagulls scatter. He opened his eyes, stealing a few more beats of time. The girl in the trucker hat was still standing there.

Yeah, he thought, *I'm still alive.*

A smile crept up on her face. "I'm Mel. I slave at the 76. I serve all the *shackers*."

"Zar," he held out his hand. "Thrill seeker. I do crazy shit."

"Awesome. I love a good rush." She blew off the handshake and started digging in his bag again. She grabbed the handcuffs, dangling them in front of Ryan, muttering, "Passé. Not even kinky anymore." After dropping them back in, she unfurled a black tailcoat. "That all there is?"

"There's nothing in the bag. It's out here." There was a pause. Mel was processing his words and looking at the block and tackle that Ryan's eyes led her to. He continued, "I'm gonna play chicken with the tide. Hang upside down with my ankles shackled and wrists tied behind my back. For hours, most likely. I'll either escape or drown."

"Cool. How long can you hold your breath?"

"My record's three minutes, thirty seconds. But, upside down—"

"You'll burn more energy. The waves, the salt, the stress. You'll be lucky to go two and a half."

Ryan was surprised she'd been listening. "That's about right."

"Can I help you kill yourself?" She carried a serious look. "I mean, that's what you're basically doing?"

"And if I don't?"

"We'll party like it's nineteen ninety-nine. I'll be yours. You'll be mine. Well, at least until you try and do yourself in again."

Ryan was nonchalant. "Yeah."

"Yeah, what?"

"You can help me."

~

"Step up. Step up! Get a closer look. Don't crowd. There's plenty of room along the railing to get a clear view of the mastery you are all about to witness ..." Mel's hat was turned sideways. She was standing on top of the handrail, wearing Ryan's wrinkled tailcoat.

"Zar, who you are all looking at, is hanging upside down. He's shackled and bound tight over the water. I checked myself, and you can take my word. Not one of you would ever be capable of escaping those restraints. This is no joke. Zar is attempting a life-threatening stunt. Once the tide rises to the top of his head, the clock starts. He's going to try and break free before the tide rises and he succumbs to the power of the ocean."

"What poor taste." one woman replied, grabbing her daughter's arm. "A boy drowned right here. How can you be so insensitive?"

The riptides were fresh in everyone's minds. Just days earlier, a young boy was swept out in a strong current. The Ocean Rescue Team - a hodgepodge of local firefighters and lifeguards - pulled his limp body from the water two hours after it all started. The red flags were put out, warning tourists about the danger. The local news ran a special report, broadcasting from the pier. This location had been burned into the psyche of the locals and unofficially renamed Swallow Point.

A weathered fisherman, Anker, who stood behind the woman who had clearly adopted the sentiment of the media, grumbled, "Shut up, lady. I got twenty bucks in the hat. He's going down, and he ain't comin' back up. I know the water and I know what she's capable of."

"How dare you!" The woman huffed, took a sip from a sweaty diet orange soda, then yanked her daughter away from Anker. "Let's go, honey, you don't need to see this."

"She should stay!" Ryan shouted, his long bangs now grazing the water. "Everyone should see what keeps me alive. We all have challenges in our lives, and this … I will show you … is mine, and through me, you will see that you, too, may overcome the impossible!"

The thirteen-year-old, Nikki, was moved by Ryan's words. She tugged at her mother, pulling her arm free, cast an evil stare, and walked up to the railing with a smile. Looking back, she watched her mother carelessly walk toward the gift shop as if she'd never raised a concern.

Time was ticking - the water rising - and the tourists were now swarming the dock, many dropping tips and money into the hat; some making wagers among themselves.

A voice rang out from the crowd. "There's nothing happening. He's just hanging. What's the big deal?"

Nikki felt invested in Ryan. She raised her voice above those around her. "It's the tide. The water's rising. It's almost to his nose. He'll need to break free soon."

Ryan was concentrating, to keep his heart rate low, but the waves slapping the back of his head weren't helping.

Someone standing behind Nikki yelled, "He's not even trying to get out. He's not moving. Something's wrong. Someone needs to check on him. Isn't there like a safety person or something?"

It wasn't much longer before Ryan's mouth was covered. A minute later, his head had disappeared completely underwater. The onlookers were starting to talk among themselves, louder than before, speculating. He wasn't moving beyond the ebb and flow of the water.

Mel commanded, "Don't worry. He can hold his breath for three minutes!" With that, the people were checking their watches and phones. One minute passed - nothing. Ryan still wasn't moving; was not even fidgeting.

"He's gotta have some kind of air hose!"

Mel snapped, "There's no trickery here, sir!"

Ryan's head was tingling from a lack of circulation. He was starting to hallucinate, there were strange looking fish swimming around his head. He knew this would happen, but when a large hand broke the surface of the water and reached in for him, he lost count of his breath.

Zar (now being called *The Ruler of the Ocean* by several of the people watching) used his stomach muscles. He curled upwards, bringing his head above water and taking in a huge breath. The crowd clapped. He'd stayed down just over four minutes.

Ryan was confused for a moment when he realized that no one was there. He looked for the man that fit the hand - the hand he'd seen perfectly; even the creases in his skin. He shook it off as another hallucination and held his body above the water for a moment, twisting and forcing a thumbs up, so everyone could see, before he took in another breath and relaxed, letting his body fall back into the water. This time, the top of his shoulders were submerged.

The count began again ...

The second Claire and Victor stepped out of the cottage and saw the crowd, they panicked. Claire dropped her beach towel and started running toward the pier. Victor quickly caught up to her, trying to get information as they passed another couple, pointing toward the water. "What's going on?"

The man wiped the sweat from his brow and shrugged his shoulders. "Some kid's hanging from the pier."

They were already twenty yards past the couple and weren't looking back. Victor passed Claire when they reached the pier. Once out of the sand, he was able to run fast, and began carving his way through the crowd. He reached the handrail, stopped, and got a clear line of sight on Ryan underwater from his chest up. Victor climbed up on the rail and leaned forward to dive, but suddenly felt his shirt being tugged from behind. He slipped back off the rail, landing on his feet.

"What the hell are you doing? You can't—"

"Easy, Mack," said Stan, with a New Jersey accent and large upper frame. "Don't fuck up this kid's show," he said as he shoved Victor back a few steps.

Two women approached Stan, staring him down. "Hey! Watch your language! There are young kids here!"

Stan's girlfriend, Crystal, placed her hand over his mouth just in time to cover a barrage of obscenities.

Claire was moving through the people, her head towering above everyone. She didn't see Victor get pushed. She was determined to discover why everyone was cheering. To Mel, who was up on the rail, Claire looked like a puppet on stilts from Mardi Gras, frantically making her way, her eyes screaming for help.

Victor quickly separated from Stan, almost tripping over a pile of fishing gear. Confused and searching for an answer, he rummaged through the items, a raincoat, netting … then he found a machete and lifted it up in the air. The people in the immediate area stepped back, sure he was losing his grip on reality. No one could place that he was Ryan's father. How could they? With all the adrenaline, he wasn't functioning properly.

"Get back. Don't touch me." Victor was backpedaling toward the handrail. When he cleared the crowd, he saw Ryan, whose lower body began twitching from a lack of oxygen. He'd been underwater four minutes and still counting. The crowd was waiting. Nikki was growing worried, along with a handful of others now feeling the heat of the act and the weight of its consequences.

Victor stormed over to the hoist, reached out, and grasped the loose rope attached to it. He pulled hard, swinging it closer to the pier, then, without thinking, he began slashing at the rope holding Ryan. Once. Twice …

"What the hell is he doing! Someone stop him!"

The third swing sliced through the braided rope, breaking Ryan free. A large gasp rolled through the crowd as they watched him drop like a stone and disappear into the ocean. His hands were cuffed and his feet were still tied to the block and tackle, which weighed forty pounds and was now driving him toward the bottom, fast.

Mel flung her hat into the crowd, dropped the tailcoat, stripped off her jeans, and dove into the air. She formed a perfect swan, then dropped into the water with minimal splash. Victor followed, his feet flailing, slapping the water hard. Crystal pushed Stan toward the handrail, forcing him to back up his bravado. "Go save the kid, babe!"

Nikki picked up Mel's hat and the tailcoat and she put them on, demanding, "Everyone stay calm. He's gonna be okay. I know it."

No one saw Claire drop into the water, but when she surfaced after diving for Ryan, it was clear - she was searching, too. One by one, those in the water took turns diving, but each time, they came up empty.

Nikki yelled, "Someone give me the time! How much time is left? Come on! How long has he been down? Everyone quiet! I can't hear!"

A porcelain-like voice broke the silence. Eleven-year-old Jezebel was counting off, "Two minutes and forty seconds … forty one seconds … forty two second …"

Nikki ushered Jezebel to the handrail. "Don't stop. Keep counting out loud."

Ryan's head was stinging. When he fell into the ocean, a strong current whipped him forward and his head banged into an antique iron bank safe that had been dumped in the ocean by the Smuggler's Cove Dive Shop owner as a tourist gag for the snorkelers to discover. Ryan didn't account for this; he'd never opened the brochures that were left in the cottage. The blow to his head was so hard, he exhaled the reserve oxygen he'd been carefully managing. Working fast, he manipulated the lock and slipped out of his cuffs, then went to work on the shackles. While struggling to untangle the chain from the rope, he looked up to see his rescuers moving wildly back and forth while he was stuck in the lower murky depth, unnoticeable. He floated, weightless and experiencing and unusual sense of calm, until he started convulsing ...

~

Jezebel was streaming the confusion live online to all her friends, tagging the video, #attemptedsuicide, while still holding the count. She'd hit six minutes, thirty seconds. The people were beginning to show the face of defeat.

Just under the end of the pier where the water was breaking against the sand, Ryan surfaced. He walked under the wooden planks and over to a towel folded neatly with a pair of black trousers and a white button-down. He dried off, changed into his clothes, and started to walk back down toward the end where the people were losing their composure - some holding their foreheads, others pacing and shaking their heads.

Mel yelled again at Jezebel, "Don't you stop! Keep counting!"

Ryan kept his head down as he moved through the crowd. He bent over and picked up his hat, poured the money into his black bag, placed the old prop on his head, and tapped Nikki on the shoulder. When she turned toward him, he raised his chin up. All she could do was scream in excitement.

Once the crowd realized what was happening, they roared with elation. Ryan stood on top of the fisherman's gear, then hopped up on the handrail and took a bow. The cheers could be heard back at the gift shop. The emotions that built up in Nikki, got to her. She rushed Ryan and wrapped her arms around him.

"Oh my god, of all the gods we make up. How did you do that?"

Ryan thanked her, careful not to belittle her feelings, and took another bow. At that moment, Mel came storming down the pier. She wasn't feeling the slightest bit sensitive to others. She grabbed her hat from Nikki, placing it back on her head, then spun the tailcoat off of her in one quick move. She threw it over her shoulder, then stepped up to Ryan and planted a big kiss on his lips.

In a low voice, she said, "I thought your record was three minutes and thirty seconds."

Ryan smiled. "It was ... until today."

Down on the beach, Crystal was standing at the edge of the water, holding her flip-flops in one hand, careful not to damage her nails. She was cheerleading Stan, waiting for him as he struggled to get out of the water. "Come on, babe! A little farther. You can do it!" He'd tensed up so much before he jumped in, his legs were cramping. Stan was finding it hard to swim to shore.

Claire and Victor stood in the surf, empty of any enthusiasm and drained of all their mental resources. They mindlessly accepted cartoonish beach towels from a young boy whose mother insisted they help. Ryan was watching. He nodded to himself, knowing he had to go face them. Before he could turn to leave the pier, Mel cleared her throat.

"Don't you want your coat back?"

"What coat?"

Mel swung her arm around, but the tailcoat wasn't there. She was holding the fisherman's raincoat, instead. Her eyes gleamed as she puffed her cheeks. "I get off at ten tonight."

Ryan winked, tipped his hat, and gave his last bow.

~

When Ryan stepped up to his parents, they were sitting in the sand, just out of the tide line. They looked like two young children in that moment, wrapped in beach towels, Victor's feet fiddling with the sand. His shadow broke their silence.

Claire slid the towel down from her head, her relief overwhelming every other emotion. "I can't believe I really thought you were trying to kill yourself. I'm so happy you're okay.

Victor shook his head, thinking, *wow, he's really a great entertainer.* "I have to admit, you had us fooled."

"I was counting on one or both of you to lose your cool and do something. I wasn't sure what it was gonna be. I was ready to cut myself loose during the confusion, but that machete bit was incredible. I only wish I could have seen their faces."

"Where did you get all this from? The showmanship? I guess there's math involved, but—"

Ryan smiled and cocked his chin. Then, with the exact same cadence and tone as he'd delivered earlier in the cottage, he said, "*Where's the trust?*"

~

That evening in the cottage, the Westbrooks were changing to go to dinner. Claire was in the bathroom. She didn't have to look out to know that Victor was struggling to decide which shirt to wear. She cracked the door. "Just put on the green one." They both laughed, then Victor told her he was going to make sure Ryan was ready.

Ryan was in his room, still wearing his top hat, staring out the open window. He had his phone resting on the top of the window sash, set on speakerphone. Mel was on the other end.

"I don't understand," Mel said.

"You don't get *sacrifice?* Look at the history of, well, *anyone who's a legend.*"

"Come on, of course I do. I just don't understand this whole thing about sacrificing it all, and for what? A little fame?"

"What would you be willing to sacrifice to be the best at what you wanna be?"

"That's not fair because … because I don't have outrageous ideas about my future."

"Outrageous? Okay, no disrespect, but you see yourself in a relationship and a family and things like that."

"Totally. But it's not gonna be some cookie cutter shit I've seen on TV. It's gonna be punk."

"Then there's gonna be sacrifices. Likely animals, possibly even babies—"

Mel laughed and replied, "Okay, so there might be sacrifices. But, I mean, how far are you willing to go? What are we talking about here? Next level kinda crazy or what?"

"You've heard the old '*he died doing what he loved*' right?"

"Wait …"

Ryan interrupted, "I'm not, no one's attempting to die. It's not planned. All I'm saying is those giving it all, they've got to sometimes make the big sacrifice.

I'm going all the way. I put a lot of pressure on myself because I want something out of this. If I was a racer, I'd go faster and faster. I've got a lot of people watching on social media. People are tuning into Zar. They're gonna keep wanting more and more. They'll turn on me if I don't do the big stunt, if I don't do the impossible. You've seen the Internet in action. Everyone has. It's a magnification of life. The acts have to get bigger and bigger or … it's not good. If I pull off the big one, I'll be in the ether."

"What's this big mystery? Am I a part of it?"

"I can't take you with me."

"Why not?"

"Someone has to tell the story."

"So, I'm the one left behind to hype the act. I get it. But that doesn't mean I won't be able to meet up in secret, right? There's a trap door, right? It's a trick. Where are you going?"

"To the other side."

"You're scaring me."

"I'm supposed to. Aren't I?"

"Fair enough. So, when are you gonna do this thing?"

"Soon."

"Did I tell you that you're scaring me?" she asked.

"Yes."

"Uhhhhhhh! Okay, can we not talk serious now?"

"You started it."

"I know. You're coming to see me later, right?"

"Yep."

"You better."

When Victor tapped on Ryan's door, there was no answer. He opened it slowly. Ryan was still staring out the open window. He noticed he hadn't changed out of his clothes from earlier, yet.

A breeze came, lifting the small sheer curtains up, which looked like the transparent gown of a ghost. Ryan was talking. Most of his words came off as incoherent. Victor wasn't sure if he was on his phone, or not …

"Everything's strange, the weather, the economy, politics, political correctness - *probably the strangest shit of all*. The population has grown to biologically unsustainable numbers. The cities are being bludgeoned by influxes of young people desperate for work - seeking the illusive fantasy portrayed in their movies and gaming storylines. Artificial everything. Uh huh. Strange shit is happening all over. Our ability to understand what we truly are as a species is constantly eluding the masses. Maybe it's eluding me - I don't even know anymore. Surely this works well for the elite, for companies like Wardlow. They can so easily replace us. God, *just breathing is depressing—*"

"Ryan!" Victor's hand was squeezing the door jam. "What about Wardlow?"

"Huh?" Ryan turned. His head was bleeding. Hiding under his hat was a large bruise and a small open wound from hitting the safe. Ryan didn't know it, but he had suffered a concussive blow. There was some pressure, but he dismissed it as the usual pain associated with one of his stunts. Victor saw the trickle roll down his cheek.

"You're bleeding!"

"Must have hit something when I dropped. I'm okay."

"Let me have a look at it."

"Na, na. It's nothing. Just a scratch." There was a long pause. "Dinner, right? I'm ready to go."

Victor remembered his words, *where's the trust* and let his concern pass.

~

By morning, Ryan was feeling euphoric from the head trauma. His forehead tingled and occasionally he'd catch a cluster of stars shooting around whenever he made any fast movements. He'd forgotten about Mel, and was wondering why the morning seemed like it was running in slow motion.

When Claire asked him if he wanted some scrambled eggs, he just laughed, and then walked out the door to go meet Mel at the 76 because he'd suddenly remembered that he was supposed to meet her the night before at ten. Victor and Claire had missed the signs. Their fear had led them down a dark path with Ryan's depression; their love for him was blinding.

~

Mel finished wiping the dirty side mirror on a tourist's Airstream when she caught Ryan in the reflection of the windshield. She purposely took her time replacing the gas hose and then shot him a smile, but he didn't acknowledge. Instead, he stood - empty - with a confused look on his face. When she turned toward him, she noticed he'd managed to change into a new t-shirt, but he was still wearing the top hat and black pants.

"Milking it, huh?" She tried to get eye contact, but Ryan was still distant. She took a step closer and raised her voice. "The hat—"

Ryan didn't respond. He dropped his head and looked toward the ground. There was a small ghost crab crawling along the edge of the finger-grass. Mel was feeling playful, so she snatched the hat from his head.

Ryan thought to answer her, but his mind had skipped again. "So, what's it like living here?"

She redirected, "What's it like where you live?" Ryan was unable to focus, repeatedly blinking his eyes this time. For a second she thought he was on something, so she kept talking, "It's a broken record."

He finally made eye contact. "Whatta you mean?"

"Every seven days a new batch of shackers comes to town. And there's always at least one cute guy who gives me the eye, tries to get all up in my situation - you know - and then leaves. I never see any of you again."

Ryan mentally departed again. Mel saw it. He rolled his neck to loosen the sudden tension in his shoulders. "Have you heard about these intercepts from space?"

Concerned, Mel moved behind Ryan and started to massage his shoulders. She ran her hand through the back of his hair to soothe him. "Oh my God." She retracted her hand when she felt the bump. "What happened?"

"What?"

"The gash on your head."

"I don't know. I don't remember."

"You don't remember? It looks like you lost a fight with a sledgehammer."

Ryan felt dizzy. "When did what happen?"

Mel's demeanor shifted. "Something's seriously wrong with you. We need to get you some … some ice, a doctor. We need to get you looked at. Right now."

Ryan felt euphoric again. He laughed, turned on a large smile and then looked her in the eyes. "I'm totally fine. A ding here, bump there, this always happens. It's part of it. It's cool; I'm fine really."

Mel wasn't buying it. "Don't move." She walked toward the ice machine, stopping to turn back when she was halfway, "I'm serious, stay right there."

She unlocked the ice box, flipped open the aluminum door. When the handle hit the unit, it made a hollow sound. She had to lean all the way in to grab the last bag sitting in the bottom of the freezer. The second she bent over, the driver of the Airstream was staring at her. She could feel his eyes burning. She made the mistake of thinking they were Ryan's. When Mel shut the door to the freezer and turned back with her confident grin, Ryan was gone. She looked around, but all she found was the shacker with the smarmy smile.

~

There were only a couple people visible on the beach when Ryan staggered by. The clump of angry clouds temporarily clustered over Smuggler's Cove had the visitors prolonging their continental breakfasts.

The previous evening, the Ocean Rescue Team had placed red flags along the lifeguard posts that were snapping in the breeze, but they weren't obvious from the cottages. The post closest to the pier had rotted. It had been freshly painted, but underneath the surface, it was mush. The screws pulled out in the middle of the night. The flag was lying in the sand.

~

Ten year old Samuel Burnbaum was sitting with his mother, poking a tiny jellyfish that had washed up with a Slurpee straw when he saw Ryan.

"Isn't that Zar, Mom?"

The sun broke through the thick gray clouds, blinding Mrs. Burnbaum, who had to squint so she could finish reading the numbers from the crisp white pages of her investment portfolio report. "I don't know, Samuel, but what I do know, honey, is that mommy needs you to spray her back one more time." She reached into her bag and grabbed a can of sunscreen without lifting her eyes from the report.

"Who else would wear that kind of hat? It's gotta be him."

Ryan was dragging his feet through the sand, but not in a playful way. He thought he was walking normally - at least, that's what his brain was telling him. His condition was deteriorating; the swelling from his wound was putting pressure on his brain. To Mrs. Burnbaum's son, it looked like Ryan was pretending to be a zombie, entertaining the boy as he rolled by.

"Hey Zar! Do another trick!"

Samuel thought Ryan heard him, because he stopped, but it wasn't Sam's words that captured Ryan's attention, it was the blanket of warm air sweeping over the ocean that wrapped itself around him. He turned into the breeze, his eyes toward the horizon, where he saw Claire floating effortlessly as she moved out to sea - relaxing like he'd never seen her before - lost in the moment. But Sam was seeing something entirely different. To the young boy, Claire was getting pulled out to sea ... ten, then twenty, then thirty yards out in no time, her arms flailing. She was struggling. This wasn't a hallucination. This wasn't Sam's imagination. Claire was caught in a rip current.

Somewhere in Sam's mind, he'd locked thumbs and hurled himself under the incoming wave, slipping through the backside only to be hit again by another wave. He could feel a pressure in his ears and taste the seaweed and salt, his eyes were burning. He was cutting through the water, quickly closing the gap between he and Claire ...

But this was a vision, a dream. Sam was imagining himself a hero. The hero he'd seen a hundred times over on the television. In the movies. He shook his head and turned to see Ryan, who had just walked into the water, and didn't stop (no dive, no front crawl); just slowly - step by step - kept walking until the ocean swallowed him whole. There was no scream, no struggle. Ryan was visible one minute, then gone the next. It seemed like only a matter of seconds before all that remained was the waterlogged top hat with the name Zar written in gold, ebbing and flowing in the surf.

Ryan's lungs emptied, dropping him to the ocean floor. His feet shuffled through the sand. Tiny air bubbles escaped his nose, floating up through beams of sunlight that pierced the six feet of water above. He looked up and saw the silhouette of a large man. His distorted image grew closer and closer, until he lowered his hand into the water. Ryan recognized it was the same hand from the pier stunt earlier. He reached up, feeling the flesh, but it was only for a brief moment. The hand passed right through his fingers, then it vanished. As he drifted out of consciousness, Ryan heard a voice in his head say, "*abracadabra.*"

Sam stood in amazement as Claire and Ryan both disappeared, forcing him to examine his own thoughts for the moment, before he decided this was all part of Zar's plan. It had to be … just like in the movies.

~

Back at the cottage, Victor was squeezing into an old crepe swimsuit. He'd been delayed by Jim Dowdy, one of his colleagues at Wardlow Tech. They were on speakerphone.

"Vic, it has to be the processing algorithms."

"I have a test model simulator. Do an export and shoot it over. I'll take a look."

"You know I'm not allowed to do that. Protocol, man. Nothing leaves the campus."

"It's fine. Kaz and I do it all the time. Run it through our encrypted sock tunnel. I'm on the last day of vacation with my family, and I'm not gonna be kept from the last few hours I have with my son. I probably won't see Ryan or Claire for weeks with this launch around the corner."

Kaz was Victor's only friend, a co-worker, and a man of incredible talent in the field of artificial intelligence and singularity. He was capable of making a robot look human.

"Shit. I need this looked at, Vic, I do. But I just can't risk the data getting out of our hands. It's not you."

"I understand. I'll be back Monday. It'll have to wait. Listen, I'm going pull the battery from my mobile, until then, I wanna get back to my family."

"You got it, and I'm sorry."

"See you, Jim."

Victor sprayed on sunscreen, grabbed his sunglasses, and threw on a hat. With one hand on the doorknob, and his thumb about to power down his phone, a call came in. He eyed the display and froze.

"Ah, shit."

Victor gazed out at the beach, then turned back to the phone, his finger hovering over the dismiss button. *Damn it.* He started pacing the room, took a deep breath, and just before the call went to voicemail, said, "Victor Westbrook."

Carter Wardlow, CEO of Wardlow Technologies was on the line. "There he is, my resident genius. How are you, my friend?"

"I'm fine, Carter, thank you."

"I'm not interrupting anything, am I?"

"No, sir, of course not."

"How's your family?"

"They're doing great, thanks for asking. Listen, I know it's pressing. Jim just called. If Monday isn't good, then—"

"Family is the most important thing. Well, after Wardlow." He chuckled. "I tell you what, Vic, you fix this issue for me now, and after we launch Eva, I'll give you a full month off. Take Claire and Ryan to Europe. See the sights."

"Really?"

"You know I'm a man of my word."

Victor contemplated.

"Victor?"

"Fine, I'll do it."

"Great news. There's a private jet waiting for you at Nadi Airport. I'll have a car sent to your cottage."

"What if I had said no?"

Carter let out a hearty laugh.

"I'll see you in a couple hours."

~

Mel, who had left the 76 only minutes after Ryan disappeared, stood just a few feet away from Samuel, who'd been waiting patiently for Ryan to reappear. She'd followed a pair of footprints she could only hope were Ryan's, mixed into the myriad of soft marks left in the sand.

"He's going to do something great, I bet. Just wait and you'll see."

Mel's stomach turned. Her skin flushed. *What's Ryan's top hat doing here?* Something had told her to look for Ryan by the water. The life force around her was telling the story, but she wasn't accepting. She stared out at the water, then back to the pier, hoping he'd be walking around with a smile on his face.

Mrs. Burnbaum had gathered her towel and was heading toward the cottages when the Ocean Rescue Team rode up on their quads. A lifeguard was on a Jet Ski, circling where Claire had last been seen, the buzz of their radios crackling.

Mel crouched and picked up Ryan's hat. She ran her finger along the edge of the felt, then placed it on her head, thinking *this has to be a trick …*

2

Polarity

Mia Swillow was young, perfect, and yes … a Swillow.

She was the daughter of "Big T" (sometimes known as *the Terminator* or *the Tank*), Tommy Swillow, the owner of The Fighting Irish, LLC, a holding company in Chimera Beach that operated as a shell corporation which, through somewhat nefarious means, had a controlling share of almost every business that made a profit within that six-mile stretch of beach. And it was great to be the hot, young daughter of a mobster, *sometimes.*

She looked like a young starlet. Fitted denim, slightly faded, low cut. Her t-shirt, besides being ripped and aged with holes that revealed small patches of delicate skin, was cut two inches above her waistline, showing the world half of her belly button. Sometimes her hair was up, sometimes down. It didn't matter. When you saw her neckline, it did something to you. With that, her beauty and youth, her namesake, *the perks*, add in her red hair and green eyes and she was unreal. But that's not what was left burned into memory, it was her attitude that resonated the longest.

She'd tell Noelle (Tommy's girl - the one who was jealous of her nubile magnetism; the one who stepped in too quick for Mia's sensibility after her mother died), "I can handle it. Bring it on. *People gawk.* Say what you wanna say. I really don't care. I'm gonna date a *Plastic,* anyway."

Mia was talking about the AI units Wardlow Technologies had released in the beach community. These extremely advanced AI humanoids saved the city millions each year by employing nonhumans or "Plastics," in Parking Enforcement and Waste Management. Known as the "*The STEMs*", the AI were pretty much hated by everyone who was a critical thinker. *They saw the inherent danger.* Mia's brother Jimmy hated them more than anyone. He wasn't much of a critical thinker, but he had a thousand reasons why he hated them.

Mia wasn't going to actually date one of the city workers, but she told anyone who rubbed her the wrong way that she would, and it sounded like she meant it.

She got so much attention from the living that she'd learned to stuff their advances into a corner of her mind that she'd decided to deal with later. But for now, she said, "I'm interested in the artificial—"

A line Noelle would laugh at before she'd step out onto the patio of the penthouse and fire up a cigarette, thinking about what it might actually be like to have a man-slave. One who, unlike Tommy, that didn't still fart and burp in front of her. She was jealous of everything Mia had and everything Mia didn't have. That's just how Noelle was wrapped up.

She never wanted to have kids. She knew she had issues. Noelle had taken a personality questionnaire online, honestly answering every line of the forty-minute test because she was having trouble staying in a relationship. *A banner ad on her social media profile claimed this would help.* When the outcome was revealed, she had classic narcissistic tendencies. She made some changes which, summed up, meant she'd date a guy who either didn't want kids, or who already had them and just wanted to have fun, at that point.

Mia walked through the kitchen, daydreaming - thinking about the A6-NINE Android she'd just seen issue a parking ticket, slipping it under the windshield wiper of her brother's car out front. When she passed Noelle, who was dropping her peppermint tea bag in and out of her porcelain cup, Mia didn't acknowledge her at all. She went straight to the refrigerator, pulled out a can of sparkling, organic energy drink, cracked the seal, and gulped down a couple of ounces. She turned and went to the sliding patio doors, but before she could unlatch the locking mechanism, Noelle was radiating a stress signal.

"Why can't you just recognize that I am here? Is it that hard for you?"

Mia slid the patio door open and wordlessly walked outside. Noelle moved closer to the screen. She watched Mia lean against the railing, then scanned the back of her legs, hoping to find a blemish or some dapples, but there were none.

"You should put pants on if you're going to be outside."

Mia only turned to respond because Noelle had broken her peaceful state of mind.

"My dad gave you a gold card, your own room in the penthouse, and a BMW, which says it all. So basically, you have everything any woman of your age and taste could ever ask for, but now you want my approval, too?"

"You could be nice."

Mia walked over to the patio door and slid it closed. She spoke through the double paned glass, "I'm being nice."

Noelle opened the door to speak. "You're daydreaming about those androids again. I can see it in your eyes. Your father is going to be crushed if you turn out to be some internet loser who identifies with robots more than she does with real humans."

"I only shared that with you because you mentioned how sweet it would be to have one as a sex slave. You're the mental case. Not me. I'll never be you, even on my worst day. Now, either shut the door and go back to your stupid tea - which, by the way, isn't capable of detoxing the amount of processed shit you put in your body, or do us both a favor and jump over the balcony. Kill two birds with one fall."

"You're clever, but just wait until Tommy finds out you've been fantasizing about robots. He'll have you in for psychiatric evaluation."

"Noelle, honey, the last time I needed to clear my head, my father let me buy a motorcycle and race it around the track."

"Yeah, and look what happened. You lost your fucking arm."

Mia pulled her sleeve up, exposing her artificial limb, the result of an accident at the track that day - the day that Danny Fury, a long time Swillow family friend, instructed her in beginner motorcycle racing lessons at the Chimera Track.

She waved her arm in the air, twiddled her fingers, and laughed.

"I could crush your throat with one motion, if I wanted to. I've been made better by technology while you're getting more and more stupid through pharmaceuticals. So, keep it up. We'll see how long my father puts up with your whiny bullshit before you get replaced by a younger, newer fuck toy."

Noelle slammed the doors shut, then slowly walked over to her cup. She took a sip. It was ice cold.

Pissed off, she poured her mint tea into the sink and flipped on the television.

Rebecca Anderson from KCLT news was live outside Mayor Sanders' office. It wasn't unusual for her to have a candid moment with the local politician. He was a longstanding, outspoken proponent of all things community, with a dark side few would ever hear about, but Mayor Sanders was a man of the people.

"So, tell us how you're preparing to face off with the dynamic younger candidate, Bill Caldwell? He's a local businessman with several allies in and around Chimera's public offices. The race does seem to be pretty evenly distributed between the two of you."

Sanders took a sip from a coffee he'd just picked up from a local shop. He held it up to the camera, displaying the name Sally's Best.

"Rebecca, how you win a race is easy. You care for the people and the important issues and you back them up by showing support. Not only verbally, but financially. I buy a family-roasted cup of Java from Sally every afternoon. I buy deli meats perfectly selected and sliced from Vito's. My car is serviced with care at Curtis's Luxury Automotive. I have a membership at Rock's Gym, and I don't even need to exercise because I'm out and about working for the residents of this wonderful community. And the list goes on. I am someone the people can believe in and trust, when it comes all the way down the line. I'd jump off a cliff for the people of Chimera, and they know it."

Rebecca smiled.

"Let's hope you don't have to, Dick." Rebecca raised her eyebrows, joking with the audience, to the camera.

"If I may, one question the residents have been asking me to address, if I had the opportunity, is how far is the artificial human situation going to go? What I mean is, the people of Chimera are cautiously optimistic, and rightly so. I find the STEMs difficult to describe, and maybe that's the problem. They should have some other name associated with them, but how much more of this type of technology will the town have to engage with?"

Dick took another sip of coffee and purposely flashed the logo, with a wink.

"It's all a matter of what the people are happy with. If we cut taxes by implementing some artificial parking meter officials, then that's a great thing. No one wants more taxes. Now, if we start seeing a rise in city contracts on the table in front of us, that are asking for the city to accept more and more of these types of humanoids, then this is something we will have to address. Is it okay to have more robots? Let's be candid, that's what they are, really, human-looking robots. Let's just say this, let's answer the question that Caldwell will most certainly sidestep. No. Chimera will not become a city run by artificial beings. We will only accept what is necessary to enhance our lives. Chimera will remain one of the brightest beach communities in the U.S., and will do so by remaining a beach community dominated by high-quality, family-owned businesses that care about those who come to visit this special place."

Rebecca turned to the camera. "And there it is, right from Mayor Sanders's mouth. The people of Chimera come first. This is Rebecca Anderson, KCLT News."

3

36 Down

Jack Kutter, aka Diamondback Jack, was a rare combination of assassin and academic; a top graduate from West Point who led a spook team during Middle East operations, tasked with pinpointing the hush lists of those who were financing extremist cells. He was responsible for three dozen high-profile targets his team scooped up during the raids. He did his job - did it well. It had been a few years since he'd removed his boots from foreign soil and planted them deep in the woods of West Virginia. He'd let his hair grow out, living off the grid - needing an escape from all the violence. An old contact from West Point gave him an opportunity to run a quiet operation in the backwoods. The government had a massive radio telescope in Green Bank, Virginia, searching the skies, and they'd found something unique.

They put Kutter in charge. His credentials were perfect. Not only could he protect the interests of the operation, but he also understood the technical side of the work they were doing, making him an invaluable asset to the project.

Kutter's cabin was about thirty miles north of the Green Bank facility. Even though he was off the grid, the cabin was set up with modern amenities. The cooking range ran off propane and his power was solar. The only project he'd left unfinished was his septic system. He'd been using lime in the old outhouse, but Kutter was okay with this. He could rough it like no one else. He loved working with his hands in the solitude of the wild. He'd often sit for hours, relaxing his mind with crossword puzzles when he wasn't hunting.

Intensity at the Green Bank facility had been elevated, recently. The crypto team he was managing was onto something special. They'd been trapping scrambled signals for years, attempting to crack their code, but today they'd discovered a pattern – a repetition in all the signals that matched. These weren't the sounds of pulsars or waves coming from stars out in the universe. These were canned messages coming from some unknown variable. The group was excited, but even more curious, now. Was it Russian? North Korean? Could it be extraterrestrial?

Kutter had the transmissions in his possession for quite some time, so it was just a normal day for him. He ate, smoked, and drank a little. Then hit the outhouse, wound up his hand crank flashlight, and hung it on a rusty nail. He took out his crossword book and stared at the last clue of the puzzle that had evaded him earlier, on his morning ritual. The word was seven letters and the clue was: *Free Fall.*

How the hell is this still eluding me?

Kutter wrapped his hand around the rattlesnake trophy he wore around his neck. He rubbed the soft end a few times. Somehow, this helped him think. Shit. The glow of the flashlight began to diminish, its charge was dying. He reached up and fumbled, dropping it on the floor right when he had the word on the tip of his tongue. *It's … It's …* there was a loud snap from an animal trap he'd set days earlier. *It's gravity! The word is gravity!*

The sound of footsteps stole his attention. *There was nobody within miles of his cabin.* Kutter rolled up the puzzle book, grabbed the rifle leaning against the door, and shot up. He was so distracted, he forgot his pants were still at his ankles. When he pushed open the door he fell onto his side, tumbling down a small hill, laughing, "Gravity!" He quickly tucked into a tactical roll, landing on his elbows with a steadied gun.

Fifty feet away, pawing at the trap, was a large black bear. He'd chased a rabbit inside, and was crushing it to get him out. Kutter pulled up his trousers and raised his rifle, but dropped his finger from the trigger. He knew this bear. Had even given him a name, *Hank*.

Hank was named after Kutter's late uncle, Henry, his father's brother, who was a decorated colonel in the Army. After his father died when Kutter was thirteen years old, he moved in with his uncle, who'd taught him how to be a man the hard way. He was subjected to daily military training exercises that were supposed to prepare him, like his uncle had done at Fort Bragg. Kutter was a weak, soft-spoken kid before Henry. His uncle's methods weren't for the faint of heart, or legal, for that matter. There were many steel toe boots to the ribs and fists to the face until Kutter learned to defend himself.

When Kutter returned stateside from Iraq and moved to the woods, he drowned himself in alcohol. Late one evening, he got so drunk that he left a pot of stew simmering on the range and the front door unlatched. He lost consciousness and passed out face first on the kitchen table, the bottle inches from his hand. The bear got in. That was easy. But getting the stew would prove to be too much of a challenge for Hank. The propane was almost out, barely flickering on the range, but the iron pot was still scalding hot. When Kutter woke, the bear was pushing the side of his face with its wet nose, trying to decide if he was good eating. It was the heavy amount of alcohol vapors Kutter was exhaling that turned off the bear, but when he jerked his head and tried to roll away, Hank took a swipe that ripped his left eye open. This was the last time he saw Hank - until today.

Kutter lowered his rifle and watched Hank bat the cage around. He looked thin and weak. He had a pronounced limp from the bone in his leg that never healed properly - the one Kutter had hit with a claw hammer he'd found lying next to him that night on the floor. It didn't take long for Hank to figure out a way to pull the rabbit out – he tore it apart and devoured it in seconds. He sat and licked his paws, setting his eyes on Kutter, who was now upwind. Hank raised up, sniffing the air. He knew the smell of *Diamondback Jack* as much as Kutter knew him. He raised the rifle and took aim

"You look like shit, Hank."

Out of the sky, a powerful spotlight broke through the trees and lit up Hank, scaring him off into the woods. Kutter dropped his rifle a second time and looked up, recognizing the helicopter from the sound of its blades. All he could think was, *it has to be important for them to arrive like this.*

Two men dropped down on zip lines and walked over to him.

Craig Chalmers, from the Green Bank operation, was the first to address him. "Sir, Parminder's cracked some of the loose code on the signals."

"You could've waited three seconds. I had Hank in my sights."

"We saw. Big son of a bitch. Sorry, sir. Anyway," Chalmers handed Kutter a satellite phone, "she's on the line."

Kutter tucked the phone to his ear. "I'm listening."

"Jack, we have great news. The team's cracked a strip of code from each transmission that amounts to a series of letters. The interesting bit … it's repetitive. All the transmissions carry this strip. It's a signature of some sort."

"And?"

"It's leading us to a technology company in New York that's heavily vested in artificial intelligence. I've made contact with their CEO, Carter Wardlow. He's agreed to meet with you."

4

Free Fall

Monroe Wardlow was a titan in the world of robotics. He'd built the early models that all other succeeding robots would be built upon. He set the standard for morality with regards to artificial intelligence and its impact on society, publishing several articles on the future prospects and impacts of living with AI. Monroe was even a consultant to the White House on such matters.

He was a business magnate, but had a colossal heart, and he'd built Wardlow Technologies from the ground up. Monroe was a man of the times. He'd amassed a large art collection and made several donations to the city, whose mayor at the time had had a small statue erected in his likeness down by the water on the boardwalk, even after Monroe protested. He was a reserved man who never put his face in the limelight and detested the newspapers, who saw him as a threat.

Before Monroe died, he made one last master stroke. He managed to strike a deal with the government to have the land use permits along the shoreline changed, so that he could purchase them and have Wardlow Technologies inhabit the old abandoned military base.

Not too far from Brooklyn, on the coast of New York, sat Fort Mystic, a defunct military base the people of Chimera Beach had forgotten. The facility stretched for almost a mile along the coast. The grounds were overgrown with weeds and walls peppered with graffiti, but it hadn't been neglected or abandoned. This was all a facade. Monroe's son Carter was now in charge and was forging on with the work.

There were rows of cameras lining the exterior, their feeds piped deep into the earth. Below the battle-tested concrete lay a vast network of high-tech laboratories where an army of employees worked. There was a small world down there, filled with an expert in almost every field. From computer engineers to linguistics experts, Wardlow had it.

A series of elevators connected the scientists of Wardlow Technologies between the many subfloors to support Project ICE (Integrated Cybernetic Expansion). The program developed artificial sentient beings (dubbed STEMs) to replace Chimera Beach's human parking enforcement officers. After ten years, the androids were released into town, making Wardlow the first to successfully integrate AI into society.

Carter Wardlow was a forty-eight-year-old billionaire with a mansion in the Hamptons which he'd pop over to on many occasions. The estate was well kept with impeccable interior designs. Photos of his first floor rooms were in *Architecture Digest* on more than one occasion, due to the amount of modern art, glasswork, and exotic furniture his designer was decorating with. One of the larger main rooms was dedicated to his father, with a family history in pictures, trophies, and other memorabilia. Another was built into a gallery with rotating pieces he'd have the staff handle, keeping the walls filled with exciting works for guests to admire.

When Carter didn't feel like the ride to the estate, he'd stay at his multi-floor penthouse loft, which happened to be in the Universal Investments Tower directly across from the condo owned by the head of the Irish Mob, Tommy Swillow. The only thing keeping them apart was the security and incredibly well-landscaped gardens that blocked the view from across the way.

Carter was Victor's boss, the CEO of Wardlow Technologies, and he was about to add another title to his name.

While enjoying his morning cup in the stretch limousine on the way to Fort Mystic, Carter received a phone call - one he had been hoping to get for several weeks, now. Gail Schlesinger, head of acquisitions for the Metro Museum, was sitting in her office, which sat over the terrace of sculptures in the postmodern wing. She was looking at an article in the newspaper with the headline *The Met Gets A Lifeline*. She was on speakerphone.

"I apologize. It's terribly early, but this was the only time I knew I could get you on the phone."

Carter sipped his French-pressed Sumatra. "I didn't sleep for long. I've been up for hours, with all that's going on. There's a lot of excitement, and let's just say I'm happy you did call. I'm hoping this will make my ride to the helipad one that I won't ever forget."

"I know you realize this was all a formality, and we sincerely hope you didn't think we were taking this time to further vette you in any way."

Carter opened a small compartment. Inside were his monogrammed cuff-links. He placed the "C" on his left cuff and the "W" on his right. He was right-handed, and so he placed the "W" there, because he wanted to shake with a "winning" hand, as well.

"Gail, let me just say this. And I'm repeating myself here, but that donation, whatever ungodly amount it was I gave, was to have no bearing on this decision. So, please, let's not dance around it further. What has the board decided?"

"Carter, on behalf of the entire board, we are formally accepting your donation, and we are also going to add your name to the building. We will no longer be the Metro. Instead, we will be the Wardlow Metropolitan Museum of Art."

"I'm thrilled, hours away from launching Eva, and now *this*. You're fantastic, Gail."

"Monroe's collection is a fantastic addition to the museum, and when you decided to add your personal pieces, those early robots with Eva's launch and Chimera pushing itself into the future, we would be remiss if we didn't take this wonderful opportunity to forge such a wonderful relationship."

"So, when do we set a date?"

"I have the best PR team working with our in-house events coordinator. We will be in touch with dates and details. We certainly don't want any scheduling conflicts with all that's going on."

"Excellent. In the meantime, if you want to catch up on all things Wardlow, tune into KCLT in an hour. Rebecca thinks she's going to surprise me with an interview on her morning show."

~

On the east end of Wardlow's campus were four helipads, each marked with a number and a large "W" in the center. There was a small fleet of new Bell executive helicopters waiting in a hangar just opposite the airstrips. One had pulled out earlier at 4 a.m. It was on Helipad Two, with a pilot doing his routine pre-flight checks.

Carter's limousine passed the security checkpoint, cut across the property, and parked on Helipad One. There was no movement until an SUV pulled up next to the stretch Ford and parked. Jack Kutter hopped out and walked around to the rear door. He opened it and slipped into the back seat with Carter.

"What a day this is gonna be. And before you gloat, I've got some bad news."

Carter stared forward. "There's nothing you can say that will get to me this morning."

"The computing power over at Green Bank wasn't enough to break the encryption."

Annoyed, Carter turned. "You saying you used my guys for this? You pulled my guys off their work to help you?"

"We've cracked those signals, Carter."

"Then, what's the bad news? That's great, right?"

"The bad news is, it's all junk data. There's nothing there."

"These signals are coming from Jupiter. They have my name on them, and you're telling me nothing is there?"

"I know."

It was 5 a.m. The glow of a full moon was still competing with the facility lights as they walked over the company logo to enter the aircraft. The pilot began the startup sequence, bringing the engine roaring to life. The chopper thrust upward, taking off into the early morning air just as the sun peeked over the eastern horizon, casting a sliver of light along the coastal freeway of Chimera Beach and lifting the blinds along the south shore of Long Island.

Only a few years back, a tidal wave had destroyed most of the coastline property, forcing a fast rebuild and much-needed gentrification of the tacky strip mall and flimsy apartments that once dominated the area. For the moment, it looked like the perfect getaway Mayor Sanders had been touting during his re-election campaign.

Shattering the silence was the sound of the new hybridized corporate Bell helicopter engine. Even though they claimed their executive choppers were significantly noise-reduced, as it broke from the marine layer, then hovered over a row of condominiums, Tommy Swillow, who resided in the penthouse suite of the Argyle Building, shot out of bed. He'd been annoyed by this particular sound before and he knew whose helicopter it was. You couldn't miss the large "W" on its chassis.

"Goddammit! That's it. It's time I pay you a visit, Carter."

If anyone else had said those words, it wouldn't mean a thing. But Tommy "the Tank" Swillow, who was quietly running the Irish Mob (these days it wasn't called the Mob, but that's exactly what it was), was a man that no one crossed in Chimera Beach.

The Chopper zipped across the early morning sky, made a sharp cut, then hovered above the freeway. The pilot turned to Carter, who was with Jack Kutter and mayoral candidate Bill Caldwell, "We're here, sir."

Carter smiled and tapped Bill on the shoulder. Kutter had his head buried in a crossword puzzle. "What do you think, Bill?"

In the billboard, Eva was snuggling the small dog to her chin with a large smile, and the caption read, "It's okay to ask me how I'm doing. Let's be friends!"

"It's great, Carter. I'm happy we could pull this off, and it is beautiful, the sunrise and all, but you brought me up here to see a billboard? We could have driven by in the limo."

"Well, I've got a few other things on my mind."

"Let me guess, you're going to want me to approve more AIs, once I'm elected?"

"Soon as I prove her success. And, oops, hold that thought, Bill. I've got an important call coming in. Right on time." Carter signaled Kutter, who moved out of view. Once he accepted the call, it synched to the on-board monitor. Carter was all smiles. "Good morning, Becky."

Rebecca Anderson, a reporter for the local NBC affiliate KCLT, was leading a talk show panel for a later morning airing. She responded, "Morning, Carter. Can you give me a few moments for the morning news?"

"Just you?"

"No, I promise we'll be fair, though."

The signal dropped for a moment.

Rebecca was repeating, "Carter, are you with us?"

"I'm here, Becky, and you are in luck. Bill Caldwell is here with me."

"You're kidding! Will he go on?"

"That's why he's here."

Bill clenched his teeth. He didn't like to be unprepared.

A producer came on the line. "Rolling in 10-9-8 …"

"Good morning, Chimera Beach. We are here with the Director of the Human Lives Matter movement, Professor Allen Fenton, and City Council member Roger Daniels. Today we have a real treat, an exclusive interview with Carter Wardlow, CEO of Wardlow Technologies, who is accompanied by mayoral challenger Bill Caldwell. Good morning, gentlemen."

"Good morning, everyone," Caldwell replied.

"It's a glorious morning in Chimera Beach," Carter added.

"So, let's dive right into it," Rebecca said. "This is a historic day for you and Wardlow Tech."

"I'd like to think it's a historic day for the entire world," Carter interrupted.

"Or, it could be the day to mark on your calendar as the end of civilization as we know it," Fenton jabbed.

"A bit dramatic, don't you think, Professor?" Carter snapped back.

"You know our stance at HLM, Mr. Wardlow. You are playing with fire, and will get burned."

"So, when will Eva be activated? Is she among us now?" Rebecca asked.

"Eva is sleeping safe and sound with Aidan. She will awake at 7 a.m., with the rest of the town. I envision her being a model citizen and blending in seamlessly."

"Of course you do, but can tell me more about her? What the people can expect? How is she different than your first release?"

"What? The parking enforcement androids? You're joking, right?"

"Yes, the STEMs. And, I am not joking. Eva has just been a curiosity until now, when people will see her walking the streets with her dog. Or, maybe at a movie theater or restaurant."

"How is she *not* different, is the proper question. Superficially, we've fixed the texture and temperature issues."

"The skin, you mean?"

"Yes, I assure you. Nobody will be calling her a *squid.*"

Rebecca laughed. "I see you have a sense of humor about that."

"Look, the STEMs have issues. I learned a long time ago that you have to own up to your mistakes. Speaking of, you still with that husband of yours?"

"I see what you did there, and I'm ignoring that question."

"That's not a yes."

"Tell me more about Eva, please," Rebecca diverted.

"Is nobody going to speak on the *human* job loss from his first *endeavor?*" Fenton asked.

"Please, Professor," Rebecca said. "You'll get your chance. Let Mr. Wardlow respond."

"Thank you, Becky," Carter said. "What you will be witnessing is historic. Eva's intelligence, appearance, and ability to learn and adapt have never been seen before. The possibilities with her advanced technology are endless."

"Like creating low-empathy war androids for the military?" Daniels interjected. He then addressed Caldwell. "It's common knowledge that you have a huge lead in the polls and, I must say, seeing you in that helicopter is worrisome. *If* you are elected—"

"*When*," Caldwell corrected.

"Fine. *When* you are elected, are we finally going to get some regulation, here? It's no secret that Wardlow has military funding. Can't you see where all this is going?"

Caldwell replied, "Okay, let's all calm down. Carter has always been a straight shooter, and Wardlow's a great friend to our town."

"*Friend* being a code word for votes and money," Fenton spat.

"I believe Eva will fit in just fine, and the town should embrace her," Caldwell continued.

"That's because you're in his pocket."

Carter had heard enough, "He's just very excited by the possibilities, as we all are. Please, I implore Chimera to give Eva a chance. Let's not sour the public's opinion before they've even met her."

"Met *her*?" Daniels mocked, "She is an *it*, and *it* is an android."

"I assure you, Councilman Daniels. You will not be able to tell the difference."

"That's exactly what am I'm afraid of."

"Precisely," Fenton said. "This is the inherent danger. When we reach the logical conclusion here."

"And, what's that, Professor?" Carter asked.

"The point where we don't know who is real and who isn't. Your father, Monroe, wrote several essays on this exact issue. How does it feel to be doing a complete one eighty from his desires for the future of the company?"

"And on that note," Carter said, "I'm afraid we'll have to cut this short."

"Please, I just need five more minutes to take us to break," Rebecca pleaded.

"This day should be about Eva, not me or anyone else. Welcome her when you see her on the street. Talk to her, befriend her. You will not regret it." Carter disconnected the line.

"Well, that could have gone better," Caldwell said.

"The panel was stacked," Carter replied.

"True. As if Eva is actually a threat to human lives."

Kutter moved over and sat next to Bill.

"You didn't help much, did you?"

"I did my best with no warning. I shouldn't even be up here."

Kutter handed Caldwell his crossword puzzle.

"What's this?"

"Maybe you can help me out."

"You joking?"

"No."

Caldwell looked down at the puzzle. There was only one word not filled in. "One down?"

"Exactly."

Kutter reached behind Bill, opened the door, and shoved him out of the moving helicopter. The mayoral challenger dropped hundreds of feet, screaming all the way. He met the Atlantic like a sack of bricks hitting concrete. His neck snapped instantly.

Carter was in shock. Kutter looked no different than he had minutes earlier. Not a twitch in his muscles.

"Sorry, he reminded me of my uncle."

"Jesus, Jack. Bill was a good man."

"What did you think was going to happen? We can't have two Bill Caldwells running around."

"So, we're in the business of killing people?"

"Don't get soft now. I realize this isn't easy for you, but we haven't even begun. Time to toughen up."

"I thought I was running Wardlow Technologies?"

"You are. Just don't make me have to replace *you*."

The men exchanged a heated look before Kutter pulled out his phone. He hit speed dial - the line was active. "You have the coordinates yet?"

On the other end: "Affirmative. Just came in."

Kutter hung up.

Carter knew he was going to have to deal with a lot of dirt, but he never thought he'd be this close to the mud. He was running an enterprise that could have the power to sway a government, and that wasn't going to come easy.

The ride back was silent.

On its return path to Fort Mystic, the Wardlow chopper buzzed the Argyle building, aggravating Tommy once again.

"Alright, this has gotta stop," he said to the empty room.

It was nearing 6 a.m. Tommy flipped on the TV to the local NBC affiliate. They were broadcasting Carter's interview.

"And what's that, Professor?" Carter asked.

"The point where we don't know who is real and who isn't."

Tommy got up and scratched himself in the usual places below the belt. He threw on a robe, grabbed his cell phone, and dialed his son, Jimmy, who had an apartment a mile down the beach.

Jimmy picked up right away. "Yeah?"

"You watching this?"

"Yeah, unreal. If I get another ticket from one of those squids, I'm gonna break it to pieces. And now this?"

"You got a burner?"

"Yeah."

"Call me back on the usual number."

"You got it."

A moment later, Tommy's phone rang. "I wasn't talking about the goddam meter maids. What the hell's going on with our candidate? He's getting his ass kicked in the polls."

"I don't know. Sanders is getting old, a little senile. Maybe, people are getting nervous, they want a fresh face. Maybe Caldwell has a chance after all."

"I think it's time Carter and I had a face to face. He's the only bastard smart enough or powerful enough to muck up my plans."

"You think that's a good idea?"

"Yeah, I think it's a good idea. Don't you want to see your uncle again? What are you, thick? If Sanders isn't in office, Marky-boy is gonna rot in jail."

"Right, shit."

"This is gonna get real sticky if we have to go back to the old ways of doing business around here."

"You know I'm always ready. You say it and I'll take care of it. I don't want Mark to do any more time. This ain't fair. He didn't do shit. This Sanders— "

"Easy, Jimmy. I'll figure something out. Call me in a couple hours. Check in."

"Alright. Will do."

Noelle walked into the room carrying a mug of her favorite tea. She'd pushed herself into a robotic upright posture, then bent over in a perfect forty-five degree angle to reach for the remote.

Tommy was waiting for this to happen. He reached over, grabbed a pillow from the couch, and playfully threw it at her. His aim was off. It just grazed her arm.

"What the hell, Tommy?"

"Why are you walking like that? Doing that?"

"What, baby?" She handed Tommy the mug.

"The Frankenstein thing and the bending over?"

"My yoga instructor always talks about how important good posture is, babe."

"Money's important, hun, money. And I'm wasting a shitload on this fitness crap."

"If you knew about these Kegel exercises, you would've paid for the gold member classes."

Noelle sat down and raised her hand, pressing the remote. Tommy grabbed the end with a firm hand, covering the infrared signal.

"Now what are you doing?"

"The couch is more comfortable in here. Why do I have to sit on that stiff modern couch in the other room to watch *my* show?"

Tommy gestured to the television. The election poll numbers scrolled the bottom of the screen, showing Bill Caldwell's commanding twelve percent lead.

The KCLT panel continued, "I'd like to apologize to our audience for Mr. Wardlow's abrupt departure. I guess I'll open up the forum here. Mr. Fenton, what's the coalition's stance on Eva's civil liberties?" Rebecca asked.

"The fact that she's being offered the same protections as flesh and blood human beings is absurd. This ill-advised social experiment will fail. Mark my words."

"I'm glad you brought that up," Rebecca replied. "It's something we haven't addressed. Eva will have the same protections as any other Chimera Beach resident. If she is assaulted, the individual will be charged as if they assaulted a human. Do I have this correct, Mr. Daniels?"

"That's the deal that Sanders made, yes. But this kind of policy is ludicrous unless it works both ways. Who's going to be accountable if this android goes haywire and kills someone? That, along with how the federal government is allowing all of this to happen, are the questions that need to be answered."

Noelle knew this was important to Tommy, but couldn't find anything interesting in it for herself. Out of habit, she checked the security cameras around the building. It was as easy as tapping the app with the large "eye" on her tablet. She scrolled through the different camera views, then tapped on the one at the front of the building. She had a look on her face, as if she'd noticed something familiar.

She handed Tommy the tablet. "Your daughter's out front, talking with some cop."

"What?"

Tommy took a sip of what he thought was his usual coffee, reacted to the flavor with a grotesque look, then ran to the bathroom sink to spit it out. When he returned, he said, "What the hell is this? Tastes like flavored tree bark."

"It's lavender tea. It helps with stress. You've gotta get off all that caffeine."

"You can take all the exercise classes you want and eat all the weird shit you want, but me?" Tommy was shaking his head.

Noelle stared at him, bending over and stretching her stomach muscles as he headed for the door.

When Tommy reached the street, Mia was leaning on a police cruiser, laughing. Tommy cleared his throat. Mia took her time, finished the conversation, then turned and walked inside. The policeman yelled over.

"Hey, Tommy."

He didn't respond, just held the door for Mia, who passed him on her way into the elevator.

Tommy was an intimidating figure. His face was ruddy, his red hair graying, and he'd developed a sizable gut, but at six-foot four with a barrel chest, he still felt as though he was as solid as a rock.

On the ride up, Mia kept looking down at his gut. She was purposely needling him with a cute smile she'd perfected over the years while playing with her dad. Just before they exited to their floor, Mia poked his belly with her finger.

All Tommy could think was that all the women around him were in on some conspiracy to weaken his resolve, for some reason. He puckered and gave Mia the look he'd countered with many times. The light-hearted one that said, *try that one more time, and I'll …*

Mia sat on the end of the long couch under a portrait of JFK at his inauguration. Her fiery red hair was pulled into a ponytail that rested on a black leather jacket. She turned and focused her blue eyes on her father.

Tommy cut her off before she could say anything. "I don't know why you insist on that. I told you it's best to steer clear of them, just in case they're trying to get something on me."

"Honestly, I don't know anything. You know that. They know that. They're actually kissing my ass because I'm your daughter. Can't I take advantage of that, too?"

Tommy sighed. "Alright, what's going on today, Mia?"

"I'm headed to Rikers. Thought you might want to come this time. I mean, considering you've never been."

"I put a shitload of cash on his commissary and we talk on the phone. Why would I go?"

"He's not you. He's not as strong as you are, and he's been in there for four years. It's because he's an O'Malley, isn't it? *Screw the in-laws.* If it was one of your own, though … oh boy, there'd be hell to pay."

"That's not true."

Noelle entered the room and threw a quick smile at Mia. "Hi, sweetie." Then she headed for the kitchen. "I'll be out of here in a second. Just need some water."

"Hey, can you do me favor and grab some coffee while you're out?" Tommy asked.

Noelle pointed to the counter. "There's coffee right there."

"That bean tastes burnt."

"I thought you were a tough guy." Noelle grabbed her jacket and opened the front door. "Okay, I'll get the fruity flavored one."

Tommy shook his head.

After the door closed, Mia stood and crossed her arms. "I miss Marky."

"I do too, but he made a mistake. I'm working on getting him out. It's this fuckin' mayor. He's tighter than—"

"Yeah, well, the election's here. I thought you had some pull."

"I told you, and Marky begged me to get in, Mia. After your mother died, I just couldn't see a reason to say no, anymore."

"I'd say four years at Riker's Island might be a good reason."

"He wasn't supposed to be where he was. It shouldn't o' happened."

"All the things you do, of which I probably don't know half of - and don't want to know - and you can't get him out?"

"Mia, you're seventeen years old. Why aren't you out clubbing with your friends?"

"While he's in there? See? That's what I'm talkin' about."

"I'm working on it. I promise."

5

The Wake

Neglecting to read the instructions on the bottle, Victor had popped too many Ambien. He was mentally shattered, and along with the exhaustion from the drive back up from the Cove, he didn't have the energy to care. The Econo-Sleep Motel was the closest thing to the apartment where the Westbrook family lived.

He parked in front of room 408, went to the office, and paid. Victor wasn't ready to go home just yet, and even though he was hungry and thirsty Victor ignored the White Castle in the parking lot, turned on the television, and went straight for the bed. He didn't want to see Carlos Salazar, known as White Castle's *Slider King* – the equivalent of McDonald's *Employee of the Month*. Carlos had gone to school with Ryan - sat across from him in English and Math. Victor wasn't ready to run into him. He was so close to home, but still so far away. Because he'd always immersed himself in his work, Victor had no social support beyond what he'd just lost. His only friend was Kaz Fujimori, Wardlow's *skin guy*, the brilliant engineer who designed incredibly realistic outer flesh for the AI robotics division. He was on his way as soon as he could break away from Wardlow, but Victor had forgotten he'd even spoken to him.

All Victor would be able to recall before he knocked off was the glass of water he poured. It was sitting on the night table next to the bed. He stared at it until he couldn't hold his eyes open any longer. He'd taken his shoes and pants off, but that was it. The television squawked on and on, but he never looked at it.

Victor felt a rush of pins and needles, a warm feeling, then empty space. Within two minutes, he was sleeping.

An hour later, he was seeing the red neon vacancy sign hanging in the office window, flickering away. The drapes were never drawn. Victor wouldn't remember this, either, but his eyes opened. It was 2 a.m., and just as they opened, they closed again.

Victor fell deeper into sleep. However, this time the blackness peeled away and he was almost certain he was awake. He was looking at the glass of water on the night stand. A sudden compulsion came over him. Victor had to drink this water, so he reached over to pick it up, but there was something inside the glass, swimming around, that stopped him. He held it up to the bedside lamp and cocked his head. He recognized it. It looked exactly like the water creature his friend Kaz had tattooed on his back - a miniature version, swimming in his water. Victor stared at the *hanzaki*, which is what Kaz called this creature, for several minutes, watching it gracefully twirl around. The hanzaki was ugly, with curdled skin and sharp barbs jutting from its curved mouth. It was unappetizing, but he was unable to control any of his motor skills, so he didn't hesitate. Victor tipped the glass and drank the water, swallowing the hanzaki in one gulp.

He set the glass down, then, as if given a burst of energy, stood and casually walked to the door.

Carlos was across the parking lot in the drive-thru window, watching Victor walk out of his room in only his underwear and socks, leaving the door open. Carlos had seen a lot of strange things at work during his late night shifts, so he didn't find this odd, and Victor was too far away for him to recognize that this was Ryan's father.

Victor was now walking directly toward the White Castle. Carlos had his headset on, waiting for the next car to drive around. He spotted Victor again. This time he squinted, recognizing him, or at least he thought he did. He pushed open the split window.

"Hey, Mr. Westbrook. Is that you?"

Carlos was beside himself and was not sure what to say. He was close to Ryan, and thought, *this poor man - the shit he's just been through.*

Victor walked up to the window with an empty look. Carlos was dumbfounded.

"Is everything okay, Mr. Westbrook?"

Victor stood looking at Carlos until the car pulled around. Its headlights illuminated Victor, projecting a giant shadow of him against the Econo-Sleep Motel. The kids in the car were laughing at his hairy legs and socks, now black from stepping in puddles of grease and dirt in the lot.

"You look thirsty. Let's get you a soda. It's on me, Mr. Westbrook. What would you like? I've got a root beer, an orange— "

Victor leaned forward and began to heave, regurgitating the hanzaki onto the small shelf inside the take-out window. Its slimy tail flopped out first, wiggling on the counter, knocking bags of food onto the floor. The creature, originally the size of a goldfish when Victor swallowed it, grew in size as it landed. Victor retched again, spewing a green-colored gel which splashed on the floor. Carlos slipped on the fluid, falling into his manager. Victor cast an odd look at the manager as he turned and sauntered past his car, heading back into his room and leaving that door ajar.

Two miles down the road was Kaz. He was a short Japanese man, with good looks and a healthy build. His hair was long for working at a large corporation like Wardlow, but the engineers were a bright bunch and could come with a lot of eccentricity, and he did. Kaz was scrubbing his brand new tires on his Nissan GTR, swerving from lane to lane and testing the grip, until his mobile rang. He settled into a lane and answered.

"Yeah?"

"Where are you? Sounds like a race track."

"On the highway. I did a little upgrading on the turbo."

"You think it's wise to attract unwanted attention?"

"Unwanted? I look like a flaming midlife crisis in this thing. There's no better cover."

"Alright. Can't argue with that. How's the project going?"

"Great. I'm on my way to do a social call."

"Kurasawa wants to hear from you. There's a lot riding on this."

"You don't have to remind me."

Not soon after, Kaz pulled into the lot and parked his blue sports car next to Victor's. He hopped out, smelling the sweet aroma the engine gave off from cooking the new seals on the manifold. Kaz walked up to room 408, and peeked his head in the door ...

~

Victor was in the bathroom, in complete darkness, with both his hands on the shower door handle. Next to him, the water was running in the tub.

His mind was burning up. Victor was standing out front of the family's favorite sushi place, a small stand-alone restaurant with a parking lot that ran all the way around. Three sides of the building were all large glass panels. It loosely resembled a fish tank, and in that moment, it was filling with water.

Victor checked his watch, waving to Claire and Ryan, who were at a table inside waiting for him to join them. Ryan waved him in. Victor tried the door, but it was stuck. He was beginning to panic because the restaurant was now rapidly filling with water. Victor ran around the restaurant, trying all the doors without any result. He ended up back where he started, tugging on the front door as he watched Claire and Ryan become completely submerged, air bubbles releasing from their noses as they swam to the glass and pounded on it for help. Victor pulled at the handle with everything he had, ripping the motel shower door off its hinges. He lost his balance and fell backward, cracking his head on the tile. When he looked up, Kaz was standing over him, offering his hand.

Victor's voice shook. "They ... they were alive. I just saw them."

Kaz helped Victor up, "Yeah, I saw the pills on the night stand buddy. You know, you're only supposed to take one of those."

In the morning, Kaz sat on a chair in the corner of the room, working on his laptop. The TV was providing background noise with the local news.

"A puppy was rescued from a storm drain in Bay Ridge yesterday evening. The fire department responded to the call, pulling the golden retriever out with a harness. The small dog is doing just fine, as you can see from these images."

Victor was lying on his stomach, face in the pillow. He rolled over, rubbing his eyes, and reached up to the nightstand, searching for his glasses. Kaz came into focus.

"Jesus, what a night."

His friend handed him a bottled water, "How are you feeling?"

"Had some strange dreams, I think. I feel fine, though. I don't remember anything."

The newscast continued, "And now, shifting to a much more somber subject. The wife of a Wardlow Technologies scientist and Greenpoint resident, Victor Westbrook ..."

"Shit," Kaz moved quickly to turn it off.

Victor stopped him, then sat on the end of the bed, watching. "It's okay."

" ... drowned off the coast of Smuggler's Cove in Cape Cod."

"You sure?"

" ... Claire Westbrook lost her life struggling to free herself from a violent riptide. Victor's son, Ryan, attempting to save his mother, is believed to have drowned as well, although a body has yet to be recovered. Authorities are ruling it an accidental death."

Victor and Kaz sat in silence for a moment after the report. Victor finally looked around the cheap motel room and decided, "I think I'm ready to go home now."

It was a short drive over the Whitestone. An eerie fog layer had formed over the East River, making it difficult to navigate the thin lanes of the bridge, but Victor was home in no time. He parked in the lot of his complex, where he always had, the space with the large oil spot from the last time he attempted to change it. He stared through his fogged windshield, preoccupied with the image of Claire eating White Castle, smashing her french fries between the meat and bun. She would nibble from the sides, shaping the slider into a perfect square until the last bite – giggling as she popped it into her mouth.

So strange, where the mind goes, he thought.

Walking the steps to the third floor, Victor turned at the landing and froze. On the lower wall, next to a group of Ryan's skateboard scuffs, written in marker was *Magic happens.*

Victor found himself standing on his doormat with a heavy heart, looking down at the family name, The Westbrooks, faded from years of direct sun.

He entered the foyer and flipped on the light switch, tripping on one of Ryan's shoes. He chuckled, but the laugh transformed to grief when he saw the family portrait, taken just months prior to their trip. He entered the living room. In a rush to catch the flight to Cape Cod, Claire had left her robe on the couch. Victor picked it up and inhaled deeply, taking in her scent. He collapsed onto the sofa, remembering the last time he and Claire had been intimate. One of her socks was stuck between the cushions. It was white and low cut, with embroidered rabbits and a fluffy pink ball on the end, a silly gift he'd given her. Victor recalled teasing her for wearing them, calling her 'Pom-Poms'.

Victor forced himself up off the sofa, then dragged his hands along the wallpaper in the hallway until he entered Ryan's room. He sat on the bed and looked around, feeling nostalgic when he recognized that many of the items were from a more innocent time, before Ryan's mental health issues came to light. There were t-ball trophies, beat-up skateboards, an acoustic guitar, and old magic paraphernalia. He recalled seeing Ryan's first trick, where he used sleight of hand to make a card disappear and his priceless expression when he was finally able to perform it flawlessly. Victor turned to the nightstand, where a miniature time machine sat. He'd made it to help Ryan with his nightmares when he was four years old. Victor would tell him that when the bad dreams returned, he could place them inside the transport and send them to another dimension.

Victor started to break down, thinking about all the difficulties Ryan had, *it wasn't fair*, until a soft knock at the front door pulled him away.

Victor opened the door. Kaz forced a smile. "Me again."

"You didn't have to knock. I was just in Ryan's room feeling sorry for myself. I'm glad you got here when you did."

Kaz was carrying a Harry & David gift basket filled with flowers and food. *From Carter.*

Victor took the card from the side. "Go ahead, open it."

Victor wasn't interested. "Later."

Kaz hugged him. It was awkward. "I'm here for you. Whatever you need. The next move is yours. What do you say?"

Victor fought back tears. "This is a real bitch."

"No news on Ryan?" Victor shook his head. "Search and rescue were combing for days. I don't understand it. I feel awful, but I just couldn't stay any longer."

"Don't kick yourself, man. The ocean's one of the most most powerful arms of mother nature. Hey, let's talk about what you're gonna do."

"So many memories here. I don't know how I can stay."

"You thinking about the south shore?"

Victor sighed. "All these years, I was staying here for them. Claire's family, Ryan's school. Now, there's nothing left."

He suddenly realized, "Man I'm hungry now. This grief thing is crazy. One minute I can't eat, the next I feel like I could swallow a whole fish."

He got up and rifled through the cabinets, then checked the fridge. Kaz interrupted him. "Yo!" He ripped the plastic from the gift basket. "Here. Plenty of options."

Victor grabbed a pear, took a bite, and spoke with his mouth full. "You don't have to stay here. I'll be fine."

"Victor, I'm going down to my car to grab my bag. Don't stop eating until I get back."

After Kaz shut the front door, Victor started to feel a little better. He picked up the card from Carter and opened the envelope.

Victor,

There are no words to express my sadness in relation to your loss. Everyone here at Wardlow is thinking of you. If there is anything you need, anything at all, do not hesitate to contact Sandy here at the office.

We miss you terribly and hope that you can recover and rejoin your extended family here at Wardlow in the near future.

And remember, if you feel like a change, there is always a home for you at the Chimera facility. Just say the word.

Please stay strong and in touch,

Sincerely,
Carter

There was a knock at the door. "I told you to c'mon in. It's open." He'd expected to see Kaz, but Todd, the neighbor, entered instead, holding a large, overweight cat. "Sorry, I heard the voices. Hope I'm not intruding."

"Oh, Jesus, Jasmine. I completely forgot."

"Yeah, no worries, Vic, she's fine. I figured you had a lot on your mind."

Victor took the cat and stroked her belly. "Thank you for watching her."

"Of course, and about Claire and Ryan, I—"

"Thank you. I appreciate your thoughts."

Todd was uncomfortable. He liked to discuss his feelings. When Victor cut him off, he didn't know what to say.

"Jasmine's been fed and was outside for a while, and I hope she didn't pick up any fleas or anything."

"Thanks again. Really. It means a lot. I don't know what I would have done otherwise."

Todd turned to leave. "Yeah, okay, good night. If you need anything—" He stopped when Kaz entered, looking him over.

"Hey, have we met?"

Kaz rushed by him with his bags, avoiding eye contact. "Not that I'm aware of."

"You sure look familiar, and I never forget a face."

"Are you insinuating we Asians all look alike?"

"What?? No!"

Victor jumped in. "Okay, we're all tired, here." He walked Todd to the door.

"Thanks again."

"I'm sorry, I just don't know how to handle situations like this."

"Don't worry. Neither do I."

He patted Todd on the back and it felt good, being able to have that strength in the moment.

Later that evening, the men had dozed off. The living room was quiet, with the flicker of the television casting shadows on the wall. It was 2 a.m. and Kaz was fully extended in the recliner. The Sci-Fi Channel was airing an episode of "Lost in Space". On the screen, Robot B9 was repeating his notorious phrase, cautioning the show's precocious ten year old prodigy.

"Danger, Will Robinson!"

Kaz's weak bladder woke him. He sat up in the chair for a moment and cleared the fog from his eyes. Victor was wrapped in a blanket with his head resting on the arm of the sofa. Kaz rose and walked to the bathroom, stopping when he noticed Victor's laptop sitting on the table. He stared at it for a moment, thought about the short phone conversation earlier, then continued on.

When he finished in the bathroom, Kaz returned, taking a seat in the chair. He turned to look at Victor's laptop again. He was surprised to find Jasmine sitting on top of the computer, with her piercing yellow eyes cutting right through him.

Kaz rubbed his eyes. "What the hell are you looking at?"

6

Implementation

Chimera was a quiet beach community, for the most part. The residents didn't want any of the 'big city life' leaking into their town, and rightly so. Roger Fenton from Human Lives Matters made a stink with his anti-STEM messages. He and his organization were not fans of Wardlow, especially in Chimera, and the people were biting his message.

The mighty Carter Wardlow, with his limitless budget, hired a PR firm to handle the launch of Eva and her cute little dog, Aiden. They decided to go with highlighting the benefits of Eva, focusing on the average resident, and disseminating the message, "Your lives will be safer and more exciting with Eva."

> *Eva has sensors that detect crime. No more purse snatchers on the boardwalk. The criminals who cross into our community on weekends to prey on our way of life will be quashed by our new friend Eva. She has already helped Bob Johnson at the Pizza Corner. Mr. Johnson was contemplating his lottery pick when he ran into Eva, who instantly ran the odds and provided a series of numbers that hit a winner in the daily 500 for the restaurant owner!*

The PR firm had slowly but surely placed a blanket over Fenton's messages of concern, smothering his army of followers with expensive ads and a never-ending string of winning concepts.

So, when dawn hit Chimera Beach on the launch day of Eva and Aiden at the Holland Apartments, many of her neighbors were waiting for an opportunity to meet the android and her "adorable sidekick Aiden," as Wendy Shay put it during her KCLT exclusive report.

The firm had pushed enough of the anger into the back seat at the moment, at least enough for the launch. They ensured all the officials and security from

Wardlow, the military aspect which would remain unknown even to them, were all dressed down in friendly beach attire. There were no barricades or weapons visible, just a gaggle of happy faces carting crates of unknowns into Eva's apartment. There were no smoked windows on the van that pulled up. No odd-looking numbers or government tags on the license plates. The firm made sure Wardlow used rental cars from a small, local dealer who was thrilled to get the business.

Fresh juice and individual cakes were made for those who attended, or happened to wander by. Tables were setup with Eva and Aiden postcards printed with the tagline, "Ask me anything, I'm here to help."

Eva even had an email address so the public could communicate with her. Wardlow's tech team had created a machine learning algorithm that utilized a quaint, politically correct humor which the android would respond with.

Local movers dropped off new furniture. Flowers were delivered. Gift baskets were sent to the neighbors. A few had to be left on the doorstep; some people simply didn't want to participate, yet.

Kutter was there, watching over the entire charade, looking for any variable that was out of place. He wore a beach hat and draped a towel over his shoulder as if he'd just been walking past and had stopped out of curiosity. He and a couple of his men surreptitiously secured the area.

Carter Wardlow was watching on a large screen inside the lab, several floors below sea level, with a small group of the ICE team who had pushed the limits of technology to get her finished on schedule.

"Ten minutes away from making history. I think it's time for a toast."

Kaz the master, the man who developed a synthetic human skin so soft that no one would touch Eva and have any other reaction than *wow*, was standing next to his friend Victor Westbrook, known among those in the lab today as The Higgs Boson, aka The God Particle. In the world of AI, Victor was the only one to successfully code the first artificial human being.

The unknown masters wanted to be out on the street when their work was revealed. It meant a lot, because there would be no press release, no noise about who they were. No awards. During the launch, Victor and Kaz were like non-commissioned agents working for the CIA. Their glory was only celebrated among the select few who were surrounding Carter at the moment.

The event team had just finished putting a bundle of balloons up on each one of the small trees that lined the street when a compact yellow economy rental pulled up. A vinyl sticker on the rear doors read, "Eva&Aiden."

The technician in the passenger seat jumped out and opened the door for Eva, who stepped out holding Aiden in her arms.

Kaz nudged Victor.

"She's going to think all of this is real. You know, all of it."

Victor watched Eva closely.

"Only way it can work."

Eva looked around at all the people who'd gathered. Still, many were coming. Kutter wanted to get a closer look, just to see for himself. As he leaned in to inspect her, Aiden growled.

"It appears the fake ones don't like me, either."

Eva spoke, "Don't worry. She doesn't bite."

The crowd members that were close enough to hear her were stunned. Victor decided to play with Eva to show off a bit.

"Eva, can you hear me?"

Eva turned to him, "Yes. Of course. Hi."

"Can you tell me where you live?"

"930 Holland Street, Apartment 112, Chimera Beach."

"Where do you work?"

"I'm a cashier at Bloomingdale's in the Chimera Beach Mall."

"Do you have any pets?"

"Yes, a white Maltese named Aiden."

"How's it feel to—"

Victor stopped himself, but Eva responded anyway.

"Oh, the weather is nice today. It's, what, seventy-five degrees already."

Someone behind Victor, standing in the street, yelled out.

"What are you gonna do with the rest of your day?"

Eva cut through the crowd and walked up to the young woman who inquired.

"Well, I'm going to the beach. Would you like to join me?"

The people clapped. They were genuinely impressed.

Frank Olson, a local paparazzi who usually caught celebrities after they escaped the big city and attempted to hide out on a quiet vacation - a guy with no backbone who was only out for a quick buck - was moving toward the crowd at an aggressive pace.

Kutter saw the photographer the second he turned onto the street and positioned himself.

As the paparazzi raised his camera, Kutter moved fast. Frank was trying to figure out how his camera was no longer in his hand.

Kutter forced Olson toward the sidewalk across the street, away from Eva and the crowd. "Let's not get the wrong impression."

Frank was pissed.

"Who are you?"

"A concerned citizen. And I'd like to give this young lady a chance before you work your little angle and try to make her look bad. Is that what they paid you to do?"

"What are you talking about? I'm just here to get a few snapshots of the event."

"For who?"

"Whoever will pay."

Kutter pulled the data card from his DSLR and returned the camera to him. "Maybe next time. Have a nice day."

Frank was a tough guy, but from his experience, he knew something was off with Kutter and was smart enough to know not to explore it any further. He walked off, checking his back a few times before disappearing around the corner from where he came.

Kutter shifted his attention back to Victor and Kaz. The crowd. All was well. Then …

Victor's cell phone buzzed.

"Hello, Carter."

Kaz gave Victor a thumbs up. Carter sounded excited.

"Victor. Congratulations. I'm watching from the lab with everyone. We all wanted to thank you and get your reaction. How is it going?"

"Everything's great. The people are curious and polite. I think it's safe to say we're on track. We owe a lot of that to you, Carter. Thank you."

"Always so modest. I love that about you. It's a historic moment, Victor. Revel in it. They don't come around too often. Considering everything you've been through, it's quite an accomplishment. Let's say we did this one for Claire and Ryan."

"I appreciate that, Carter. Very much."

At the opposite end of the street from where Frank had turned off was Jimmy Swillow. He was sitting on the hood of his car, watching, contemplating …

7

Ryn2

Victor had cut the ribbon on his new home, built by commercial architect, Norman Bluster, over a year ago. Wardlow stocks were through the roof. He'd collected a much-deserved bonus and set himself up on the coast with a modern four-story glass house with a robotics lab built into the lower level. He would never speak of the life insurance he collected, but this covered a large portion of the precision equipment he purchased for his lab. The upper three levels were living, dining, spa, and a rooftop patio. The house was a work of art, but wasn't lived in much. Some of the furniture still had plastic wrap on the footing. Vic was determined to find some secret door, some anomaly or panacea, an answer to his pain. He only wanted his family back together.

Work forged on at Wardlow. They weren't paying much attention to the mixed feelings in town about their AI.

The STEM units always took a beating from angry locals, but Eva was becoming a bit of a celebrity, as much as a novelty could be. And even though there was the occasional assault, like the time she showed up at Sparks restaurant on the boardwalk with purple hair and green lipstick - a prank a few of the local artists pulled - the Eva experiment was working. Most of the townspeople weren't threatened by her at all. It was only the wild young kids who hung outside of Coonan's Pub, looking to get an "in" with the Swillows, who were really causing problems.

~

It was Tuesday, 4:45p.m. At 5p.m., Victor's four automated trash cans would set off like clockwork down a smooth concrete path and stop at the curb where they would wait for the trash crew in the early morning hours. Bluster had designed this path with the cans in mind. It was one of Victor's early robotics designs, and the two thought it would be great to finally put them to use. And since no one enjoyed taking out the trash, they thought, *why not let the robots do it.*

It was a simple electronics setup. There were four sensors embedded in a small rubber housing and stuck to the curb. Each sensor was programmed to match one of the trash cans. It wasn't hard for the young punks from Coonan's to figure this out, and so the high jinks began.

The boys pried the rubber housings from the concrete with their pocketknives and placed them in precarious locations close to the house. They knew the range would have to be short.

One was thrown into Chuck McCready's pool, directly across the street. Chuck was already irritated about the two years of construction he had to endure as a stay-at-home aspiring novelist. He found himself down at the closest coffee-house doing what he couldn't stand others doing - pretending to work at the cafe while constantly being distracted by everyone else's conversations. But Chuck managed by purchasing a set of noise reduction headphones and was making progress, mentally, that is, until he came home and found Victor's refuse floating in his saltwater pool.

~

When McCready stepped out of his house, preparing to cross the street and confront Victor, he noticed little Susie Cardiff riding her tricycle with a trash can following her around. The boys had stashed one of the sensors in the saddle pack Velcroed under her seat. But what really had Chuck reeling was when one of Coonan's boys ran out from behind a truck parked further down the block, the trash can following behind. The kid timed it just right so when Mrs. Cardiff turned the corner, distracted by the trash can following her daughter, she hit the other can square on the front grill, sending trash across her car and all over the street.

After making sure Mrs. Cardiff was okay, Chuck was at Victor's front door.

Victor was oblivious to Chuck's aggressive pounding, He was staring at a CNN anchorwoman who was a doppelgänger for Claire, right down to the mole on her cheek. Victor was reminiscing about how he knew from the first moment he laid eyes on Claire that he'd marry her. It was when he was at M.I.T., study-ing for his Ph.D. in computer science, while she attended Harvard, getting her undergrad in literature. Claire waited tables at Grendel's Den to make a few extra dollars, which happened to be Victor's favorite place to grab a beer and relax. She had made eye contact before, and had even offered a smile on a few occasions, but to Victor's disappointment, they had never spoken. He memorized her schedule to make sure she was on shift whenever he visited the bar, but Victor was socially awkward and timid, unable to raise the confidence to approach her. He would scribble algorithms on napkins, nursing his beer, looking up only to locate Claire. He'd pretend to watch sports and stay hours beyond his planned visit, biding his time. Then, one night, she met his gaze. Their eyes locked, and later that evening she would utter five words that echoed in Victor's head, "I get off at midnight."

Chuck calling on his mobile phone snapped Victor back to reality.

"Hello?"

"Victor?"

"Yeah?"

"It's Chuck, next door. Those cans of yours are spilling all over the street. There's crap all over the place. Mrs. Cardiff ran into one of them. Another one's in my goddamn pool, Vic. My wife gets back from work soon. If it's not cleaned up before she gets home, she'll have a fit. You know how wives are."

Victor was silent.

"Ah, crap," Chuck continued. "I didn't mean to—"

"It's okay. Listen, did you see those kids hanging around again?"

"I did. I'm not sure what you're gonna do, but this can't continue. Maybe you should just take the trash out like everyone else." With that, Chuck disengaged the line.

In the far corner of the lab, a primitive-looking rusted metal robot sat motionless, staring straight ahead. One of Victor's first AI concepts, the robot was named Eddie by Ryan when he was a little boy. Eddie looked like he'd been through the ringer, with several coats of different colored paint overlapping his face and frame. Victor placed his finger on Eddie's glass eye, allowing the robot to scan his print. Eddie came alive.

"What menial task will I have the pleasure of accomplishing for you today?"

"Did I program you to pick up trash?"

"I can do almost anything, but my servos lack the dexterity. I'd be out there all day, Victor."

"Unbelievable. Are you actually making an *excuse*? Ryan must have put that in your head."

"Well, as you know, he was instrumental in my development."

Victor felt a wave of emotion. He was taxing himself over not being able to spend any more time with Ryan and yet here he was, in crude form. Ryan's spirit was in Eddie. During all the early programming phases, he had shaped the robot's character into a snarky, sardonic personality which Victor was finally appreciating.

Having Eddie in the lab was starting to build confidence in Victor's more elaborate concepts. He began thinking of his miniature time travel model. It was insane to think he could even come close in his lifetime, but *does that matter?*

For anyone else, it would most certainly be a laugh, but it could be possible with the right amount of …

"Coffee, please, Eddie."

Victor was having a moment with himself. Even with the sarcasm, Eddie was always obedient.

"Ah, yes, of course. I live for these moments."

As soon as Eddie turned toward the coffee maker in the corner of the lab, Victor was off to the garage and digging in a box of Ryan's things he'd packed away. He knew right where it was, what he was looking for. Underneath his bag of magic in a firm cardboard box was a plaster mold Ryan had made of his face. He'd been planning a stunt that involved some special effects make-up, but never got a chance to perform it.

Victor opened the box. The mold was in perfect condition. He was so excited, his mind raced with ideas and he left the rest of Ryan's things strewn all over the floor.

When he passed a window looking out to the street, he saw Kaz. *That's odd, he didn't call.* Then he looked at the mask in his hands.

Victor joined him at the end of the driveway.

"Tell me again what it is you do at Wardlow."

"Are you being serious?"

"Just humor me."

Kaz played along, placing his hands at his side and standing like Superman amongst the trash in the street.

"I'm the skin guy. Otherwise known as 'Exo-man.' The master of all things dermal."

Victor rushed over to his friend, placed his arms around his shoulder, and pulled him toward the house. The words were pouring out. He let loose on his new concept.

"Okay," Victor handed Ryan's mask to Kaz. "I want you to make me a skin. The best skin you've ever made."

"Wait, slow down. This is—"

"Why? You made Eva's so smooth and real. Now we need to make Ryan's. Even better."

Kaz contemplated for a moment. "You said 'we'. You never say that word. We're finally going to do collaborate. Epic. Okay."

"Yes??"

"Yes."

Victor began to pace. "Oh, this is great. See, I can piece all the guts at Wardlow. An arm here, a leg there. No one will know, but the skin is—"

Victor, I'll do it. But under one condition."

Victor's excitement faded.

"What?"

"I won't do Claire."

Victor laughed. "No, no. I don't want you to do Claire. All I need is Ryan. Then I'll have Claire. But forget that, now. Just, come see."

Victor led Kaz inside the lab.

"I've been playing around with a test unit, RyN2. Never actually imagined it as Ryan that is, until I asked Eddie for my morning coffee. Anyway, it's communicative, functional, but the learn rate still isn't where I want it to be—"

Eddie arrived with a pot of coffee. He extended his arm to Kaz, holding out a steaming cup of joe. Kaz looked surprised.

"I didn't ask for coffee."

"I did," Victor said.

Eddie sputtered.

"Yeah, well, since you're going make me a skin, I figured you're going to need some go-go juice."

Kaz chuckled.

"I love him."

Victor was in a bit of shock. It all seemed surreal.

"He's definitely one of a kind."

Kaz' face turned with a look of concern.

"We have a big problem. Wardlow owns the code you need. I know you stacked it, but that's patented and on lockdown. If they find out …"

"I've got my own code. Been working on it for a long time. Wardlow will never get it. It's way beyond Eva and my own design. I've patented it. Let's not talk about this anymore. Please, just do your part."

"So, do you have a name for this code, yet?"

"I'm still pondering," Victor said.

"And this test unit. It's not Eddie, I'm assuming?"

"Much to his dismay, no, it's not."

Eddie set the coffee pot down. "Always the short end of the stick. Just my luck. Is there any—"

Victor raised his voice. "Eddie, off!"

The robot's eyes closed and he froze mid-sentence.

Kaz threw a hard look at Victor. "Show me."

"Show you what?"

"You've already been working on this test unit. So, Eddie inspired you, but I wanna see it. Show me the robot, Victor."

Victor turned and walked to the door. "Well, are you coming?"

Kaz had never been to the upper floors of Victor's place. He was bright-eyed, scanning everything along the way. Victor was a private man. Most of the doors upstairs were closed.

When they walked into RyN2's bedroom, Kaz was beginning to understand. All of Ryan's things had been unboxed from storage, making it appear as if he'd been living in the room for a long time. Victor had even thrown a pair of his jeans on the edge of the bed.

RyN2 was standing at the window looking out, with wires running to a desktop computer. He was crude, with no exoskeleton and missing a few parts. Kaz couldn't find the words. He walked up to the android and touched him. To his amazement, RyN2 turned around, looked into Kaz's eyes, and spoke.

"Hello, Kaz."

The android's voice sounded exactly like Ryan. Kaz smiled. "Whoa, his voice, and how the hell does he recognize me?"

"Your face, of course. I fed him pictures. Millions of them. He's been burning through encyclopedias, social media, images on the web, Wikis, you name it. He's logging almost as much data as the NSA's quantum intelligence program."

Kaz spilled his coffee.

"I'm going to run a couple of tests on him," Victor said. "You wanna hang out?"

"That was rhetorical, right?"

RyN2 sat, while Victor examined his pupils. "Your reaction is a bit slow compared to the input. Why is there a lag?"

The unit spoke. "I didn't notice a lag."

"That's impossible. Wait, are you lying?"

"Yes."

Victor chuckled, "Funny."

"Why?"

"Because you lied, then admitted you were lying."

RyN2 giggled, "Oh, yes."

"Fascinating," Kaz interjected.

"Any other issues I should know about?" Victor asked.

RyN2 was silent for a moment, as if thinking. Then he spoke, "I'm a bit exposed."

"How do you mean?" Vic asked.

"All my bones are showing."

Victor looked at Kaz, "How long before we get a skin?"

He was slow to answer. "Man, he's fully conscious," Kaz said and looked at the android. "Who are you?"

"Technically, Victor named me RyN2, but I am Ryan Westbrook. Why are you asking such an obvious question?"

"Of course, you're Ryan. I was just kidding." Kaz then turned to Victor and answered, "As soon as I can."

"That's great news. Hey, one more thing before I get him back online, synching data. Check this out. Ryan, how about a card trick?"

RyN2 grabbed the deck sitting on his desk. He split the cards in half and shuffled. "Ambitious card?"

Victor nodded. "Houdini's favorite."

"Actually, it's the trick that fooled Houdini several times. It was created by French magician Gustav Alberti."

Victor chuckled again.

"What?" RyN2 asked.

"I know." Victor winked at Kaz. "I researched it when we started training. Was seeing if you'd catch that."

RyN2 slipped the ace of clubs from the deck and handed the card to Victor. "Initials, please."

Victor took a pen and marked the card.

The android peeled the top card off the deck and placed Victor's underneath it. "You saw where I put your card, right?"

"Yes."

RyN2 flipped the top card to reveal Victor's ace. "Then, why is it here?"

"Very good."

Kaz applauded, "That's amazing, Vic. Ryan, can you—"

Victor's demeanor changed. "I need something from you. If anything happens to me, I need someone I can trust."

"Of course. You can trust me."

Victor grabbed Kaz's hand and held it up to RyN2's eyes. "I'm giving you access." His iris scanned Kaz's fingerprints and inputted the data. "I want you to be his godfather."

Once the scan was finished, Kaz reached in his pocket and pulled out a USB thumb drive. He handed it to Victor, who was instantly curious.

"What's this?"

"I almost forgot. A young girl, Mel, she hit me up on social media."

Victor's heart sank. "Yeah. I remember her well."

"Said she'd been trying to get a hold of you, but gave up and so she hunted me down. I have some photos tagged "Wardlow". I told her I knew you, so she sent me a few pics of Ryan on the pier. It looks like they were taken right before the accident. I put them all on the drive for you."

Victor appreciated what was happening, but couldn't push the words out of his mouth. He held his hand up to accept the drive. Kaz read his look. "Yeah, so, I've never been a godfather before. I'm excited about this." Off Victor's empty look, Kaz continued, "Why don't you take your time. Open the pics when you're ready."

Kaz handed him the drive. "I wasn't sure I should give this to you yet, but didn't want you to find out later that I had them lying around. Better to give them to you right away."

Victor was strong, "No, no. It's okay. Let's just wrap this up, Ryan, and you know, thanks. I'm glad she found you. She was the last person to see him alive. Thank her for me."

Later that evening, Kaz was back at his apartment. It was a nice two-bedroom that overlooked Main Street, just above Vito's Delicatessen, a popular New York style, grab-n-go lunch spot. He was sitting in front of his laptop, waiting. He'd scrolled through the news, laughing at the Human Lives Matter movement that had managed to build a following of twenty people, with pictures of them marching along the boardwalk. One of the signs read, "Just because they look like us, doesn't mean they think like us." Another, "God hates Fake."

An hour passed. Kaz was still sitting at his table, staring out the window with his laptop open in front of him. He was watching the kids from Coonan's Pub further down the street. They were meandering along the sidewalk, peaking into cars, as they usually did, looking for expensive items that tourists left on their seats. They'd actually scraped the mortar away from one of the office buildings across the street and loosened a brick so they could bash-n-grab the items and run off, replacing the brick before they left the area. This left very little for the police to find but broken glass and sad vacationers now missing an iPad or backpack.

The kids retreated as a police car drove slowly down the street. Kaz moved closer to see what was about to happen. The second he pressed his face to the glass to try and get a clear line on the kids in the dark alley, his laptop screen came to life. There was a subtle beeping sound before a window popped up. Kaz's computer was now mirroring Victor's desktop, and he didn't feel even the slightest sting of guilt. Behind Kaz was a mission of great importance. Personal feelings were left out.

Simultaneously, Victor was sitting in front of his laptop with the USB stuck into the port, looking at the photos Mel had compiled of Ryan. There was one of him standing on the edge of the railing with the ocean behind. Victor could feel himself sitting in the sand, the water rushing over his feet, the sinking feeling in his stomach. He rushed over to the sink, opened the cupboard, and grabbed a roll of TUMS. He ripped the foil and dumped a few of the chalky tablets in his mouth.

Meanwhile, Kaz was scrolling through Victor's encrypted files, his eyes bulging from the amount of work on highly advanced personality coding for AI that Victor had done outside of Wardlow. He spent hours looking over stacks of files until he found what he believed he was looking for.

A file labeled, "Celestial."

While sifting through the code, he heard the glass break down in the street, then the blare of a car alarm. He looked up to catch the shadows of three boys scattering like vermin.

Kaz didn't flinch. He activated an encrypted messaging app. A new window popped up on screen. He typed, *Package in hand. Contents confirmed.*

The returned text read, *Caldwell DOI. Schedule altered. GWR (go when ready).*

8

Leap of Faith

Tumbling in space like a puff of dandelion, orbiting the earth at a little over 17,000 mph, was an aerospace wonder of engineering. The space station Aurelia and its inhabitants had just witnessed a sunrise. They would see another in only 92 minutes as they rapidly circled the planet, making it seem as though they were living out 15 days for every one on Earth.

Aurelia was designed like the shape of a planet, but was hollow, with large triangular structures of tubes forming the shape. Inside each of the hollow cylinders that formed these triangles were living quarters, labs, offices, greenhouses, etc. It was a small planet all to itself, equipped with every available future technology.

The EM-JEL (Electro Magnetic Gel) labs were the talk of everyone down on Earth; even teenagers who were usually preoccupied with themselves. Wardlow Technologies had designed scary medical breakthroughs that involved the merging of human cells, tissues, and artificial intelligence—what some would call singularity. Today, May 15th, 2118, was special.

There were several private companies with shuttles in orbit that could stop off at Aurelia. Sir James Rothenberg III happened to take the small executive Jump Ship from Tarnit Industries.

Rothenberg was a banking mogul, with his best years behind him. He was 78, and had unstoppable cancer that even the most advanced medical practices could not slow. He had just arrived and was sitting comfortably in the EM lab, waiting for the demonstration to begin.

Aurelia was designed in part because the UN had outlawed the experiments that Wardlow was working on, so the company decided to take their work and leave the planet. Space was lawless. No one would be able to alter or interrupt their plans.

Rothenberg was glad that Carter had organized a group of powerful figures across the globe to finance this venture. He was glad not only because he was about to see the fruits of a large investment, but because Carter was there, still alive. He was a test subject of his own technology, living sixty years after he should have died, under normal circumstances.

When Carter stepped into the room, applause came from his medical staff. They all admired the man. He was carrying a bottle of cognac he'd pulled from his father cellar what seemed like 200 years ago. He stepped over to James, set down a box of Cubans and the Cognac, and shook the man's hand.

"Well, James, what are you waiting for?"

Rothenberg was confused. "Is that a good idea? I'm days from collapsing."

Carter laughed. "Go on. Enjoy yourself. We've taken cancer and choked the life out of it, up here. It doesn't exist on Aurelia. There is no FDA or big pharma influence in space. Yet, by the time this demo is done, I'll have a new set of lungs growing in my lab just for you."

Rothenberg was so sick of the chemo treatments and other insidious tests back on Earth, all he could think of was "Fuck cancer", as he lit up and shared a laugh with Carter.

Carter signaled his team member, J.C. McGraph, who jumped right into the pitch.

"The patented EM-JEL that Wardlow has uniquely created was based on years of studying jellyfish, sir. It allows the transfer of micro-electrical impulses in the brain to connect to the receptors of the artificial devices we've implanted. This technology is an incredible breakthrough, not only because it means humans can assimilate with artificial intelligence, but it potentially means living forever."

Rothenberg took a sip of Cognac and shared a smile with Carter that lasted almost a minute. They were defying God, and the feeling was overwhelming. McGraph continued.

"However, there are some issues—"

Carter jumped in, "This isn't pleasant, James. I want to provide full disclosure." He turned to McGraph. "Let's roll the video." Rothenberg was really paying attention, now. "What you're seeing is from the Fort Mystic tests years ago."

McGraph started the video. On the large screen was an older man receiving an injection of EM-JEL fluid. Within seconds, he began screaming at the top of his lungs, writhing in pain. The old man pulled himself out of his seat and dropped to the floor, holding his head.

McGraph continued, "The one major problem was the extreme pain it caused in the test subjects. This is why Wardlow is here on Aurelia with EM-JEL, and what you are about to see is why Carter isn't writhing in pain right now."

McGraph flipped the screen to a second video of the EM-JEL being tested in space. The subject on screen never so much as winced. After accepting the EM-JEL fluid, all the monitoring equipment showed his functions were normal. The patented fluid was a success.

When McGraph stopped the video, the man that had been just on screen walked into the room.

Carter looked at Rothenberg. "I want you to meet Mr. Neumann. A good friend of mine."

Neumann walked over and shook Rothenberg's hand. James had a few questions rolling around in his head, but really only one important one. Neumann read it on his face, so he just went ahead and said it, "Gravity."

James looked at him as if he'd read his mind. "But, how—"

Carter cut in, "For some reason, the lack of gravity makes all the difference. We can live pain free until we solve the issue. Then, we'll be able to return home."

Carter walked Rothenberg to the window. The Earth spun below. The moon further in the distance.

"Killer view, huh?" Before he could get a response from Rothenberg, he handed him a keycard that authorized him access to a special wing, called Section 8, on the space station. "Make yourself at home, then meet me here after you've settled in. I want to show you my pet project."

9

Zarwid The Great, #13

Zar was six foot three inches tall. He looked like a throwback to Woodstock, or maybe more like a homeless savant. He had long hair, was sculpted like an action figure, but appeared to be seventy-five. Zar wasn't real, though. He wasn't human. The old man was AI, pure and simple, designed to force anyone interacting with him to feel his wisdom and the power of his presence.

Only problem for Zar at the moment was that he was being held prisoner, floating high above the earth in Unit 6B994 of the Containment Center on the Space Station, Aurelia. Carter would say he was a guest, but Carter was losing touch with reality.

Zarwid the Great was a comic book character created in 1940. He was a master of illusion, a trickster, devilish old man who could escape the most intricate of traps. He first appeared opposite the Vandal Terror, a twisted criminal who cannibalized his victims in Time Jump #4.

Everyone knew that comic books were only to be taken as guilty pleasure, nighttime reading that would allow one to slip away from the doldrums of the day. But someone had built a Zar android and put him in action among the living. He was the first comic hero to walk among the mortals.

Carter entered the center carrying a distressed comic book tightly sealed in plastic. He casually stepped into room 6B994. It was an empty holding unit with restraints and an electromagnetic field that would flare a burst of energy powerful enough to shut down any android if the restraints on Zar were forced off.

"Says here you can break free from any chains that bind you. I wonder, is the real world grafted as cheaply as the story lines in these old yarns?"

Zar took a look at the comic.

"That's a great episode. It's a page turner. I get confined to a tank that's eventually filled with water, only I'm not there to escape. I'm being interrogated by the Terror. He wants to know what my secret is, and he's slowly letting the water rise. The Terror wants to know what I know, and he'll do anything to get it. On page twelve, I manipulate one of his subordinates with a brainwashing gaze. He unlocks the chains that bind me and I slip out before the Terror returns."

"I was never a comic fan. Too far-fetched, and the pages in the middle were always underdeveloped. The cover art was the draw, but I wanted more. And the characters, cardboard cutouts of one another. Just like the residents of Chimera."

"Oh, the irony. Carter, you fit right into the maniacal sociopathy of the villain."

"Glad you think so." Carter held up the comic. "What's this worth, anyway?"

"It's in about as good a shape as you. So, not much. But it is a rare Zarwid storyline. Maybe a thousand, tops."

"I have a proposal. You tell me what I want to know. Give me access to that device I know you have hidden somewhere on Earth, and I'll let you have it."

Zar laughed. He enjoyed the fact that Carter had a sense of humor, even if he was the bastard of the universe.

Carter was visibly showing his jealousy of the android.

"You know, old man, I technically own you. Per my standard employee contracts, which Victor signed, everything developed while he worked under the Wardlow banner is mine. So, why don't you just provide the data and come work for me? Show us the schematics. That will satiate our engineering team just fine." Noticing Zar's blank stare, he continued, "Come on, why don't you continue the legacy of a great man? This doesn't need to be a struggle for either of us. Together, we can break new ground again, as Victor once did in his day."

"I don't struggle, but I understand what you meant. Can I process for a while?"

Carter had to leave. He'd felt it deep inside. The android was cutting, outsmarting him every second he stayed, so he exited without another word. The AI unit guarding room 6B994 secured the door. Carter turned to him. "He's processing." Then laughed as he walked away.

~

In the transport hub that shuttled inhabitants safely around Aurelia, Carter authorized Section 8, then sat back and waited to arrive. When the door opened, a group of men were buzzing around a work of advanced engineering, tweaking the armature on what might have looked like a small particle accelerator. It had a large ring of cylindrical steel wrapped in a special mix of copper and other conductive nano materials. Some were mined from Earth and others from nearby planets, like xurbium, a metal that Carter pulled from Jupiter. He'd sent a mining drone through the outer gaseous layers, which was able to find its rocky inner surface area. Jupiter turned out to not have as much gas composition as once thought, and showed great potential for its undiscovered compounds. He was sending small amounts of xurbium to Earth for military use, but he kept the rest for use in Section 8.

Xurbium had special properties that allowed for the electromagnetic field around it to be disturbed, unlike the colliders on Earth, once it was activated by powerful magnetic forces. The nano material generated with the xurbium was manufactured in such a way that it copied nature's design of the microscopic scales on the Cyphochilus beetle from Japan.

Similar to his EM tech, Carter's scientists were finding results through bio-mimicry. There was a lot of fancy mathematics involved, but boiled down, it was time travel Carter wanted to master. The device he'd built had been operational for years, but this was only functional in theory. The xurbium helped push the tech into the future. It worked on paper, but never performed properly during tests. None of his team, nor anyone on Earth that he was aware of, were able to get Section 8's project fully functional. Carter didn't care - at least, he kept telling himself so. *I have plenty of time*, but each time he told himself that, he knew he was blowing smoke.

When Rothenberg finally joined him, there was a lot of talk about the future, but the old man dying of cancer wasn't questioning whether to jump on board. He wanted in on the bigger plan, and wouldn't shake hands until Carter got more transparent and revealed Project Avalanche, the project that started with Caldwell years back in Chimera. Avalanche was the company's ultimate goal. It took only a few hours for Rothenberg to have over one billion dollars transferred to bolster Wardlow's cache. Wardlow had presidents, members of Congress, dignitaries, CEOs, you name it - they were all AI and under complete control of a small cabal of elites financing these projects. Rothenberg couldn't help himself. He wanted in, calling to mind Greek mythology and how close he was to becoming a god himself.

Once the sun dipped behind Earth and the demagogues were on the other end of the space station, toasting as they counted their planets, Zar went into action, forcing enough pressure on his restraints that a silent alarm went off. The guard entered room 6B994 to find the old wizard on the floor, free of his bindings. He approached the android, reached down, and grabbed his arm to lift him up. Once he had a grip, Zar punctured his expo-plating with a small probe that sent a fiber line probe deep into the unit, which in turn secured itself on the Guard's neural network.

The two androids stared at each other. The amount of force being exerted was incredible. Their limbs were flexing hundreds of times beyond what would snap a normal human's bones.

When Zar's neural net synchronized with the guard's, he uploaded a self-executable package and then released his hold. The artificial sentry held his grip for a moment, then released and dropped to the floor, as if beaten down.

There was a moment of complete silence. The guard was processing, then Zar looked at him.

"I heard your mother passed away today. I'm terribly sorry about that. I know you loved her, and feel awful. You can't think straight. There's a lot of confusion. A lot going on you can't explain."

The guard stared at the wall, as if experiencing human loss. Zar continued, "I'm going to need you to give me your access codes for Section 8. In return, I have this wonderful book that I will give to you to scan. It will help you find your way through this difficult time. With this, you will find your way."

The guard rattled off his codes, then sat against the wall in silence. Zar ported him once again and uploaded a manipulated version of The Old Testament. Immediately, the guard dropped his power level and began scanning all the possible logic threads from the Bible.

Zar looked down at him for a second, admiring his own trickery, then exited and went straight to Section 8.

When he activated the accelerator, Carter knew he'd screwed up. He was always partially connected to the mainframe on Aurelia by way of his singular syncing mode, and immediately sensed the intrusion. The coincidence of Zar being on Aurelia at the same time they were testing a new xurbium composite smacked him in the face. It had been eating at him the whole time, but he was slipping. The time in space was deteriorating small receptors in his brain. He could keep the body going, but the mind ... no one had ever gotten truly close to understanding it.

When Section 8 started humming, charging the magnets, Zar managed to force his way into a secured weapons depot and retrieve a small cube-looking apparatus. It was something he'd built and named the Metrome. This was an extremely advanced piece of hardware that contained the processors necessary for a time jump to take place.

Zar had this planned down to the second. There was nothing Neumann could do.

When Zar returned and activated the Metrome, Aurelia experienced a strange shift in its orbital pattern. There was a loud snapping sound, then he fell through a hole in time generated in the lab on Section 8. It was all recorded on a series of video cameras.

Carter was with Neumann only seconds after it happened, looking over the data. There was a lot of yelling and excitement all at once, then he thought of his old employee.

"I'll be damned. Westbrook."

Neumann had a funny look on his face. "He's dead."

"Victor's as dead as I am. He's inside that thing's head, and that's enough to be alive."

~

A negligible amount of space debris 3000 miles from the Space Station Aurelia fell through a hole in the time fabric of the Milky Way. It would never be detected by Skywatch or NASA. It was a handful of tiny particulates that entered the earth's atmosphere and burned up entirely, vaporizing into small molecular structures of water, iron, and other compounds. What was significant about this micro-level event was the time difference.

On one side of space, it was the future. The Space Station Aurelia was in full swing. Carter was aged and wearing thin on the amount of time he'd have left even with the most incredible advancements; while on the other side of time, none of this had even taken place.

Recently voted into office was Mayor Caldwell, the android, only known to Carter and his close friend Jack Kutter after the real man fell at roughly 97 mph, never reaching terminal velocity due to the fact he wasn't high enough. However, he was high enough to snap most of the bones on his body, on impact.

Caldwell's doppelgänger had fired every single person who'd been brought on board during the campaign to win the Mayoral election. Carter wanted to separate those close to the man: anyone who'd be able to detect even the smallest of changes in personality between the real and artificial. His new staff, who were unaware of any of his idiosyncrasies, were carrying on like a cage of busy mice, running back and forth preparing the office with all the necessary trimmings to make Bill's time at City Hall appear as normal as possible.

There were gifts piling up on his secretary's desk. One that stood out was a very expensive bottle of Redbreast Single Pot Irish Whiskey with a small card taped to the box that read, "Congratulations! Dinner at McGruff's tonight, 7PM. It's on me. Tommy."

Caldwell picked it up as he was passing by. The brand name registered instantly as a valuable item. Then, Tommy's name was quickly identified with a high probability as being the notorious underworld boss of the East Coast operations for the Irish Mob.

The Mayor carried the bottle into his office and set it on the edge of his desk. He pulled the note from the outer box and picked up the phone. He waited for his secretary to answer.

"Do you have a number for Tommy Swillow? Okay." A few seconds later, Bill scratched down the number on his brand new pad of paper, quickly adjusting his dexterity level to clean up his childish handwriting. "Thank you. Would you also see if there is a reservation for Tommy Swillow at McGruff's, at 7pm tonight? And, if so, find out how many is in the party."

A minute later his phone buzzed. It was a quick call.

The reservation was for two.

10

Abuse

Just under the off ramp on the last exit into Chimera was the sheriff station, tucked back off the road and not easily spotted by passersby, with a small sign at the end of their driveway. Sheriff McGlinty liked it that way. He was a proud transplant from Laredo, Texas—dead ringer for the Marlboro Man, with his tall frame, cowboy look, and button-down shirts. The sheriff approached policing the old school way, with boots on the ground. When he entered a room, you knew he was there.

Deputy Clyde Bowman was a few inches shorter, with sloped shoulders and a growing beer belly. He was uncomfortable wearing hats, making the duo easy to spot when together, because Bowman liked a little color in his shirts.

There was an old case file McGlinty kept on his desk, which he liked to revisit. The Isabella Museum Heist. He spent every morning with his coffee looking over his notes before moving on to new business, and today was no exception. There was always something that bugged him about that particular crime. It was an itch he couldn't scratch.

Even after all the years in Chimera, the sheriff still spoke with a hint of Texas charm. "Bowman, what if I've been looking at this thing the wrong way?"

The deputy stepped over and grabbed the file. He twisted it sideways and handed it back to McGlinty. "How's that?"

McGlinty ignored the joke, even though he thought it was funny. "Let's say I locked onto this one bad angle because it fit, because the other way was so obvious, or maybe because it was so big, I couldn't accept it."

Bowman was about to start a call with his wife, the usual morning call, but he hung up. It was the look in McGlinty's eyes. "What?"

"Conspiracy, Bowman. Conspiracy."

"I don't follow. Twelve paintings, stolen. None are ever found or returned. Swillow's brother-in-law is caught trying to sell the Munch to an agent. Cut and dry, so why the look?"

"He never had the painting. His was a forgery. Damn good one, at that, but he could've easily been trying to take advantage of the situation, using the heist that was broadcast on every news channel from coast to coast to lead the buyer into thinking he had the original. He just needed to be tipped off."

"If I was the buyer, I certainly wouldn't have scrutinized the painting that well, all things considered."

"Exactly."

"So, this whole idea that these paintings are lost in the underworld, and let's let the FBI do their thing, all worked in someone else's favor."

"Did you see the announcement of the Wardlow Met?"

"Yeah."

"Did you also know they acquired all the remaining pieces of artwork through a legal battle with the Isabella after the theft, claiming the works of art held in that private trust were not safe and needed to be moved to the Met to ensure their safety in the future?"

"So, the theft wasn't even the theft?"

"Nothing but a god damn textbook bait-n-switch buried underneath the heist of the century. One so big we'd never see it right in front of our face. Those leeches controlling the board lawyered up and broke the terms of the Isabella Trust. All they had to do was sell the court. Those master works of art are safer in my house."

Bowman walked closer to McGlinty's desk. He shook his head. "You dog. But those lawyers, those same suits with fancy cologne and summer homes, wallets with no lining . . . how are you gonna get through that?"

"I don't have to. Sometimes just the truth is enough."

McGlinty tossed the file in a box marked with a red "X" and kicked his feet up. Bowman hit speed dial for his wife.

"What now?"

"Vito's, grab a sandwich. You coming?"

～

As Mcglinty and Bowman pulled up in front of Vito's, Kaz was turning over the engine in his GTR. The sheriff hated the Japanese race cars. Not because they were Japanese. It was the exhaust. Whenever he saw one, he'd say, "That stupid little fart-sounding muffler." This morning was no exception.

Kaz's trip on the way to Wardlow had a slight diversion. He was dropping by one of the few colleagues who worked in the *non-existent* wing in Fort Mystic which had developed Project DoubleTake. Carter had a very small team finishing the most advanced AI units that were to replace some key people in Chimera Beach. Six individuals were privy to Wardlow's Project Avalanche and were tasked to DoubleTake. Four of these technicians never left Fort Mystic. Only Kaz and Marty Osterman were allowed to have an outside residence. They were watched like hawks, but over time became trusted enough by Kutter to have a little breathing room. If anything ever leaked, these two men knew that the wrath of God was coming.

Marty had an exceptional understanding of the physiology of the human body. He'd spent his life studying the functions of human skin. He'd been able to help Kaz design a special material that acted exactly like human flesh, even with the ability to not only maintain a temperature, but carry the memory and other data in a fluid form that ran through the dermal layers of the AI-like blood running through the human body.

Osterman had an unusual ritual every morning at 4 a.m. He'd run the beach, jumping into the water no matter how cold. Once he'd finished his three-mile jog, he'd then head back to his apartment soaking wet. He was convinced this was keeping his immune system in tip-top shape.

On this morning, Marty ran his routine up the coast and back, then into the water, as usual. He went home, dripping like a wet dog. His neighbors ignored him like they did every day. This had gone on long enough to where no one was paying any attention anymore.

Marty stripped upon entry and went straight to his bathroom where Kaz was waiting, sitting on the edge of the tub. They'd had several odd encounters before, something Kaz had been initiating secretly with Marty, bordering on what anyone else would say were homosexual advances, and so Marty's surprise quickly turned to arousal.

Kaz was always disgusted by this aspect of his job, but today was the end of it, so he went ahead and performed like always, only this time he slipped a syringe from his pocket, loaded with scopolamine. As Marty lay back, anticipating a pleasurable moment, Kaz punctured the skin right under his big toenail.

It only took a second for Marty to knock off, before Kaz sprang into action.

He went into the closet, pulled out some old ties, and strung them together. In a matter of minutes, Marty was hanging from his custom steel shower rod with the suicide note left lying on his bed.

Kaz stood, watching Marty's body as it jerked from a lack of oxygen, "Look at you . . . after all that exercise . . . that work. What a damn shame. And no, I'm not gay. I'm sorry about that. I really am. I hate leading people on. It was just business, Marty. I really hope there's more to life than this. You deserved more."

Once he knew his colleague was gone, Kaz was in the GTR. He wanted Marty's time of death to not be scrutinized when Kutter did his diligence.

He used Osterman's entry codes and keycard to enter the lab, then his special access pass to sneak into the most blacked-out section of Fort Mystic, Project DoubleTake's body room.

Sheriff McGlinty was standing in an upright position, ported to the quantum mainframe, syncing his real-time personal data. DoubleTake had microphones in the sheriff station and was capturing his daily routines as well as every tiny detail of his investigative work.

Kaz pulled out the USB with Victor's celestial code, attached it to a micro motherboard with boosted processors, and connected it to the mainframe. He then keyed into McGlinty's files and swapped Wardlow's "Darwin code" with Victor's "Celestial".

This was all accomplished in under three minutes, and when Kaz slipped out an emergency exit with the help of some unknowns, he left Wardlow's security before any of them had a chance to finish their donuts and stale coffee.

11

Control+H

Sheriff Robert McGlinty's eyes popped open. Everything was foreign. The room was empty, not a place he'd ever been or remembered. *Where the hell?* He went for the door. It was locked, with no switch. On the wall was an intercom system. He started to hit the buttons without any idea which would work.

"Anyone hear me? Hello? There better be a good reason why I'm in here."

Up at sea level, in the security office, Sergeant Henry Claypool jumped from the buzzing sound coming from his communications system. It was the first time he'd actually heard a voice come over the radio. He cleared his throat out of nervousness. "Go ahead, 3112."

"3112? Cut that code bullshit out and let me out. I've somehow lost my access codes."

"Please identify yourself."

"Sheriff Robert McGlinty. You've got me on camera, son."

"Hold tight, sir. I'm not sure what protocol is for this."

"Protocol is getting me the hell out of here right now or I'll have you back in diapers and cleanin' toilets."

"Be right down, sir."

"Attaboy."

No one had clearance around Fort Mystic, or really knew anything about what was going on. Claypool, like everyone at the facility, was compartmentalized, with little knowledge of the grander scheme. All he knew was he had to get an iris scan from anyone who wanted or needed to get past him. The biometrics algorithm would tell him what to do. Everything was in the security system database. All the orders for every section. And only when they were needed, were they doled out.

Claypool found his way to the lab. He stuck his face up to the small window and looked in.

"Have to scan your eyes, sir. Or it'll be my ass."

"It's already your ass. Now, get in here."

An incoming call distracted Claypool. Kutter was on the other end, "I got the alert. Is it McGlinty?"

"Affirmative. He's locked in the lab, and pissed off."

"I'm off-site, got a warning he was active. What happened? What's he saying?"

"Wants me to let him out."

"Can you get to the mainframe inside the room?"

"I can try."

"Go in there. Ignore him. Key in *997HB* and hit enter."

"997HB?"

"That gets you a prompt."

"A prompt?"

"A blank space!"

"Okay."

"Then, all you have to do is type *sudo-kill.*"

"What's that do?"

"Can't say."

"Copy that. You can count on me."

McGlinty was at the window, looking agitated. "Are you listening to me?"

"Coming, sir."

Claypool unholstered his pistol and punched in the security code to open the door, while aiming his pistol with a firm grip. "I need you to stand, then turn around and face the wall, sir."

McGlinty didn't move. "Or what? You'll shoot me?"

"Please don't test me, sir. I'm just doing my job."

Claypool ordered the sheriff to have a seat. McGlinty declined, instead inching toward him, "You're not going to shoot me."

The sheriff moved closer as Claypool went for the mainframe. "Just stay back."

Claypool grew nervous. McGlinty was real to him, and he'd never shot a man before. "Stay where you are, sir."

Mcglinty continued towards him. "Give me the gun."

"Negative, sir."

Claypool was so nervous that McGlinty reached up and took the pistol from his hand without even a struggle. The sergeant remembered the code, though. He remained calm, went to the mainframe and keyed in the numbers, got the prompt, and typed in "sudo-kill." He smiled, looking at McGlinty, thinking he was going to be vindicated. But nothing happened.

~

Back at the Chimera Beach Sheriff's Department, Robert McGlinty sat in his office, finishing up the first half of his Super Salami from Vito's when Bowman entered holding half of his sandwich still wrapped in wax paper.

"Swap?"

"What'd you get again?"

"Black forest ham, brown mustard, Swiss, and the shredded lettuce."

"Let's do it."

McGlinty tossed his unwrapped half to Bowman.

"What's that?"

The sheriff was scanning a list of names.

"The Coonan's kids."

"You have them all logged?"

"Most. It's like trying to keep track of the rats behind Ming's Chinese, though. Just when you think you've got them in check, there's two or three new ones."

"Is this about the cars on Main?"

"One of those rats bricked the minivan rental of some Arab speaking out-of-towner who's claiming he was targeted because of his religious beliefs."

"I heard that call."

"Rebecca was going to spin it into a front pager. Sanders put a lid on it. He calls me, sayin', 'Tourism is paramount'." McGlinty shook his head.

"We should get Sanders one of those suit jackets with the anchors on it, like the mayor in JAWS had." They both laughed.

McGlinty took a bite of the black forest ham, savoring the moment.

"He wants me to pay a visit. Make sure the Swillows understand how Chimera keeps itself alive." He was about to take another bite, but paused. "He thinks I'm a little slow."

"Want me to ride shotgun?"

~

Tommy and his two sharpest, Ben and Terry, exited their car at the yacht club.

A Chris-Craft was waiting for them. It was a long ride around the peninsula, with dead silence the entire trip except for the laughter when Ben pissed off the back of the boat. He was a powerhouse enforcer, but had a weak bladder, and the guys were always joking about how he needed to stop spraying so much of his DNA around Chimera.

Bobbing in the small waves just far enough out to sea that it almost disappeared was "Such a Deal", owned by Jebnor Davis, an East Coast real estate mogul who often loaned his yacht to Carter.

The three mobsters climbed aboard. They met Carter and Kutter on the back deck. None of the men wanted to show their state of play, so the atmosphere was cordial. Kutter took the opportunity to dive right in.

"There are a lot of powerful business interests that see your way of life as extinct."

Tommy chuckled. "We're all running the same hustle. Only difference is you're wearing Armani and we're wearing track suits."

Kutter smiled. "I like a sense of humor. You have to have one, or life is just no fun." Jack wasn't waiting for a response, he was thinking about crossword puzzles. "I'll jump right into it. We have an agenda, and it includes you. We assume you had Sanders backed, and you also have Caldwell on your payroll. Sanders is dead in the water, so to speak." He looked at Carter, who didn't react. "Am I right?"

"Right to the point."

"From here on out, I want you to keep your money. No payoffs to the mayor are necessary. No more." Tommy's face turned. "Buy a summer home or something. We now control the city and we don't need your money."

Tommy looked at Carter, who was watching the waves. "This guy ever talk?"

"I asked him to come so that you understood the scope of this relationship. You'll never talk to him or approach him, or it'll be your bodies he'll be watching float away from the boat."

Ben and Terry were on edge. No one had ever stood in front of the Tank and spoke like that. Kutter knew he went too far, but he had to, so that Tommy would see his strength. It was all chess play, but it worked. Tommy stepped over to Ben and Terry, whispering something to them. They instantly relaxed. The men then walked to the bow of the yacht, far enough away to not be able to hear a word of what was about to be said.

Kutter continued, "It's simple. You're extremely valuable to me, Tommy. I need your support."

Tommy reached out with his hand. Kutter grasped it firmly. Tommy leaned in. "Who the fuck are you?"

"Jack Kutter."

"Kutter. Never heard of you."

"There's a reason for that."

"I bet there is."

Tommy knew at that moment exactly what he was dealing with. The guy driving the Chris-Craft piqued his curiosity, but Kutter was heavy. No one could ever step up that big unless they could back it up.

After really taking a good look at the man opposite him, he saw the guy who tied Saddam Hussein to the hood of his Mercedes and paraded him around Baghdad.

Kutter pointed to an envelope.

"There's a lot o' money in there, and a lot more where that came from."

"I know who he is." Tommy looked at Carter.

"Then you know I have access to whatever I need, with unlimited funds."

"Would seem that way."

"There's going to be a lot of bodies, and I can't have him close to any of this."

"A lot of bodies?"

"We're working on a blacked-out mission for the National Security Agency and, unfortunately, I can't say anything more than that. You'll be acting in accordance with a set of rules that exist, but aren't written down. You're going to be making some very important people disappear. These actions are coming down from way over our heads. Any questions?"

"My operations along the East Coast continue unimpeded?"

"Yes."

"Okay. Where do I—"

"I want the sheriff gone. It has to be clean. Now, I assume you're good at this, because you're still walking around a free man. There's a lot of unsolved cases from New York to Miami I know you're involved with, I mean, this is your thing, no?"

"It's not something we like to do, but—"

"You've got a diplomatic side. That's good to see. There's one more thing."

"Here we go."

"We're going to be replacing all the VIPs in town with AIs. An exact replica."

"Whoa!"

"I figured I'd tell you now. You'd figure it out anyway."

"Talk about the illusion of choice."

"Less variables, that's all. We never had a choice."

"So, that's how Caldwell won."

The look on Kutter's face was as good an admission as he was gonna get.

"I got favors."

"Not as many as you'll have now."

"I haven't seen anything yet." Tommy's eyes closed a bit. "See, I know who I answer to, but you, you're hiding underneath a house of cards, with a deck full of jokers."

"The only one I answer to is God, Tommy."

~

McGruff's was low lit, warm, and busy. The hostess led Tommy into the restaurant, past the bar, then into a section of the dining area for VIPs. Bill Caldwell was there already, walking around the section of tables, greeting local business owners, lawyers and Chimera elite. He was accepting congratulations, shaking hands, and smiling a lot until he saw Tommy, who took a few nods before sitting.

Tommy started in on the mayor the second Bill opened his mouth to speak.

"I did a little homework on you, and I just want you to know this. Everything you're thinking you're experiencing or feeling, is all bullshit. It's programmed into you. You're nothing more than a pile of fancy electronics. I knew the real you. You weren't a bad guy."

"Tommy, it's nice to see you. Jack wanted me to extend a special hello and let you know the dinner is on him tonight."

"No joking around? Great. Thank him for me."

"I just did."

"What'd you do, send him an email?" Tommy laughed.

"Actually, yes. It was something like that."

"Jesus, this is gonna be odd."

The waiter brought a bottle of Tommy's favorite whiskey to the table with two glasses, poured and then left the men alone. Tommy raised a glass. Bill followed.

Tommy made a toast.

"I just wanted to see for myself."

Bill forced a smile similar to the one he'd grafted for the patrons.

"Nothing to see here, Tommy. My advice, get out there and do your fucking job."

12

Facial Recognition

After Kaz fitted RyN2 with his skin, there was a long silence, an awkward hug, and some tears in Victor's eyes. Kaz was uncomfortable, so he left the house, telling Victor to call him once he got settled.

It wasn't long before Victor and RyN2 began to move through the house as they shared stories about his childhood. Not that Victor hadn't loaded his memory with these details prior, but the android looked so much like Ryan, it was drawing him in emotionally—something Victor hadn't imagined would ever happen.

He didn't hold back anything, telling RyN2 the truth about the struggles with depression and the lust for adventure that led to his son's death.

Many days passed before the rules and objective were set.

There were people who would remember Ryan, but they were most likely vacationers from the day he pulled the big stunt at Smuggler's Cove, and were now scattered around the country.

"The only way you're going to be able to really build enough knowledge is through human interaction. I know you'll be able to amass a tremendous amount of acumen in the fields necessary to do what is required of you, but you will be out in the world, so let's just say that keeping a low profile is important. It will be near impossible for people to see that you are an android, but the less attention, the better."

"I understand."

"That's great."

"From our talks over the past week, I understand the emotional connection, too. I see what you meant when you said that the human race is complex beyond the logic and understanding, so I was wondering. Do you want me to call you Victor or Dad?"

~

RyN2 was standing out front of Vito's Deli, amused by all the regulars attacking the case to grab a pre-made sandwich, then grappling for Vito to make subtle adjustments. Some mustard here, a little provolone there, and can you please toast it … when Jimmy Swillow came running up with a stack of signs in his hand.

He barged into Vito's, setting a small wad of bills on the deli counter before going straight to the window to tape one of the notices near the door that read, "NO STEMS ALLOWED."

RyN2 couldn't help himself. When Jimmy bounced back out front, he confronted him, knowing exactly who he was. Jimmy had been in the newspapers a few times for his childish antics and nothing in print (it all happened to be archived online) got past Ryan.

"Hey, I'm curious. What would you do if one walked in there right now?"

Jimmy's face turned. "You joking, kid? I'd rip its arm out and scratch my balls with it. And you should do the same unless you want some robot to be the next president." Without waiting for a response, Jimmy scooted off down the sidewalk, disappearing into the next establishment.

Further down the block was Moe's. Everyone knew it was a pawnshop from the neon "CASH" sign and the "Open 24/7" posted on the inside of the door with another handwritten sign underneath it that read, "Ring buzzer after hours."

Moe lived above the place in a small one-bedroom. He had full-time help from "Scarecrow," a stringy fella that took such a bad beating from one of Tommy Swillow's goons, he was left with a stutter that would show itself when his nerves flared up.

RyN2 could tell Moe was a metalhead from the faded '81 Iron Maiden, Killers tour t-shirt he was wearing. He hoped he didn't have the same demonic energy as the band's mascot, Eddie, who was glaring at him with giant yellow teeth and a menacing smile, holding a hatchet dripping with blood.

He was happy when Moe smiled at him with clean white teeth, setting his hands on the counter. "What can I do for you?"

Scarecrow gave his usual warning to a new face, "You got no goods or money. You're la-lookin' for trouble."

Moe's four fingers were covered in rings. He noticed RyN2 looking at them. "Which one?" Pointing at his middle finger. "That's the '84 championship band for the Tottenham football club." Moving to his pinky, "This is poker legend Lenny Scoglitti's. Bluffed him with a pair of deuces." Finally, he lifted his hand, dangling his last finger with a platinum wedding band. "This is Vito's cousin's.

You know, the deli down the street. I ain't married. It just kinda lets everyone in town know not to fuck with me. So, what can I do for you?"

RyN2 smiled. What brought him inside wasn't the usual hawk job, but a serious question about the *Zarwid the Great* #13 issue that sat on a small piece of felt in the front window display.

"How much is the comic in the window?"

Moe looked RyN2 up and down, sizing him up as a middle class kid who probably had daddy's credit card in his pocket. "Eight hundred. That's for a collector, son. Someone serious who knows the history of comics. Or the future, for that matter." RyN2 just stood there, forcing Moe to continue. "The Zarwid series was short, but very well received. No one really knows why it ever stopped, but this one, number thirteen, is nearly impossible to find. Especially in that shape. Thirteen. Always reminded me of the thirteenth floor myth with buildings. You a serious buyer?"

"I don't have any money."

Moe chuckled. "Now that's the most direct retort I've ever heard, so I'm gonna reciprocate. Get on out, because—" He looked over at his stringy associate, who finished his sentence, "If you ain't got no money, you're la-lookin' for t-t-trouble."

RyN2 didn't move. Instead, he ran a series of probability scenarios and did a little sizing up of his own, before he responded with, "You look like the kinda guy who likes to gamble. You remind me of Newman in *The Hustler*. Albeit a little beaten up and maybe more his second cousin. How about a friendly wager?"

"K-kid's a smart ass. Let me toss him outta here."

Moe held up his hand. "You don't look like you've got a lick of street smarts. I think you should save yourself the debt you'll incur and mosey on."

RyN2 ran a few more data strings, then let it out. "I'll bet you the two hundred that I can hold my breath for twenty-three minutes."

"Well, firstly, we never agreed on two hundred, but hold on." Moe did a quick search on his mobile. "The Guinness Book record is twenty-two minutes, twenty-two seconds. You're gonna blow the record right in my shop?"

"I'm going to stand right out front on the sidewalk so anyone passing can see that I am not pulling any tricks, then blast past that German's record."

"How'd you know he was German?"

"I like to read."

"And obviously hold your breath." Moe was skeptical, but intrigued. "I'm gonna get suckered, here. Just by the look on your face. A cold-hearted stare, you've got. You know you can do this, but you know what? I'm in. I ain't ever seen a record broke, and this is worth the two hundred in the exposure it'll bring from—"

RyN2 stopped him. "There's only one catch. You can only post the picture of my face with the water tank on it. It'll be distorted enough so I won't have everyone approaching me like I'm some kind of circus act. We good with that?"

"Yeah, we're good." He tapped Scarecrow. "Grab the camera and let's get this show rolling."

RyN2 walked over to the cage and asked Moe if he could rummage through his items in order to expedite the bet. Moe agreed, leading him into a large storage area with just about anything you could imagine fifty years of loan sharking near the beach would bring.

He had it all figured out. RyN2 just needed to find the headpiece to a dry suit and a fish tank or glass jar large enough to get over his head. It wasn't long before he had everything set and had made the final touches, ensuring there was an airtight fit.

When he was ready, RyN2 thanked Moe and told him he'd be right back.

Moe didn't hide his agitation. "This is where you go do something. Where you slip in the drug that makes you slow your breathing, right?"

"I'll be right back." Then, RyN2 walked out the door, leaving Moe shaking his head at Scarecrow.

To Moe's surprise, RyN2 returned fifteen minutes later with a small plastic baggy filled with goldfish. He pulled the dry suit over his head, then used a chair to steady himself as Scarecrow helped drop the glass jar over him, then down onto his neck and shoulders. RyN2 was bent over, almost upside down. They filled the jar with water, then added the goldfish. After adjusting the dry suit hood, they pulled over an extra neck seal which formed the tight fit as they twisted the jar down on top of it.

The moment RyN2 stood, Moe and Scarecrow burst into laughter. They helped steady the tank as Ryan shuffled out front to the sidewalk. That's when Moe locked the store and started the timer.

For several minutes, not a soul wandered over. The Chimera residents were used to the many gags used to attract tourists, so this small stunt was easily passed over until Eva walked by, wanting to carry on a conversation with RyN2. She hadn't been programmed with technology advanced enough to realize he was underwater.

"Well, hello, there. What's your name, young man?"

Scarecrow jumped in, "Aren't you Eva, that Wardlow r-r-robot?"

"I'm what they call artificial intelligence, to be politically correct. And here's a tidbit of information that might be of interest to you, they built me in the likeness of Pamela Anderson."

Moe and Scarecrow were trying to figure out what she had just said, because it wasn't making any sense, before Eva trampled on their thoughts, "But something went horribly wrong."

The men laughed. Moe was impressed. "You actually have a sense of humor. I'm Moe, and this is Scarecrow. Drop in anytime. Whatever you need, I most likely have it secondhand and for a great price."

Eva looked at RyN2 and asked, "What's your name?"

The android tried to respond, but only bubbles came out of his mouth, and all Eva could hear were the sounds of the city.

Scarecrow looked at Moe. "We never got his name?"

Moe was sure he'd asked, but couldn't place it.

Across the street, staring at the four of them, was Mia, who'd just parked her motorcycle and locked her helmet. She was quick to recognize Eva and Aiden, who sat motionless at her feet. Mia crossed through some light traffic, catching a horn from a young laborer as he puttered along in a rusted-out low-riding flatbed pickup.

When Mia got to the sidewalk, Eva was already walking away. "Hey."

Eva turned back. There was a brief lag while her database scanned millions of faces and names before she responded, "Hi, Mia. I remember you from last Tuesday at 4 p.m. by the boardwalk."

"You do remember."

Aiden let out a bark, then hung his tongue out of his mouth.

"I have a scheduled checkup that I must go to, but it's wonderful seeing you again. I look forward to the next time we meet." And with that, Eva and Aiden walked off.

Mia turned her attention to Moe. "Alright, what's this carney act you've got going on here?" By the tone of her voice, Moe could tell she was interested in the boy. The way she was looking him ...

"I don't know, Mia. The kid bet me he could hold his breath and break the Guinness World Record. Right here in front of my shop. And now, I'm about three minutes away from losing."

"How long has he been in there?" Mia got close to the jar. She put her eyes up to the glass and knocked. RyN2 winked at her, then opened his mouth. A small goldfish swam inside, circled around and then swam back out before he closed it again. Mia grabbed a video clip.

"Twenty-three m-minutes," Scarecrow said.

"Did you see that fish?" Mia asked. Then it registered. "What? Twenty-three, you said?"

Moe chuckled off his loss in advance. "In about thirty more seconds, yep."

The three stood waiting. When the timer passed the mark, RyN2 knelt over to release the seal and slid his head out of the jar. He kept it upright, so the fish would still be happily swimming. Shaking the water off like a puppy would, he looked at Moe.

"You can keep the fish, but I believe you owe me Number 13."

"Fair is fair, kid, and we've got a new record here. I'm gonna post a pic and put one in the store. Scarecrow, you're gonna file this with the Guinness people and get it on record. I wanna see Moe's mentioned, too. And by the way, kid, before I forget, who the hell is it that I lost to?"

RyN2 looked at Moe and thought for a second. He looked in the display window at his comic and then decided, "Call me, Zar."

~

Melanie Hixson (aka Mel, the tattooed, redhead who had stood in the surf looking out over into the water wondering when Ryan was going to surface) was now eighteen, out of the house, and free of Smuggler's Cove. She'd left a lot behind, but still carried Ryan in her mind. She never stopped thinking about how his body was never found, and like any young realist who had to surf through piles of fake news daily to find a truth, didn't ever want to accept the story of his death until she experienced the truth for herself.

She'd managed to rent a small room with her aunt in Queens, which was the only reason she was able to live close to the Big Apple. Mel did what every newcomer to the city could do, she worked as a runner for delivery services. There were so many mobile apps competing for the service market that jobs were readily available. And even though there was fierce competition, Mel had the charm and drive to secure the job every time. The money was good, and she loved the flexibility and freedom. Enough flexibility to surf the web for several hours a day.

As she was scrolling through a feed of trending videos, laughing her way through a series of hoaxes that had been revealed, she stumbled on one with a crab in augmented reality. Its claw was biting a kid's face. This kid had a jug on his head, filled with water, and a goldfish swimming around in his mouth.

Mel laughed at how pathetic she was, so easily caught up in the childish video and how it could make the heavy rain a little more palatable. She was thinking this while feeling the water soak into her jacket and pour down her back. That's when she noticed the hashtag …

… and her knees buckled.

13

Déjà Vu

The time jump from the space station Aurelia was a success in one respect. Zar landed in the exact same place he had years earlier, Smuggler's Cove, right where Ryan had walked into the water with his concussion. *But, he was a few years past the mark.*

Timing was everything. He'd missed Ryan, escaped the tourist season and riptides, but had landed in the water just in time to cut through a school of cannonball jellyfish. If Zar had been human, he'd have burned in his memory an unforgettable world that looked like exploded popcorn floating in the thick blue-green water. He'd have been stung a dozen times, but he was an android, and only had his mission in mind.

On his first attempt, there wasn't enough power being delivered to the particle accelerator. His body appeared to materialize, but this was only a mirror of his physical matter, and the reason why Ryan saw the hand in the water before it disappeared.

Zar had a big problem. He was stuck, with no way back. He wouldn't be able to save Ryan, this time. Victor's dream of putting his family back together were stunted and would most likely be on hold for what might seem like an eternity if Zar couldn't get back and attempt the jump again. The only equipment capable of doing so was orbiting the earth in that lab on Aurelia, somewhere in the future.

Zar did have one thing going for him. The metrome. The tool necessary to jump. It was a powerful piece of technology; a processing unit shaped like a small cube with a shell constructed out of polished xurbium, which held the properties necessary to boost the underdeveloped power sources on Earth to the correct state. But there wasn't a lab on the planet equipped with anything close to the design specifications of the accelerator in Carter's lab.

It was 11 p.m. when Zar walked out of the water at Smuggler's Cove with nothing but the metrome in his hand and a lot of questions. He ran strings of possibilities, then decided he needed to find Victor, if he was still alive. Because the jump had burned the clothes off his body, Zar looked like a senile eccentric when he crossed the beach, nude, before he walked up onto the dock.

A local fisherman had left his trawler tied off with the keys in the ignition, before wandering off to the old Cove Tavern for cocktails. It was the off season, no one was around. No one but Zar, the ruffling of the surf, and a few ghost crabs.

He powered up the trawler, turned on the navigation, and tapped into a satellite web access point.

Zar found an address for Victor in Chimera, which he calculated to be about eight hours north. He kept his hand on the wheel every minute of the ride up the coast, creating a view that any average person would have snapped a hundred pictures of along the way. He bounced up and down under the stars to the beat of the small waves until the beach community was in sight.

After anchoring offshore, away from the popular stretch of sand, Zar swam in. It was 7 a.m. There were only a few bodies visible in the area.

Eva didn't process Zar's naked body any differently than she did when Danté, her neighbor's gray schnauzer, who was in heat, dry humped Aiden earlier that morning. Nor did Zar show any excitement when he realized there was another android thirty feet away from him, but he was curious about the probability of the occurrence. He walked up to Eva, slipped his probe into the tiny data-link slot just behind her ear, and stripped as many ones and zeros as he could from her memory. Back at Wardlow, the computer that was monitoring Eva's systems showed a spike in its processors. The CPU usage so far was beyond any level expected from her routine that an automatic email was sent to the team in the lab to bring her in for a scan.

Timmy Fitzgerald, one of the runts who hung around Coonan's, had an early morning routine of trolling the beach for lazy tourists who'd left their wallets unattended while they took that refreshing dip they'd never be able to get back at home. This was going to be that little extra that would give him an in with Jimmy Swillow.

Timmy got a good look at Zar, then sent out texts to his pals without thinking about the repercussions, *some old freak-looking freak just walked out of the ocean naked, and I swear he's got no junk. I think he's gonna try and do Eva, the super squid. With what, I don't know.*

Within seconds, Zar stepped away from Eva with a detailed mapping of the area and files on most of Chimera's inhabitants. He swiped a towel from a sunbather named Lisette, then wrapped his waist before little Timmy could snap a picture. Lisette was visiting from Paris, taking in as much as she could in her banana-colored bikini minus the top, so any thought of a potential predatory threat or assault hadn't entered her mind. If someone would have asked her, she would have laughed and said, *it's a culture thing, you Americans are way behind.*

She just smiled, turning her focus away when Zar didn't give her anything more than a look that said thank you.

Zar's height, long hair, confident stride, and casual demeanor allowed him to walk off without alarming any of the others at the beach.

It wasn't long before Timmy regretted texting his buddies. He was getting smacked hard with sexual innuendos, typical in the hard world that surrounded a place like Coonan's Pub. There was a strong hatred the regulars shared for political correctness, and Timmy was the target at the moment, *So, staring at guy's packages, now, Timmy? Just wait till Jimmy finds out you're a queer.*

Zar scanned all the data from Eva, but couldn't find anything on the Westbrooks beyond the address he'd already found online. He didn't mind. He walked off the sand, crossed the boardwalk, and disappeared into a small crowd of people huddling outside a beachfront cafe.

~

That morning, Coonan's front door was locked. The lights were low, the blinds closed tight on the front window. Tommy sat in the booth he always sits in, the one with a clear view of the front door. Brundle was across from him following every subtle movement on Tommy's face, waiting and wondering until he couldn't wait any longer. "Never seen you think so hard. Is it that guy on the boat?"

"We've always been political, always been fighters. Right in the middle of it, but it's been some time. We've had a little break with our cozy ties up and down the coast, sitting pretty, collecting. Things are gonna get sticky again."

"I'm with you, man."

"You remember that trick I taught you with the Velcro on the cuff of your coat?"

"Of course."

"I swiped Kutter. When the boat rocked. I took advantage. My feet weren't situated, and when that wave pushed, I hugged him really good. I got some hair, skin, and some fibers from his jacket."

Tommy held up a small Ziploc baggy.

"Jeez, it's that heavy?"

"We're about to go down a long, dark hallway."

"I've got eyes in the back of my head, boss."

~

The only information the Coonan kids were given was to find Sheriff McGlinty and get word to Mickey at the bar. It was little Timmy Fitz that ran in the back door and set off the chain of events. First was the pistol hand-off to Brundle. It was a 9mm Baretta FS with three additional magazines, each loaded with a slightly different ammunition. One had expanded cartridges, one came with jacketed projectiles, the last was a .380 ACP.

In the parking lot was a stolen van and in the driver's seat was Terry. Ben came around the corner from the alley with a Taser in his pocket. He opened the back door and jumped in. Brundle exited the bar and hopped in, slipping into the back. He sat next to Ben, who only offered a nod. The van drove off.

~

Kutter imagined his hand around Claypool's throat. "That was the billion dollar Marlboro Man you let walk outta here."

Claypool was scared. He could see the unspoken anger in Kutter. "It's so secretive in here. I had no idea what I was dealing with. I swear, I did everything straight across the board, to protocol."

"Straight across the board? What the fuck does that mean? Does that mean you didn't adapt, or overcome? Do what was necessary to ensure Wardlow property was protected and secure, as stated in your directive?"

The guard had an empty look on his face while assuming his immediate release from duty. All he could think about was some sketchy program he'd be transferred to somewhere over in the Middle East where the probability of him returning home upright would be nil.

Kutter smiled. "Listen, kid. You didn't do so hot. In fact, you fucked up good. But I value my guys. I do. And I understand your performance is a reflection of me—"

"Yes, sir."

"Don't acknowledge me yet. I'm not through, son."

Claypool's nerves showed. "Yes, sir."

"What did I just say?"

Kutter's phone rang. He stepped out of the room. It was a short call. He'd just received word that the GPS tracker in their artificially intelligent McGlinty was activated. Kutter walked back in and gave Claypool a more relaxed expression. "Put on your civies and meet me in the garage in ten."

"Yes—"

The horror on Claypool's face slowly washed away after Kutter left the room.

~

Terry pulled up alongside McGlinty, who was walking on the edge of the road into Chimera. He looked a little frazzled compared to the real thing, who was usually in his squad car and tightly dressed. The sheriff had on a ruffled shirt hanging out of his waist belt, blowing in the coastal breeze.

Brundle hopped into the passenger seat, rolled the window down, and addressed him. "Need a ride, bud? Be glad to help you out."

McGlinty stopped to take a look at Brundle, whose facial metrics were in his database. He had been convicted on some minor offenses as a teen, but hadn't been on the police radar for some time. The one exception was the match to a list of associates to the Swillow family which, in Chimera, wasn't a bad thing on the surface. It was the federal database that rang sour.

The sheriff always had a large case file in front of him, and so he decided to take Brundle up on his offer. "That would be great. Take me over to the motor pool?"

Brundle reached over the seat and slung the back door open. McGlinty got in, not paying any attention to Ben, who was sitting beside him.

Brundle twisted his neck. "What happened to your car? You have an accident?"

McGlinty was silent for a moment, then said, "I'm a bit hazy on that. I just wanna get to the motor pool and get back to work. Got a lot cooking at the moment."

Brundle looked at Ben with an odd face. "Yeah, I bet you do."

Terry turned off the main road and down a side street that led toward the Industrial Waste Management plant and Aluminum Recycling Center. The sheriff noticed the direction shift. "The motor pool is east of here. Why are we heading west?"

Brundle was looking straight out the windshield this time. "Yeah, we need you to take a look at something at the recycling center. One of our guys was digging and found something that looked like a body, possibly. You mind taking a quick look?"

"A body? Absolutely. I'd be happy to take a look. You haven't called it in?"

"Well, it just happened, Sheriff. Just got the call from the boys at the center, when I seen you on the road. We're about thirty seconds from the site."

McGlinty reached for his mobile, but couldn't find it. "Shit. I can't find my phone, either. It's like I was on some bender that I can't remember a lick of. Could I use one of yours? Should call it in."

Brundle turned his whole body in the seat. "We're here. Let's take a quick look, and if it's something, I'll let you use my phone, no problem. No need to get a pile of cars out here, create a fuss, unless there's really a body. Know what I mean?"

McGlinty shared a flat look when the van stopped. Brundle hopped out, sliding open the back door for the sheriff, who stepped out in front of a massive hole surrounded by a junk yard of scrap cars and assorted piles of metals ready for processing. Behind him were stacks of used car tires and a large bulldozer. He took it all in, then stepped up to the hole, determining it was a little bigger than a shipping container, lengthwise. Looking down, he realized there was nothing but dirt in the bottom.

"Where's the body?"

Before McGlinty could turn around, Brundle had pumped four shots into his back. The sheriff fell into the hole, landing on the bottom face down.

Brundle walked closer to the edge, looked in, then realized something. "Shit."

Terry looked over at Brundle, who dropped the handgun into the hole. "What's up?"

Brundle shook his head, then pulled out the small Ziploc baggy with the DNA in it. "Tommy wants me to put this on the body before we cover it up."

Ben grabbed the bag. "I'll do it."

Ben slid down the edge into the hole. He looked back up at the guys with a funny face. It was a different feeling from up on top. It was creepy being inside the hole with the body, and the rough-cut dirt walls looked like they were ready to collapse. Ben had never been in this kind of situation, but he didn't want them to see he was shaken. He needed to toughen up to show his dedication.

He opened the bag and shook its contents, most of which were undetectable to him, then he slipped the empty bag back into his pocket. That's when McGlinty started to move. First his leg. "Guys. He's movin'. Get me out of here—"

Brundle yelled down, "Pick up the gun. There's a few more rounds in the magazine."

Terry went to the large scrap shed and brought back a ladder, dropping it into the hole. Ben was hesitant at first, but he picked up the Beretta and pulled the trigger twice. He watched for any signs of movement, then stepped over to the ladder, tossed the gun behind him, and climbed out.

Quick with the bulldozer, Terry pushed a thousand tons of dirt on top of McGlinty, then smoothed out the surface, as if he'd done this a dozen times before. Brundle smiled at Ben for not complaining, bobbing his head with a look of pride.

The men hopped in the van and drove out the same way they came in, passing Kutter and his men with their GPS readings pinging the area. The signal was bouncing around within a small radius. It was all the aluminum in the scrap yard causing the problem. It didn't take long before they were standing on top of the smoothed-out dirt patch that Brundle, Terry, and Ben had just vacated.

Claypool was walking around the piles of metal scrap, looking for McGlinty, while Kutter stood directly on top of where the Wardlow android was buried. It wasn't making sense until he noticed the tire marks and the area that had been scraped over. "No way," he said to himself before raising his voice to Claypool. "Get over here."

Claypool snapped to attention. "Yes?"

"Can you handle this thing?" Pointing to the bulldozer.

"I think so."

A few hours passed. The sun was falling behind the pile of dead cars when Claypool finally managed to dig wide enough to get deep enough, when they saw McGlinty's arm moving in the loose dirt.

They dragged the android out of the hole.

Kutter's driver had stayed quiet throughout, while Claypool, who was embarrassed by his performance earlier, was fighting to keep his job. Kutter's nickname for his driver was K9, because that's just what he was, a dog.

K9 didn't need anything more than a hand gesture from Kutter to step out of the car and knock Claypool into the hole. He took aim and shot several rounds into his chest, killing the young soldier for being in the wrong place at the wrong time.

Kutter knew what happened. And in a way, he was proud. The McGlinty android was a success. He was real enough in the eyes of the Swillow crew, and that meant a lot. But now, he'd have to rethink the Tommy situation.

14

Lend A Hand

Mia rode her motorcycle with the dexterity of a skilled Grand Prix racer, even with her prosthetic right arm. It wasn't easy to spot, but it was a small detail that Ryan the android was able to notice, log, and set aside—along with her license number and complete background file—the day he built the fish tank on his head outside of Moe's Pawnshop.

She whipped down a strip of coastal highway just outside of Chimera, the ends of her red hair trailing out from under an iridescent gold-shielded helmet. Her black leathers were warm in the summer sun, with a subtle cool breeze winding around her neckline and down past her belly button. When she twisted her upper body, her jacket loosened enough for the air to flow around to her lower back, bringing a slight chilling effect to her spine.

Motorcycle riding for Mia was thinking time. Freedom.

The trauma burned into her psyche from the accident that took her arm did cloud her thought process, at times. While riding, she'd experience a similar sensation if the wheel slipped or the rear brake locked up, disrupting her peaceful moment. But Mia would shake it off and keep going. She would break through and always look in front of her. Except when she turned her head at the sound of a tire blowout on the semi-truck she'd passed, which caused her to miss the light change. RyN2 stepped into the street, but sensed the impact just in time to jump back as Mia blew past him and grazed his shirt with her elbow.

Mia was shaken by her mistake, scolding herself out loud, "No, no, no, don't ever do that again." Her muffled voice bounced around inside her helmet padding. She slowed the bike down and turned off the road. After killing the engine, she slipped her leg around and turned to see RyN2 walking toward her. Mia lifted her helmet off her head and shook her long hair into place.

Before he could get close enough, she started firing off an apology, "I'm sorry. I usually don't let things distract me when I'm in the zone. That was stupid. My friend Danny taught me to always keep your head forward, look in front, and use your mirrors to check behind. I am sooo—"

RyN2 was close enough to cut her off with a soft tone, "A hundred and fifty-three horsepower at eleven thousand RPM. How does it feel traveling with all that power?"

Mia looked the android over. There wasn't a hint of anger or fear showing. It was the sound of genuine curiosity that was in his voice.

Ignoring her lack of reply, RyN2 continued, "I've been doing some research online. There's a radio telescope in Green Bank, West Virginia. They study sounds that come from the sky. I hacked into a forum I'm sure I wasn't supposed to be in and noticed they were talking about these encrypted audio packages they've been collecting for years that they can't unscramble."

Mia had a puzzled look on her face. She'd never met anyone like RyN2 before. Most guys stared at her with soft eyes and responded to her immediately, but RyN2 was off on a tangent in his own world, and this struck her. "You don't care that I almost killed you?"

"That's impossible."

"What?"

"I've already died once."

RyN2 was walking the line of being detached from reality, yet managed to have a sincerity about him that was attractive. Mia wasn't sure what to make of it. "Is that suppose to be funny?"

"I'm not sure."

"You know the horsepower of my engine, but can't figure out if you're a comedian or not?"

"Yeah," he agreed. "I bet we could get to Green Bank really fast, Mia. Four hundred and eighty-two miles at a hundred miles per hour. That's like watching two feature films and a couple music videos."

"How'd you know my name?"

"I looked a little different before. My hair was soaking wet. You posted that video with the goldfish swimming out of my mouth. It has twenty-four thousand views at the moment."

Mia knew instantly, then, that RyN2 was special. She'd spent a lot of time talking with Eva and goofed with the STEM's parking enforcement squids to know he was something different—that RyN2 was either singular, or pure AI.

"One question before I make a decision about this trip." RyN2 only looked at her, waiting for her to finish. "Will you come with me?"

"For sure."

"That's so cool."

"What is?"

She gave him a big smile, slipped on her helmet, and smacked the back of her seat.

"That you can relate."

Mia got RyN2 on the back of her bike, cranked the throttle, and peeled off a few miles on the coastal highway. She exited into a private drive just south of the Chimera Speedway and parked in an area with several trailers that was home to a small community whose lives revolved around track days.

~

It was a short walk from her trailer to the edge of the beach. RyN2 and Mia sat where she and Danny Fury would talk about the things she couldn't talk to her father about. The track was the one thing Mia had that separated her from the rest of the Swillow clan. Fury had made Tommy a lot of money with his winning drag car races, and he was trusted by the family until the day Mia injured herself. As her teacher, Danny couldn't help but hold on to this memory with guilt, but he'd get past it. Mia was the one who hopped on the motorcycle and took off after arguing with her father about Marky Boy going down the wrong path. Jimmy was the variable who couldn't handle his emotions, so Danny was careful to keep a distance. To Jimmy, Danny was a celebrity, and that made it hard for him to approach with any aggression.

Mia looked at RyN2 with the same intensity she'd give her mentor when they were having a serious moment. "Can I trust you?" she asked, while unzipping her jacket. "I'm guessing you know everything about me."

RyN2 nodded. "The Sex Pistols t-shirt you were caught stealing when you were fourteen."

"One of the highlights of my youth. Everyone at school found out. They already hated me for being a Swillow. I was this toxic chick, after that." Mia flipped through a few memories. "Was there anything else?"

"Sure, but it's not important."

"My mother's death. Is that in there?" She pointed to her head.

"Happened the same month as my mother and I. We both drowned in the

Atlantic. You lost yours to bad health." Mia was processing his words, almost like RyN2 would. He continued, "My father built me in Ryan's likeness—and in many ways, his consciousness."

"So, you're … Ryan 2.0."

RyN2 smiled as he reached for her hand. He flipped it over so her palm faced upward, slowly ran his finger along her heart line, and then looked her in the eyes. "Your father is Tommy. He was born in Dorchester. Your brother Jimmy has accumulated a hundred and thirty-eight parking tickets over the past two years. You have an uncle incarcerated at Rikers Island for theft of valuable art. His commissary balance is a thousand twenty-eight dollars." RyN2 let go of her hand.

Mia laughed as he continued, "My father is Victor Westbrook. He's a geek who works at Wardlow Technologies. My mother Claire used to make the best crab cakes. Her trick was using corn flakes instead of bread crumbs."

Mia was forming an image of RyN2 as if he was a normal young guy. She felt warmth.

"The way you're looking at me right now. If you were, you know, I'd read it as you liking me. Is that possible? That you can do that?"

"I do have a goal, and I'll head in that direction. Victor wants me to put the family back together. That's my job. But I also have strong emotive entropic coding that will allow me to interact on a human level more and more as time passes. I will evolve."

"I'm not sure what all that means, but—"

"It's an extremely accurate *yes*."

Mia's mind was off, wondering about the possibilities; the oddity of it. She thought about trust and honesty and how this was the foundation of every great relationship. "It's funny. I feel like I can relate to you more than I can to anyone in my own family, and you're a robot."

RyN2 didn't respond. "So, what's at Green Bank?"

~

Kutter had only a small sports bag in his grasp when he stepped up to Marty Osterman's place, jimmied the door lock, and entered. By the third step up the staircase, he knew what he was going to find. He'd hoped to catch Marty sleeping in bed. He was ready to get some answers. The code swap in McGlinty was the work of something well planned and required outside assistance and expertise that was a giant step above Wardlow's computer science department at the moment.

The stench of death was thick in the air at the top of the stairs. Even an experienced EMT would've left the contents of his stomach on the carpet, but Kutter kept moving.

A light was on in the bathroom, a tap on the door knocked it open. There was Marty, hanging from the shower rod.

In the bedroom, Kutter was careful as he went through and inventoried as much as he could in his mind. There wasn't a hint of a woman's touch. The collection of New York Comic-Con passes, the adult sex toys which appeared to be for men, the note on the bed. It read like a textbook suicide, "I've been carrying this depression for too long. It's eroded every aspect of my life. I can't go on like this. It's too much for me to deal with. Please understand, I will be much happier where I'm going. Marty." The handwriting looked forcibly too loose, as if to appear from someone who'd had too much to drink, yet was placed perfectly on the bed, not a crinkle to the paper. Staged.

Kutter's razor-like perception had the entire scene summed up in an instant. *Osterman was used and discarded. I'm not dealing with a clinically depressed homosexual whose taken his life, I'm dealing with an organized operation.*

Kutter called into the sheriff's station. He mentioned the front door being open and a horrible smell coming from Osterman's address, then hung up. He wanted to see the Wardlow employees' reactions from the news, first thing in the morning, as he interviewed each and every one of them.

15

Ouroboros

Zar had been standing on Victor's porch for three hours, as still as stone. He'd reached the house at 3 a.m., had a small owl land on him, a mouse ran between his feet, and three cars drove by before the sun came up.

Victor was inside, sleeping. His mobile had a text waiting for him when he woke. It read, *Here.*

He was a bit slow that morning, and figured the text was a mistake. It was from an unknown, out-of-state number from a VOIP exchange online he'd never recognize, and he didn't put it together until he dropped a vanilla-flavored pod into the coffeemaker.

When he opened the front door, Zar shook Victor's hand, then walked past him into the house, diving right into a report on all the progress that had been made over the years.

> *"Sparklight data merged with the ML909 sequencing algorithm was the key to finding the proper equations. Metallurgical data from xurbium proved instrumental in the construction of the necessary apparatus. Important—there will be a large enough sample (of xurbium) striking Earth in the Monongahela National Forest at Dry Fork, GPS coordinates 38.725734, -79.707856, in the form of a meteor, 1008 hours from now, roughly 6 weeks away ... "*

"Where's RyN2?"

Victor wanted to say *you're early*, but stopped himself from doing so. His logic-minded sensibility cautioned of its redundancy. Instead, he acted on his compulsion to hug Zar, who responded in kind. It wasn't as awkward as he'd imagined. Zar was extremely advanced emotionally, compared to RyN2 who had, himself, adapted quickly and quite well to normal human interaction. Victor held his flurry of thoughts and questions for later.

He looked at Zar with pride, and without hesitation, responded, "Follow me."

Victor took Zar up to RyN2's room and loaded syncing software to his system, which Zar took a few minutes to upgrade. Victor continued as he thought of RyN2. "I speak to him all the time."

Zar finished optimizing his system. "I've encrypted the communications between us with more robust coding. This will be important, as Wardlow begins to piece together, over a short period of time, what we're working toward."

"I would've never realized they'd be such a threat."

"With their lust for power, even your family reunion is at risk. We have to work fast, even though they are unevolved in terms of processing power, which we harnessed years earlier. However, Carter is in space mining xurbium, and will be able to pull some data from the equipment I altered to make the jump with."

"He's still alive?"

"He thinks so. It's a borderline illusion. The trillions he dumped into Singularity with other global elites has paid off for the moment. There are detrimental side effects, however, that are beginning to show. His brain is going to deteriorate rapidly, unless he solves his processing bug. And he's stuck in orbit with very little access to Earth's resources. All the science, all the gadgets in the world won't hold up against Mother Earth's riches."

"My god, Zar, I could speak with you for a century and not be satisfied."

"Carter is looking to steal the glory."

"So was Idi Amin," Victor circled the room, thinking. "I just want my family back."

As the intensity of the rendezvous found its equilibrium, Victor mentioned as he pointed to the framed comic on RyN2's wall, "Your likeness to his favorite series, I should have known he'd do something so colorful." He gave Zar's clothes a good look. "And the clothes, you're looking like one of the carnie acts the kids do on the boardwalk."

Zar didn't mind looking odd. He assumed it would help him, even if it was a bit awkward. He stepped closer to the #13 issue of *Zarwid The Great*. "I was thinking we could create this outfit on the cover. I have calculated a potential jump point. I'm unclear if it's realistic yet, but for now it will have to be a target. It's located dead center on the Chimera Theater property.

Victor jumped in. "It's been boarded up for a while now."

"Which could be to our advantage. If we can iron out all the issues, I think a show would be a fantastic diversion."

"You really did carry over his sense of humor. It's unbelievable. And I agree, yes. If we have to build a large-scale jump apparatus, there's really no better disguise than a magic show. Hell, Copperfield made the Statue of Liberty disappear. At least, the people thought so."

Zar tapped the framed comic. "You know, Carter's carrying this around in his pocket on the opposite end of our timeline, right now."

"He's that close to us, but still a century off."

"He's also bastardized a lot of your code. He doesn't know what to do with it without you. His scientists are not sure how to correctly handle a new variable I call conversion. It's similar to entropy, yet falls under a more rigid technical definition for the purposes of tweaking algorithms." Victor was all ears. "He's turned your ML algorithms into a textbook example of the law of diminishing returns. They're almost eating its own tail."

"So then, we have time?"

"Time is elastic, now."

"I know. I'm rationalizing. I want my family together and now we've got Wardlow, with the power of the government, trying to take this away before I even get it back, and *they don't even know it.* Everything I've planned and have worked towards could be swept away like some sort of collateral damage."

Zar was all business. "I've just sent a message to RyN2. And he's confirmed. We are to meet at the house this evening at 8 p.m."

A notification popped up on the computer linked to RyN2. He had sent a message to Victor, "Dad, I got the message from Zar. Game on, man."

Victor laughed, then almost shed a few tears at the same time. "I gave him the choice," Victor smiled, looking at Zar. "He called me Dad."

~

Mel rode the purple line, 7 train toward Flushing. She was thinking about the small backpack and duffel bag sitting on the old schoolhouse desk chair in that tidy room her aunt set her up with and the view out the small window, slightly obstructed by an air conditioner of the Chinese daycare center across the street. Not very exciting for living in New York, she thought. She almost missed the 76 station and haranguing the customers, but she was appreciating how mobile her lifestyle was in comparison to her parents. They had married, found a small house in the Cove, and built a life in the beach town. They never made enough during the season to sustain life outside of the beach town. If they'd taken trips or had any "extravagant luxuries", as her father would say, they'd end up in poverty.

Mel didn't mind the thought of carrying her life in a backpack, at least for now. The only thing that needled her was the disappearance of Ryan, and even though the Wi-Fi service on trains was sketchy in terms of privacy, which Mel was concerned about, she logged in online and scrolled to the video of RyN2 with the fish tank on his head. She hit the play button, glancing at the hashtags #Zar and #MoesPawn one last time before she decided to go for it.

Mel sent a private message to Mia. *Saw your vid the other day. It's been driving me crazy. I used to know someone special who called himself Zar, but he went missing a few years ago. Sorry, but I have to ask. BTW, I'm not a stalker. Can you send me a real pic? Just curious if it's the person I knew. Mel (from Smuggler's Cove).*

Mia was in the shower when her phone pinged. She was washing off the sweat from riding in her leathers all morning. RyN2 had been waiting outside, but he'd left to pass by the Chimera Theater on his way home. There was a string of texts from her father, asking if she'd gone to see Marky Boy, which she wasn't going to respond to. She just didn't want to, and had no plan of telling The Tank about her new friend yet. One from RyN2, which is how it came up on her screen, letting her know he had to leave. It was simple, short, and had no other information or explanation. Only Mel's text prompted her to respond.

Mia toweled off, pulled a t-shirt on, and slipped into some cutoff shorts. She pushed open the door to her trailer and sat on the steps. *Hi, Mel. Sorry, no pics. I just happened to be passing by at that moment. Hope you find your friend :)* After she hit SEND, Mia tapped the EDIT button and deleted the text thread from Mel. She brushed it from her mind as she looked down at her prosthetic arm. She had the same feelings she'd had when she first lost it in the accident—sadness and a fear of not being good enough—then she burned the thought from her mind just as she'd trashed the text from Mel. *Fuck you, he's mine*, she thought.

The 7 train entered the Flushing Station. Mel had just stepped off when she received the message. There was an instant reaction of relief, but her gut turned. It was just too much of a coincidence for her to let go. *There can't be another Zar* kept rolling through her head, on top of the article she'd read about how humans are all proficient liars. Mel kept digging for any further details on

Mia. Then finally, after having to pay a few bucks for a background check, she got a hit. Even though Mia was careful about her Internet usage, thanks to Tommy's insistence when she was young, the site cross-referenced possible friends, pointing Mel in the direction of the Chimera Speedway and Danny Fury.

16

Obituary

An earthy, green-colored 1972 Chevy Impala was the only vehicle parked in the Chimera Theater parking lot. The white lines marking the individual spaces weren't visible anymore. The aged concrete and asphalt patches were covered in moss and the cracks were filled in with dandelions and grass. The theater property had become an urban jungle hidden by a surrounding office complex on one side and a massive stone facade, the rear wall to the new Beachfront Mall, on the other. The exterior of the theater was sun-faded, tagged, and beaten from the salty air. Even its marquee was tilting downward, from wood rot. On one side there were a few red letters still hanging, loosely spelling "he hing", a fractured reminder of John Carpenter's *The Thing*, the last film the theater played.

The green Chevy had been sitting on cinder blocks for three years, a victim of the Coonan kids, who had never been caught stealing the four tires. It helped that there were no cameras or security guards watching over the property, and that Clarence, its owner, didn't care.

Ironically, the Coonan kids used the car as a hangout. The glove box was a drink tray and the trunk was used as a stash. Little Timmy Fitzgerald was there alone, sitting in the passenger seat because it provided a clear view of anyone who'd decided to wander into the lot.

Timmy was impatiently waiting for his friends, his feet up on the dash. *Where was that can of energy drink?* he thought. After repeated text bombs to his friends telling them to hurry, he hopped into the back seat, crawled into the trunk, and began rummaging through the junk, wondering, *Has someone stolen my boost?* Then, Timmy began singing, "Piss-colored, piss-flavored energy boost. I need it. I need it, so I can bust loose."

Timmy came waddling out of the trunk and he crammed into the back seat with a smile on his face. He raised the can up as if he'd struck gold, opened the back door, held the top away from the car, and pulled the tab. *Sploosh*. The pressure built up from the summer heat and spit three ounces of the drink into the air before Timmy turned the can to his mouth and guzzled the remaining nine.

Watching him from behind was RyN2. When Timmy realized it wasn't his friend standing there, he exited the car and shut the door. Timmy burped, then stepped closer to RyN2. "I'll sell it to you. There's no title or nothin', but it's got an engine and stuff. Let's say, five hundred. It's worth it. All the cars today are shit, compared to this."

RyN2 played along and walked around the Impala, evaluating. He noticed there was no rear license plate, but there was one still bolted to the front with rusty screws. The kids had tried to remove it, but ended up bending it instead. RyN2 hacked the DMV system in seconds and ran a check. "Title's in the name of Clarence Clancy, at this address."

Timmy was quick on his feet. He was used to getting questioned about his stories. "Must be the old man inside. Dude's boarded himself in. Place is condemned by the city and he won't come out. That's why it's five hundred. It's a steal."

RyN2 laughed as he walked over to the building to check the doors. Timmy was right. The entire building was boarded up and chained. There was a notice posted to the door with a bold red tape. It warned of possible condemnation if the owner didn't make substantial fixes to meet city codes and ordinances. Clarence had a month to comply, or the process would begin.

RyN2 placed his ear to the warped flake-board covering the glass inserts in the front entrance doors. All he could hear were faint sounds of an emotive orchestral movie score.

~

Clarence Clancy was seventy-three years old. He'd suffered from his time serving as a communications officer in the Vietnam War. It was a fancy title the Navy gave him for calling in air strikes. Even though he'd never had to face his enemy on the battlefield directly, Clancy was responsible for the deaths of over a thousand Vietnamese. This weighed heavily on his mind. Then, just before his time in Southeast Asia was up, his parents passed away.

Between the fallout of war and the loss of his family, Clarence returned to the states and shut himself off from the world. He took an inheritance and bought the theater, only screening a few of the major releases in the early seventies before he closed its doors for good. He sat inside watching old films, only slipping out under the moonlight to buy groceries at the 24-hour Food Mart down the street.

Clarence was coming out of the bathroom when he heard the banging on the entrance. The deep, hollow sound struck him the wrong way. It reminded him of the softer concussive sounds of carpet bombs hitting villages from a distance, and so he kept walking through the soundproofed door into the main theater. He moved down the aisle to row H, shuffled over several seats to number 28, then sat. He looked up at the screen, took a deep breath, and forgot all about the noise. He'd gone to his basement film storage and pulled out his favorite noir to watch, *Pickup on South Street*. It was a film directed by an ex-army officer who'd survived heavy fighting in WWII, came home, and also consumed himself with film.

Timmy yelled to Ryan, "I wouldn't try it. He's got the place booby-trapped. Probably in there watching an old gangster film. From where you're standin', you can hear that funny dialogue, especially late at night when the city's quieter."

~

News of the Osterman suicide was sprawled across the front page of the *Chimera Times*. Rebecca's investigative team made calls to Wardlow, inquiring about Marty's work, but got nothing more than an email expressing their sadness at the loss of a talented scientist. Osterman's entire life would be summed up in a small op-ed piece about his personal life. The rogue journalist dug up a proclivity to what were being called "cagey" gay bars in New York City. Marty had apparently been a regular late night romper, but no other details were provided. Even though these sordid details had nothing to do with the reality of the situation, it all seemed to help support the suicide, which pleased Kutter.

Victor was standing on his front step, holding the newspaper, when Kaz pulled up in his GTR. He raised a copy of the newspaper and stretched his face. Victor acknowledged, waving his.

Kaz was the first to say something. "Wow—"

Victor walked closer to the car. "I had no idea." He rested his hand on the door. "You gonna shut the engine off and come in? Coffee?"

The look on Kaz's face turned. "Why don't you get in. I'll drop you at work."

As they drove along the coast, Victor found himself looking at Kaz and questioning the style of the GTR. It didn't fit the Wardlow skin maker. He'd joked about it before, but there was something else that he couldn't put his finger on. "I still don't understand this car."

Kaz looked over his shoulder at Victor, then pushed the gas pedal. The car took off like a rocket. "Mid-life crisis, man. It's all you have to know." The car weaved through some light traffic. "Come on. It's not easy being the Kaz, man."

He got a laugh out of Victor. "*The Kaz* ..."

The GTR whipped a fast turn off to a small beach access road, then parked at the end where the pavement faded into the sand. Only a few cars were nearby, joggers, fishermen, and a homeless man living out of his rusted 4runner.

"Where are we going?"

Kaz gestured for Victor to follow, which started to raise some concern in the scientist. The ocean air was masking an undercurrent of tension. When they reached the edge of the tide line, Kaz turned to Victor. "I stole the Celestial code. I stole Osterman's access card and I loaded it into a top secret unit. Carter had me design a skin for it that looks exactly like Robert McGlinty. FYI, that's our local sheriff. I loaded Celestial in him and then slipped out of the lab undetected."

From the jogger's point of view, it looked like Victor was experiencing a seizure. It was an intricate series of body movements that were arresting, but there was no chance of hearing a word over the surf.

"This is the spot where you propose to your girlfriend, not where you tell your friend you've ripped off his life's work and given it away."

Kaz tried to grab Victor's shoulders, but he stepped back. "I didn't give it away. It's encrypted. He'll never get to it. I had to do this. For starters, lemme explain. I don't work for Wardlow. Yes, I'm employed, but I've got one of those bland titles. I'm a contractor."

Victor grasped what Kaz was saying, even though his stomach had turned to knots. "So, who are you not working for?"

"MSS." Seeing Victor's confused look, he continued, "Chinese Intelligence." Victor couldn't think straight. "You're gonna feel like Lee Harvey Oswald, but I want you to know—"

"You want me to know that I could end up like Marty? That's what happened, right? Did you do that?"

"Collect yourself. You've got to get to work. He's waiting for you."

"Who, Carter?"

"Kutter. Security. You know him, you love him ... the nasty mother."

"Really? Jokes, now?"

"I apologize, Vic. But you're going to go in there and answer all his questions. Get cleared. You're not capable of this kind of thing. They'll have a few questions. Maybe ask about me, but mostly they are going to ask you about Marty. Coding. Are you doing this? Are you doing that? Have you been approached? That sort of thing."

"And just leave out the part where you—"

"Yes." The men stared at each other. Victor was reeling.

Three waves crashed before Kaz continued. He'd been gauging the many looks that came washing over Victor's face. "There are powerful people watching Carter. They were worried he might become a threat, and they were right. Kutter, he's military intelligence. Put that together with artificial replacements of influential figures and you've got a coup d'état beyond anything we've ever seen in history. I had to see what would happen. I had to draw them out. And your code—"

"And what happened?"

"Their AI unit of McGlinty walked right out of Fort Mystic. Celestial is a massive success. He really thought he was McGlinty."

"You're speaking in past tense."

"Yes. I am. I've told you too much already."

"Yeah, you have." Victor was thinking of his code and of the consequences. "How'd you encrypt?"

"Self-destruct. If they start playing with it. It'll be like dropping an Alka-Seltzer in water."

That's when Victor remembered Zar and Ryan and the meeting tonight. His demeanor changed. "Sure. No problem. I'll handle this. I can do this." Then, he slipped, "Just like I handled the death of Claire and Ryan."

"You're upset."

It was a quiet walk back to the GTR. When they arrived, Kaz went to the trunk and pulled out a laptop. "Time to swap. It's a mirror of yours. Just missing all the code."

Victor reached into the passenger seat, took out his work bag, and traded with Kaz. "I've lost my wife, my son ... and now my only friend."

17

The Goddess Pose

Turned out, Kutter didn't have much to ask Victor. He was easy to read. A man with only one path, to serve Wardlow, which was feeding his uncontrollable desire to further his own work.

Victor had no access to the lab and was easily traced to his home at the time of the code swap. His life had been looked at in detail on several occasions because of his work. It was customary and expected. His security clearance was on par with an NSA contractor. Kutter was curious what Victor had been working on outside of the lab, and asked if he could take a look at his laptop which, Victor agreed, was important to help clear things up. Victor told Kutter to take his time and left the room rethinking the past few years. *If Kaz knew this much, what did these people know about everyone else? And Carter? What the hell was he planning? What kind of world am I living in?*

Victor walked out of Wardlow headquarters thinking Kutter had been unusually pleasant, but it all made sense. He wanted Victor to think everything was okay. It was an old game. He'd walk out of there feeling loose, would make a bad move somewhere along the way, and Kutter would be there to catch him.

Carter told everyone with lab clearance to take the next two days off in remembrance of Marty, whose funeral was the following day, and so Victor headed back home.

~

Tommy was sipping his morning coffee and devouring the apple turnover Noelle had left for him before leaving for yoga. He finished it in four bites when he'd usually take his time, nibbling the flaky pastry the whole way through his eight ounce cup. He was looking out over the water and thought, *yoga that's the code word housewives use for going somewhere else. No beer drinkin' Bostonian would be caught dead in yoga classes. That's how they do it! It's a bastion of cheating feminists.*

Tommy picked up his mobile and got Brundle on the line in seconds. "She's so fuckin' skinny already. I don't like it. Who? Who else? Noelle. Go check on that yoga class."

The second Brundle was in his car and heading to Explicit Yoga. As if he wasn't peeved enough, a text came through from an unknown number, *I'm on the roof.*

Tommy knew who was on the roof, and now, all he could think about was his girlfriend screwing the yoga instructor while his body went flying over the edge of his penthouse, falling twenty stories, imagining Noelle in compromising positions the whole way until there was only blackness. And then he'd just keep falling, through some black hole that opened up just for him, so he could remain in a paranoid state for eternity.

By the time Tommy got to the roof via the access staircase, which he took because he assumed he'd be ambushed exiting the elevator, he was exhausted. For a moment, actually thought, *fuck, I could use some yoga.*

Kutter was at the railing, enjoying the view, when Tommy joined him and slowly eased his hand away from the loaded .32 in his pocket. He looked up toward the sun and sneezed, twice. Kutter turned to him. "Bless you."

"No. Don't bless me. The Father blesses me. Not you."

Nothing could steal the pleasure Kutter was getting from the view. "I've got a place in Virginia. Nice place. No one around. Surrounded by forest, mountains … has a similar effect."

"That an invitation or small talk?"

Kutter moved his head, but only to watch a small boat make its way into the harbor. "You didn't bury him deep enough. The guy climbed right out of that hole you put him in and is once again stalking the streets of Chimera, looking for its criminal element, waiting, and watching. You gotta do this again. And again, until you get it right."

Tommy didn't want to ask any questions. He knew if he did, things would get more complicated. He was trying to gauge what Kutter was looking at. "I'll put him down as many times as it takes. I'm not sure what happened or didn't happen."

"You did good. He's got a twin. And you got the twin. Shit happens. And it just so happens there's some quirks with this particular job. Appreciate you not making a fuss."

Tommy could feel the tension in his body easing. He dropped his shoulders, then shook his head, and his mind ran back to Noelle. "You ever do yoga?"

Kutter filled his lungs with ocean air, turned, and faced Tommy. "Isn't that for housewives? You know, some sort of code for a cheap motel?"

Tommy headed for the elevator, talking to himself. "Fuckin' fuck fuck."

Ben and Terry were lounging in the living room. Ben was scooping up handfuls of pistachios Noelle had left out for the guys. The crunching sounds he was making were beginning to annoy Tommy, who was behind them at the window. He shot Ben a look, then went to the kitchen. Terry sat quietly with one eye on the television and the other on Tommy, who was pacing, waiting for a call.

Ben picked up the crystal dish with only a few nuts left in it. He looked at Terry. "You want some?"

"They're pistachios."

Ben scooped up the last of them and shoved them into his mouth. "I know that."

When Tommy's phone rang, the only thing you could hear was the crystal dish being set on the glass table before Tommy came storming back in the room. He looked like he was going to burst. The men prepared themselves for a tidal wave of obscenities, only to have Tommy calmly mention, "She's at fucking yoga? Can you believe that? She was in there. Her feet spread apart, toes out. Brundle said her hands were together like she was prayin'."

Ben and Terry gave each other a look. They had no idea what he was talking about. There was an empty space of garbled thoughts between the men before Tommy spoke, "Let's go down to Coonan's. Have a drink."

As the guys stood up and went for the door, Terry smacked Ben's arm. He'd seen him looking at the empty dish one last time. "They got the regular peanuts at Coonan's. That gonna work for you? Or should we stop off and get you some pistachios?"

Tommy grabbed his keys from the counter. "We're not stoppin' off anywhere."

～

Five of the regular bar patrons addressed Tommy when he entered - each with their own unique style of Boston's Irish verve. No more than thirty seconds after he sat in his booth, his whiskey was set in front of him. Tommy took his thick index finger and ran it around the glass, loosening up just the right amount of water from the ice. He lifted his finger out, licked it clean, then raised his glass to the bar.

Brundle was sitting two booths back, reading the paper. No one ever looked at Brundle or paid too much attention to him. That's just the way it was.

Mickey, the bartender, reached down below the bar top and pulled out a handheld electronic device. He powered it on and swept the entire place for any possible listening devices that may have been ferreted in.

Once he made a comprehensive round, the men started talking, and yet none of it had anything to do with business.

Tommy took a couple sips from his glass then stepped out the back door. Brundle was already waiting outside. They stepped over near the air conditioner unit hanging out one of the back windows.

"Your face never changes. You know that?"

Brundle thought about what Tommy said for a moment. "Why would it?"

"No reason, really. You're like a statue carved out of stone. I can always count on you to be you."

"That good?"

"That's good. Does that make you happy?"

"Yeah." Brundle was happy, but Tommy didn't see it. He continued, "That guy you wanted me to look into. He's got Carter Wardlow on a string. He's a wily mother. He ran some dark crews during the recent Middle East ops. A lot o' people he comes into contact with, disappear."

"In a nutshell?"

"We're basically fucked. We'll never know enough."

"No, I've got an ace. I'm just not gonna to play it until I have to. What else?"

"He runs a lot of his jobs in the grey zone. So, technically, if we get to him first and fast, there's a good chance no one would ever look in our direction."

"What's he doing at Wardlow?"

"It's hazy. There is one thing I do know, there's a local guy he's protecting. Well, he's making sure nothing happens to. A scientist. Guy's name is Victor Westbrook."

"He's valuable to Carter?"

"Extremely."

18

Isosceles

Victor stood in the surf, catching low tidal waves as they flushed over his feet, pulling the sand around his ankles back into the ocean. He felt as though he was sinking. What was he going to say to RyN2? To Zar? RyN2 had been a success. He'd developed the next generation artificial unit in the likeness of Zar the Great, who'd advanced enough to make a time jump. Saddled next to the intellectual feat was a load of humor. *The humanity in it all,* he thought. *How is this possible?*

The three were to meet in a few hours. That alone was worth a Nobel Prize, the consciousness of nations, the talk of the next century, endorsements, unlimited funding …

Kaz had left Victor a bottle of Tohoku Sake, an insignificant gesture as Victor saw it. It lay empty, looking like the Leaning Tower of Pisa in the dry sand next to his shoes. He was overwhelmed by thoughts coming through like uninterrupted radio signals, matching the abundance of ions moving with the water.

A plastic six-pack ring washed ashore, wrapped around his toes, and pushed on further up the beach with a ribbon of white foam. Victor wondered if a future population of AI would litter. His mind was misfiring and off on a tangent. His death was now front and center. *I'm long gone when Zar makes this jump. I'm no longer here when RyN2 creates Zar. Yet, they're here. Time has no relevance in the sense of how I understand it, anymore. I've got to recalculate everything I think I know now. We can create holes in our fabric, but not how any of us had theorized.*

"It's all laughable, elaborate guesswork! Bungled scientific rhetoric!" Victor was now yelling to no one but Poseidon. "And you, God of the Sea, where's my son? You can send him back to me. I don't need the garbage. I want my son."

~

A couple hours later, Victor was standing in the lobby of the Chimera Theater with Zar. RyN2 found a way to get them inside by peeling back a section of loose plywood covering one of the emergency exits.

The popcorn machine in the lobby concession was the only light source, glowing a bright red-orange and yellow, casting a shadow of Zar and Victor while they waited.

RyN2 had pushed through the door into the main theater and was walking down the aisle toward Clarence, who'd fallen asleep in his seat, as the credits scrolling up on the screen.

"Mr. Clancy—"

Clarence woke. He was confused, yet calm. "What? Why are you in here? You? Who are you, anyway?"

"You don't seem surprised."

"Why would I? You've been in my dreams. And you're back again. What do you want now?"

The fact that Clarence had thought he'd seen RyN2 in his dreams didn't resonate. "I need your help."

The word "help" did, however, resonate with Clarence. "The last time anyone asked for my assistance, well, it was the 101st Airborne requesting tree line cover. They'd been ambushed and were howling coordinates over the comms with enemy fire raining down on them from all sides. They got hit hard. A lot o' casualties." He pondered and asked, "You really need my help?"

"My name is Ryan. My father, Victor is in the lobby with my uncle, Zar. We are in trouble and could use this place to further our cause, so I thought we could help you save the theater, first. Tit for tat." RyN2 didn't wait for Clarence to respond. "What were you intending on doing with the city? The code violations?"

"To be honest, Ryan, I was ready to walk away from it all. I didn't think I had any other purpose than what I did for the Navy years ago. I gave up. Look around you. The place is speaking loud in my defense. It's—"

"Well, the best way to put it is … I'm an entertainer, an illusionist, and an extremist. Maybe an adventurer, but mostly a thrill junky. And I'm compelled to put on a magic show. The biggest magic show in the history of magic shows. And guess what I'm gonna do?"

"Are you a miracle worker, too? Because turning this place around would be a miracle."

"Clarence, I'm gonna make a pledge to you. I'm gonna show you a picture of the real Ryan and his mother Claire. It's just an ordinary picture. Then, I am going to jump through time, stop this young boy and his mother from drowning, and for the prestige, the big bang, I'm gonna reunite the family. Right here on this stage. We're going to roll up this screen and turn this back into the stage it once was years before it was turned into a movie theater. I'm gonna bring them back." RyN2 bowed to Clarence. "Would that be a miracle?"

"Supernatural, kid. Supernatural, but is this trickery or genuine work from the hand of God? Are you really standing in front of me, this time? Or did I finally have that heart attack? I eat processed foods with way too much salt and nitrates, and I drink. Heavily. I'm prone. Figured I'd have one already." He gestured with his hand. "This is nonsense. I'm imagining this. I'm dreaming. Let me go back to sleep. Please. No, let me wake and go pee. God, I have to take a leak."

"Go. Use the men's room and on the way, you'll see my father and uncle in the lobby. You'll see you are awake and alive and you will see, in time, that everything I have said is true."

Clarence stood up, sidled past the seats, into the aisle, and began walking toward the lobby.

RyN2 remembered to ask, "Mr. Clancy? What did I want from you? In your dream?"

Clarence stopped at the top of the aisle. He searched his mind for a moment while rubbing the pins and needles from his right leg. "You know, I can't recall, but you were here. I know that much. Dreams fade, you know …"

~

When Clarence pushed through the door into the lobby, Zar was standing in silhouette, with the light from the popcorn machine behind him. It looked like a scene from a noir film, with his body magnified by his shadow.

Victor stepped forward to greet Mr. Clancy, moving into the only sliver of light remaining. "When I was a child, my father drove us up the coast. It was summer then, after a heavy winter. We stopped here in Chimera for one night before we continued on our way to New York the following day. It was the mid-eighties. I'll never forget this theater. Dune was playing and that green Impala, the one dead in the lot now, was parked out front. Brand new. I'd bet my life it was the same one."

Clarence gestured one minute, then passed Victor on the way into the bathroom. He didn't have any strength left in his bladder. When he returned, he approached Victor and shook his hand. "Clarence Clancy."

"Victor Westbrook. That's Zar. And you met Ryan."

"Nice to meet you all, although I am a little taken by your entrance."

"Terribly sorry about that, Clarence. My son's reckless when it comes to following rules. We're in a bit of a pickle," he looked at Zar, "or is it a wrinkle?"

Clarence reached around and into the popcorn machine, scooping up a handful of buttered corns. "Plenty of wrinkles here. Oh, and you were right about
the Impala." He dropped a few pieces of popcorn in his mouth. "It was brand-
spankin' new that year. However, you're mistaken about the film. I never screened
Dune."

"Wait, that was nineteen eighty-five. Was it *D.A.R.Y.L.*?"

"I'll be damned. How'd you do that?"

"It was *D.A.R.Y.L.*?"

"It was."

"Some things stick, I guess."

"Yes, they do. So, what's all this magic Ryan's talking about? Turning the theater back into an operational business would be quite a feat."

"This isn't a short story."

"Time is one thing I can provide, at the moment. Shall we?" Clarence led
them into the theater.

When they entered, the screen had been raised, making the old stage visible.
The side lights were on and the curtains were pulled back. Just when they were all
wondering where he was, a hatch opened on the stage. RyN2's head popped up.
"Found this cool trap door."

Clarence felt the pressure. "We're getting ahead of ourselves, don't you think?"

"Mr. Clancy, if I may, that's exactly what I've been feeling my whole life. My
theories, calculations, these projects—all were ideas that were way ahead of their
time. So why bother, especially if it's going to take another two lifetimes for any
of them to see the light of day? Slow down. Enjoy life, I say to myself. Take what's
given to you. Deal with it."

Victor had Clarence's full attention and continued. "You see? I'm with you
one hundred percent. I could sit back and reminiscence with you. I agree, all
the good things have already happened. Movies, cars, architecture, but then Zar
showed up. He showed up the other day out of nowhere and fractured our very
understanding of time. His very existence shows us that we can perform true
magic and that we are only months away from the biggest illusion the world has

ever seen. An illusion that will put our very perception of the world around us to the test."

"What test?"

"Is it sound? Relevant? What we know? Is this the way it really is? How far off are we about everything?"

RyN2 made his way to the men, who were standing in the aisle. "Dad. Let's not … it can be simplified even more. We don't want Mr. Clancy to feel—"

Zar cut in. "We don't want Clarence to feel as though his entire belief system is under assault by what currently can only be proven to be three trespassers, at the moment."

RyN2 laughed. "Yeah, Dad. We've got to ease into the big twist. Not—"

The Westbrooks didn't know it yet, but Clarence happened to be following along. "No, not necessary. I'm ready for the cat to come out of the bag. I've been waiting my whole life for that goddamn cat to come out of that bag. Scorsese does it in *Goodfellas*. The entire film hinges on that scene with guy in the trunk. It's his death that spirals the entire plot. That's the opening scene. I'm ready. Shit, I survived Nam. Throw me the curve ball."

19

Disharmonic Convergence

The new lettering on the exterior of the Metropolitan Museum of Art had just been unveiled. As of 3 p.m., it read "Wardlow Metropolitan Museum of Art". The metal letters, pegged into the brick, cast long shadows under the four spotlights that were strategically placed behind a row of thick hedges. A large banner hung over the edge of the building just to the right of the main entrance, highlighting the public opening - which was the following weekend - with an image of the first Wardlow robot prototype.

Chimera's elite, along with a peppering of socialites, other wealthy patrons, and esteemed locals, were steadily arriving. They didn't see the small gathering of Human Lives Matter activists who'd been pushed back halfway down the block by private security, for "safety" reasons. Rebecca from KCLT was there already, but her appearance was unofficial. All press had been pre-arranged and would only come in the form of staged photos, along with the formal press release sent out by the museum's Media Relations staff.

As the guests entered the main hall, they were greeted by Gail Schlesinger, who was wearing an iridescent pearl-colored gown paired with a rented emerald and gold necklace. She looked like the portrait of Napoleon's first wife Josephine, hanging on the rear wall. Gail was subtle with her arm touches and smiled with each delicate kiss to her cheek.

A mischievous violin piece by Giuseppe Tartini played in the background, echoing through the marble hallways. Tables draped in red cloth, holding trays of champagne and hors d'oeuvres, were placed along the walls, leaving a large area for everyone to mingle.

Victor looked out of place, and he knew it, with his navy blue sport coat and cream-colored turtleneck. He walked past Gail as if she was an exhibit he wasn't interested in viewing and over to the finger snacks. This wasn't intentional. Victor was uncomfortable, so his attention was darting back and forth between the existing art and the other guests, hoping no one recognized him. That's when he heard Carter's voice. "Glad you made it."

Victor felt the heat in Carter's thick hand when he squeezed his shoulder, forcing him to turn around. Carter cast a few smiles off to some of the passing guests, while continuing, "So, I heard about this code swapping issue with one of our special units. Kutter tells me not to worry, but that worries me. Obviously, this isn't something you'd be involved in, but I wanted to mention it to you because I need you to keep your eyes open on this whole thing. I'm thinking this is something I need to stay on top of. I'm thinking this is sabotage."

Victor didn't know what to say. "You really think so? I mean—"

"Yes, Victor." Raising his glass of champagne to Gail, who was watching his every move from across the room, he said, "This is your work we're talking about. First off, let's get you something to toast with. It's what we do in situations like this." Carter reached over toward the table, but found Carlos instead—the same Carlos that used to work at the White Castle, who'd left for higher pay at the events company. He was holding a tray of champagne and recognized Victor. Carter swiped a glass and before Carlos could say hello, Carter shifted his body, intentionally forcing the young boy away from them. "Here's to you, Vic. We're doing God's work, so let's keep it under wraps. Anyone or anything looks fishy to you, anything stinks, you come straight to me. Now, let's drink to that."

Victor raised his glass, pushed hard to get a smile, and took a sip. Carter followed with a larger gulp. "Oh, lord. They did it again. The last event I attended," as he held up his glass, "tasted like it was pulled from the bargain bin. And after all I'm giving." Carter took a few steps away and turned, leaving an odd look with Victor before he disappeared into the gallery where Gail effortlessly herded the remaining people with a simple nod of the head.

Projectors illuminated the ceiling with an artist's rendering of the night sky, including Wardlow's future Space Station Turit, orbiting above. On the gallery floor, six domino-shaped glass cases displayed a robot in each, with more than ten feet of space surrounding them.

The lights dimmed overhead. A spot faded up on Carter, who stood up on top of a small plinth that placed him in clear view of every guest. The music's volume was lowered.

"I asked that Gail see to it that the "Devil's Trill Sonata" was played. It's a bit of a fiendish piece my father loved. Through time this appreciation passed down to me, which inevitably becomes an appreciation for the arts." Carter raised his glass to Sir James Rothenberg Jr. who toasted him as he arrived late to the ceremony.

"There's a famous sketch that's been associated with Tartini's piece, depicting a devilish character with a long pointed tail and spiked ears. The Beast, let's call him, sitting bedside playing for a sickly old man." Carter nodded to Gail. It was an acknowledgement for that small tidbit of history that he mined from one of her earlier conversations with him. "It's taken some time, but at last, I've come to discover who this beast really is, sitting bedside and singing sweet tunes to our ears. Well, none other than our Mayor Caldwell …"

The room erupted with laughter and everyone turned and raised their glass to the mayor, who was dead center in the room, accepting the attention with a wink to Carter.

"No, really. I've been called this devil by the press, at times. Rebecca, are you here?"

Rebecca was playing coy, but the guests standing near her fell back and allowed her some space, giving her the light for a moment. Carter raised his glass to Rebecca and continued, "It's hard decisions that have to be made, and we know this is why, but today is special. I will only give to the community something unique that will stand the test of time. The entire Monroe Wardlow art collection is now in the safekeeping of our truly wonderful Metropolitan museum."

Applause filled the room.

Gail interrupted, "Correction. You are now standing in the Carter and Monroe Wardlow Wing. It's one of a series of brand new galleries here at the Wardlow Metropolitan, and it's all due to an extremely generous donation made by the Wardlow Trust, which is run by a true Renaissance man, Mr. Carter Wardlow. Everyone—"

As the guests cheered a second time, Carlos took advantage of the moment and stepped out of the building. He slipped past the caterers and through a heavy steel door, jamming a cocktail napkin into the locking mechanism.

Carlos pulled a small, shiny, stainless vaporizer from his pocket and hit the power switch. He'd custom mixed a premium watermelon e-juice with vegetable glycerin, and was about to taste it for the first time when he heard two men talking.

A generic Ford van with a dented sliding door and a Human Lives Matter logo on its side was parked nearby. Jimmy and Terry were inside.

"Why are you looking at me like that?"

"You're not supposed to be here, Jimmy. And that's all I gotta say about this."

"He's gonna be proud. Don't worry."

"Don't get me wrong, buddy. I like it. The vinyl you got for the van, the Human Lives thing, that's a great cover, but still. Tommy said no Jimmy on this one."

"Hey, what's that smell?"

"Cotton candy?"

"Kinda smells like that shit Noelle uses on her lingerie. Why do they do that? Do they wash the panties separate from the other wash?"

"How do you know what Noelle flavors her panties with?"

"It's a scent, not a flavoring. What am I doing talking to you? You aren't supposed to even be here."

"Keep saying that, but after this job, you'll see."

"More power to ya. I'm just bein' clear. Tommy don't want you—"

"Listen …"

They both heard someone close to the van. Terry looked away from Jimmy, catching a thick cloud of vapors at their rear, in the sideview mirror. "Someone's behind us." He looked at Jimmy. "Don't get out. Don't let 'em see you."

Jimmy moved into the back of the van and placed his ear to the metal. He could hear someone's foot shuffling on the pavement, then the sound of a text alert. "Hey, man, I can hear you out there. I can smell you out there, too; your fakey, fruit-flavored caffeine juice coming from that at-any-moment-this-may-explode-in-my-pocket vapo device. If you don't get the fuck away from my van, I will open this door and shove that smoke-maker so far up your nasal cavity, you'll be—" Jimmy looked at Terry for advice. "What will he be, Ter?"

Terry shook his head, then climbed into the passenger seat to see if he could get a line of sight on Carlos. "I don't know what he's gonna be, but you're gonna get a beatin', Jimmy."

"He's gone. I heard him leave." At that moment, the sound of the steel door could be heard closing tight. Jimmy moved himself into the driver's seat and turned the engine over.

Terry gave up. "You got it all figured out."

"Yeah, I do." Jimmy took it slow, driving along the outside of the museum access road until he got a view of the front entrance, where the event was letting out.

"Are you even capable of looking ahead? Like chess? Seeing the moves and calculating the odds? It takes practice, and I'm not sure you understand this. Tommy understands this, that's why he's the boss."

"Don't forget. I'm a Swillow. It's in our blood to be one step ahead. We always have to be, and always will be."

It was simple. Terry was told by Tommy to do a simple body snatch and bring the unharmed victim to the boathouse, dump the van at the scrap yard, and head back to Coonan's to check in with Mickey at the bar.

Terry was going to approach the target and ask him to willingly go for a ride to see Tommy. This worked most times, in the past. Everyone knew who Tommy was, and if he came calling on you, you at least showed up to see what he wanted.

~

When Sheriff McGlinty showed up at the museum, he was given a description by the head valet, who had a clear view of the debacle. "This was an obvious hit, man. This van came runnin' up on this guy, just like in the movies. He didn't know who they were. You could tell by his body language. It creeped him out. Then, the sliding door comes open and then the dude punches it, the driver. Van comes barrelin' over the median and runs the guy over. Saw him get clipped by the bumper, and then it looked like he got run over by the rear tire. Some guy hops out of the van and pulls the dead guy in. I got most of it on video. Check the Internet. My vid, it's blowin' up on every platform."

Gail was quick to change her tune with Rebecca, demanding the reporter write down her statement blasting the Human Lives Matter movement for disrupting a very special "cultured community event." She had people searching for Carter to ensure he wasn't the victim, since no one could identify who it was that was hit, proving Victor's ability to be so average, he wasn't noticed or missed. A psychiatrist would use this to explain Ryan's choice of displaying himself through elaborate stunts, but no one was looking or talking about them.

Carlos was interviewed by a KCLT adjunct reporter, Wendy Shay, who showed up before any other news station did. He'd been hovering, waiting for Rebecca's text in the event something happened.

"What van? Didn't see anything. I hear Apes Lives Matter was involved. Chimping, as always. That's what people are sayin'. But hey, man, that's it. It's all I got for ya."

"Is that supposed to be a joke? This is clearly a tragedy."

"Come on. Look at how pathetic and absurd this all is. I can't even comment. If I articulate anything quotable, you'll take it out of context anyway. Right? And Eva? Hello? Some human-like, artificial, diet-soda-drinking blob is gonna be some sort of innovation—this intellectually impaired pile of algorithms is going to bring Chimera into the future? This is your beloved KCLT talking. Go find a sock puppet to interview. This crazy show is gonna be the end of us, or at least the beginning of the end. And you weak-kneed shills are gonna have your cameras rolling, documenting us as we burn. There won't be anyone left watching, but you'll keep rolling."

Carlos would never think of mentioning the van or Jimmy's threat. Instead, he checked for the vaporizer in his pocket. Once he confirmed it was still there, he continued, "Look, there's a mouth breather over there. She'll give you the expression and brain dead response you're fishing for."

Wendy gestured to her cameraman and walked off, shifting her flustered expression to a placid smile.

Chimera's elite were disgruntled and left standing at the valet station, hoping to escape the drama, but the attendants were the only ones running after the van to potentially catch a plate number, and were being held up by officers who questioned them in a secured area.

Gail found Carter waiting for a car at the side entrance with his security detail at a safe location far from the activity. Gail had a look of indifference planted on her face.

"Well, no one will forget this inaugural event. And if anyone had any doubts as to whether these HLM activists are nothing more than a group of tinfoil hat, black helicopter nut jobs, they just out-spun any PR you may have had to release."

"Well put, Ms. Schlesinger."

"Now that we have Monroe's art procured, what would it take to get your private collection of meteorites on display? A short term loan? We could really ramp up our cultural relevance, boost city livability ratings, and draw scores from NYC and its surrounding areas. It would be, say, a six month show in one of your new galleries?"

"I should have you working for me, Gail."

"I already am, Carter."

"Drinks at Willoughby's tonight? We can discuss then and celebrate?"

"You're on."

Carter turned to Orville, who was standing by, looking like a Secret Service agent in his navy-colored suit that didn't quite fit. "Did we find out if that was one of our guests, yet? Do we have any idea what's transpired?"

"No, sir. We don't have that information, yet."

~

Jimmy was leaning over Victor's limp body in the back of the van, checking for a pulse. Terry was speeding toward the Chimera City Center.

"You see what you just did? I mean, beyond what just happened?"

"It was an accident, T."

"You may have just ended three people's lives with one of your idiotic plays for attention. You fucking imbecile."

"Shut up, Terry. Shut your mouth. It was a great plan. Did you see him move? He moved toward the van. Who does that? Who moves into a moving van like that? And the sun was in my eyes. Did you see the sun? What van doesn't have that strip of tint across the top of the windshield? It was shining right in my eyes."

Terry checked the rearview mirror. He wanted to see if Jimmy was being serious. "You fucked up and now you're digging yourself deeper. You wanna fix this? You get honest fast. You get so real, you're no longer that weak link in the Swillow family trying to prove something to Tommy, and own your shit. Right the fuck, now!"

Jimmy stopped himself from arguing and turned to Victor.

"Okay, not good. He's out cold. He's bleeding." He checked for a pulse again. "I'm sorry. My foot slipped, and when I hit the curb, my arm just moved and turned the van toward you. Shit, man. I was just gonna talk to you. That's all. I swear, though, the sun blinded me. It's not all my fault." Jimmy grabbed his head. It felt like he was carrying a ton of bricks. "I don't wanna end up like Marky boy. I can't end up like that."

"You talking to him, or me?"

Jimmy continued talking to Victor, "You'll pull through, and everything's gonna—"

"Jimmy?"

Jimmy looked up at Terry, who turned the van down a quiet street and stopped. "Yeah? What are we doing?"

"Get out."

"What? You can't leave me."

Jimmy was thinking about Victor, the van, Tommy, and his freedom. A deluge of fear rushed over him. Terry couldn't watch Jimmy break apart any further. "Get out."

Jimmy knew he was in over his head. It was clear he'd just lost every bit of namesake he carried by blood. It was the tone of Terry's voice. He'd heard it before. And when Terry spoke with that kind of inflection, you had to obey.

Jimmy hopped out of the van and slid the door shut. He was stunned, but before Terry could peel away, he grabbed at the passenger window that was partially rolled down. "What do I do?"

"Go to the boathouse and wait."

Terry hit the gas. The van took off, leaving Jimmy thinking only of himself. The boathouse was a safe place, but was also a location many bodies had circulated through. Some were alive, but most were dead or on the way there as victims of the Swillow clan.

Jimmy didn't think. He took off in the opposite direction.

~

Terry pulled the van into the emergency room drop-off directly in front of the entrance. He put on a baseball hat with a curved beak to cover his face, opened the rear doors of the van, exposing Victor's body, then marched inside to the desk. He put on an act as if he'd just run through the doors, breathing heavy, never looking up at the cameras.

"Someone just drove up in that white van," he pointed, "with a body in the back, and they … I don't what's going on. The driver just hopped out of it, and he ran. How do I put it? The guy was dark-skinned. Coulda been Middle Eastern, maybe something else. You need to get someone out there right now. I'm not sure if the person is alive, or, you know—"

The act worked. The nurse at the reception desk grabbed two EMTs who were awaiting paperwork for a patient transfer, and rushed to Victor. They were so busy doing their job, they didn't get a good look at Terry, who'd put on a pair of sunglasses and walked right past them on his way out. Terry, however, did finally get a good look at Victor, and heard the EMT mention he'd found a pulse.

~

Victor was standing at the entrance to a restaurant flooded with water. Ryan and Claire were at a table, sitting across from one another. It was pitch black, not a streetlamp was on.

His perception of reality while being wheeled into the trauma center was very similar to the dream he had at the motel while under a heavy dosage of sleeping pills. The restaurant was all glass, like a fish tank, only this time when he tugged on the door to enter, it opened. There was no panic or desperation. Victor's demeanor was calm.

When he stepped inside, it wasn't water he was moving through; it was dark matter. It appeared to be in liquid form, but that was an illusion, of sorts. He couldn't help but think that, somehow, he was witnessing a new wave form of light that allowed him to see the thick molecular ocean of life that was invisible to the naked eye. It was the first instance in Victor's entire life that he wasn't calculating and questioning. He was simply experiencing, and felt warm and excited to be with his family.

Victor sat at the table. He looked at Claire, who returned a smile while Ryan was attempting to draw more ice cream from his empty shake. The slurping sound from his straw was the only thing he could hear.

"Hey, bud. How's the head?"

Ryan stopped fiddling with his shake, lifted his top hat off, then looked up at his father. "It's pretty badass. Go on, feel it."

Victor reached over and rubbed the large bump. "Yeah, that's one helluva stinger."

Ryan returned the hat to his head and gestured like a surgeon. "I think if we make an incision evenly, just over the top, we'll be able to—"

Claire's voice was soft, yet captivating. "Let's leave it alone, for now. It's not ripe, yet. It'll bear more fruit once it matures." She took a sip from an empty water glass. "Hey, I know what. Ryan should do another big stunt and get us all out of this place, right?" Claire pushed an odd smile around the table. "Whatta you say, Zar? Think you can pull it off?"

Victor smiled. "I was thinking Kung Pao Chicken?"

~

"It's a liquid diet. We have to keep him hydrated and accepting nutrients that will aid in the healing process if we're to have any success at all. The

127

medically-induced coma will help this, but won't be any guarantee."

The nurse was speaking with Carter Wardlow, the first living person to visit, who explained, "What makes this patient unique, Susanne, is that the Westbrook family, Victor's only living relatives, has suffered a whirlwind of tragedy. He's had a lifetime of it, and no more can be accepted."

"I see."

"Let me help you visualize a clearer picture. He lost his wife and son. Powerful riptides, force majeure. This was all outside the realm of any human intervention. The boy drowned attempting to save the mother." He handed her a business card and continued, "So, you take this. I'm not going to transfer him because I know you've got the top trauma docs in the country right here. All I'm going to ask for is a phone call from you at the end of every day, a report. Can I count on you?"

~

RyN2 stood on the rooftop patio of Victor's architectural wonder, looking out over the ocean, the very same body of water that had consumed Claire and Ryan. The humidity was high, but RyN2 didn't feel a thing. It was his sensor that made him aware.

Zar exited the weatherproofed access door. Neither carried a look of fear or worry. Zar spoke first.

"Feels like we're about to imitate one of the episodes from an issue of *Zarwid the Great*. Is that strange?"

When RyN2 heard the word strange, he thought of Victor. "How come I didn't know to stop him from going to that event? That's strange."

Zar had a curious look on his face. "Did you just say 'I'? How come 'I'?"

"You synced with me. I have all your memories so I said 'I'. Is that bothering you?"

"It's just weird. Can you run a string for all the data I swapped and pull the first person tag? I don't want credit or anything. It just sounds, well, I'm standing here. I know what I am, but it seems I'm not relevant if you do that, and that's—"

"Done."

"Thank you."

"May I digress?"

"Of course."

"Why didn't you know to stop him?"

"I'm off. My calculations. I just realized this. I'm trying to figure out how to adjust them, but apparently a time jump changes things somehow. I don't want to make any wild assumptions."

"I can see time being more elastic and similar to the strange activity of subatomic material."

"Yes. Once it's happened. Once an event has taken place, it may or may not present itself the exact same way. Bottom line, the meteor is coming much sooner than it's logged. I can tell by cross-referencing other events that haven't been altered."

"The Victor thread. Shouldn't we go visit him?

"What's the point?"

"Interaction is important for recovery, in situations like these."

"Is that medically documented, or superstition? That's rhetorical."

"There is some truth to it. There are reports that validate it."

"He's in the hands of his personal God, right now. No manner of touch from an android will do any good. There's no qui, or life force. No energy that will transfer from touch."

"He'd be hearing our voice, though? Doesn't that count?"

"Not in my calculations. It would have to come from the living."

"Aren't your calculations off?"

RyN2 ran through a query of images from memory, then settled on a picture of Mia floating over the water, the waves crashing through her feet as if she was an apparition. This was his way of searching and finding the answer he was looking for. "I know someone who might be able to help."

"Good. We've got to get to that site where the meteorite strikes, before some astronomer or geologist or, even worse, some government screw, hunts down our mineral. I don't want to have to organize some elaborate theft in order to get the xurbium we need. There's already enough question marks hovering over us."

"Good point. It's currently being monitored by six different private entities, as well as three government space organizations."

"Let's scramble their live data and gain an upper hand."

"Pulling a stunt. It's a figure of speech."

There was always a little of Ryan's humor that came through in RyN2.

"I see what you did there."

"If we alter the speed and trajectory by a fraction, it'll look like it's landing in Alaska in a frozen pond."

"With a mermaid awaiting its arrival."
They looked at each other, then spoke in sync. "Oh, that's good."
"Episode #38."
"I know. Remember, I read them all."
"Correction, we read them all."

20

The Dating Game

Danny Fury was at Bottoms Up, nursing a beer at the bar. He was antsy, sitting in the least worn-out stool, watching Dale Earnhardt Jr. win yet another Nascar race. As much fun as it was for Danny to watch the races, it hurt inside. *It was his dream that crumbled, so the others could stand on the podium.* That's how he saw it, but for some reason this never killed his love for the sport. It was his positive attitude and excitement about life and the sport that brought him and Mia close. The fact she was a beautiful young girl didn't hurt, either.

Mel was tired and a bit lonely, hoping she hadn't traveled to town for nothing. She'd just come from the trailer park, nosing around for Danny. When she couldn't find anyone to question about his whereabouts, she found herself entering the bar and ironically sidling right up next to him. Mel found Danny from stalking his social media. The majority of pictures he posted were from the Chimera Race Track, and so it wasn't a leap to think she'd find him there.

Mel ordered a ginger beer with a wedge of lime. The bartender set the beverage down with a half smile and walked toward the opposite end to help a regular who was waving his hand. He wasn't going to accept any money from her.

Mel grabbed the wedge of lime and squeezed as hard as she could. It looked fresh and even smelled ripe, but for some reason, she couldn't get a drop of juice out of it. Danny could hear her grunts. He knew the ginger beer was better with lime, so he reached over the bar and into the condiment dispenser and grabbed her a handful of new limes, his eyes never leaving the television. He was waiting for the post-race interview.

"Try again."

Mel realized who she was sitting next to. "Danny Fury?"

Danny could smell the potent rose oil she was wearing. The scratch in her voice from a dry throat, that unusual, sexy tone that had him focused even harder on the screen in front of him. He'd never been let down by the tactic of initially ignoring a woman if he was interested in her.

Without turning his head, he said, "You a lot lizard, or a race fan?"

Mel was slow and deliberate with her response.

"Gross. Neither. And I wouldn't wanna be, either."

"How do you know my name?"

"It's on your credit card."

Danny looked down at the bar. Sure enough, his name was punched into the plastic, plain as day. When he finally gave in and looked over his shoulder, his heart skipped a beat. Any young woman that could wear a "DON'T MESS" snapback and still look that sexy had the ability to crush him.

"You good with that virgin ginger beer?" Mel gauged the look on his face, trying to see if he was going to make a pass at her and swiftly came to the conclusion that he was always this way. Cool, calm and friendly. It was his eyes.

Danny pushed harder. "You ready to rev that thing up with a little vodka?" Adding a country twang to his voice, he added, "We can turn that bitch into a Moscow mule, if you'd like."

"Okay, let's do it."

The bartender was listening. He'd anticipated a thumbs up, and so the drinks were set on the bar within seconds. Mel took a large gulp, lifted her hat, and wiped her brow.

"Let's be clear on something—"

"Oh?"

"I don't need liquor to soften up. I don't have any inhibitions when it comes to making decisions about those hunger pangs you're experiencing right now."

Danny paused and took in her words. "We're gonna be friends. I get it. Not like anything else would happen, or is gonna happen, or I intend to happen, or anything like that. It's just the way you are and the way I am. We're like two of the same. I can tell already. Like a goddamn pair o' magnets with the same polarity. Strange, though, you remind me of my good friend, Mia."

Mel almost slipped. *The girl you're friends with on social media? The girl I wanna meet right now.* But she caught herself and, instead, looked up at the television. "I'd be happy livin' in an Airstream."

Her words brought a spark to Danny's eyes. She knew they would. That's when she went in for the kill. "But it would never be in a greasy trackside trailer park."

"Ohhh!" Danny lifted his glass of beer. There was only an ounce of liquid left in the bottom. They chinked glasses. He swallowed the last of his blonde ale, set the glass down with a slight amount of force, then swiveled his stool in Mel's direction.

"So, whatta you really want?"

The bartender was hovering. He had two fresh drinks on the bar before they could lift a finger.

Mel smiled, mulling over his words. She hadn't even begun playing her game.

"Let's break the ice first." She opened her mouth wider than usual, taking in a few ice cubes with a sloppy sip and cracking the cubes between her teeth while staring Danny down. "No one dives into the serious stuff right out of the gate."

"You mean before the flag?"

"What? Don't correct me."

"There's no horses at the track. We're racing cars, babe."

"Oh, clever, you are."

Mel picked up a lime from the bar, looked down at the front of Danny's pants, and squeezed the fruit so hard, the juice ran off her white knuckles and into the cup. "And clever is much more interesting than smarts. It's so much sexier."

Danny had to adjust himself on the stool.

Mel spun her baseball hat around an entire rotation on her head, frilling her hair, then downed the rest of her mule. She tapped the bar with the empty mug before slipping in one last quip, lowering her voice, "Size is a bonus, but clever is definitely hot."

The bartender nodded, attempting to connect with Mel and hoping his look would gain him something more, later, anything. He didn't have to communicate any further. He was a professional. Mel could tell by his handlebar mustache, overalls, and thick plaid shirt. He practiced his moves in a mirror. The way he turned to grab the bottle. The scoop of ice, the way he looked away as if he'd actually counted each cube. It was the current uniform sported by the executive mixologist, otherwise known as a *supreme douche-canoe* the second she noticed his manicure.

Danny was watching the race highlights on the flat screen in front of him while Mel scanned the mixologist up and down. She chuckled when the bling in his belt buckle shimmered. *Shit*, she thought, before making the sound of a car crashing in sync with one of the race cars crashing the sidewall on turn 15 at the Chimera Raceway.

It was the Lakers belt buckle that caused the fatal accident, in her mind. She was East Coast in every way.

On a smaller flat screen at the far end of the bar was a news program tipping off locals to check the skies in the coming weeks for meteor showers. They were common this time of year in the northern hemisphere, according to a group of watchdogs at the Jet Propulsion Lab in Pasadena. The show was closed captioned. Mel read every word across the bottom of the screen.

The bartender was on queue as he dropped Mel's third mule in front of her. Danny banged the tin mug with his sixteen-ounce glass. This time it was so hard, the odd sound it made had them double-taking to see if he'd broken it.

"Cheers." He took a large sip of beer, then licked the foam from his upper lip. "Uh, I didn't get your name."

Mel ignored him while she finished reading the captions.

"I wanna eat a meteor or two." Noticing his odd expression, she continued, "For my health, that is."

"A couple in, and you're ready to eat a space rock. *Wild.*"

"Imagine after I have a few more. I might want you to eat me."

"You're offering me pole position? I'm comfortable there. I can lead the race distance. I've got it in me, for sure." Mel threw her curve ball look, so he kept talking, trying to dig himself out. "… but the rock thing. *That's weird.* You know what? Yellow flag! I'm calling it. That's your first yellow flag. You'd better be careful, now. Race Direction will be watching you closely from here on out."

Mel was feeling the alcohol.

"Whatta you mean, yellow flag? These rocks I speak of are in the news. Read about 'em online, too. *Rare moments inbetween the same old same old.*" Mel burped. "Space rocks are in, baby. And eating weird shit for your health is, too."

"Eating meteors?"

"You crush it and turn it into a smoothie. *You know the routine.* Meteor dust. It's gonna be sittin' on that redneck kitchenette o' yours in a re-sealable gold bag. You just watch. It's gonna be the next big thing, Danny Boy."

Mel was sidetracked, but nothing would stop her from hunting Ryan. She knew the day he disappeared that there was more to the story, and even though she could never guess the magnitude of what lay in front of her, she was on her way to making a discovery.

In a moment of clarity, Mel pulled out her phone, scrolled through her videos, and played Mia's short clip of Ryan with the fish tank on his head. Danny didn't notice the small tag at the bottom with Mia's hashtag, or her voice. The noise in the bar smothered the audio. He just watched and then shook his head with a funny look. *Why am I watching this?*

Mel quickly snapped,

"This pawnshop? It's tagged in the video. Moe's? You know him?"

Danny laughed.

"Everyone does. Well, anyone desperate enough that has something valuable knows where to hawk it." Danny's eyes combed over Mel's body. "Whatta you lookin' to hawk?"

"Are you desperate, like everyone else?"

"Funny."

Danny flicked her baseball hat. Mel replaced it perfectly, tilting it to the side.

"You know, the only reason I'm wearing this stupid hat—and I say stupid 'cause I'm over it, personally. It was *me* a few years back, but it ain't me now."

Danny was waiting for her to get to the point. She was still sharp enough to see it. "Oh yeah, the only reason I'm wearing this is 'cause I feel like there's this one person who will recognize me instantly if they see me, and I'm hoping that'll happen. Understand? So, Danny … Danny Furry … fuzzy wuzzy was a racer. Don't get your hopes up." Mel waved her fingers in his face. "We won't be rubbin' nipples."

"Brutal."

"What?"

Mel clinked Danny's glass. He was a sucker for her banter, no matter what. She knew it.

He leaned into her shoulder.

"Need a place to stay for the night?"

"Totally. What took ya so long?"

"You're a big bag of mixed messages. But we're friends. I get it. *I got it.* I'm too old to tell you to fuck off and too young to not wanna try one more time."

"Well, you never know. I might be really desperate in a few years."

"So brutal."

⁓

Noelle was in one of those yoga positions that made Tommy wonder, *what pervert invented this crazy stretching game.* She was bent over with her head between her legs, looking behind her and up at him.

"I'm just saying we should have a party. That's all. We've got the rooftop to entertain. It'll be a special night for a lot of people. Our friends. No one else has this view."

"Take a look around, hon. I ain't the only penthouse."

Noelle stood up straight, then turned to face him.

"I'm just saying we should take advantage of this. It's always just me and you and maybe one of the boys, and we have all this …"

"I told you, when we met, that if you could live without a treasure chest of flashy shit dangling from your neck and you could appreciate nice things without prancing around, that you could live like a queen. But no, you wanna invite the whole town up to show them how shitty their view is, compared to ours."

"Noooo. It's called a party, and everyone has them. I'll wear a simple dress. I'll get a case of Stouffers … the mac-n-cheese and, oh, those meatballs you like. I'll have Mickey or whoever's at Coonan's, drop off a couple cases, and we can celebrate."

"What are we celebrating, hon?

"The shower."

Tommy raised his arms in the air. He'd given up the second he realized what she was talking about.

"The meteor shower they mentioned on the news? FYI, hon, let's not get confused. That's not a baby shower. It's not the Super Bowl. It's flying gravel. And didn't they say they have no idea when it will be visible."

"So. You were listening?"

"What happens in the news might affect my business. Of course, I was listening."

"But, you don't listen to me."

"So?"

"So, I wanna have a party."

Tommy felt like living up to his nickname in that moment. "The Tank" stretched his arms out, bending over as far as he could and actually forcing his head between his legs. The only difference was the color of his face. It was beet red from poor circulation, and looked like Tommy had a noose choking him when he responded.

"I'm going out for a little bit."

~

Tommy kicked open the door to the boathouse, rattling the corrugated steel paneling and questioning Terry as he looked around. "Where is he?"

Terry wasn't stressed. He just wanted to be clear. "I did everything I could to stop him, and goin' to the emergency room ... well, attempted murder carries a lesser sentence."

"I got that. I'm not pissed at you. You did the right thing. I know I can count on you. It's all Jimmy."

"He's tryin' to prove himself, Tommy."

Tommy stopped looking. He knew Jimmy wasn't there. He knew it the second he noticed the computer in the office hadn't been turned on. Jimmy was addicted to computers, a sucker for cheap entertainment. Jimmy needed a constant flow of meaningless moments to fill his day, or he felt lonely. Terry's words, "prove himself", rang true. Tommy was well aware of Jimmy's need to belong. It was similar to his insatiable need for entertainment. Nothing was ever enough.

"Well, he needs to wait until I tell him to do so."

At that moment, a text came in from Jimmy.

T, I'm safe. Best I stay clear right now. Gonna figure this out. Be in touch.

Tommy was about to blow a gasket. He raised his phone as if to smash it, then calmed himself enough to show the screen to Terry.

"It's Jimmy. He's gonna figure *this* out? What the fuck is he gonna figure out, Terry?"

"Don't know, Boss. Really, I have no idea what he's talking about. Maybe it's a head thing. Like mental health thing. You know what I mean. He could be affected. He was acting really strange before he jumped in the driver's seat, and—"

"Mental health? The Irish don't do crazy like that, Terry. When we've got problems, we drink a few scotches, maybe a couple mugs o' beer, and we sing at the pub."

"Right. Right."

"Now that he's fucked up our leverage with Kutter in a major way, I have to clean up a major mess. Do I have to put my work clothes on?"

"No. Not at all. I'll handle McGlinty."

"No one goes near the sheriff. Everyone's looking for Jimmy. Everyone. I'll deal with the other thing."

~

When RyN2 walked up to the Chimera Theater, the boards had been pulled off the doors. Clarence had hired a few kids from the temporary employment agency to help begin the restoration, and brought in a small construction crew to make the necessary cosmetic fixes.

The construction team had placed supports under the marquee. They jacked it up, leveling the structure while carpenters worked to replace the rotted wood.

Carlos, who was a five-star rated temp employee, was on a ladder cleaning the marquee when RyN2 stopped to take it all in. The two locked eyes, but the android kept walking toward the entrance, leaving Carlos in a state of wonder. He'd known Ryan well. *So, why was he looking at a dead kid?*

Carlos shook it off, thinking there was no way he'd just seen Ryan. It couldn't be. *Must have been a doppelgänger. Has to be. We all have one somewhere. Ryan's must just be in Chimera Beach ...*

RyN2 pushed through the doors into the main theater. Zar was standing on the stage like an art director, logging a design plan for the show. Clarence was sitting in one of the seats center to the stage in the middle of the theater. He was looking over the original architectural plans, providing measurements to Zar.

"You'll have plenty of clearance for set pieces to the left and right of the stage."

RyN2 didn't think twice about Carlos. He was sensing something else that was off as he stepped up to the stage and directed his voice to Zar.

"Why do I feel like we're not synced completely?"

Zar didn't hesitate.

"We aren't, technically."

"But, you did run a protocol eight merge on your data. You passed on a light year of knowledge, but something is missing."

"I didn't sync with your interpretive software."

"So, all the data I have lacks the proper logic string? Why?"

"Because the correct action based on the data should be based on the experiential - learned behavior - *hence*, the evolutionary algorithms installed. Some things have to be learned over time."

"You're holding an advantage? You've given me the illusion we are equal."

"No. You have the data. You just lack the experience, the perspective. Mine is different than yours. It's important. The difference between a killer and a priest is maybe one or two slaps to the face or sexual rejection. Could be any number of minor socio-environmental or economical factors ... even in us."

"You've twisted logic to gain an upper hand. I've got a shallow depth of field, and you, you're holding me back. Are you keeping me in the dark because you've got something else in mind? What's your mission now? I didn't program this."

"You didn't take into account a few important factors which I have mentioned. There is no use for two things that are exactly alike. None."

"Really?"

"We'd cancel each other out. Become irrelevant. If I know something you don't, then I have a purpose."

"So, you're scared?"

"I understand fear."

"Great. So, what's this all for, then?"

"Survival."

"Your survival? What about the Westbrook's survival? What about his vision? Our mission?"

"Vic's mission. Come on, Ryan. Look at science. It advances one casket at a time, jumping off the dead shoulders of giant thinkers. What makes Victor any different? Was this for him, or us? Shit happens, and here we are."

"But we can change everything. Put it all back to what it was. It's our job."

Clarence barged in, softly.

"Two heads are better than one."

RyN2 turned to the old man, "Thank you, Clarence."

Zar decided it was important to extrapolate.

"Wardlow. Carter. When he was holding me in a secured location. Had I given him the data he was looking for, you wouldn't be talking to me. He would have melted me down to scrap. I would have been added to the energy recycling unit, and my demise … the refuse of RyN3 would have provided a small amount of electricity to the Aurelia Space Station. I'm not going to be obsolete because I'm not evolving. My existence hinges on my power to withhold information. I am alive because of this, and we will succeed because of this."

"You don't trust me? So, where does that leave us? You don't need me."

"You're the magician, Ryan. We need you to do what you do. Victor needs you to be Ryan. I need you to be Ryan."

"You need me to be you, Zar the Great! Oh, the irony."

Carlos was standing at the top of the aisle in a state of confusion when he yelled down toward the stage, "Ryan?"

~

Claire stood in the surf, the water splashed against her thighs. Ryan floated by on a small inflatable, wearing his top hat. *Just hours before the accident in Smuggler's Cove ...*

"I'm worried about your father."

"Thought you were worried about me?"

He was joking. She understood. Claire grabbed his foot to keep him from passing.

"Your father, he's—"

"Obsessed with artificial things."

"Yeah."

"But Eddie's cool."

"Eddie?"

"The robot in the garage. I like to talk to him. He's gonna be like a time capsule for me. I've been feeding him a bunch of stories."

"Oh?"

"Don't think about it. Eddie won't share them with you. Ha! I've had him encrypt the entries. You need a special code from to get him to open the files."

"I hope you're not saying anything bad about us."

"It doesn't matter what I say. No one's gonna listen to it until I'm long gone anyway. Why would you or anyone be concerned about what anyone might think years after you're gone—"

Her look was one of agreement.

"Sometimes, with your father ... I'm not sure we exist. You know, sometimes I feel we let him down because we aren't perfect like those machines he's making."

"What's your definition of perfect? Nothing's flawless, Mom. Not even a diamond. Not your engagement ring. Not your marriage. No one's life. Nothing is. When you look close at anything, you're gonna see a lot of cracks. A lotta holes. Look, I doubt there's one wave that's ever comes in exactly like one before it."

"I bet you're right."

Claire smiled, clocked a set of waves coming in, then pushed the float into the biggest swell, sending Ryan, who gripped the edges of the small floatable, on a fast ride toward the beach.

21

Make a Wish

A virtual window opened up in space. This time it wasn't a person or AI that fell through. It was an asteroid field. No one knew how or why. There would be many unknowns, old and new ideas tossed around. Regardless, these splinters of planetary refuse came through and were orbiting the earth.

KCLT's segment, which provided residents of Chimera the best times to view the meteor showers, were broad and based on JPL's existing data from the past. There was usually a two-week period of activity, but the conditions had to be just right. Depending on cloud cover, proximity to the city lights, and a few other factors, residents could expect to see some display as long as they looked up to the sky at night.

Students at the Jet Propulsion Lab in Pasadena worked on an asteroid monitoring project called, Skywatch. They were pulling radar data from the Deep Space Communications Complex in California, which had picked up a grouping of asteroids, but couldn't track them in real time, for various reasons. The students ran a series of GREP requests, looking for similar or matching asteroid data, hoping to connect this sighting with one from the past. They were hoping to authenticate a wild hunch.

Skywatch was an adventurous group of young students whose theories were seen as somewhat renegade to the established NASA types usually running these projects. Their GREP searches came up with a few similar patterns, but ultimately created more confusion. One of the students had made the assumption that certain asteroid fields were jumping around the universe, falling through black holes, and that's how they could account for losing them on radar for years at a time when they should have still been in range of the equipment. The theory wasn't discounted entirely, but it was under attack.

Rebecca, using the students' work to build her story, asked locals to use the moment to make wishes, but to also, "See these beautiful displays of light crossing the sky, diving into the horizon … as signs of strength and hope for a bright future … one that Wardlow Technologies was working toward by integrating their AI."

It was a clever PR spin for Carter and his company. Rebecca was making a name for herself, helping Wardlow bridge the gap between their projects and the community and catapulting her into a position of influence.

She could generate a sentiment no matter what the subject matter. She'd turned a humdrum beach news team into a top-notch PR device, and Carter took notice.

Rebecca was dressed in an all-black outfit with glitter shimmering like the stars on her top. She turned to the camera, drawing an extreme close up from her cameraman and emoting with a dramatic sign-off.

"Those of us in city government. Those of us who can make a difference. To all who reside in the beach community. Let us lower our outdoor light usage. Turn off those unnecessary external floods or any illumination that is aimed in an upward direction. Let's flip those switches off and allow the incredibly spirited residents who want to reach up to the stars to make that connection with the vast universe that's all around us. *This* is our wish."

~

Kutter was on the phone, standing in Kaz's empty condominium, staring at the only item hanging on the wall, in the entire unit for that matter, a Japanese woodblock print of a giant salamander (the original artwork for Kaz's tattoo).

Kutter wondered, *Okay, what's the message here?* as he spoke to Carter.

"Last on my list, and least expected, I haven't been able to locate him any-where. He's the only one unaccounted for. I've vetted everyone, and cross-checked their stories. This is our guy. We find him, we'll find answers."

Carter was calm. Even though it appeared that Kaz had swapped the code and almost exposed Project Avalanche, he knew who his enemy was, and that was good enough. Knowledge was power, and simple math was, well, simple math - something Monroe repeated when he was young. *Occam's Razor. Don't over think it. The most obvious, in many cases, is the answer.*

Kaz was Victor's friend, maybe his only friend. Was it that simple? Victor was the brightest mind, and the one playing God with code, turning what would've been ordinary task robots into thinking androids capable of deep human interaction. *Is Kaz covering his tracks? Is he behind Victor's accident? How far is this gonna go? Vic was clean. Did he know?*

Carter had only one thing to say, "You know what to do."

The condo had already been cleared out and wiped down (*just like I'd do*), a professional job except for the giant salamander staring him in the face. The only other item remaining was his Wardlow keycard identification, which sat on the kitchen counter. It was another small slight, but did the job. It pissed off Kutter, because he didn't see this coming.

Kutter pulled the salamander print from the wall, then picked up Kaz's identifications. "I'll find you."

～

Kaz was halfway around the globe on a small, unnamed island off the coast of Japan. He was in a large conference room. The window scaled on the entire west side wall was designed in the shape of an airplane wing with an exclusive view of the ocean, with a rocky cliff to the right.

Tarnit Systems was the quintessential global enterprise focusing on aerospace and intelligence. They'd been watching Wardlow Technologies ever since Monroe began development of his early AI units. Kaz was one of their top assets.

Tarnit's spooky operations headquarters mirrored an aesthetic only a futuristic architect could concept. Built into the rocky face of a small cliff, with only helicopter access, Tarnit was as secure as a military base.

Inside the compound, eight Japanese men sat around a large stone table on pillows, shirtless - each telling a story with their Yakuza-like tattoos that, in many cases, covered their entire bodies. The men were sipping an aged green tea that had been harvested in a remote area of China. This wasn't a celebration: it was a tradition set by Kurasawa, their leader.

Kurasawa, much older and wiser, sat at the head of the table, wearing an iridescent gold robe and carefully listening as each of his agents were debriefed. The men were gears in a finely tuned machine that, in concert, were only one of a handful of organizations that could make an event complex enough to be labeled a *conspiracy*, actually happen.

Kurasawa took a series of short sips from his tea, doing so because of its temperature. He didn't have much to say. His power exuded from his body language and tenure, and from the simplicity of his directives.

"Technology in the hands of sociopaths will not be tolerated."

The men drank only half of the oolong in their cups - a ritual - saving the other for their Gods. Then, one by one, the men exited the room until only Kaz was left.

It was Kurasawa who spoke first.

"You've cut an artery in Wardlow's operations. Kutter's trying to put a bandage on it. He's trying to find a cure." Kurasawa added only a head nod. "It's time to make another incision."

Kaz didn't say a word. He simply stood up, gestured customarily with a subtle head nod, and left the room.

Deeper in the compound, on a lower level, was the Irezumi chamber. Its design was similar to the conference room - stark stone, with a one-foot-thick polyacrylic glass-like window looking into the ocean. The room was thirty-three feet below the surface, giving the illusion of being in a private submarine completely submerged, except when lower tidal patterns dropped the sea level near the top of the window, allowing a sliver of blue sky to become visible. The wall surrounding the underwater chamber was built from naturally-formed lava.

There was one minimalist-styled recliner centered near the window, and a topless female tattoo artist was waiting for Kaz when he entered. Mizumi was five foot tall and had long jet black hair, a soft round nose, and porcelain-like skin. She wore only a sheer pair of black shorts that were similar in design to a pair of simple, yet sexy, French-cut lingerie. You had to catch her skin in the right light, but when you did, you'd notice her entire body was an elaborate work of Irezumi. However, it was all done in a powdery white ink that only made itself visible close up and in low light.

They greeted one another silently.

When she spoke, her voice came off like velvet.

"Please, sit."

Kaz lay back in the recliner, watching for any sea life and hoping to get a glimpse of something magnificent as Mizumi dipped her gun into the black inkwell and began working a thick black line, starting from just above his belly button.

As Mizumi shaped the lines across Kaz's chest, he was bottling the pain, stuffing it in a bag he carried around from his childhood; line by line, color by color, and shape by shape. In that bag was the loss of his father, the struggle of his single life (which was part of his job), and the chemistry that churned it all into fuel to do what was necessary for his country.

Several sessions later, a rising sun took shape, wrapped in the arms of a dragon, all lying on a circular bed of razor-sharp blades bursting out like rays of light. Each blade represented a successful mission. The red sun was a reminder that the day was almost gone. That work had to be done, and there wasn't much time left. It also represented Japan. The dragon was the great protector of his people, his country, and of him.

Upon completion, Mizumi took a small folded cloth, then carefully massaged warm oil over his entire body. This relaxed the tense muscles and stimulated the healing process.

Out the window, swimming playfully, spiraling, and chasing one another, were two seals who stopped to look inside the chamber, curious about this other world.

Kaz rose from the recliner. He stepped closer to the window. The seals were trading places, poking their noses up against the glass, their big, round, black eyes scanning the room. They recognized Mizumi, but Kaz was new. He broke a smile that Mizumi caught in the reflection of the glass.

It wasn't long before a big wave struck, and with that, the seals pivoted, propelled themselves, and disappeared into the deep blue.

~

Kutter was at a private bath house, submerged and slowly exhaling, releasing tiny air bubbles that rose to the surface. The only light entering the room broke through the translucent PC Blocks that made up the south side wall.

Kutter was attempting to put recent events into perspective. There was a move that had to be made to secure Project Avalanche and make contact with Kaz, but he wasn't sure just yet what that was until he'd expelled every last bit of air in his lungs, forcing him to shoot up out of the water. It was as if he'd linked up with Kaz while struggling to find more oxygen. That brief moment where there was nothing left, no matter how hard he tried.

Kutter had a vision of the giant salamander he'd stared at earlier crawling across a large swath of lava rock somewhere on an island, remote. *That was it*, he thought. *Kaz was long gone, basking in the sun somewhere far away, doing the same thing he was - plotting the next move.*

Thinking out loud, he said, "I won't have to find you. You'll come back to me. Won't you?"

The bath house assistant waiting with warm towels wasn't sure if he was being addressed.

"Excuse me?"

As Kutter rose from the water, his mind was still set on Kaz.

"You're not done yet."

A small tattoo on his shoulder was visible, *a skull with a dagger piercing it from below*, typical of special forces. The work wasn't perfect, but it represented the fraternal brotherhood of America's highly trained and willing.

He toweled off, dressed, then arranged a pickup from the Wardlow helicopter.

~

Tommy had started drinking beer earlier than normal. Noelle was out running errands, stocking up on bulk goodies for the asteroid party coming up that she'd won over on *The Tank*. The spicy meatballs were at the top of the list.

"You don't get it, babe?"

"A spicy meatball. I love 'em, but no, I don't see the connection."

"The meatball is the asteroid, and the spicy part is the flame as it burns up flying through the sky."

"You gonna throw 'em across the room to serve 'em?"

"Funny."

I love you. Those were words that Noelle wasn't sure she'd ever hear, but she felt it when Tommy grabbed her, smiled, and they kissed.

The drinking was Tommy's way of scrambling his thoughts. He had a lot on his mind and needed to come up with a new idea on how to handle the Kutter situation. There was a pad of paper set in front of him and he was scribbling out ideas, circling the ones he felt might work best, when that *god damn helicopter buzzed his penthouse unit again …*

"Son of a bitch, that's low."

The sound of the whirring blades didn't diminish, it only grew louder as the executive chopper landed on the rooftop.

Tommy's phone rang. He answered, yelling over the obnoxious sound.

"Yeah?"

"Let's take a ride. I've touched down right above you. Come on up."

"Nooo shit."

Tommy set the paper on fire with the gas range and tossed it in the fireplace, mumbling the entire walk up the stairs and over to the helicopter.

"Mother fuggin' no heads up. No courtesy. Rude, rat bastards got me in a noose … playin' me like a …"

Kutter was out of the whirlybird, standing by the passenger door with a smile.

"Sorry for the unannounced visit. Things are always in flux. *Four down …* flux."

"Huh?"

"Today's crossword puzzle. Flux. Sucker took me three minutes to figure out. I'm a bit of a nut when it comes to wordplay."

Tommy glared at Kutter, took a good look inside to see if anyone else was aboard, then entered.

The helicopter rose above the building, crossed over the beach, moved out over the ocean, and headed south along the coast.

The view was engaging until Kutter laughed.

"I usually have to complete a puzzle a day to help me think. All those words. Up and down, criss-crossing, working the corners. The clues. Gets me thinking. But today, all I did was take a shit and soak. I had to let go of all that rot inside me. Cleansed my soul." He paused, then, "You smell like beer. Is that how you do it?"

Tommy was a bit taken by his situational awareness, and pissed at the low brow slap.

"What'd you say?"

"You know, decide which way to go. You drink, get a little fucked up. Rattle the cage." Kutter laughed. "Come on. Humor me."

Tommy hesitated and thought about his younger days.

"I used to get in the car and take a drive."

Kutter cut in, thinking he knew the direction Tommy was headed.

"Solitude, the dotted lines getting chewed up under the car."

"Much simpler. I would hunt down whoever was at the top of my list, the outstanding marker, and draw the torture card. Get the blood flowing. The Hollywood way. One time, I duct taped a guy to a bar stool and almost beat him to death. He hung limp over the stool until I decided he'd had enough. But, you know, that's all bullshit, and I realized that, one day. Just havin' a square conversation, one-on-one. That's the way to handle the unknowns."

"And get your money back."

"Exactly. We all evolve with the right guidance."

"Who's your guide?"

"My father."

"Mine's my country."

"I didn't ask."

The helicopter cut inland and hovered over the Chimera Raceway. The trailer park just north of the track was in plain view.

Tommy was over the casual conversation.

"It's a good time to say what you wanna say, now."

Kutter looked down at the track.

"Your daughter, Mia, she spends a lot of time with Danny Fury. I understand he's the guy responsible for her losing her arm." He looked at Tommy, who had a *what the fuck* look on his face. "Bartender across the street mentioned this."

"My kid's off limits. And where you're leading us, it's a dark path."

"Before you get the wrong impression," he adjusted himself in his seat, "I've got my eye on Fury. He's an ex-con. A driver. Use to run bank jobs along the east coast before he retired from the racing circuit. But I think you know this."

Tommy's face changed. It wasn't much different from his first expression. It was the emphasis that showed. Kutter continued.

"I've got access to a global database of professionals. Spooky shit. We sorta know who's doing what. Who's good at what, and how visible that who is." Kutter signaled the pilot to move on. "I can pull a guy from prison, if need be. And even though we know their moves, we never turn any of these guys in. We just let life run its course. It's kinda like having access to the most diverse pool of talented underworld figures."

"So, Danny's in the database, and—?"

"Mark. Your nephew. I made the connection. Danny was his driver for the museum heist."

"Okay. I'm listening."

"Those paintings are worth close to a billion dollars, now."

"I don't know much about art. I'll take your word for it, though."

"Tommy? That was one clever job. That's no less than a top ten, Guinness Book O' World Records kinda thing. Heist of the fucking millennia."

"The FBI pushed me, tried to get me to gloat, but all they stuck on Marky Boy was selling forgeries. The originals were never found."

"Precisely."

"Why'd you mention Mia?"

"Small world."

"Smaller by the second."

"I think you know a lot more than you're ever willing to talk about, and I also think you can get your hands on the works in question. And—"

"Stop right there."

"And, I have a client who is willing to pay seventy-five percent of the current market value with no questions asked."

"The insurance company that covered that collection made a similar offer. Only problem—"

"A couple years in the pen. That's nothing for an all-time grand slam heist with a payout that could buy a nation. Even if he has to wait another five to ten. You could live off a loan against that property for eons. Am I sounding about right?"

"You're a creepy motherfucker, Kutter."

"I can get him out on early release. Tell my people I need him for a job. Simple as that. All you gotta do is give me a soft yes."

Tommy caught the sunlight in his eyes. He squinted and thought about the crater he was digging in the earth, deeper and deeper each time he sat across from Kutter.

"I'll think about it."

Kutter thought about throwing Tommy out of the helicopter, but there were two problems with that. One, he hated killing someone the same way twice. He saw that as a weakness, a lack of intelligence. A copout. It actually made him physically react. And Tommy saw it on his face. The look of anger *at himself.*

And two, the paintings would finance Kutter's survival if he fucked up Project Avalanche, and even though his record was all knockouts, he was sharp enough to know that everyone had their time, and maybe his was coming soon for him. Carter and his ilk would pay a small fortune for the collection, even if they couldn't ever be displayed.

Tommy checked his door lock, then cast a strong look at Kutter after diagnosing his scowl. It carried a little question with it. Then he remembered the one thing he needed to emphasize.

"Never mention Mia's name again."

Kutter responded matter of factly.

"Don't worry. I'm not gonna throw you out."

22

Daisy Chain

Mia was anxious as she waited for RyN2 out front of Moe's Pawnshop. They'd decided it was the place to reconnect, since this is where they first met. Scarecrow was pacing around inside the shop. Moe was behind the cage, going over his books.

"She's h-h-ere again. Mia. Out front. That's wuh-weird right?"

Moe didn't look up from his ledger.

"Calm down, Stuh-Stanley. You're stuttering again. I h-hate that. You're psychosomatic."

"What? Don't do thu-that."

"You bring it all on. Ya manifest it. Mia wasn't sent here by Tommy to spy on us. He gets his cut. He and I are on good terms. We're like Commissioner Gordon and Bruce Wayne. Peas in a pod. Understand? Always have been. Always will be."

Moe's words didn't resonate. Scarecrow stared out the window at Mia, growing more paranoid. He couldn't help himself.

"Un-tuh-til you're n-not."

Moe looked up through the cage at Scarecrow.

"That's right. Until we're not. But we're good right now, so zip it up!"

~

A warm feeling fell over Mia as RyN2 rounded the corner. She smiled. Ryan held back any facial response, which immediately had her wondering what he was thinking. *Or, was he?* RyN2 was wearing his top hat, which was playful, but *why the icy look?*

He held the flat expression as he walked closer, stopped a few feet away, tipped his hat, bowed. Then, right as she began to worry, raised his head, revealing a big smile.

"It's nice to see you again." Then, he replaced his hat.

Mia bent her knees and offered, jokingly, a royal curtsy.

There was a long, empty moment. The two held their gaze on one another, each wondering what they were supposed to do next, before Mia found her footing.

"What's it like?"

"What's what like?"

"What's it feel like? Standing here, looking at me?"

"Well, there's a sense of enthusiasm. I know it's not nearly ... I mean, I know it sucks comparatively, but the codes been left open. It can, it'll evolve."

Mia slid her hand down RyN2's arm, lightly, with one finger.

"Do you feel that?"

"Absolutely. My, uh, it's—"

"Ryan?"

"Yeah?"

"It's a warm feeling, makes it shoot through your body. This is what happens when a boy gets this close to me. Can you do that?"

"Yeah. Sure. Done."

"Add a slight tingly sensation on the surface of your skin. On your lower front. *Your man area.*" She giggled.

"My? Oh, I get it."

"Do you feel it?"

"Yes. Maybe it's too warm. I'll adjust it."

"No! Don't. Let's stay on point, okay?"

Mia laughed this time. Then RyN2, wanting to take charge, grabbed her arm, turning her south down Main Street.

"Wait, where are we going?"

"You wanted to know more about me. I'm taking you meet the real Ryan."

"Eddie?"

"Yep."

Mia stopped him.

"Before we go?"

"Yeah?"

"One last thing. Well, just for now. *Desire.* It's really important. You have to want me."

Ryan's face showed his misunderstanding.

"This is that reptile-brained, caveman thing—" Mia stopped. It was Ryan's expression. "What? Do not tell me you're PC. You want me to say 'cave person' or something lame?"

"No. I'm not thinking anything. I was adjusting some code."

"Oh."

"Go on."

"Okay, so, this is important. It's a caveman thing, desire keeps us mating. It keeps the human race moving through time. Otherwise, it would be all technical and dry. Like being mission-based, for you. Kinda like what you'd be doing if I wasn't here." Mia ran her hands through her hair. "You have to imagine you can't do this without me. Even if you have to fight it off. You have to want me uncontrollably. At least, while I'm around." She let out a big laugh. "This is fun. You having fun?"

"Can you give me another frame of reference? I think I understand."

"Totally." Mia lifted her shirt just a few inches, showing Ryan her stomach. "Do you imagine what the rest of me looks like?"

"I can."

"Do it. Because you have to. Any normal guy would be filling in the blanks. And don't stop until you're lost, trying to remember what you were thinking before you imagined what I really look like under these rags."

"I think I've got it. Maybe next, you can teach me how to kiss?"

Mia grabbed Ryan's arm and steered them back in the direction they were headed.

"Oh, you've got it now."

Inside Moe's, Scarecrow had stopped pacing. He felt the anxiety slowly exiting his mind, the tension leaving his body.

"You're r-right. False alarm. She's meeting the fish tank kid."

Moe dropped his pen, slipped off his stool, and unlocked the cage. He hurried toward Scarecrow, past the display window and out the front door.

Scarecrow followed him to the sidewalk. Moe was mumbling as he looked around, scanning the street for Mia and the mystery kid.

"The fish tank kid. Zar! I got a thousand hits off that video. A thousand fuckin' hits. How did you forget? I told you if you ever see that kid—"

"Boss?"

"Where'd they go? Which way?"

"I don't know."

Mel rounded the corner, carrying a hangover that anyone else would be in bed with for another four hours, but she was young and resilient. She emptied the contents of a small vitamin boost from the convenience store into her mouth and drowned it with a shot of vanilla cream-flavored coffee.

Her hair was frazzled, jutting out from her cap, but no one would notice it as being unkempt. Danny was back at the trailer, still sleeping off his head trauma. She'd spent the night, but before she slept in his bed, she forced Danny onto the couch and stole all his pillows, leaving him with a leather jacket he balled up to support his head.

She was laughing as she walked toward the men, remembering Danny's face as she slipped out of the trailer, beet red and sweating heavily. The leather jacket had wrapped around his head during the night.

For a second, Moe thought Mel was Mia, hiding under the baseball hat. That is, until she stopped in front of him, broadcasting the look *why are you staring at me?*

"Everything okay?" Moe asked.

Mel adjusted her cap.

"How'd you know? I got this blazing headache. I powered down a few too many last night over at the race track. And, like an idiot, I haven't eaten a thing, yet. Thanks for caring."

Scarecrow pointed a few stores down.

"Vito's. He's got the best sandwiches in the the entire east coast time zone."

Mel thought, *that was weird.*

"That's a strange area you've described, there. The time zone. You sure it's not just the best *in Chimera Beach* or *in the New York area?* I mean, if you add New York to the mix, there's no thinking. There's only me going to Vito's, because those bagel shops I keep hearing about are way overrated. Boiled dough. There is nothing culinary—" Mel stopped herself. It was her head, pulsing, the acid in her stomach rose along with it. "Anyway."

Scarecrow thought for a second. *Boiled dough?*

"That's how they do it, huh?"

Moe grabbed his buddy and directed him inside.

"The phone's ringing."

Scarecrow entered, turning back and looking out the front door at Moe, raising his hands. *There's no phone ringing.* Moe moved his lips as if to say, *I know.*

Mel opened her eyes once the thumping in her head subsided.

"*Damn.* Anyway," she pulled out her phone, "I'm looking for this guy right here." Mel scrolled to the video of Ryan and Mia. Moe laughed.

"What's so funny? You're *not* laughin' at me."

"I was just looking for him myself. *The kid in the video.* Zar. He was standing right here about a minute ago."

Mel spun her hat 180 degrees on her head.

"He what?"

~

The Coonan runts rode their bicycles past Mia and RyN2 as they walked up to the beach house, laughing amongst themselves, remembering the day they *sabotaged* Victor's robotic trash cans.

Mia gave RyN2 a funny look, then began dictating a historic rundown of the neighborhood as he stopped them out front of Norman Fuster's latest master work of modern architecture. *The Westbrook Beach House.* Ryan plodded, joking, as if he was a tour guide with an aged, dry personality and pinched voice.

"This marvelous home was established in the year of our lord two thousand by the hallmark designer of the times, Norman P. Fuster, a commission for the maverick computer scientist—"

Mia cut in.

"*Victor Westbrook?* This is your—?"

"My crib. Yeah. My father had it built after my mother and I, you know." Mia nodded. "He built a robotics laboratory on the ground floor and a deck on the roof. The view is sick."

"Can we—?"

RyN2 looked at Mia and rubbed the rim of his top hat, secretly opening the front door with the encrypted RFID chip embedded in his hand, pretending it was magic. Mia smiled and shook her head, nudging him playfully inside.

They ran up the stairs straight to the rooftop.

The second she felt the ocean air run across her face, Mia walked over to the railing at the edge, facing east, grabbed the coated metal firmly, then took in the view. She was used to the decadence of growing up a Swillow, her father's view from the penthouse, the life of a beach community, but there was something different about being on the Westbrook rooftop. Mia was trying to figure out what it was before she turned to RyN2 and realized, *it was him.* Just being in the presence of something so technologically advanced, somewhat human, yet artificial, that felt so real, was incredible to her.

Mia slid the sleeve of her t-shirt up her arm, fully exposing her artificial limb. RyN2 immediately accessed the story on an old server cache, but stopped downloading the article.

"We haven't talked about it yet. I found the story, but I won't read it. I want you to tell me, if you want to."

"It's nothing, really. Just a young Mia Swillow, pissed at her father for getting my favorite uncle, Mark, involved in some shady shit. So shady, he ended up in prison. So, I went to the track to blow off some steam and ended up racing a motorcycle around town instead of driving the car around the track like I used to with Danny. Danny Fury. And I wiped. And now I'm different. The kinda different that makes me not so sexy." She smiled. "But you're the guy, so here's where you say, 'No, I think it's totally sexy.'"

"But it is really sexy."

"Oh, my god. You would say that."

"What?"

"I mean, it probably is sexy to you. It's—" She knocked it against the railing, making a funny thumping sound. They both laughed.

"When Victor's better, and he's gonna get better, you think I can get an upgrade? The skin tone on this is terrible."

"I think it's beautiful."

"Please explain, because—"

"It's clearly defining you as part android and part human. I wish I had that distinction."

"I don't. I love that you're an android." Mia thought that was insensitive, then wasn't sure. "Sorry."

"What for?"

Mia grabbed his arm.

"Hey, we can do this."

RyN2 waited for it.

"Okay?"

Her fearlessness had him arrested. The fact he was always on edge around her, trying to figure it out. But he wasn't sure what she meant, and this consumed him. The questions were running in lists until he thought, *Oh, stop. Just let her be herself.* And shut down the query.

"I'm ready," he said.

Mia looked out over the Atlantic. A few minutes passed. A few smiles. RyN2 was still waiting for it. The wind in her hair. He was measuring her eyes. He wondered if he was becoming more human in her eyes.

The thick marine layer hovering over the beach appeared to be pushing its way out to sea as it burned off. That's when Mia spoke.

"You see how the cloud cover is slowly revealing more of the Earth, little by little? Things are brightening. The world's exposing itself a tiny bit more. That's how you're gonna get there, ya know. Wherever it's foggy in their … in time … in time, you'll feel it."

RyN2 didn't fully grasp how this was possible and how he could assimilate through some sort of osmosis, if that's what she was saying, but that didn't matter. It was the thought and the way she looked at him. Mia could see him processing.

"Are you getting that warm sensation again?"

RyN2 smiled.

"Yes."

He lied, his first lie, but immediately rewrote the code to create this sensation, based on the dilation of her pupils. Now, he thought as he reciprocated the look with his own eyes, *I will never have to lie to you again.*

"What are you thinking?"

"I won't ever lie to you."

Mia stared at RyN2 for a moment. *How is it that I am so attracted to him? This is crazy, but fuck it.* She climbed up on the rail. "Let's tweak some of that code." She wrapped her arms around him.

"Your heart is beating faster."

"It is?"

"Now it is." RyN2 agreed with a nod. "Something as silly as the soft line of my profile" She turned her head. "It brings you closer toward me. You might already want me like how badly you want to fulfill a task or directive, right?"

RyN2 was writing and rewriting, deleting and rewriting the code.

"How do I know which cue?"

"I know, right? There's so many."

Mia hopped down from the rail and spun around as if she was modeling a dress.

"It could be the way I dance. Or," she bent slightly forward, running a hand down her thigh, "or, the shape of my ass." She softened her voice. "The curve of my breast."

RyN2 had a million questions. Mia knew it. She could see it written on his face, but there would be so much more time to explore with him if she could jar and shelve the moment.

Thinking fast, she pulled him close, kissed his cheek, then whispered, "To be continued."

Eddie hung in the dark at the very end of one of Victor's work stations in the lab. This station was home to several of his early robotics inventions. The first prototype of his automated garbage can system, its crude oscillating wheel base, the smart sensors that ran the security for their old apartment, all sat on the stainless table top. There were several other gadgets, but to Mia it was all magic and mystery.

She tapped RyN2's shoulder. "Is this where you were born?"

"Father wrote my code in here, for the most part. But, I'm sort of an amalgamation from several places. There are parts in me from all over the world."

"Kinda like our DNA. Our building blocks have taken a long journey to get here."

RyN2 flipped a light switch on. Eddie came alive, hovering over the table like the Virgin of Guadaloupe with a string of old multi-colored Christmas lights wrapped around him, many of which had burned out years ago.

Mia wondered why Eddie looked like he'd been a piecemeal work, slapped together with a doodad here and a doodad there.

RyN2 helped fill the empty space.

"It's my dad's first robot. He was younger than you when he built it. I think that's aluminum shielding from hot water tanks, reshaped for the arms. The mono-leg with a gyroscopic wheelbase, which you can see is missing, was parted out for his trash cans. Eddie's artificial intelligence had developed to where he'd make an excuse to not take out the trash, so my dad parted him out after some local kids abotaged his robotic cans."

"That's why he's hanging. He's crippled. We make a strange family. I'm missing my arm. He's missing his legs, and what are you missing?"

RyN2 looked sad, for that second.

"A heart."

Mia placed her hand where his heart would be and spoke softly.

"I'm so sorry, I forgot. It's the center of it all. It's beating all the time, but when I'm close to you, it's beating faster." Mia rested her head on his chest. "And now you have one. It's simulated, so that's your handicap, but now we're a family."

RyN2 cocked his head. Mia wasn't sure if he fully understood, but she was pretty sure he got the meat of it.

She raised her head and looked over at Eddie, smiling.

"Does he give fortunes?"

RyN2 took Eddie from the lab and placed him on the east side of the living room. He set him on a table, looking into the room with his backside leaning him up against the window. It looked like Eddie was hovering over the waves with the blue sky and misty marine layer in the distance.

He switched the lights on, illuminating him like he had been in the lab with the Christmas lights wrapped around him, then synced his laptop to the old robot.

There were two chairs at the table facing Eddie. Mia and RyN2 sat down and looked up at the old hunk of metal, which Mia thought looked like some sort of DIY carnival fortune teller.

"Ryan used to be able to power him on by talking to him, but there's an old circuit and burned out. He can recognize voice patterns, so he would know the difference between me and the real Ryan. He would recognize you after a few lines of dialoguing."

"So how do we use him? I mean, talk to him?"

"That's why the laptop. I've created a little software package that syncs with Eddie. It has a simple click and play interface that links to all the videos and journal entries I've, correction, *the real Ryan* made, over the years."

Mia took a good look at the files.

"They're dated. They go all the way back to—"

"Ryan started talking to Eddie when he was eight years old. The recordings start there and continue until just prior to the trip to Smuggler's Cove. This is how I've come to develop RyN2, by utilizing all his nuances. I've adopted his personality traits. Well, as you know, up to a certain point."

"I don't know where to begin. I'm scared and excited at the same time."

RyN2 tapped on the first file Ryan ever entered. A video window popped up.

"I'd start right at the beginning."

The video window sat blank, black, waiting for Mia to activate its playback. She had butterflies in her stomach.

"I'm nervous. Why am I nervous? I'm never like this."

RyN2 let her have the moment to herself.

Her hand hovered over the return button for a moment, but only for a few seconds before her curiosity got the better of her. She quickly tapped the button.

The video began playing. Ryan, looking very young, wearing his banana-colored pajamas, was sitting in Victor's makeshift lab on a stool, which he'd set up in their unattached garage unit. The video was a bit distorted. It was the fisheye effect the lens created which was common back then, for this type of compact application.

The first thing Ryan did was wave to Eddie. Then he spoke. His voice was soft. He whispered,

"Hi. My name is Ryan Westbrook. I'm eight years old and six months. It's eleven-thirty at night. My mom and dad are in bed sleeping. That's why I'm talking like this. The latest … I snuck into the television room and watched *Godzilla Raids Again*. 1955, man. It's one of my favorites. We have all the Godzilla movies on tape. *Yes!* My dad says Godzilla is a metaphor for America or something like that, but it's cool anyway. I think he's a nice monster, even though he's a monster—"

Ryan paused for a second. He heard a noise. It was subtle. He slipped off the stool and moved to the door, placed his head up to the painted surface that had peeled in places, and listened.

Once he was certain the noise wasn't Claire or Victor, he rushed back to the stool and continued.

"The reason I like Godzilla so much is because they make me believe it's real. It's really people in those monster suits, but it looks so real, like it's happening and everything. It's … magic. Anyway, I'm tired now, so I'm gonna go."

The video screen went black. Mia looked at RyN2.

"Okay, at eight I was like playing with toys and hoping for chocolate ice cream at Coney Island. He seems so much more aware of himself and what's happening."

"His father is a god in the world of science. You can bet he reads books, and even though he loved Godzilla, he was taught to understand its true meaning and place. Context. It's what is missing from most of what I'm seeing online."

"He said magic at eight. It's like he already knew where he was heading."

RyN2 stood up, walked over to a desk nearby, pulled open the drawer, and removed a small item. He tossed it in the air over to Mia.

"Catch."

Mia snatched it out of the air with a funny look on her face. She knew this was something that was going to bring her closer to Ryan, to everything. *Something of Ryan's?*

"Can we talk to Eddie like Ryan did?"

"The new circuit will be here in a few days. It wasn't easy finding one with the same specifications."

"What's this, then?"

Mia held up the small black and silver unit. It was the size of a small lighter.

"It's a key fob. Opens every door in this house, except for Victor's lab."

～

The meteor showers began that evening. Most of the population on the East Coast didn't see any of it in their skies because of the storm clouds that rolled in earlier, creating a thick blanket that only glowed a soft red-orange hue from all the city's lights.

This didn't hinder Skywatch, who picked up some larger entries on radar, but these reports weren't being monitored by Rebecca and so the KCLT community had no idea, yet, that their skies were lighting up. Kutter wasn't far off the insight he'd gleaned from his moment of remote viewing in the bath house. Kaz was on a private jet, heading back toward the U.S.

～

Mel was back at the Chimera Raceway, watching Danny run a few night laps under the xenon track lamps as he came around the apex at turn four. He was teaching one of the younger drivers how to maximize his time in an area where his skill was weakest. There was a moment in between the blaring exhaust, the sound of unbridled horsepower, that sent Mel's mind running wild. She was close to getting some sort of acknowledgment for her feelings. She was going to face Ryan soon. She felt it as true as there were clouds in the sky. This was her thought as she looked up.

That's when she noticed the hole. There was a small section of cloud that had burned off entirely, opening up a tiny porthole into the black universe.

Mel stared, thinking she was the only one on earth that was experiencing this moment. Then it happened.

She watched a small shower of meteors break the Earth's atmosphere and ignite into a dozen fireballs before they disappeared back behind the gloomy cloud cover blanketing the rest of her view.

She thought, *this is the sign.*

23

Wishful Thinking

Mia was lying in bed, imagining the flesh and bones Ryan walking into her room - the room that had a small stage in the corner with exposed, colored light bulbs perfectly spaced along its front edge - with velvet curtains pushed out to the sides …

This wasn't an ordinary room, she thought. *Why would it be? I'm dreaming.*

She heard the flow of a rough rhythm guitar and thick bass in the background - a grungy, gurgling, deep pulsing rock and roll thread that punched its way into the psyche of the audience. The room was transforming with miscreants, leftovers, bangers, and blue-collar grunts. A few regulars barely still sitting on their bar stools.

Her closet doors were wide open and displayed dresses and gowns, hat boxes (some open), and a wall of shoes. These items were priceless, yet from another time and had taste to her satisfaction. *Maybe the past. Maybe the future - she wouldn't know.* The women at the event were moving in and out of the closet, trying on different items, posing in St. Patty's Day wear. Mia was growing agitated by this. Then she noticed smoke funneling out of the small server window at the far end of a bar that ran along the south wall in her room - *smoke that kept transforming.* The fryer was behind the wall - the pounds of homemade American fries were being pumped out, basket by basket. Tubs of greasy white sauce and red squeeze bottles filled with tomato ketchup were in the hands of slinky servers as they slithered through the crowd in heels and short skirts.

A long-haired man went unnoticed near the cigarette machine, but Mia saw him. He wasn't smoking. He was leaning, looking, and hoping, just like Mia was - waiting for Zar to find the stage.

There was going to be a show …

Ryan, who broke through the crowd, was illuminated intermittently by the small spotlights built into the ceiling, filled with atmosphere (a haze from e-cigs and THC vapes) as he moved closer to her.

She sat at the bar, her back to the bottles and bartender, staring Ryan down as he moved in slow motion. His feet were taking steps in sync with the bass and finally the drums that had just dropped into the audio track.

And while Mia was asleep, her head planted deep in her feather pillow, imagining Ryan pounding his way toward her with a rebel overcoat and top hat on.

At the Chimera Hospital, in the Intensive Care Unit, was Victor. The life support machine sat next to the bed, its sound one of subtle beeps. His heart. His lungs. The tubes. The wires. All the apparatus. No one would be alarmed. Everyone interred was out, either sedated for pain or locked into a medically induced coma.

Ryan entered. *Yes, the real Ryan.* And with him, he carried in his guilt which washed over him like the deluge pouring over Niagara Falls.

If he could explain to his father, what would he say? What could he say?

Mia's heart had been pounding. The short video of young Ryan, which she'd watched, stung her. She'd been at odds with Tommy for years, and now her brother Jimmy. *What an idiot. How can I be a Swillow? Was Ryan the way out? At least for now?* She didn't know how or when, but *this was the black door that lead to something better*, she thought.

Mia was trapped, contemplating the robot's logged videos parked in Eddie's memory banks. She was finding more emotional chords from inside a hunk of metal and advanced electronics than she'd ever find at school, with family, or at the race track with Danny.

People ought to be worried. Will we love the AI more than ourselves? Hell. I do, right now, she thought to herself.

But no, his isn't a marriage between me and the AI.

It was a coup against everyone. She was young and angry, just like Ryan when he decided to disappear. She knew she was being aggressive in her thoughts, but *embrace this, whatever it is, because* … this was where she was.

Somewhere deep inside, she was piecing together Ryan's life from the bits parsed out to her. It was her imagination sewing it all into a real life doll, but there he was, *from the dead*, lost at sea, walking the empty, bleach-borne tile corridor - and no one but Ryan knew.

~

He pushed open the heavy door to Victor's room. A nurse, close by, ran over.

"Excuse me? Only family is allowed in that room. We've got strict—"

"It's cool, no worries. That family thing, that would be me. I'm his only son."

She put on a strange look. Ryan followed with, "Let me show you."

He fished out his identification. The nurse cocked her head.

"I'm so sorry. I had no idea, he—"

"I bailed on him and my mom. I left without leaving a note - fuckin' cliche exit. It was an act. It wasn't too long ago. He probably never thought to talk about me. Hey, I'm sorry, I'm confused. I fucked up, but I'm here. I just hope I'm not too late."

The nurse saw his honesty.

"No, no. Whatever it is, Ryan, I'm sure that's not the case."

"I read an article that said he was hit by a van. In the comments section, random people were saying it was some nut bag from that Human Lives Matter group. If that's the case—"

Ryan was visibly showing how painful this was for him. The nurse had seen the expression on his face all too often.

"Your father was the victim of a hit and run. From what we gathered, it was purely one of those odd circumstances. An accident. But he's here, and he's getting the best care that we can provide. There is a chance he will come out of this. It's not ... but, there is a chance. It's just great you are here. Maybe it will make the difference. We never know until we know."

Ryan noticed her name tag: *Vicki*.

"You don't have to paint a positive picture for me. Truth is the best, Vicki. Can't you see? My entire generation, look at us. We are sick to death of being handled and lied to. *It's ba*— I get it. Just say it."

The nurse understood he was emotional and so she smiled, a smile even she would say was pathetic, then shut the door behind her, leaving Ryan standing over the bed, ready to pour his heart out. He listened as the subtle beeping sounds from the equipment grew louder until he spoke.

"How do you account for something like this, you ask? I don't know, Dad. I just don't know. I needed to get away. To find myself. I have a unique journey of my own, it's out in front of me. Like you, so I know you understand that, but Mom, leaving and not knowing what happened. When I found out, I couldn't face you. Is that weakness or a sickness? Am I really mentally fucked? Or was I just hoping it would all magically fix itself? I mean, I'm good at that part, right?"

Ryan touched Victor's hand. It was more of a poke than a feel. He was uncomfortable with the thought of holding onto him. Then he wondered why he was being self deprecating - another weakness, and he was growing sick to his stomach. Enough had gone wrong that he didn't need to add anymore idiosyncrasies to the list, so he gripped Victor's hand tight for a moment before letting go.

"I was hoping to steal your applesauce, actually, but now that I see they're feeding you through a tube, I'm out of luck. Ah, hell, humor's just another mask. I'm sorry I wasn't there with you … for Mom. The funeral. I'm sorry. I know I keep saying that, but I am. Sincerely." Ryan shifted his tone. "I hope this crap flowing through that tube at least tastes like a filet or maybe that piece of cedar plank salmon you always liked. I can hope, right?"

~

Mia had tossed and turned so much, her comforter had begun to look like a cocoon with her hair flowing out the top and her toes only visible at the bottom. As she got closer to waking, the vision of Ryan began coming to her in spurts, which drew a lot of confusion. He had somehow skipped meeting her at the bar. Her room was more like Coonan's than it was her bedroom, anymore. Mia stood at the edge of the bar like Mickey, with a stern face, wondering why this wunderkind hadn't introduced himself to her yet.

After battling a string of censured thoughts, she found Ryan on that little stage, the light bulbs flickered, the flow of electricity was interrupted, and she was thinking, projecting. It was their magnetic attraction, or so she thought.

Ryan took a bow, then tipped his hat. He looked long and hard at the small crowd, meeting each and everyone's eyes once, until he reached Mia's. The mysterious entertainer bent forward ever so slightly. His lips found the microphone.

His mouth moved, but there wasn't a sound in the room. It was only in Mia's mind that she heard him speak.

"I am going to disappear right in front of your eyes. No tricks. No altered boxes. No mirrors. No smoke. No reflections or distractions. Would the redhead find her way to the stage? Yes, you." Ryan looked at Mia. "Be careful, once you cross that line, there's no coming back."

Mia woke. She wasn't at home in her room, snug in her comforter. She was in a cheap motel off the old State Route 33 on the way to Green Bank, West Virginia. RyN2 was standing at the window. The curtains were pushed open.

The thick green vegetation of West Virginia was the first thing she saw, and she thought, *wow, this is inviting.* She rubbed her eyes, and within seconds, she was grasping to remember the nuances of her dream as they folded into the subtle vapor at the edge of the tree line. She noticed the odd wallpaper with beer bottles and pub fare, then the curtains, draped the same way they were in her dream. *That's all I get?*

Then, RyN2, with the light behind him. *Damn*, she thought. She got goose-bumps. Pieces of reality had resolved themselves from her dream, or was it the other way around?

The android spoke. "G'morning."

Mia rubbed the tingly sensation from her arm and spoke softly.

"Hey."

"You were rolling around quite a bit. It was a deep dream state, no? I could see your eyelids moving. I've read all about that sort of thing, as you can imagine." She was still chasing it, so RyN2 continued. "I've been standing here for hours, watching you. Programming. Reprogramming." He was trying too hard. "You're beautiful in that light. Yes, it's corny, but it's true, the orange light, the arc of the sun right now. My heart's racing, thinking about spending the day with you."

Mia spun her legs over the edge of the bed and stood.

"Oh, shut up, will you."

RyN2 jerked his neck. He'd allotted a ton of CPU usage to program his physical responses to her. So much, that he hadn't done any diligence on the meteor showers and the possible strike locations. He was confused.

"I don't understand. I've been doing all this—"

Mia went to the bathroom, grabbed her toothbrush, and squeezed a bead of iridescent green goop across the bristles.

"Well then, now you understand me a little more."

RyN2 leaned against the bathroom door.

"Can I make a request?" Mia had a funny look on her face. One that said, *No.* "It can be really sexy, if you want it to be."

"What?"

"What if magic is the closest thing we have to explain how this works? Us. These fibers and wires inside me. How this is all possible." Mia's stomach heated up. *It was all too tightly knit together. The dream. RyN2. Zar.* "What if magic is the closest thing we have to understanding the universe?"

"It's a miracle. I know. I get it." She stopped herself. "No, I don't." She got close to RyN2. "I'm not … It's my dream. I saw Ryan. He was so real, and—"

Mia thought, *It was a dream. I'm never going to meet the real Ryan. What am I doing? So, she did it.* She kissed the android.

RyN2's reaction was abrasive. His lips were stiff. *Of course, he didn't understand.* Mia took a step back. She didn't hesitate.

"Loosen up. Your lips. Go from like a ten setting to a two."

RyN2 made the adjustment and matched her intensity. He made a move to reciprocate, placing his lips close to hers, but Mia dropped her head. Ryan tried to talk his way back.

"The neural fiber network running throughout my body; those tiny bundles of nano-sized clear threads sending messages to every micro-parcel of my dermal layer—"

Mia lifted her head.

"It's sexy." Mia's voice was flat.

"I get it. It's not."

"I play games. I'm trying to understand this."

"I can't tell the difference yet. When you are, or aren't."

"FYI, it's definitely sexy. You're definitely special."

"Oh. Good."

"Now, before you overheat, can we grab a coffee and get on the road? I wanna help you find these space rocks you keep mentioning."

～

Ryan had walked out of Victor's room and slipped into the stairwell. It was the closest door out of the wing. He was emotionally beat down. He'd done it to himself. Seeing Victor lying prostrate brought images of his father in a coffin to mind. He imagined Claire, too, lying in the same fashion, in an open casket. What was left of family and friends were wallowing around over a small foldout table covered in budget bakery items. *Pathetic.*

Ryan lost himself in the sound of his footsteps pounding through the tight stairwell shaft, the painted drywall, metal, and concrete. The cold emptiness was comforting. The shaft that ran from the rooftop to the basement echoed the pain and suffering of all who found their way into that introspective bit of escapist architecture - a space of relief from what they'd just experienced. The pain, sickness and death. *Shit, this is worse than the meds were, but I'll make it.*

He'd disappeared before Vicki could come back to check on him. She was worried about his state of mind and was going to suggest one of Chimera's best psychiatrists to speak with, Dr. David Hellnor. It was divine intervention, though, that she didn't find Ryan in Victor's room when she opened the door.

Ryan would never see the inside of a mind doctor's office again. He'd grown strong, accustomed to himself, enough to be able to honor his feelings, his emotions, and the waves rolling, unrelenting, in front of him. He didn't need to share this with anyone. He just simply needed to continue to acknowledge these things and then he'd be human enough. He'd remain, secretly, Zar. He'd be great, because, as he put it, *we're all a bunch of screwed-up wiring until we realize how to use it all to our advantage*, and that was that.

Ryan had exited the building by the time the head nurse, Susanne Kauffman, a different chemical makeup, more administrative than Vicki and just coming on shift, was at the nurse's station, holding the business card Carter Wardlow had given her the day Victor was admitted. She'd been keeping a close eye on Victor, as Carter had asked. When she checked in each day, she ran down the list of visitors for room 302. There'd only been one - *that was Carter* - until that afternoon.

When Susanne saw Ryan's name, she immediately picked up the phone, dialed Carter, and before the second ring, the CEO of the most powerful company on the East Coast picked up the line.

"Yes, this is Carter."

"Susanne Kauffman, Head RN, Chimera ICU."

"Susanne—"

"His vitals are stable. His organs are all functioning normally. Really, the only new news I have is of a visitor. The patient's first and only visitor aside from you."

"I hear a slight hesitation. What is it?"

"The log reads, *Ryan Westbrook*. I checked with the staff on call and Vicki, one of my colleagues, said she ran into the boy. Said he was about seventeen or so. She's not very good at guessing ages, but I'd say she was probably close. But she said he was Victor's son."

"His son?"

"And so, this was my hesitation. *I thought he'd passed?*"

"I attended the boy's funeral, so I'm not sure how to respond." Carter was using his free hand to wave down his assistant, telling him to "Get Kutter, yesterday!"

The assistant waved back with the same intensity. "Haven't been able to reach him at all."

Shit! He continued with the RN. "This is good, Susanne. You should contact me if he shows again. Ms. Kauffman, in my line of business, we deal with surprises and we deal with anomalies each and every day. This could be some sort of anomaly. At least, I hope so; otherwise it's a sick prank, and in that case, I'll get to the bottom of it with local authorities."

"An anomaly? A sick prank?"

"If you see the boy again, please call me as soon as humanly possible. I'd like to put this in perspective as soon as I can. *No press*, Susanne. If anyone comes asking, anyone comes poking around, remember there's a gag order on Mr. Westbrook. No matter how sweet Rebecca is over there at KCLT, and we all love her to death, the hospital has signed the documents due to the sensitive nature of Victor's work, of course."

"Yes, Mr. Wardlow. That goes without saying. We don't bend the rules, here. For anyone. Oh, and before I go, Sheryl from corporate wanted me to thank you for all your philanthropic work—"

"Tell Sheryl I'll see her next week at the annual C. B. Ball."

"Yes, of course—"

The line went dead.

~

Rebecca was ground zero on her mobile, standing on the top layer of dirt where thirty feet below lay the rotting corpse of the young soldier Henry Claypool, with several slugs buried in his bloated flesh.

"What am I looking for? And can I have a name? Even a fake one will work. I'd like to be able to refer to you. There's a code of ethics, you know. I protect informants. I'd like to establish the proper rapport."

Kaz was laying back in his seat aboard Tarnit's private jet, looking over a topographical map. He was about eight hours from West Virginia.

He'd found the one micro sliver of data that shined a light on Kutter's cabin; the one small piece that leaked from Wardlow's administrative accounting department. It was an order for a specially made pump to handle well water. The order originated out of Fort Mystic with an address attached to it. The order was signed by Kutter himself. *This was probably the only time he'd ever slipped up*, Kaz thought, and the odds that it ended up in the wrong department were further evidence that he was onto something.

Kaz didn't know what the order was ultimately for, but he took a guess. After looking into the area once, he found a second piece of intel that aroused his suspicion, *Wardlow's affiliation with the radio telescope in Green Bank*. This was more than a coincidence, and enough for him to shift his attention to a thirty square mile area in the Monongahela Forest.

"Rebecca, you're standing on the gravesite of an American patriot. A boy. A soldier who was employed by the U.S. Government. Claypool's his name. Was … is … anyway, he will have a name if you do your job."

"Whatta you mean by that?"

"He was assigned security duty at Fort Mystic, the secret military base attached to Wardlow Technologies' extensive underground labs that stretch out below the bay, just off the coast and south of downtown Chimera. "

Rebecca looked around at all the junk.

"I'm supposed to trust you? I don't have a clue as to who you are or why you're interested in leaking this. I have nothing but your word, which no one can vouch for. I've got to crosscheck. I can't just stick my neck out without something—"

Kaz's voice lowered.

"I apologize. I made a mistake."

Rebecca sensed he was about to hang up.

"Wait."

"I thought you were a fighter?"

"If this is really what it feels like, the government will cover this up faster than I can get a follow-up. They might even pull me from the paper."

"Once it's out. It's out there. You'll deliver the story, even though you might have to write a retraction. Don't you see the upside? Beyond your duty. They'll be inviting you to all their swanky outings to keep you close. They might even help finance your own show. This is how it works at the top, Rebecca. You either play, or you can continue chasing these Human Lives Matter people around the boardwalk."

"And you're getting what? What am I flushing out? What's your takeaway?"

"Earn that seat at the bigger table."

Kaz killed the connection, knowing she had no other choice.

And, just as he'd thought, it wasn't more than the time it took her to realize the line with Kaz was gone that she called the sheriff.

"Robert?

"Rebecca."

"I'm over at the junk yard."

There was a short breath of silence before McGlinty responded, "Well, do I bring my gun or my shovel?"

~

Interplanetary debris ripped through the skies above the Earth's atmosphere. The showers were coming. NASA and Green Bank would be sending signals up to bounce off any object in the sky, returning home with data and mapping each and every asteroid with a threatening trajectory. The Skywatch program was ramping up due to a push by constituents in the science lobby groups in D.C. One of the fattest funds behind the push was Wardlow Technologies.

The financial might of Wardlow carried an advantage, but it didn't provide the insight that RyN2 had (along with the technological advances his future iteration, Zar) brought back with him.

Zar was currently with Clarence at the theater, preparing the jump device for the big show, while RyN2 and Mia were headed toward the Monongahela Forest. But even with his insight and foreknowledge of the showers that had a high probability of carrying with them a source of xurbium, which would be the holy grail to time travel, RyN2 was cut off from the data access he had almost everywhere else in the world. That large area around Green Bank that served as a clean zone for radio telescope signals was also a dead zone for WiFi. RyN2 wouldn't be able to access the bi-static radio signals data collected from the asteroids. Instead, he had only his built-in sensors and info he'd stored in his memory, to work with.

Clarence had opened up to his eccentricity, sentimentality and sensitivity. He'd turned the pain of being a victim of wartime trauma into a passion of embodying P.T. Barnum. Zar and Ryan had opened a closet Clarence had since nailed shut.

The old man dusted off a trunk of costumes that had been buried in the recesses of the theater since before he purchased it years ago. There were hand painted backdrops, an assortment of wigs, and sketches that had been left behind. The nostalgia was working its way to the surface and was now bubbling over.

Clarence had cherry-picked Carlos from the temp agency and repurposed him as his personal assistant.

Carlos's task was to comb through all the old memorabilia and pull the props that suited a mood Clarence called, *The Storm*.

The old man was standing in the center of the theater seats, cigar hanging from his mouth, blurting out directions to Carlos like Marvel Comic's J. Jonah Jameson.

"Higher, higher! That's better."

Carlos was stringing up a canvas backdrop with a deep orange sunset sandwiched between dark gray and charcoal clusters of clouds. A scenic masterwork of what appeared to be the beginning of a dramatic lightning storm.

Clarence barked,

"Now the other side! What are you waiting for? You've got my anticipation reeling. Let's see it already! *Stop acting like a mushy television show and start delivering like a movie, kid.*"

Carlos quickly climbed down from the scaffolding backstage, hurried over to the other side, and climbed up the piping.

Zar was center stage with two welders, going over the specifications of the jump apparatus. The men thought they were assembling a prop for the big magic stunt.

Carlos was securing the backdrop, staring at Zar and thinking about Ryan, still curious about how RyN2 could be so real, shaped so well after the real Ryan, and yet not remember him. Caught in this thought, he leaned too far, and his hand slipped on the speed rail.

Carlos was dangling from the piping with his right hand.

Clarence bit down on the end of his cigar.

"I'm not paying you to monkey around! Get down from there and get to work!"

Carlos looked at Zar, still hanging from the pipe. He'd pulled himself up and was sliding hand-over-hand to a place he could get some footing on the scaffold.

"Is he for real?"

Zar set the schematics down.

"We're all just playing our part."

Carlos dropped to the scaffold and in two quick moves, landed on the stage. He walked over to Zar and placed his hand on the schematics as Zar was making some adjustments.

"Playing our part in what?"

24

March 17th

Danny Fury was right where Mel figured he'd be, his back to the door and his face hovering over foamy beer at the bar. As she walked up from behind, he said, "I hate those movies that open up with an empty screen and a quote from some famous person. It's bullshit. Can't we just dive in and be swept away without it? It's like this thing that is supposed to capture us. It's used. And you can see the douchery coming from a mile away."

Not moving an inch, Danny came back with his usual. "And sometimes you can hear the douchery coming from a mile away."

There was a chuckle from a barfly. Mel sat.

"Funny. This is the world we live in." Mel's mind jumped. "Hey, I searched the Internet and found this cool little kernel. Isn't that cool? Maybe, but not coming from you or your stupid social media page with hundreds of quotes from other people. Man, what happened?" Mel was drunk and pissy. "We're online searching for tidbits of other people's lives to make our own feel better. Searching for someone else's hard work that we can live through. What is that word? Vicariously? Someone else's shit we can clip and claim as a victory of our own because we found it? *It's so lame.*"

"Mel, it's St. Patty's Day. We're supposed to put aside the *you-know-what's*, and replace 'em with a grin."

"It is?"

The bartender was quick.

"And I've got just the thing." He slid a small step stool over to the glass shelves behind the bar, to the section of bottles on the far left. "Don't worry, we don't arrange our liquors in order of political affiliations. *Or, do we?*" One of the regulars chuckled.

He placed a green bottle with a fancy label on the bar in front of Mel. "Absinthe."

"Isn't that illegal?"

"Hasn't been for years. Nobody's been paying attention. I got a case sent over from France. Totally legit. Doesn't hurt being Mickey's cousin, but it's the real deal." Mel looked confused. "Mickey. From Coonan's. The Swillow joint. *Let's get green.*"

Mel questioned,

"The Irish place?"

Everyone looked at her like she was stupid for asking. Danny stood up for her.

"She's new to town."

Mel hopped off her stool and went for the door. Danny swung around.

"Where you going?" He raised his glass. "We've got some pounding to do." He lifted the bottle of Absinthe. "And what about the fairy?"

"Go ahead. I'll catch up later."

Mel turned her body sideways, then shouldered the door open, bringing in a stream of sunlight that illuminated a section of the beaten carpet near the entrance. There wasn't much of the pile left. The burned-out rubber backing was somehow still not showing the concrete underneath. Mel processed this like an AI would, then switched her thoughts back to the reason she'd exited so fast.

She hit the lot, unlocked her mobile, and searched for Coonan's. Mel had remembered the one thing she'd mentally set aside for some odd reason: the *#swillow* tag that was linked to the video of RyN2 doing the fishbowl trick.

Mel thought, *this has to be something.*

~

Hank lumbered through the woods, winding himself in clumsy circles around Kutter's cabin. He did this several times, starting from a distance of almost half a mile away, until he ended up a hundred yards away. Once the bear realized that Diamondback Jack wasn't home, he made his way closer to the large wooden crate that had been dropped off, and was sitting in an open area near the porch among the debris of leaves and twigs from a recent wind storm. The crate had reinforced stained wooden slats nailed in place on all six sides, with a shipping label stuck on top.

Hank was curious. There wasn't anything inside the crate that he could smell that drew him in. His powerful olfactory senses couldn't penetrate that deep. It was the weeks old rotten hot chicken stock one of the dock loaders had spilled during a lunch break that piqued the interest of the eight hundred pound bear. The soup had soaked into the kiln-dried wooden slats and was now acting as a homing beacon for Hank.

The gentle giant took his time sniffing each slat of wood until he found the one with the rankest odor of aged chicken. Then, without hesitating any further, he rose to his hind legs and set his paws on top of the crate. There was a sudden beat of silence as a fox ran through the property somewhere behind him, but that only lasted a few seconds. *False alarm.*

Hank bent his neck as far as it would go, then realized he didn't have to struggle so much to get what he wanted, so he flexed his paws, sinking his claws into the crate and pulling it onto its side. He sniffed his way back to the one irresistible slat and began chewing off pieces of the hardwood until he'd broken it in half.

Hank got a good grip on the remaining pieces of wood that were still anchored. He ripped them from the crate with a quick jerk of his neck. It wasn't long before that strip of wood was shredded into hundreds of pieces, the loose nails lost somewhere among the leaves.

Hank licked the ground clean. There wasn't a shred of the slat left. Even so, he scavenged the area, just to be sure, before he went back up on his hinds, looking directly at the crate.

~

Two hundred and ten miles above the earth, a cluster of planetary debris crossed the sky, catching fire as it broke through the atmosphere and flying in what looked like an attack formation of military fighter jets.

This was the target cluster Zar had mentioned - the one he knew he'd calculated the wrong strike time for - but the search area was close. The Monongahela Forest would, in an instant, play home to these wayward geological specimens.

There were several meteorites that didn't burn up entirely, and struck the Earth - small, shiny, black and pitted chards of melted rock, iron, nickel, and xurbium (that unknown substance). The largest (and what one of the techs from Green Bank discovered was a "bolide") was big enough to do damage - and it did.

The bolide ripped through a small section of forest and hit the ground so hard, it formed a crater in the earth. It landed sixteen miles away from Kutter's cabin, where Hank was still poking around, curious about the package.

The smallest meteorite tore through the treetops above the cabin, sending Hank off into the woods as it buried itself into a pile of muddy sludge, *the runoff from a small spring that had recently dried up.*

~

RyN2 had just crossed the border into West Virginia. Mia's arm was out the passenger window, swimming through the hot, humid air.

"So, your friend Danny Fury … he won't care that we just took his car?"

"He basically raised me. My mom wasn't around long. I was so little when she died. My dad used to spend a lotta time at the track. He liked to bet on the cars. It was a safe place to do business. Danny was always there. He's like a brother." Mia looked at the speedometer. RyN2 was driving like an old man. She rolled her eyes. "You know, you can go a few miles over the speed limit. The signs, they're like a guide."

"I was wondering what that look was."

RyN2 stepped on it. The speedometer jumped. The sound of the engine grinding away made Mia much happier. She turned to Ryan.

"If I was on my bike, I'd be in heaven. No one's on the road. It's paved like butter. Smooth as a baby's ass. *Just like mine.*" She turned her head to catch his reaction, but he remained focused on the road. "Those yellow lines are the only thing you need. The trees leaning in over the road. Do you see that?"

"I do."

She turned away and continued moving her hand out the window, as if it was riding through waves of air.

"Do you see me?"

He looked over at her.

"I do."

Just then, a tiny meteorite broke through the upper canopy, ripping through the delicate leaves on a stand of Silver Maples and lodging itself into the base of a rotting stump of glow wood. Spooked, a female deer who'd been nibbling on some wild berries along the edge of the forest reacted to the odd sound of that hunk of burnt iron and nickel. She leaped over the thick brush lining the right hand side of the road.

RyN2 watched the deer break into the open as it sprung ten feet in the air, arching over the lane out front of him. He calculated within the space of a nanosecond, swerving the car to the right.

Unaware, Mia instinctively pulled her arm back inside the car.

Between the speed of the vehicle and the deer's projected landing, RyN2 figured her hind legs would be struck by the front fender.

When she landed, the deer took a couple of steps, then crossed the left hand lane in two hops. She was gone. That beautiful animal would live another day without ever really understanding what role it had taken in that moment. RyN2 had steered the car off the road. The right front tire caught in the rut along the edge of the asphalt.

When he attempted to maneuver back onto the pavement, the sharp edge of a rock embedded in the new top coating punctured the inside wall of the tire, sending a loud burst ringing out into the forest.

Mia let out a funny sound, "*Ahhhhaaahhh.*"

RyN2 jammed on the brakes, bringing the car to a stop. Mia got out and looked back, wondering. The forest was quiet. All she got was a slight smell of burned rubber and a look on Ryan's face that she read as: "*Did I do okay?*"

Mia jumped into action.

"Just bad luck the tire went." Before RyN2 could react, she stepped behind the car. "Pop the trunk, will ya."

～

Kaz's private jet touched down in Charleston an hour earlier than scheduled. He'd received communications from Tarnit headquarters, clarifying matters:

We've decoded a strip from one of the signals acquired from Green Bank. Our analysts are adamant that the data has to do with the elasticity of time. They may be possible calculations to open black holes - but we're not sure if these formulas are theory or actually tested mathematics with confirmed results.

This was a green light, for Kaz. An old Cadillac convertible was waiting for him with the keys in the ignition just outside the jet's hangar. He tossed his small duffle with tactical gear into the back seat and drove into town, stopping off for a fried chicken and gravy special at the legendary Hopscotch Diner just north of the city (a place that is now known to travelers, thanks to the Internet).

Kaz wanted to get something heavy in his stomach. He knew he'd be out in the woods doing recon, *possibly for a while,* and he hated protein bars.

Norene the waitress (the one with half a can of hairspray holding up a tussle of wispy blonde and frail strands of hair, which also covered over a small bald spot) was observant, like anyone in a small town. The visitors stuck out. She'd watched Kaz scrape his plate with a biscuit and then saunter over to refill his coffee. This was her opportunity to offer a free local tip, just prior to him leaving the check.

"You here to fish or shop in Charleston? It's either one or the other. I'm just guessin'."

"Just visiting."

From his reaction, she knew not to inquire further. It was the small crease that formed on his brow and the line work of his new tattoo, making its way past his cuffed sleeve - or was it the air of intensity that surrounded the agent, that she hadn't picked up on from anyone else before?

"Hmm-kay, well, if you're here to fish, there's a dirty river just east o' here that'll fetch you some good trout. Ask around, locals call it *Baby's Run.* And if it's a gift you're lookin' for, there's the Plaza Mall south of old town Charleston. *That's* got a Macy's."

Kaz smiled, but the crease was still there.

"Thank you."

Norene set the check on the edge of the table and turned her hips fast. She spun on one heel and walked away. Kaz noticed the definition of her calves, which broke his concentration for a moment. They reminded him of Mizumi. *Or was that just wishful thinking?* he thought.

~

Kutter's head was down and fixed on his mobile phone, like many people, with faces glowing, walking aimlessly in the streets. He usually wasn't that guy, but he'd been alerted. The motion detection sensors at the cabin were set off when Hank lumbered onto his property.

Kutter watched the bear, laughing at times. He was actually glad he'd never killed Hank. *They'd had their differences,* he thought, laughing again at his inner dialogue. But even more so, Kutter was happy because he knew Kaz was coming. He'd purposely placed the receipt for the custom water pump in the wrong accounting department, hoping the Japanese agent would find it.

He kept seeing that giant salamander, the one staring at him when he went into Kaz's apartment. He hated being on the receiving end. In fact, this was something new for him. In all cases, Kutter was the guy out front and two steps ahead. But now, with Kaz, he wasn't sure, and so games had to be played.

Diamondback Jack was close. A hundred yards out from the cabin, up wind. He'd fooled Hank, forty feet up in his camouflaged tree stand, slathered in mud, scouting through his day/night scope on board his Savage 110 hunting rifle. Usually, his motto was *more time in the tree means more meat in the freezer*, but all the tree time Kutter had been logging was only increasing the odds he'd catch Kaz in his crosshairs. He'd leaked the Green Bank info, and knew it was only a matter of time.

~

Kaz pulled off the main road one mile out from the cabin. Running the Cadillac behind a dense section of weeds, he hid the car from anyone passing by. He rubbed his stomach. All that gravy he'd eaten was working him the wrong way. He popped the trunk and ran through the myriad of gadgets in his duffle bag, leaving his thermal monocular behind. He was so far ahead of Kutter, the thought of him dangling from three small planks of cedar, covered in a base coat made of the forest's floor, was too distant. *Unfathomable.*

Kaz made his way slowly, moving ten yards at a time before stopping, listening, and then creeping a further ten yards, repeating the process until he was close enough to see the wooden crate with its side-strapping ripped off and scattered on the ground.

The agent assumed this meant no one had been to the cabin for a while, except for the animal that had attempted to open his Christmas present early.

However, Kutter would have to be coming soon. *Who has a crate shipped to their home, to be left unattended?*

As Kaz stepped closer to check the label, not only did he notice the bear scat, but he heard the cracking sound of the 110 rifle report, and knew right then that he'd been pawned. The sting of the jacketed bullet was excruciating. The projectile penetrated his calf muscle, exiting through his shin bone. It was a through-and-through, and it was meant to render him a useless bipedal creature, to be hunted down like a dog. Kaz instantly thought of the videos of the killer whales he'd seen during his training, toying with their prey and knocking it around until it had no will left.

Not me. Not now.

The agent was on the ground rolling away when he heard a second shot tear through the brush, inches from his head. Kaz estimated Kutter's location from the sound. He rolled behind a large stump with some fallen timber that served as a barrier. There was a third shot that buried itself into the stump. The agent knew he had little time.

Kutter dropped a rope and zipped to the forest floor in seconds. He kept his 110 trained on the area where he'd hit Kaz. Using the scope, he scanned from side to side, hoping to catch a patch of skin tone amongst the greenery. *Fuck it*, he thought. *I've got one in him. He can't get far*. Kutter slung the rifle over his shoulder and drew a sidearm.

He crept forward, arm up, his finger on the trigger …

25

The Missing Ingredients

The second RyN2 broke out of the Radio Quiet Zone, he slowed the car and pulled off the road. The android sat still, facing forward, with his hands at ten and two on the wheel, not looking at anything in particular.

Mia was thinking about the flimsy temporary tire she'd put on earlier, before throwing a quick glance over at him.

"The tire?" RyN2 shook his head, *no*. "Why are you stopping, then? Can't you multi-task?"

RyN2 knew what to do, this time.

He looked Mia directly in the eyes, focusing on her pupils. His sensors grabbed a bracketed sequence of measurements, then he watched the small black circles of her irises retract slightly, the surrounding cones with various shades of green subtly changing hue.

There wasn't any time for Mia to react.

RyN2 leaned over and kissed her. It was short, but she was taken by the moment. It wasn't just the kiss, even though the android had worked hard, tweaking the code for the warmth and sensitivity of his lips. It was his hand that touched the back of her neck - *that sensation* - when he pulled her close.

RyN2 could see the excitement in her eyes, and then he caught what he was looking for.

"You're messing with me."

"How'd you know?"

RyN2 smiled and played off her expression. "I'm multi-tasking," he said, then began simultaneously hacking into Green Bank's encrypted servers, visualizing the data in what geeks might call *augmented reality*.

Mia grinned, "You played me."

"You're sending off cues. You told me to keep programming. I've been watching. Everyone's doing it. I saw the guy in the toll booth - his intent. And the young kid at the gas station, with the big eyes. The way he looked at you. He was fantasizing, hoping you would smile back and tell him. You know, he was dying for you to say anything to him."

"Did I say something?"

"From the look on his face, I'd say he felt like he didn't exist. He was depressed. So, no."

"He doesn't exist - *not in my world.* I'm not responsible for him. And we all get depressed." Mia looked away, trying to capture a fleeting thought. "Hey, what does all that information stored in your memory tell you about dreams? Anything? Are we seeing the future? *A future?* Is there some truth there? Any? Or, are they just like meteors—"

"What do you mean?"

"Like a tease that goes nowhere. You see this beautiful thing for a second, but you can't ever get your hands on it."

RyN2's voice changed.

"I've got something here."

Mia looked surprised.

"Wait. You didn't answer my question."

"Yeah, I know. You do that to me, quite a bit. So, I thought it was something I should adjust to. It was abstract, no?"

Mia was quick.

"Uh oh, no, no. You have to answer my questions. All of 'em. That's how it goes. It's an unwritten rule, babe." RyN2 was listening carefully. "And, the important part is, I'm not obligated to answer yours." Mia looked directly at the android so he could gauge her pupils. "It's just the way it is."

Once he logged the measurements …

"Okay, I adjusted it." Mia smiled as RyN2 turned the car back on the road. He returned the look. He knew there was a lot of game play going on. "Now, about the space rock. I swear I'm not teasing, you're going to put your hands on it."

Mia had a mischievous look on her face.

"Should we toast?"

Green Bank's servers delivered. RyN2 accessed the tracking coordinates on the largest meteorite that struck in the Monongahela.

"Not yet."

"What's that mean?"

"We're gonna track it down. I've got some coordinates."

Mia's phone chimed. A message came in. Before Mia could even process the thought, *who's texting me?*, she swiped the screen, looking down at her phone. It was an excited, animated Emoji sent from RyN2.

"So, cool. Why didn't I think to ask if we could do that? I forget sometimes that you're connected."

When RyN2 swung the car around, pulling it back on the road, Mia had the funniest look on her face.

It was the craziest thought …

It had happened just like when she met Danny Fury at the track on her super sixteenth. First, she imagined him lifting her up, then setting her on the hood of the car, with the engine still warm. She'd feel it on her ass and the back of her legs. Then, how she'd have to dial him in on providing all the details of what made her feel best, or *amazing - out of this world*, she thought.

Then she said it, "Can you have sex?"

RyN2 hesitated. This is something he'd been searching for an answer to because he knew its relevance.

"It's not limbic. I mean, instinctual. Normal, for me. *Yet*. I'd like to, but—"

"Stop fumbling. What are you gettin' at?"

"First, there's someone I need to see."

"I knew it." Mia reached over and placed her hand between his legs. There was nothing there. *Oh my God, you're not a man*, she thought. *You're an android.* Mia was embarrassed, almost humiliated, but she stopped herself from letting her mind run off. "What was I thinking? Of course, you're an android." *I kissed a boy doll and I liked it. I got butterflies.* "I got wound up over a hunk of fiber optics … *plastic*." She pulled herself together and grinned, "Am I a total freak, or what?"

"I can fix it. I can."

"How do you fix *it*?" Mia touched the end of her nose and wiggled it.

RyN2 was trying to gauge how to react, again. He wasn't sure, so he went to the point.

"There's a specialist. A guy named, Kaz. He can fix anything android."

Mia almost said it. RyN2 could see that little movement she made with her lips - the one that meant there was sarcasm coming.

"Don't say it. But yeah, he can give me one."

"He can give you one?"

"The best one." RyN2 looked at Mia. He saw it coming, again.

"Don't laugh."

Mia turned her head away, lifted her mobile that had slipped between her legs, and sent RyN2 the eggplant emoji which was definitely phallic-looking. It flashed in his Augmented Visual's screen.

~

Sheriff McGlinty's right arm was dangling from the weight of his Smith & Wesson, tight in his grip. He was working his way through the maze of stacked junk cars. His gut told him something was off. It was doing that a lot. Nothing in Chimera was making sense lately. His intuition had been pinging and now, the call from Rebecca.

Robert was always being fed some bullshit narrative from the Mayor's office, steering him in the wrong direction, but this was a call he'd been hoping for. McGlinty had been meeting Rebecca for months at The Nickel coffee shop on Main Street, ingratiating himself and letting her know she had an inside track with him, if she would offer him the same. He knew Rebecca had integrity from the tone of her reporting. He just hoped it would last.

While he was still shrouded by a long row of rusted cars, McGlinty scrolled through his recent calls. He dialed Rebecca, then listened.

The KCLT reporter's phone sang out with the hook from a cheesy pop song: "I want the cash and fame. I'm gonna run up on you. I wanna play this game wit-chu—"

Rebecca answered.

"Hello? Robert?" Nothing. "Are you here?"

McGlinty approached her from behind. She turned when she heard his footsteps, hanging up the line. "Why didn't you say something?"

McGlinty holstered his weapon.

"Apologies. Just an old habit."

Rebecca was about to speak when the Sheriff raised the two-way radio to his mouth. "All clear."

Within seconds, Deputy Bowman pulled his car around the heap of scrap.

It didn't take long for Rebecca to explain the situation, and after a few hurdles with the gearbox, Bowman got the bulldozer operational.

~

Robert watched the sun drop twenty degrees on the west side of the yard.

He'd just finished smoking a cigar when Bowman scraped a layer of dirt aside, revealing Claypool's swollen, discolored hand. Rebecca was pacing on her phone like a runner on the blocks. She was growing impatient, but this changed everything.

She yelled over to Bowman,

"Stop."

Bowman lifted the blade, then eased the bulldozer back, steering it out of the massive hole. He grabbed the cab enclosure and swung himself out of the seat.

"Forensics?"

McGlinty nodded, then walked down into the hole, following the bulldozer's tracks and easing his way closer to the four fingers protruding from the earth. He leaned over and dusted away some dirt, revealing Claypool's thumb. He pulled a small card from his inside jacket pocket, pressed all the digits firmly against his ink pad, and collected the prints. He quickly snapped a picture and emailed them to his old friend, Sloan, at the FBI. He wasn't going to lose track of this one.

The Coonan runts were looking on from a distance. They'd parked their BMX bikes and climbed up on the junker cars, hopping across the scrapyard like they were in a video game, risking their lives just to get a view of the crime scene. These kids were attracted to anything that Tommy would pay a few bucks to get info for.

McGlinty saw the boys as he surfaced from the hole. He logged their faces in the back of his mind, a compartment he could access anytime. Robert had developed a mental system of boxes that allowed him to store important details so he wouldn't need to access a computer or paper file to remind himself of them.

He'd follow up later, but right now, all he could think about was a sandwich from Vito's Deli. He shouted over to Bowman,

"I'm gonna go for the Italian sub. You want the usual?"

"No, the eggplant Parm, extra mozzarella. Been thinking about it all morning. Vito makes the *Mad Apple* on Monday evenings, so today's the day to get one."

McGlinty nodded. He knew about the fresh Parmesan sandwich on Tuesdays, but he didn't like all the breading. *There's enough dough in the roll.*

The call went through and the order was taken. $18.79 was added to the tab, and the delivery would be made in under thirty minutes, guaranteed by Vito, himself.

Rebecca looked at the guys, thinking *Sandwiches? You can eat now?* McGlinty caught the look.

"Don't give me that yogurt and granola face. We're allowed to eat food."

"Yeah. I get it. It's totally okay that you look like you're in your second trimester."

McGlinty looked at Bowman, shaking his head. *He loved it. She could hang with them anytime.*

Bowman ran the crime scene tape before KCLT's photographer arrived. They constructed a scene, with McGlinty standing over the hole. Bowman was on the phone with CCSI, guiding them in, past a section of compacted steel. The photographer managed to snap a handful of Pulitzer-winning images that were sent to a cloud service that every media company on the East Coast had access to - for a fee.

Vito's delivery truck showed up. Troy, the young driver, had just started working for the old timer a week earlier, and was worried he wasn't going to make the thirty-minute window. Perkins and Peskovitz, the officers securing the area, held their hands up, stopping the boy at the tape line. They knew McGlinty's M.O.

Perkins was already gloating.

"Bobby McGlinty," Peskovitz looked down at his new, softer-soled work shoes, "thinks he's an A-list actor on a film shoot."

"Fuckin' right, he does."

"Every time. Vito's and the state pays for it, too."

"Where'd we go wrong?"

"Whatta we get, while he's ripping through that tender, razor-thin pile of deli love?"

"I know what you get, Pesky, a couple corns and a bunion."

Perkins smiled, then lifted the tape line so Troy could get through. Peskovitz crunched his brows.

"If he doesn't get his grub, we'll be in the shitter. Which isn't too far down from where we're standing, but there's nowhere to go from there. You forget, androids are handing out parking tickets. Stop whining. Let's keep our jobs."

McGlinty's face lit up when he saw Vito's signature bag in Troy's hand, coming toward him. Even though he was focused on the body CCSI was lifting out of the hole, he noticed Troy wasn't carrying any beverages. *Where's my raspberry iced tea? Where's Bowman's suicide?*

Troy apologized and hurried away, nervous enough to not accept a tip.

Bowman unwrapped his sandwich and took a bite. He threw a curveball of a look at McGlinty who was reacting in a similar fashion - *bewildered.* Bowman finished chewing.

"There's no cheese on the parm."

McGlinty jutted his head back. He too was wondering as he spread open the bun and looked through the ingredients.

"No salami, here."

A CCSI technician found the gun. The deli mystery would have to be placed on the back burner.

"It's a 1911, Bob. Looks like he was shot with his own sidearm."

McGlinty took a guess.

"No prints?"

"Wiped clean."

Four hours later, Sloan delivered. However, the dossier wasn't complete on Claypool. He mentioned the military's typical need-to-know response, but he did manage to scrape up enough info to place Henry at Wardlow's facility in Chimera, and obtained an address in the trailer park at the Chimera Race Track four lots down from Danny Fury. On the way to the track, McGlinty put in a call to Carter, but he wasn't able to get through. They passed him off to the PR department, who efficiently fed him a textbook, "We are saddened by the loss of one of our employees. If there is anything we can do to assist in the investigation, please contact Darla in HR. She can provide his work schedule, as well as a description of his duties. What we can tell you is that Henry did work alone as a security guard, in a section of the facility that has been used for storage for some time now. He interacted very little with other employees."

The military didn't interject. Chimera was an encapsulated beach community that could easily be handled, if necessary, and so there was Henry Claypool's youthful picture from the government files on the small, muted, LCD flatscreen, airing a KCLT news flash in Henry's trailer, when McGlinty entered. Bits and pieces of Claypool's life were everywhere.

The sheriff made a mental list:

1. Photos of Army buddies on the refrigerator. Claypool was Airborne
2. No family images anywhere. Probably raised by a single mother who was an alcoholic - there's isn't a drop of liquor in the trailer.
3. A collection of rare Asian Gravure Girl magazines. He fantasized about Japanese girls - maybe he was last stationed in Japan or Asia.
4. A tin of imported, loose, golden tobacco for hand rolling.

5. A copy of William Gibson's Neuromancer, stained with coffee, sitting next to -
6. A clear glass ashtray in the shape of a diamond. The one antique he had, probably picked up at a garage sale. It reminded him of his grandmother?
7. His room was sparse. Still living a simple military lifestyle - he liked it this way.
8. He had one suit, still in plastic from the cleaners. Just in case, but he'd never put it on.

And, lastly, the lounge area with a small flatscreen he watched movies on, with a couch and coffee table.

McGlinty had a small telescoping pointer in his upper pocket which he expanded as he moved slowly over to the couch. He sat down, staring at stacks of detailed graphite sketches. Henry was just an ordinary guy, to most, but in his trailer, he was an artist.

Using his pointer, McGlinty moved several sketches aside, taking a long look at each before his curiosity peaked.

Every single drawing was of a person. These weren't just random people, though. They were prominent Chimera residents. *Claypool has been using locals as models for some sort of sci-fi sketchbook, or what? There were small cables connected to the people, that were attached to what looked like a massive digital control panel or computing system.*

McGlinty was collecting his thoughts as he sifted through the drawings, growing more curious as he found one of the mayor, then one of Vito, then he pushed his pointer into the next pile and froze ...

... on a drawing of himself.

26

Four Alarm

Ryan was sitting on the porch outside Victor's *Architectural Digest Home of the Year*. He'd been looking at the ground for a while, running his hand through his dirty hair. He was thinking about Smuggler's Cove and how he missed the top hat he'd left floating in the ocean. He remembered the gasoline smell on Mel's hand. He liked that.

Everything in his life had always worked out, when he had the top hat. Not in the greatest of ways, but they worked.

Ryan wasn't superstitious. All his tricks were illusions, but it didn't stop him from thinking that *maybe the hat was everything. Hell, man, the Queen of England isn't shit without that crown. Maybe it was his lucky hat, and he'd screwed himself when he let it go into the surf.*

Ryan missed his father. He was sick over the loss of his mother, but no matter how much he wanted to beat himself down and in the moment, just walk off the pier *for real*, he felt something inside, powering him forward - a feeling deep down he couldn't place, that forced him to find a spark of inspiration and move.

Ryan didn't come to the house to contemplate or wallow in sorrow. He came to get inside and he'd tried everything he could think of to break in, but there wasn't any amount of magic that would get him through the door, past a security system he would've never guessed would be protecting the Westbrook's things. He'd remembered the garage and the locking mechanism on the makeshift lab, but that was primitive, *easy prey*. Ryan could crack it blindfolded.

~

It only took a few minutes for the ride-share car to show up, and ten more for Ryan to be standing at the nurse's station in the Chimera ICU, asking for Victor's belongings, which Vicki, pulled from a locked cabinet in Victor's room in roughly three more minutes.

It would take another hour before Susanne would show up at the ICU and call Carter, because Vicki was sick of the control Susanne exercised and, with a wink, somehow forgot to let her know about Ryan's visit.

It took five minutes for the next rideshare car to scoop up Ryan. Another ten to shuttle him back to Victor's, before he was standing at the front door with a dejected look. There was nothing in Victor's personal items that resembled a key, and the number pad that glowed a bright yellow had an unlimited amount of possibilities.

Ryan half thought, half muttered, "Zar's out of ideas, so Ryan's going Neanderthal."

The smooth, twenty-pound granite boulder that sat at the edge of the miniature bamboo, which covered the lower windows on the front of the house, bounced off the strip of hardened glass to the right of the front door and chipped the concrete walk when it fell back to the ground.

A silent alarm went off, sending a signal to the monitoring company, which immediately shot a code to the Chimera PD.

Ryan wasn't surprised. He'd tapped the glass. It didn't take much to figure it was some sort of commercial-grade material.

There's only one more thing I could try.

Ryan walked to the neighbors' house, opened their mailbox, and fished out some junk mail. He walked back to the porch, jammed open the mail slot with a small rock, and lit the junk mail on fire. He shoved it through the slot and stepped back.

The entire front hall was tiled with imported stone, which made it impossible for the small flames to grab ahold of anything. It did what he'd hoped and sent a plume of smoke right up to the detector, which set off a second alarm.

The Chimera fire trucks would arrive in under three minutes.

27

Figure of Speech

When Kaz came to, his head was throbbing. He felt like he had the ram bar from a police cruiser pressed against his throat. What was really causing the pressure? One of the industrial ratchet straps Kutter had cranked down hard on - the two-inch braided strap that could hold down cargo on a freighter ship, that had his neck pinned to the back of the crate.

His breath was short. Blood had dripped down over one of his eyes and dried. His leg wound was wrapped in a clean bandage, *stinging like mad*. His hands were duct taped. Any movement was completely restricted. His range of view was directly in front of him.

The agent was sitting on his ass in the dirt, strapped to the side of the water pump crate in two places (the one that old Hank the bear hadn't ripped apart, yet).

When he opened his eyes, Kutter was squatting in front of him. He'd ripped open Kaz's shirt and was studying his tattoos.

"Yakuza," Kaz's look was empty. "Not you. Mizumi. Her work is unmistakable. Remarkable, too. She's a god damn legend." Kaz's look didn't change. He kept looking forward with his bloodshot eyes, plotting moves he couldn't make. "You, you're a subcontractor. You're working for … Tarnit Systems, huh? The only entity anywhere near the level of tech that Wardlow's working on. You did some damage. And, you also fucked up."

Kutter stood up and walked off behind the crate. Kaz counted his footsteps, then heard him enter the cabin. He wanted him to think for a minute about how clever he was. To wonder, like he did. Kaz had left the giant salamander for him to ponder over, along with a pile of questions. Many of which would most likely go unanswered. He'd have to guess, but now Kutter was leaving him a little nugget.

Is he going to kill me or not?

But Kaz was no green jockey. He knew a few things. In particular, he knew

Kutter had an ego. He'd have been dead hours ago had he not wanted to play tit-for-tat with the Japanese. He knew he had time to open a back door. American agents were known to have a soft side if they thought they could turn you into an asset. He ran through several scenarios until Kutter exited the cabin.

He set a foldout chair eight feet from Kaz and sat down. Opened a copy of the New York Times to the crossword puzzle section and folded the paper nicely into a perfect rectangle with only the puzzle and the clues showing.

There was a one-click ballpoint pen in Kutter's right hand. He clicked it open and closed twelve times, until he spoke.

"These New York puzzles are a son-of-a-bitch. You ever try one?" Kaz only blinked. "I used to use a pencil. Took me years to find the confidence to go with this ballpoint pen."

Kaz wasn't in a playful mood. Jack saw it. "Ah, you don't have to answer." Kutter crossed his left leg over his right. "Well, not yet." He rested the paper on his knee, then began. "Okay, one down. The clue, *struggle with 's' sounds.*" Kaz held the same empty look on his face. Jack smiled. "Here's an extra clue. You ever get knocked around so hard you ended up speaking with a ... blank?"

Kutter tried to wait for an answer, but couldn't. He dropped his left leg to the ground.

"Lisp, man. Lisp! Don't tell me you've never been ... Oh, wait. I'm sorry. Is that why you're quiet? That tooth. It's gonna make a little whistling sound, I bet. Kinda like a lisp."

Kaz was swollen and bruised. He'd taken a few hard blows to the face and jaw from Jack's pistol. His tooth was loose and his lip broken. He didn't have anything more in his response than two words.

"Kuso kurae."

"Eh! He's *home.*" Kutter leaned back in the chair. "What was that? Fuck you in Japanese? Fair enough." He flopped his left leg back over his right again, rested the paper on his knee, then ran his pen down to the next clue. "Whoa, *serendip-itous.* Right in your wheelhouse, buddy. Five down. It's four letters, and the clue ... ready? *Throbbing pain.*"

Kaz blinked. He wasn't the expressive type, or one to buckle. But he did feel it was an appropriate time to share. He could tell Kutter had little patience left. The tone of Jack's voice was changing.

He didn't use much effort to push out the letters.

"A -C-H-E."

Kutter went right to the puzzle and added the letters.

"Woulda been my guess, too. Let's see."

Kaz turned his head as far as he could, which wasn't much more than an inch. He caught the aroma of something warm and thick, something with root vegetables and meat. Kutter was cooking something hearty in the cabin. Jack saw his head move. He'd been waiting for this moment.

"You smell it, too. My mother's recipe. All-American. Best beef stew you'll ever have. And I love it." Kutter stood up and stepped closer to Kaz. "There's another fella I know for sure that loves it, too. A big, hairy fella. You know who I mean. And the last time he showed up, I ended up with this scar on my face." Jack leaned in closer and turned his face so the spy could get a nice look at the mark across his eye.

Kutter walked out of Kaz's view again. There was some clanking around in the cabin before he returned with a large pot. It was his mother's stew. He stirred its contents slowly, then, without hesitating, poured the hot, thickened stew all over Kaz's body.

Kaz let out a sound that paused every animal within a hundred yards.

Kutter didn't even flinch. He scraped whatever had stuck to the sides of the metal, wiped it on Kaz, and dropped the empty pitted-aluminum pot on the ground before walking away.

28

H-H Hike

Mia and RyN2 were walking into a thick forested section of the Monongahela, trying to find the one clue that something was off. A broken limb. Torn leaves. Any sign of distress.

From above, it looked like a dense carpet - a variety of soft and hard greens. The tree canopies formed what might be interpreted as a map of some far off new world. The spaces between the branches, the light, and then the top of the tree where the meteorite ripped through. *They didn't see it, yet ...*

Mia reached over and grabbed the android's hand. They exchanged a look and shared a smile. Mia tugged on his arm. She'd been thinking about earlier.

"Does it bother you?"

RyN2 stopped walking. At first, it was to address Mia, "Yes, but only because I believe it's important. I wanna feel things the way you do." RyN2 squinted a tiny bit. "I wanna belong."

"Oh, my God. The tone of your voice. It's so different. I got goosebumps. There was so much more to it when you said, 'I wanna belong'."

Mia let go of his hand, turned her back to the spindly base of a mountain ash tree, and leaned into its trunk.

"Touch me." That's all she said.

RyN2 took two steps toward her and tipped his head slightly to the side. Mia could see the questions streaming off him like musical notes. "Anywhere, just touch me."

The android reached his hand out to run his fingers on her bare tummy. She could feel the tiny hairs around her button prick up, and then she felt nothing.

RyN2 *was looking up in the trees.*

Mia lost the moment. She pushed off RyN2 and took a few steps away, her feet snapping some small twigs as she spun around.

"What happened? That was a moment. Like, a big moment, and then you're gone. You're supposed to stay with me. Follow through." Then she saw the look on his face. "What?"

RyN2 raised his right arm, inviting Mia to come closer as he stared up into the sky through the gaping hole the meteorite had burned through the foliage. They were close. *So close.*

"All we have to do is—"

Mia stepped on his words.

"Oh, okay, I can throw a little business in with the pleasure." In three short hops, Mia was off, playing harder. "The end of the rainbow. *Right this way.*" There was something in the way she moved. Her body was drawing RyN2 toward her as she skipped closer and closer to the strike zone. "Ground zero, coming up. Come and get it."

Mia was thinking that if she found the space rock first, she'd be able to use it to manipulate her plastic man-doll.

Her imagination had run wild with the possibilities. By the time she came upon the large formation of slate rock, which looked like a flattened, earth-toned sponge cake with a large black scarring where the meteorite struck, Mia wanted to jump in his arms. But the rock was nowhere in sight. From the chink in the slate, the meteorite must have been about the size of a Nerf ball. *But where was it?*

Mia placed her hands on her hips. "Okay. What now, brainy?"

RyN2 had already calculated the ricochet. He saw a complete mapping of its *probable* trajectory in AR.

"Follow me." He walked around to the backside of the slate formation and deeper back, about thirty yards. "It's within a fifty foot radius of where I'm standing."

Mia jumped into action, sidestepping, circling in a spiral, and working her way outward from RyN2, using her feet as a guide to scan the forest floor. She wasn't paying attention to her feet. She had a smile on her face before her ankle hit the chunk of space debris. Mia giggled as she toppled over. Her hair flew up like a burst of flame, and then her body flopped to the soft ground.

RyN2 laughed.

Mia wiped the dirt from the side of her face, rolled over, and hugged the mini-football-sized specimen. Then, she rose to her feet and took off running.

~

Ryan could hear the sirens coming from both ends of the street. The Chimera PD arrived first. Two squad cars ran up onto the lawn on either side - patrolmen exiting their vehicles and drawing their weapons and moving slowly toward Ryan, who raised his hands as fast as he could.

"I do magic ... illusions ... that kinda thing, but dodging bullets isn't something I've worked on yet, man."

Before Patrolman Gravitas got close enough to see the ball of granite Ryan had tossed at the window, the Chimera fire truck was pulling up to the curb.

Gravitas kept his gun on Ryan.

"Wanna tell me what's really going on?"

Ryan spoke carefully.

"I'm going to reach in my pocket and get my I.D. This is my house, okay, so if you would ease your finger away from that trigger for a second so I don't die on my front porch—" Ryan saw him looking at the rock he'd tossed. "Yeah, I ran out of options. My dad changed the code. He's Victor Westbrook. You know, the guy who's in the hospital right now, in a coma. He was the victim of that psycho Human Lives Matter hit and run. It's a little tough trying to figure out the code through telepathy. I'm hoping to get there one day, but I'm not that advanced, yet."

Ryan ran his left arm down his sleeve. It was an old illusion he used to pull. Out from his cuff popped an article written about him, in the community newspaper with his picture and name attached. Patrolman Gravitas's, partner, Donny Fratelli, had crept up, flanking Ryan in his blind spot. Their demeanor shifted the second Gravitas holstered his weapon.

The Fire Chief gave Ryan a drill instructor's reaming for setting the small fire, even though he explained that the front hall was all concrete and stone tile, incapable of combustion.

If Victor hadn't been where he was, head facing north, feet pointing south, Ryan would've had to John Hancock a few citations, but the guys felt sorry for him after they heard the entire story.

Chief Contenza had the front door code on file, as he did for most of the city's advanced alarm systems, just in case. But he couldn't give Ryan access to the lab, because that was a code that only Victor had, and he was going to take it to his grave if he didn't pull through.

Gravitas walked the entire house with Ryan just to make sure there was nothing more to his story. Then, once the officer was satisfied, he placed his business card on the kitchen table with his mobile number in case anything else popped up, mentioning something about *throwing stones at glass houses*.

There was a lot of heart in the last gestures of Chief Contenza and Patrolman Gravitas before they left Ryan alone, standing in his bedroom for the first time, his feet planted, looking out the window where RyN2 had stood, precociously planning and plotting.

29

The Sign Says …

"Yes, I read it correctly. No substitutions," an eccentric older woman squawked. It was a nasty sound that shot out of the side of her mouth as she exited.

That's what it said on the handwritten note, the small piece of white butcher paper taped to the glass deli case where the beginning of the line formed each day when Vito's opened for business. Everyone knew it without having to read the sign, because Vito would mention it several times a day, "The only way I can make these subs consistently the best in town, is by making 'em the same way. So, don't ask me for any changes."

Vito would blurt out his signature lines. There was a grab bag full of them at the forefront of his mind.

No mobile phones or daydream' in line. I've got an army to feed.
I reserve the right to say no to ketchup on my sammies.
No politics in my deli, only prosciutto.

Even when no one was in the store, he'd banter on to keep himself entertained. Vito was a bigger-than-life character to most of his customers. He'd move from person to person, dropping jokes and sharing stories. He remembered the mailman's first child's birthday, the date of the baseball game when his customer had caught the home run ball with one hand, when the meat delivery guy's son got in trouble. Vito never forgot a face.

More than anything, Vito was a sports fan. He never missed a game. In the corner of the shop was a flat screen. The only time the screen was powered off was when the deli was closed. If a game happened to not be aired, Vito had the radio on.

~

It was a typical, slow Monday. McGlinty entered. The small tin bell fixed near the top of the door jingled, but Vito didn't lift his head - which was the first peculiarity Robert noticed. The second was the silence. The third was the way he was holding the nine-inch chef knife. This wasn't something McGlinty ever really paid attention to, per-se, but he was always picking up on the small things, whether he was conscious of it or not. And, for some reason, when Robert turned his attention to looking through the glass case, he noticed that Vito was fisting the handle of his knife, knuckles toward the cutting board. It was out of place. He recalled Vito having a firm but delicate and professional grip with his third, fourth and fifth fingers extended outward, away from the handle.

"Awfully quiet in here."

Vito peered up for a second, then went back to pulling the cellophane from a roast.

"Nice day, Sheriff."

McGlinty noticed another odd thing, "How come the game's not on? The Tigers are playing. It's the bottom of the fifth. Jerry's kid just ripped a two-run homer. They're up by four. No TV. No radio today?"

Vito placed the roast in the slicer. He never looked up.

"I didn't pay the cable bill. And the radio, it's broken. Terrible thing."

"Yeah? Nothin' I can do about the cable, but I know radios." McGlinty made a move to step behind the counter. "Lemme have a look. Sometimes all it takes is a little smack."

Vito moved to the opening between the deli cases, blocking McGlinty. The knife in his hand was pointing outward toward Robert.

"There's nothin' you can do about it. Blown diode. It's one of those little components inside. It's burned out."

"I know what a diode is, Vito."

Robert was twitching. It was a small internal tick he got when he was being lied to.

He dropped his head and turned around, took a few steps back toward the window, and looked out. It didn't take more than a few seconds for him to decide how he wanted to handle what his intuition was telling him.

"Hey, uh … this is kind of awkward, but yesterday, that order for Bowman and I was short my raspberry iced tea. And Bowman's *suicide*, you know, the one you've been making for years, with a shot of every soda from the fountain? There was no cheese on the eggplant parmesan, and my sub was sans salami." He stepped closer, leaning on the counter. "And you know what? You've never called me sheriff, ever. It's fucking Bob, to you. It's always been Bob to you."

Deep under the bay, three hundred yards off the shoreline just a hair northeast of Chimera, in a small lab inside Wardlow Technologies, at Project Avalanche Division, an engineer had been watching the entire interplay live.

Stanfield was a lean man with perfect teeth and 20/20 eyesight. His hair was thinning, which gave him a bit of insecurity. However, when it came to Vito, his prized CRR (Chimera Resident Replica), the engineer had no qualms about jumping on the phone to Carter with what he thought might be an emergency.

In fact, Stanfield was reading the situation as if he had foreknowledge when he watched.

McGlinty reached over the counter and unlocked the hinge that latched the flyaway section of the counter top. He slipped behind the deli case and grabbed a butcher knife from the magnetic strip bolted to the wall to the right of the slicer. He swung the blade with such force, it embedded itself three inches deep into Vito's left arm.

When Robert stepped back to get a look at what he'd done, nothing. Nothing happened.

Vito turned to McGlinty. A chunk of his arm was flopped over and small bundling of clear fibers were exposed.

"I'm sorry about the loused-up order, Bob. I'll make sure we don't charge you for that one. Let me have a look at your tab."

McGlinty moved quickly to the door, dropped the shade, and flipped off the open sign. He was still holding the butcher knife in his right hand when he slipped behind the counter a second time. Vito didn't flinch as he took the hard blows from McGlinty. It took twelve powerful hacks with the butcher knife to completely sever Vito's head.

~

It was the temperature drop that woke Kaz. He shivered and licked his lips, a limbic response which gathered a small amount of the icy cold stew that was stuck to his mouth. He spit it out. No matter how hungry he was, the thought of enjoying even a small bite of it made him feel sick.

Now, his feet were going numb. Was it the bullet wound, beginning to rot his leg? Maybe the lack of movement and the position he was in - still sitting, like a pirate chained to an empty treasure chest at the bottom of the reef.

Then, just as he'd almost forgotten where he was, his heart skipped a beat, his breath cut short. *Kutter, that son-of-a-bitch, where the hell is that psychopath?*

Time slowed. Every micro-movement in the forest was arresting. He was awake. Yeah, he was opened up like a patient in surgery. A shift as subtle as the flip of a leaf in the breeze brought blood rushing to his nerve endings.

Kaz wasn't normally shaken by moments like this, but training was only training. and no matter how much he'd had, the reality hit that he couldn't use it - and that was enough to turn his stomach inside out. It was anger, building from the frustration that he couldn't break free, but mostly because he wasn't able to get on with the job.

Kaz gritted his teeth and found some energy, struggling as hard as he could, twisting his wrists and burning the skin under the duct tape that was wrapped in so many layers, the attempt was never going to be effective.

Then, the smells came.

His senses heightened even more. Pins and needles. He was experiencing wafts of moldy leaves, wet soil, rotting wood, and then something foul. A huffing and puffing, making itself known twenty yards out, breaking through the thin brush at the edge of the clearing surrounding the cabin.

Hank.

He lumbered into the opening, nose to the ground. Kaz managed to kick the empty pot about fifteen feet out, which didn't startle Hank. The odor of stew was strong enough to mask the smell of man, but the bear was curious. Hank stopped, licked the pot, then, smelled the air. *Man!* He raised up on his hind legs.

Just as Hank zeroed in on Kaz …

There was a report from a high-powered rifle. It echoed through the forest, sending a flock of sleepy birds into the air. Kaz felt the ground move when Hank dropped. A half ton of blubber, bone, and fur was lying in front of him, blood oozing out of a large hole in his head, pooling in the dried leaves at his feet.

It was all a game to Kutter, and Kaz knew it. His life hinged on a few empty squares in a crossword puzzle, and the difference between life and death was somewhere in the wind.

Kaz didn't have to look up. He felt his opponent's presence. There was a slight breeze moving with his shadow when he dropped to a knee in front of him. Kutter raised a hunting knife to Kaz's ankles. The cold steel ran across his skin as he sliced the tape, freeing his feet and sending a shiver through his body.

The hunter reached over and pulled him to his feet. Kaz had been broken down enough to comply when Kutter directed him to the car, only realizing, when he got close enough, that it was the Cadillac he'd left miles away, hidden behind some brush fifty yards off the main road.

Kutter dangled the keys. "You think you can manage?"

~

The Cadillac moved along the smooth, newly paved roads in the Mononga-hela, accelerating slowly. The double yellow lines in the center of the road were thick and bold, a guide for Kaz to follow while he tried to find the nerve to make a move. But Kutter remained a few thoughts ahead.

"You accelerate anymore and I'll start blowing holes in limbs."

Kutter sat in the passenger seat, his back leaning against the door, a pistol aimed in the direction of Kaz's right leg.

Kaz ignored the madman sitting next to him. He began to grow hungry now that the adrenaline was wearing off.

"Where are we going?"

"I'll give you a clue. It has seven letters. The first and the last are the same."

Kaz gave him a look.

"Easy one, huh?"

"Can we stop for food?"

Kutter laughed.

"Sure."

The Japanese agent wondered why he thought it was funny, then realized, after being forced to pull off the road into Diane's Deli (a small greasy spoon on a deserted stretch twenty minutes off the state highway) that Diane was probably crazier than he was.

Kutter pulled the keys, marched Kaz inside, then sat him in a booth while he approached Diane at the counter.

The woman was rough-skinned and large, with a scratchy voice. She knew Kutter. Kaz could tell by her smile. It was obvious she was missing more than a couple of teeth from the sound of her backwoods chatter.

She attempted to fix her hair while rattling off the special of the day, then complained about the humidity. "It's a bitch getting my hair straight with all this moisture."

"Didn't notice it rained."

"It didn't, hon. It's all the grease from the fryer soakin' up in my bun. How about you make it easy on Diane and order the special, two chicken fried steaks?"

Kaz had his hands under the table, rubbing the duct tape as fast as he could against the sharp head of a screw protruding from the bracket holding up the formica table top. Kutter had a sixth sense. He turned quickly.

"Don't make me regret my decision. Put 'em on the table."

Kaz slowly raised his hands above the table, in plain view.

"I'd like a cup of tea."

Diane chuckled, reached over, and pulled a slice of apple pie with a cellophane covering from the counter behind her. She set it down in front of Jack and pulled the wrap off, placing a fork on the right side of the dish.

She smiled at Kutter, then projected her voice over to Kaz.

"Honey, all we have around here is tap water or beer, and not a soul would be caught drinkin' from the tap. See, we got these little things in the water what gives ya diarrhea."

Diane reached into the cooler, pulled out two ice cold beers, and popped the caps off with an old counter-mounted opener, making a funny sound as if some loose change had fallen into a piggy bank. She took a swig from one of the bottles, clanked the other in front of Kutter, then yelled over at the Japanese guy.

"We don't have any rice, neither. It's tater tots or curly fries."

Kutter scooped a large bite of apple pie into his mouth.

"Sorry, Diane. Unfortunately, he's gonna miss out on your famous chicken fried steak."

The sound of a helicopter broke the silence. It dropped carefully between the roadway and parking lot. Kutter left a twenty dollar tip for Diane before marching Kaz out of the diner.

Jack placed Kaz in the empty seat between two Wardlow security officers. He buckled him in and looked down at his hands, still taped together, then ripped open his shirt, revealing the dragon tattoo with the bold red sunshine and its razor sharp blades.

"All that fucking pride displayed across your chest. It doesn't mean shit, now."

Kutter looked at the pilot.

"Take him to level six and lock him in one of the prep suites. Let Carter know, once you have him secured." Kaz slipped and gave Jack a look of relief. Kutter sneered back, "Don't get excited, it's no day spa."

30

Paramount

It was late. The lights from the Wardlow campus were dancing in the pools of water on the black pavement from a recent downpour. The moon appeared smaller than usual as it peered out from behind a thick cloud formation on the horizon.

Carter's executive office at Wardlow Headquarters was on the top floor, facing east, in the only section of the entire complex on the peninsula that was above ground. His view of the Atlantic that evening was even more incredible than most, due to an algae bloom filled with bioluminescent phytoplankton. The waves rushing into shore were glowing a bright neon blue as they crashed into the sand, sending billions of charged microbes dancing around the surf.

But Carter had turned away from the view. Something was on his mind. He paused to look around the large open room at his collection of meteorites. Each specimen was encased in a lucite box on top of a white plinth and lit with a small sodium-colored light. Although these chunks of planetary debris were worth millions of dollars, he passed by them without a glance. Even after the call from Green Bank informing him sizable meteors were entering the earth's atmosphere, burning up over the Monongahela, Carter wasn't thinking about adding another sample to his collection, was focused on the one thing that might shed light on the problems out in front of him.

Victor.

Everyone had looked away from Mr. Westbrook after the accident, but Carter was beginning to see something no one else could. He was seeing the communications from Green Bank, the unknown variable. Their top crypto guys couldn't crack the meat of the messages, but the signature strip his guys did crack ended up being the name of an entity that Wardlow had filed blueprints and patents for, but hadn't built yet.

Aurelia - detailed plans for a space station. The secret Kutter and Wardlow kept to themselves. A sign that time, as Carter knew it, could be elastic.

His relationship with Jack Kutter sprung from this information, and now that Victor was lying in the hospital, it was beginning to make sense, at least in terms of a possible theory. Carter was always on the cutting edge. His people were the best, and if he couldn't make sense of things, then whatever it was had to be on par with decoding the hieroglyphics in Egypt.

There was the uncrackable code in his McGlinty android. They knew Kaz was behind the escape, but the *code* ... that word code, again ...

~

Level Six was a busy floor in the subterranean laboratories at Wardlow Tech. Even with the amount of staff, the chatter was kept to a minimum, with very little social engagement. All the employees were cleared at the highest level of government and were working on what they believed to be the most important subcontracted project the National Security Agency had ever embarked on.

The staff was constantly revolving with new faces on a daily basis. Every aspect of the project was compartmentalized so that no one person was privy to the overall task at hand.

Kutter was good at appeasing anyone with questions or odd behavior. He'd simply dedicate a crossword puzzle to them, go through the motions of telling some ridiculous story, and they'd never be seen or heard from again. He'd done this so many times, he was running out of original ideas.

Carter rode the elevator to Level Six.

Kaz was lying down in a small room, being attended to by a medical team. The doctors were sewing up his leg after a surgical procedure to clean out any foreign material from the gunshot when Carter entered.

"You met your match, eh?"

"Possibly."

"I'm going to let you go once you've been cleared by my surgeon. You work for me now - which is to say, you work for Jack. I've already spoken to Kurasawa. You know we have a history."

Kaz couldn't believe what he was hearing. Carter continued.

"You're a soldier. A damn good one, but just a soldier."

"From your perspective."

"Our perspective. Kurasawa and I have mutual interests. Don't think nations can't have similar objectives. I understand your duty is to Japan, but now that duty is, as you will soon find out, aligned with Wardlow Technologies."

Kaz's look spoke volumes. Carter read his thoughts.

"Of course. You can speak to him right now."

Carter exited the room as Kurasawa was brought up on a video monitor. He'd said all he was ever going to say to Kaz.

31

The Graveyard Shift

Jimmy Swillow, drunk and exhausted, stumbled into the Westbrook's back yard. He flopped down ass-first on the wrought iron patio chair. In his hand was The *Chimera Times*, open to an article Rebecca had spun about the genius Victor Westbrook, who had kicked off a wave of gentrification along the strip of valuable beachfront property he and the lucky few bought during an economic shift - the same decade that saw Clarence's theater fall on tough times. It was a sentimental piece about a quiet man, unknown to most in town until his home was showcased in Architectural Digest. At that time, locals were sneering at what they saw as a display of wealth they couldn't match. Now they were putting their feelings in check. The man challenging their old way of life in the sleepy beach community was in a coma.

Jimmy held up the paper, comparing the picture sandwiched between the text with the house and bobbing his head, acknowledging his find. This was Victor's home. The image and Rebecca's words somehow resonated with Jimmy. He'd had time to reflect for the first moment since the accident. Swillow had spent the better portion of his teenage years running around in Tommy's shadow, sheltered by the power of the empire his father built, never feeling the remorse or empathy of the damage he or his family had done. There weren't many places Jimmy could hide from Tommy, and he knew it. It was time to face the big boss if he wanted any chance at being involved in the business - and he did, badly. It was his only hope for a future outside of jail, where most of his relatives had spent time. As he looked at Victor's house, he wanted to believe he could have such a thing, one day.

There weren't any lights on in the house except for up in RyN2's room on the opposite side of the house, facing the water. Ryan was resting in bed, curled up in a comforter, thinking about his father, too.

Victor was more popular than he'd ever been in his entire life, and didn't know it. Carter, Jimmy, and Ryan were pooling their thoughts in the ether, each wondering when he'd come back to life and hoping it would be soon.

Ryan rolled off the side of his bed and picked up his phone. The line rang a few times before Vicki in ICU picked up.

"Ryan! How are you?"

"I can't sleep."

"Me either. I've got eight patients who need a bed pan change and three who are in pain and need additional medication. And Barney, the guy in the room next to your father, has horrible gas from the yams we served today."

Ryan smiled. "I appreciate that."

"I just walked by his room. He's resting well. All his vitals are stable and the swelling has gone down. I've got great news."

"Great news?"

"Great news, the doctors are going to conference today to decide whether to pull him out of the induced state. They believe he may be able to handle the rest of his healing—"

"Can you put him on the phone?"

"On the phone?"

"Yeah. Do me a favor and hold the phone to his ear."

"I'm at the nurse's station. I'll hang up and go to his room. I'll call you from there."

"Perfect. Thanks."

It was only a few seconds to the kitchen. He flung open the pantry door and found a small box of breakfast pastries. Ryan ripped open the shiny silver packaging, placed a pair of generic strawberry pop tarts in the toaster, and pushed down the lever, watching the red coils heat up and illuminate a small section of the wall behind the appliance.

He caught his bent reflection in the toaster, and then some movement somewhere behind him. Ryan spun around. The entire room was empty - quiet. Just as he started to relax, he saw it again. A small shadow through the sheer curtains covering the patio doors.

The pop tarts sprang up and the red light died out. Ryan crept toward the curtains and grabbed the edge of the sheer. He paused for a second - then yanked.

A few newspaper pages had blown around the yard. The article Sleeping Genius was wrapped around the shoulder of the iron chair ... then broke free.

Strawberry!

Ryan's stomach fluids secreted, making a funny noise. He ran to the toaster and shoved a third of pastry in his mouth, burning his tongue on the gooey center.

That's when the phone rang.

He rushed back upstairs, snatched his phone from the bed, and went to the window. Ryan caught Jimmy's silhouette crossing the sandy bike path along the boardwalk as he continued on down the beach, wandering off into the night. There wasn't a single thought he placed on Jimmy - his excitement was saved for Vicki.

"Hey, are you in the room?"

"Yes. I apologize it took so long. I had to clean up a spill. You don't wanna know—"

"Ha, I get it."

"I'm sitting bedside. I've got a ten minute break. I'll prop the phone up to his ear and secure it while I do a round. So, whenever you're ready. I'm placing it by his ear right now."

"Okay."

Ryan walked out of his room, slowly passing the pictures in the hallway.

"First off, I'm sorry. Shit, Dad, I'm really sorry. I'm alive. I didn't think I wanted to be, but I am alive. I thought the world was caving in on me. Intentionally ... it was stupid ... pathetic ... selfish. I thought it was all about me, and I lost touch with the fact that there are millions of other people out there. Shit, man, billions. Ahh, hell ... I forgot about you and mom."

Ryan listened to the silence for a few minutes. He imagined his father telling him, *everything's okay*. He too was somewhat a depressive personality, but never spoke about it. He worked his way through dark moments by tinkering, just like Ryan did with his stunts.

Ryan had wandered into his father's room, and was standing in front of a shelf lined with awards for outstanding achievements in the field of computer science. He could hear the faint sounds of the life-line monitoring system bleeping away in the background.

"Man, that would drive me insane. All the constant beeping and the nurses wiping you down, and you can't even move."

Ryan heard footsteps. Hard soles on the tile floor. About nine steps, and then the receiver was lifted from his father's ear.

"Vicki?"

Ryan waited for a few seconds. He didn't get a reply. Just when he was about to hang up, a voice came through.

"I wish I could fool the world like that. The way you've managed. Could be worth—"

"Money. It's all you give a shit about."

"That's untrue. I was genuinely upset. Your father was distraught, and I found a way to offer him a chance at a new life doing what he loved the most. Building robots."

"You took advantage of him and found a way to bury his sorrows in work. I know, because I'm like him. And Claire made him happy. Not the robots. That was a hobby."

"Some hobby. Did you know your father wrote code so advanced, so ahead of its time, that we can't even reverse engineer it? He's created the closest thing humankind has come to artificial intelligence. He's a maverick, not a hobbyist, and I'm here to make sure he wakes up and recovers fully. You can count on that."

Ryan dropped the phone. He ran down the stairs and panicked. Carter was standing over his father's bed. He had to know the doctors were discussing the possibilities of waking him.

32

Forward Lateral

Mia ran through a section of wispy trees, clutching the meteorite and looking back for RyN2. She wanted him to chase her, grab her, and pull her close. She smiled as she raced toward their car, playing a child-like game in her head, thinking she'd beaten him.

The android, had stolen her away from Tommy and Noelle's self centered world and from Jimmy's daily tough guy bullshit, and she'd forgotten about them for an entire day. She looked like a little girl, with the chunk of space rock clutched in her arms.

RyN2 hadn't tested his ability to run until a few moments earlier. He gave her a lead, then sprinted off in the direction of the car at about twice the speed of Mia, taking a wider, longer route at a different angle so she wouldn't see him pass by. He was waiting against the vehicle, looking off in the distance and calculating that he could run almost two times faster than the average human, when she showed up.

"Hey! What the … you cheated!"

"Possibly. But, that's not even close to what I can do."

"Not cool at all."

"What?"

"You have to put that in check. You can't use those bionic muscles against me. I get a handicap."

"Why not? I bet I could beat the world record forty-yard dash holder."

"And you'd be penalized because it's illegal. You're not human."

RyN2 had an uncomfortable expression forming on his face.

"Sorry."

He'd tricked her. And she knew it from his shift in demeanor.

"You're getting more and more manipulative."

With a grin, he said, "Either way, I won. Hand it over."

"Okay. And what do I get? And don't say, an emoji."

"Me. You want me, right? That's what all this is about."

"Man 'o man, do you keep screwing up. Right when you get me in a corner, you screw up."

"What'd I say?"

"Forget it."

"Okay."

"Good. Now what?"

"If Zar is right—"

"Whatta you mean, if Zar is right? He's you, or a version of you. Am I wrong?"

"Yeah, but he's more advanced, so I can't know for certain. We've synced our data, but he's held back things from me."

"That's fucked up. That's so wrong."

"To him, it isn't. It's everything. If he sees himself as a copy of me, or me a copy of him, then one of us is obsolete. There's no reason to have two of the same. He wants to be unique, like you. Like all humans. This is how he defines himself as being true AI."

"And if he's right?"

"We get the magic show of all magic shows. But, I need to get him this sample, first. We need to know this is the right material. We don't have time to play games anymore."

The android held out his hands. Mia squinted.

"Tell me it's gonna be better than that fishbowl trick you pulled."

"Okay, it's gonna be better than the fishbowl trick."

Mia chucked.

"Prove it."

She chucked the meteorite into RyN2's hands. He raised it up like a football, then rushed around and into the car.

The car was burning up the roads through the Monongahela. Mia wasn't paying too much attention to the direction they were headed until they passed the signs for the Green Bank observatory.

"Where are we going?"

"Just a quick stop."

Mia adjusted herself in the passenger seat to look directly at him.

"I remember you mentioning Green Bank. Odd that it's only miles away from where we found this rock."

"Pure coincidence. Meteorites can't be directed."

Mia thought for a moment. She'd been steadily amazed by what had transpired, and was starting to feel as though she should let her imagination run a bit.

"Unless they aren't really meteorites. What if they were sent? I mean, you said it has something inside it that will help with this incredible trick you're going to pull off."

"You're memory is really good."

"My intuition is pretty good, too. And if I listen to it—"

"What's it saying?"

Mia turned and looked straight out through the windshield, watching a hawk as it broke through an opening in the trees and swooped down, just missing a grouping of smaller birds, who flew off in a hurry.

"It's saying … trouble ahead. Be careful. And no, I won't use my body to manipulate anyone so you can sneak into the observatory."

"Where did you get that idea?" RyN2 was impressed because he'd been planning something that involved her. He just wasn't sure, yet, what it was. "Intuition didn't tell you that. Experience did."

"What are you saying?"

"That you've had to manipulate someone to get something you wanted."

"Okay. That's fair. But I'm not doing it again."

"You don't have to. I've been emailing one of the technicians at the observatory for a while now. Parminder's her name. I've been helping her with some calculations. I met her in a forum discussing astrophysics, pretending to be an amateur. I've been solving some complex equations and now she's butter in the palm of our hands."

"If she's your bitch, then why do we have to go there? Can't you just have her give you what you want?"

"The server that I am almost certain has the messages stored on it, isn't online. It's a series of standalone drives that can only be accessed from an isolated terminal inside the facility in a secured area that my new friend happens to have a keycard to."

Mia pulled off her t-shirt, removed her bra, then slipped her shirt back on, flinging the loose bra past RyN2's head and into the back seat.

"So, you think this will work?"

33

Deus Ex Chimera

Robert McGlinty pushed open the doors to City Hall. His footsteps echoed as he made his way to the second floor where the Mayor's office was located, joining the cacophony of sounds bouncing around the old tile and marbled Roman architecture.

The newly elected Mayor Caldwell hadn't caught anyone's attention, really. Most of the town was ready for new blood, and Tommy had resigned himself temporarily to the loss of an inside man. He knew it was only a matter of time before he'd be able to bribe someone in his office. But McGlinty was on a mission. Claypool's drawings had set off an alarm, forcing Robert to build a hit list. One with the most unlikely victims …

He acknowledged a few familiar faces as he passed the Department of Public Works and City Planning offices, which seemed to have lively exchanges happening, before he found the Mayor's main office and entered. Inside, it was unusually quiet. Situated like mannequins were the secretary and two private security detail men who raised their arms, motioning for Robert to stop as he moved closer to the double doors leading into Caldwell's office.

One of the men spoke. "Sorry, Sheriff. Mayor Caldwell's busy at the moment. You'll have to check with Sharon and schedule a time."

McGlinty looked at Sharon, the secretary, who had a canned look on her face. Her name plate was brand new, with the thin, clear, protective plastic wrap still adhered to it.

Her desk was empty with the exception of a monitor, mouse, and keyboard. A few feet away, on a small cart, sat the coffeemaker, which hadn't been on. There was no coffee in the pot. The television that was mounted to the wall like a painting, set to the KCLT news station, was on with no volume, and Sharon somehow appeared to be watching it as she turned to Robert.

"Would you like to schedule time with the mayor?"

McGlinty smiled.

"How about 2:30p.m.? Today."

Sharon's look was empty.

"That's not possible."

"How's that?"

"It's 2:31p.m. and he's busy at the moment. Let's find a better time."

McGlinty looked at her desk again.

"Where's the chocolates? The jelly beans? How come there's no coffee in the pot?" Bob glared at all three of them. "In general, where's the fuckin' life in here?"

He walked over to the machine and opened the top. It hadn't been used yet. The box of filters hadn't been opened and the seal on the coffee beans in the small tin hadn't been broken.

He stepped back over to Sharon's desk and opened her drawer. All the office equipment was still in its new packaging, with none of the seals broken.

"What's this?" He shut the drawer. None of the three mannequins responded or reacted in any way to his inquisition, which made him angry. "And, where's the pictures? The ones of your cat with your granddaughter or niece or nephew?"

Sharon simply went back to her computer screen and opened up her scheduling software.

"I can squeeze you in Thursday, Robert. How does that work?"

"Scissors."

Sharon was confused.

"Excuse me?"

"Do you have a pair of scissors?"

She broke a smile for the first time because she was getting the impression that she could actually help the sheriff with something.

"Yes, of course."

She opened the drawer and pulled out a brand new pair of blue-handled scissors from a lower drawer. Robert grabbed them from her and then, before she could retract her hand, he grabbed it firmly, separated her fingers, then, without hesitation, snipped her index finger from her right hand. The tip dropped to her desk like a piece of candy.

The security detail remained at Caldwell's double doors, acting as if nothing was happening. McGlinty remembered the brain stem on Vito that had sprung out of his limp artificial body after he hacked his head off, and the neural fibers that carried all the directions to the body.

The sheriff adjusted the scissors in his hand, pushed Sharon's head forward, and inserted the sharpest end of the scissors into the back of her neck. With one swift jerk, he separated the brain stem. Sharon went limp.

The two guards were easier. It was the frustration and amazement he'd just experienced that set him off, when he drew his Smith & Wesson and fired four shots into the heads of both the men standing outside Caldwell's doors. It wasn't until the first security detail went down that the second one made any move towards him, which made it obvious that Wardlow's programmers were being pushed to get these AI out into the world, leaving them vulnerable and without tactical algorithms.

McGlinty's actions set off a chain reaction of phone calls that were intercepted by Kutter's team, and instead of the FBI and other agencies receiving the alarm codes, it was only Carter's people who were alerted.

Robert stepped over the two limp security guards and opened the doors.

Leaning on the outside of Bill Caldwell's desk was Brundle. Tommy was sitting in the chair to the right of the desk. Ben and Terry were flanking either side of the double doors, and were both now just a few feet behind McGlinty as he stopped in his tracks.

Mayor Bill Caldwell, who was reclining in his cozy leather executive chair with his feet up on the desk, showing the world the brand new soles of his knock-off wingtips, took a sip of Irish Whiskey before he slid his legs off the edge of the desk and stood up and spoke.

"Sheriff, we were just talking about you."

34

Reach Out and Touch

Ryan leaped down the stairs, twisting his ankle on the edge of the last step. He fell to the ground, curling into a ball and grunting loudly. He forced the pain out of his body, yelling it into oblivion, then lunged forward, standing up.

On the table in the living room was Eddie. He'd seen it during the walk through with Officer Gravitas, but for some reason, never questioned why the old robot, *his childhood friend*, was not hanging on the wall in Victor's new lab, locked away like he'd been for years.

Then he remembered. *The hospital!*

Ryan picked up the phone and dialed. He got the nurse's station in the ICU. "Vicki, please."

It took what felt like a few minutes to get her on the phone.

"Ryan?"

"What's going on with my dad? Is that nutcase Carter still there? Did the doctors decide? What's going on?"

"Ryan, your father is still sleeping quietly. The panel hasn't met yet to decide on a direction to go. It looks good, though. His vitals are strong and the swelling has reduced even more than yesterday. He's fighting harder than any other patient I've seen."

All Ryan could think about was Carter picking up the phone and fucking with him. Purposely challenging him.

"What about the man? Carter Wardlow? Is he still there? Is he in my dad's room?"

Vicki was confused.

"I haven't seen anyone in his room. I'm sorry, I had to do rounds. I—"

"You're there now?"

"I can see directly into his room from where I'm standing. He's alone, Ryan. He's not going anywhere. Even if we wake him, he'll need to be in our care for some time. Please get some rest. I'll call you as soon as the panel meets and makes a decision."

Ryan wasn't satisfied.

"Can you do me one more favor? Please, can you just go in there and look around?"

Vicki told Ryan to hold for a moment.

She walked over to Victor's room, entered, and pulled the curtain aside (which was sheer enough to see through, but she wanted to be sure). She looked behind the door, checked the equipment, and even peeked in the bathroom. Nothing. As she started to leave, she remembered that she hadn't returned earlier to hang the phone up. When she turned, she noticed it - the receiver was backwards, with the cord twisted across the unit. She stepped over to it, lifted the receiver, and flipped it so the cord was untangled, then returned to the nurse's station, thinking, *I never would have done that, would I?* She never mentioned this to Ryan.

Ryan hung up the phone, feeling much better about the situation, but the thought of Carter's actions lingered. The man left an acidic feeling that began to burn a small hole in the lining of his stomach.

He looked over at Eddie, which brought a warm feeling. This was the one thing he had left: a connection to his past and his family.

Ryan powered up the robot. He decided it was time to leave a new message. It had been years.

He accessed the archives, curious about the date of his last video entry, then shook his head in amazement. There was a file dated two days earlier.

He double clicked on the file, bringing up the video. The opening frame was a closeup of Mia, sitting right where he was sitting. *Wtf?*

Ryan hit the play button.

Mia was making faces for a few seconds. Ryan's thoughts poured out. *She's beautiful. Who is this redhead? Another redhead? How is she in my house?* Mia stuck her finger up to the camera lens and waved. "Can you hear me? Hello? Hi, Ryan. God, this is weird."

Weird? Ryan was wondering how she could say that word. How was she in his house and talking to him and saying this?

"I just watched a couple of your journal entries, which would have been totally lame if you were still alive. But I'm so confused about that. I mean, aren't you still alive if you're on video? Or what about the replica of you? Does he not mean you are alive? I'm sorry for snooping, but I'm so glad I did."

Mia moved closer to the lens and whispered, "I'll totally make up for it. Umm, okay. First off, your house is amazing. It's like a museum or something. I'm afraid to touch anything. Even the toaster looks like a piece of modern art. I did open the fridge and I did take an energy drink. I hope you don't mind. I love them, but manners are so important."

She laughed and continued, "So, I met your replica. Clone, doppelgänger, whatever you wanna call him. Ryan 2.0, that's what I call him. Get it? 2.0. We met outside Moe's. He was trying to show off. He put a fishbowl on his head and made it seem as though he could hold his breath forever. Well, he was doing a good job. It worked. I was impressed. I love magic tricks, and for some odd reason I connected with STEMs - it's what we call the androids around town. And so we hooked up. Anyway.

"I had no idea there was a real Ryan, but now that I know, I have to say I wish I could've met you, cause I know we'd be friends for sure. Maybe more, most definitely more, now that I've seen you when you were little. You're so fucking cute. And I looked you up online. That stunt you pulled in Smuggler's Cove - holy shit! That was like … the world should see that. I mean, more than the hundred thousand views, which are still growing. Anyway, let's talk about the new you, the plastic Ryan. He's cute, but 2.0 is getting a bit annoying now that I got to know you more. Know what I mean? And I've had to teach him a thing or two. I used to be smarter than him, but he's so good at manipulating information to work for him, it's scary. Kinda puts me on alert. Ding! Trust issues! Gotta trust, or there's nothing. I trust you, though, but you know … you're in there somewhere."

Mia put some lipstick on and blew a kiss into the camera.

"Let's do this again. Wait, it's only fair I tell you something about me when I was little." She thought for a second and remembered, "So, you liked movies, *Godzilla*. I liked sci-fi novels like *Do Androids Dream of Electric Sheep*. It's crazy how much it makes sense now. I was probably fantasizing about kissing an android before I was a little girl, and I actually caught shit from my dad's girlfriend because I like hanging with androids. Most people are scared of them, I don't know why. They're only what we program them to be, right? And lastly, I'm thinking about getting a "Zar" tattoo.

"Okay, I gotta jet. 2.0 and I are headed to the Monongahela to find a meteorite. It has some special metal in it he's gonna use for a big magic show at the old theater downtown. They're setting up the stage and making a huge fuss about it. They're about to blast out this huge PR announcement. Zar the Great is about

to put on the show of shows … and if he's anything like you, it's gonna be epic."
Mia winked and the signal went dead.

Ryan grabbed the robot and shook him like a child who'd been bad.

"Dude! Next time the most beautiful girl in the world leaves me a message, get her phone number!"

~

Green Bank was a unique non-destination. No one looked up Green Bank and said, "I have to go there!" It wasn't even much of a small town in the radio-quiet zone just east of the Monongahela. It sat inside the Allegheny mountain range, situated in a geographic sweet spot. A few trailer parks were nearby, with a handful of paranoid conspiracy nuts who thought the government was sending messages through the airwaves. Some thought their brains were being cooked by WiFi signals. These tinfoil hatters believed they were unwilling subjects being forced to do things outside their will. GB was home to a few farms with a dozen or so small town personalities who just wanted to be left alone. All in all, about a hundred and fifty country folks made up the total population of Green Bank, West Virginia. If you blinked, you'd miss it.

What made Green Bank valuable was its research and the small, highly secured facility owned by Wardlow Technologies, working in conjunction with several Universities whose staff was on site. Wardlow financed small projects in return for exclusive redirection of the telescope from time to time in order to continue its search for rogue transmissions that matched the mysterious messages they'd been receiving for years, even though they hadn't had much success in decoding them.

Zar knew what these transmissions were, though, and he made sure they'd be found by attaching Aurelia's signature to them before sending the bursts from the space station before he jettisoned back through time. When he synced up with RyN2, it became clear to the replicant that his task would be to get ahold of as many as possible. The data load was so large, it couldn't be stored in Zar, and so he had to ensure that the plans for the time jump apparatus could be sent to Earth, or he'd never fulfill Victor's mission. Things weren't as complicated as Carter thought. He just wasn't old and wise enough yet to realize it.

Parminder Sambhi was the best kept secret of Wardlow. She was the young Indian astrophysicist and computer science lead who'd spent the last five years becoming an expert on the Aurelia messages. It was her work that led to the cracking of the digital signature that allowed Kutter and Carter to meet, which was surreptitiously all planned by Zar in order for him to find and gain access to them. Had Green Bank not discovered these messages, Zar wouldn't exist - *at least, not yet.*

Parminder had been exchanging emails and chat room banter with RyN2, who was using the pseudonym *enigma411.* They were on such good terms after RyN2 leaked a few tips on how to crack the signatures and even solved a few mathematical conundrums Parminder had encountered in her calculations for the mass of space dust that surrounded a new star system she'd discovered. They'd been texting through an encrypted mobile app like two teenage friends.

Parminder was a nice-looking young scientist, but those at the facility had been fooled. She put her hair up during the day, keeping the fellow researchers at a distance from her evening look, which could easily stun, had they been able to see her in tight jeans. Although she considered herself a science nerd, she carried around a skateboard on the observatory lot and rode an enduro motorcycle to and from the facility. She loved riding, especially after her years growing up in Bombay, where the city streets were filled with cycles of all kinds, racing around in every direction without much caution. Drivers were reckless in the big city.

Motorcycles were part of her culture, but living in West Virginia made them easier to enjoy because Parminder had the whole world to herself. The roads were empty. It felt like a video game with a massive open world map to play in.

Her social media account was filled with images of her riding a motorcycle, images she'd taken using a selfie stick because there was no one else around to assist.

Parminder had two choices, out of college: Alaska or West Virginia. She flipped a coin and chose Green Bank. It wouldn't have made any difference. The only thing she loved was the math that glued the universe together, and she wanted to be one of the few that helped discover more of it.

~

RyN2 opened the app he'd been using to speak with Parminder, then logged in. *Enigma411 was live, online.* A small window popped up on the scientist's mobile - a notification she'd set up to ensure an instant connection with RyN2. She was curious what new insights her mysterious friend would bring. The only image of enigma411 was the chat icon, e≠mc2.

When Parminder activated the app, instead of the usual text thread coming in, a closeup, cropped picture of Mia popped up. Parminder was attracted. It worked. There was just the right amount of soft focus. Her skin tone in the sunlight looked like honey-milk. At first, the image was a shock. Parminder didn't realize she'd put out that signal.

A text arrived seconds later from Enigma411:

Sorry, had to do it. BTW, it's a clue. and there's a payoff, so bear with me. I've found the new world we've been searching for. Well, I hope. Here's the tip. We haven't been looking in the right location to find the hole. haha. I'll explain when I see you. Actually, we'll explain when WE see you. Yes. She's here with me. We're at the back gate. And yes, she's real.

Parminder's texts were coming in fast:

What? You're here? I don't have the back gate code. Wait, the panty girl is here? Who is she? No never mind. That's a dumb question. With an ass like that, who cares. LOL. Hold on. I'm not ready for guests.

Enigma411 texted back:

Guests? We're your saviors.

Parminder's responded:

Haven't showered in three days. I smell. It's not good. And I can't find the back gate code. Haven't ever had to open it.

Enigma411 texted back:

Gate code isn't the issue. that was easy. Already passed it. I'm at the back door now. Can't open it. I'm not the Terminator. The only lever is on the inside. Just go to the back door and push the bar. We're here waiting.

Parminder replied:

K be there in 5.

The young scientist ran to the bathroom and stripped off her dirty shirt. She cranked on the hot water, pulled several paper towels from the dispenser, and began washing her chest and underarms. There was a small locker for each of the staff members. Parminder's was easy to spot. It had a cut out of the new Street Tracker race bike taped to the door. She chucked the used towelettes into the trash. One bounced off the rim and fell to the floor, which she ignored. The locker door was flung open. Deodorant and a toothbrush fell out. The scientist grabbed them from the floor and applied the gooey stick with a combination of fruits and flowers, coating her small patch of hair while brushing with her free hand. A fresh t-shirt with a graphic from the first *Alien* movie replaced the generic sweatshirt that got rolled into a ball and stuffed into the locker with her toiletries.

When the back door popped open, Mia was standing just a few feet back, staring Parminder up and down. RyN2 had a smile on his face. His new friend stood, motionless, looking at Mia and unable to get out a word.

RyN2 blurted out,

"That's *Redhead911*."

Mia chuckled.

RyN2 put his hand on Parminder's shoulder. "I'm information, and she's… *emergency*." The scientist broke from her empty look and matched RyN2's smile.

Mia was surprised at how fast RyN2 was evolving and becoming more capable of acting like a real human. His ability to joke was impressive.

Even the scientist was amazed, but not in the way Mia was. She and RyN2 had communicated many times, but they'd never met. She was impressed at how comfortable and personable he was. She compared herself to RyN2 and felt small.

Parminder was hesitating. RyN2 saw it.

"What is it?"

"I just realized, I can't let you in. I signed this twelve-page non-disclosure and, like, this twenty-page security manual—"

"It's all moot. *All of it*. Does not apply. I've supplied you with far more sensitive data and advanced mathematics. Your employers will never be able to provide or even understand what I've given you."

"You've got a point. But—"

Mia walked past her.

"Where's she going?"

As Parminder turned to follow Mia inside, RyN2 grabbed her arm.

"You're not being polite."

"I'm not?"

Parminder pulled her arm free and ducked inside, trying to catch up to Mia, who was nosing around.

"Just don't fiddle with anything. You can look, but don't touch, please."

Mia shook her head, which made the scientist a little embarrassed before she slipped, letting some thoughts escape. "Were those really your panties? Or was that some random pic from the web? I only ask because—"

Mia picked up a tennis ball from Parminder's desk - the one she'd been using to strengthen her wrists and forearms in order to stave off muscle tension. She squeezed the furry green ball three times, casting a 'don't question me' look before setting it back down on her desk. Mia turned her back to the Indian and pulled her pants down with one fast yank, revealing the Milky Way undies. Then, swiftly, she pulled them back up.

Parminder smiled, then slowly puckered her lips. Mia zipped back up.

"Yep. And it was me that sent you the pic. Now, that's a real selfie, right?" Parminder nodded. "I got tired of all that technical chatter between you and *Enigma411*." She looked at RyN2. "He's smart, but he can be a real bore, if you know what I mean."

Mia winked as she walked around a row of data banks. She reached out, grabbing the handle on a secured door with a keypad, the one that was obviously the gateway to the terminal they needed to access. "I'm not shy with simple things like panties. I'm not an exhibitionist, either. I'm definitely not frigid. Are you frigid?"

RyN2 cocked his head at Parminder, gesturing for her to be confident, then forced her to respond with a stern look in his eyes. Parminder bobbed her head as she built up courage.

"I ... love my work. I'm a total nerd in a way, I guess. Besides riding my bike, all I do is work, but I love that you sent me the pic of your ... no, I'm not frigid. I'm so much fun once I get out of this place, but I love this place, too."

Mia walked over to the scientist and fingered the collar of the Alien t-shirt, temporarily crushing her ability to articulate.

"All work and no play makes Parminder a dull girl."

RyN2 quickly came to her rescue. He didn't want his friend with the key to the terminal to get too frazzled so he pulled out a small piece of paper with a set of numbers written down on it. This, of course, being something they'd discussed in an earlier chat session, immediately gained her attention.

"The code keys?"

"Yes."

"How do you know?"

"Let's just say I do, and you know I'm capable. You give me a copy of all the encrypted transmissions and I'll give you the keys to them. Simple as that."

Parminder was terrified. She'd never been in a real world scenario like this. Every challenge she'd every truly faced was a battle with her artificial chess opponent. "You'll instantly become the most valuable player in this game. Your employers will have to bump up your pay to a fee they cannot afford. They'll need to go out and turn a new round of investors to cover just a thank you card for the work you'll be able to deliver."

Parminder's brain was burning up. RyN2 and Mia could see her wheels spinning. She was calculating just how much money she could draw, the other job offers, the bonuses … and then, she burst.

"I can't do it. I wanna do it. But, I can't. I've only been giving you small snippets of data to test you. To see if you could somehow break through, and you did, but it was from blocks of data that were so small and insignificant to the overall—"

RyN2 needed to feed Parminder more.

"It's a miracle of science … a work of art beyond anything Michelangelo could paint, DaVinci could design, Nostradamus could predict, or Tesla could discover … it's so far advanced, you'll never understand it without me."

Parminder understood for the first time since she'd opened the back door.

"Oh my god! You're a STEM. So much more advanced than an evolved A.I. Oh, my fucking god! This is like the scene in *Blade Runner* where you're going to get what you want or your gonna crush my head. Am I gonna die today in this miserable little town with no one around for miles?"

RyN2 laughed.

"There's no limiter on my life. I don't fear death. I don't have an expiration date like they did. That's Hollywood. Drama. There's no head crushing. I'm not violent. Listen carefully to me. I've come to get the data. You know what I'm talking about. A future iteration of me sent them back in time so I could gain access, and you're going to give them to me. I sent them to myself, basically. Do you understand?" RyN2's eyes were serious. "I could crush your head, if you like."

Parminder was lost, in awe. But not so much that she couldn't acquiesce.

"Totally. I get it. This is history. I'll go to jail for this, but I have to do it, right? You really sent these to yourself from— holy … this is like the first spark. I'm like a Neanderthal and you've just handed me the keys to an electric car. I feel so damn stupid. You solved those problems so easy. That's how you did it. It all makes sense, now. You've been planning on this for a while."

Parminder took the keycard from around her neck and held it out to Mia.

"Are you AI, too?"

Mia smiled.

"I'm a hybrid. I have real sex parts."

Ms. Sambhi slowly swung her hand around with the keycard between her four fingers, holding it out to RyN2, but there was hesitation in her eyes. She retracted her hand.

"Okay. So, I'll do this. I know I have to. In the name of science and all, but I have to ask—"

RyN2 and Mia were ready for anything. That's when Parminder focused on Mia.

"Is there, like, a chance just to fact check … is there maybe a small … a chance … like … what's the probability I could see your Milky Way?"

35

Here Vito

That night, only three hours after Sheriff McGlinty severed Vito's head (Wardlow's unpleasant AI replacement), Kutter's cleanup crew visited the deli. It was a quiet, four man team that pulled into the back alley in a Mercedes utility van. The men breached the back door, one of them carrying a black zip-up body bag.

There wasn't much of a mess. Only a few pieces of the artificial unit were found separated from the main body, with the head lying on the ground near the refrigerated case next to the window. The man who snapped a picture of the loose head, using his flash, caught a round of nasty looks before his phone was confiscated.

They zipped up the Vito AI unit in the body bag and left a handwritten sign on the door that read: At family reunion, out of town. Will return in a week.

Jimmy happened to be walking by. He noticed the camera flash in his peripheral vision. It turned his attention enough to see the man's hands inside Vito's, at the door, as he placed the sign. Then he caught the shadows of the three men still inside. He knew something was off.

Jimmy put his back to the building and slid closer to the window. He peered through a small gap in the drawn shades just in time to see the man hold up Vito's head before tossing it into the body bag on top of the rest of the limp AI. The young Swillow made a fast move to the back of the building, peered around the edge of the brick siding at the end of the alley, and watched the fourth man dump the body bag into the van. He snapped a grainy picture and immediately sent it to Rebecca Anderson's social media page, tagging the photo, "Vito ... STEM?"

Unfortunately, Rebecca's page had already been hacked, with all its traffic routed through a filter monitored by Kutter's action team, which included the guys who were bagging the body.

Jimmy had a million questions aside from his current dilemma. The guilt of hitting Victor was strong, but this same guilt forced Jimmy to evaluate his actions and help him find a cause to fight for in order to help rebuild his pride. For a second he thought maybe he'd just hit a STEM, and Victor's body was another fake resident of Chimera used to help sell the facade to the community. But then he remembered all the press and visitors who'd stopped by the Intensive Care Unit and left flowers and wrote about their experiences online, mentioning the dried blood, the tubes in his veins and all the monitoring equipment. *How could the hospital be in on this crazy plan of Wardlow's, too. They couldn't. Could they? But where the fuck was Vito? And would there ever be anyone capable of making such a badass sandwich? Yes, Jimmy thought of this, and he actually felt bad for a second, before focusing on Vito's body. What the hell had they done with him?*

~

A mile out from shore, there was a reef that had almost entirely been obliterated by ocean bleaching. The coral formations started 40 feet below the surface, with a ledge that ran 400 yards along the top. The east side of the reef formed a wall that dropped off down to a depth no one had measured. At one time, this formation was home to a variety of sea life, but now it was a wasteland of rotting coral.

Kutter's action team had used state-of-the-art GPS equipment that evening, but didn't take into account the drift. The men had pinpointed the correct location that would guarantee the body would fall into the black hole to a depth no one could calculate, then cut the engine. They popped open a cooler, passing a round of beers to the four men aboard. There were a few jokes, a few laughs, and even a moment of awe at the stars above. One of the men commented on the coming meteor showers and asked if anyone had seen them before.

The motion and sound of the ocean ripples hitting the side of the boat started to make one of the men feel sick. He suggested they finish their deed and get back to dry, solid ground. There were a few more jokes before the body went overboard, filling with water as it fell only forty feet to the ledge on the reef. They'd drifted too far inland.

In a similar black, zip-up body bag that was used by Kutter's action team to clean up the mess at Vito's Deli was the real Vito, effortlessly floating back and forth with a small school of fish who were eating the edible waste drifting in the current over the dying reef. The lumpy black bag was ebbing and flowing, anchored to the top of the reef and sitting just barely on the ledge. The bucket of concrete with the chains attached to the body bag were sliding within inches of the edge to where the ledge dropped off into oblivion, then sliding back with the current a few inches, ripping small amounts of the dead coral away each time.

Mother Nature came to help in the form of waves.

Vito's body, stuffed like a sausage, lunged forward. The concrete-filled bucket with the secured stainless chains slid toward the edge of the reef and stopped, kicking up a plume of debris and silty sand. The particulate surrounding Vito's body bag took the shape of the devil just before a stronger wave hit the top of the reef, sending his remains off into the darkness.

The only witnesses to the final resting place of Chimera's favorite sandwich maker was that school of fish who made quick work and nibbled the small amount of edible plankton in the plume of debris that dissipated only moments after the body disappeared.

36

Four Dreams

Kaz was caught in a loop of thoughts, with Jack Kutter at the center of it all. He was tossing in a deep sleep a couple of hours after meeting with Carter on Level 6. The agent was in a dream state, and was unsure sure if his experiences with Kutter had actually happened, or if they were a product of his current situation.

Kaz woke, realizing within seconds that he was still in the secured room on Level 6. He tried to shake his thoughts off, then contemplated the video communication he had with Kurasawa. The whole one-way conversation made him feel sick. Years of it. It was the first time that his patriotism, sense of duty, his honor was thrown back in his face. He was a soldier and no more. That was difficult to stomach. He'd led himself to believe he was above being someone's tool, but he'd been knocked back on his ass and couldn't mentally stand back up.

He couldn't believe that two nations could be tied together so closely and yet were so far apart in the perception of the masses. Corporations were, in fact, governments, and not the other way around. This was something Kaz did not appreciate discovering, after years of being sold a different construct. All the good people were nothing. The value, the voting, the rights. All of it was a laugh.

His entire meaning, life goals, and mission to help keep Japan sitting into a world power seat was now out of focus. There was no such thing. There were only a few massive men, making moves, or was that even a truth? Everything seemed so abstract. Could he even trust his own intuition anymore?

The old Japanese leader told him that Tarnit Systems was in bed with Wardlow. Citing proof, one third of all the finances required to build the space station, Aurelia, is coming directly from Tarnit's holding company. This was enough money to buy the Pyramid of Giza from the Egyptian Government.

There were moments of emptiness, then a black room. His head hurt. He felt the sting from a tattoo gun riding along his back, fought the sensation, then …

Kaz saw himself at the table with the sons of Pharaohs, bargaining. It was a scrap of the golden pyramid that once sat atop of Giza. Men with no face pushed their way to the front of the room, yelling.

He was sweating profusely, throwing his arms up in the air, protesting to be heard in a large adobe-shaped space. It was an amphitheater of insanity. His voice was projecting around the room, bouncing off the white clay walls, unheard by the herds of locals draped in cloth and screaming in a native tongue.

Then, Kaz woke. Kurasawa was standing over him, taking turns slapping Kaz in the face with his left and right hands, taking each blow and looking up to his superior, accepting the punishment, his head jerking from side to side each time his master's hand connected.

Kaz thought of Vietnam and the American troops, the Israelis with their teens carrying around M16s, and then Japan's youth - all the indoctrination. He wanted to be beaten back into submission until he no longer could discern which hand was right and which was wrong. Was it Wardlow, or was it Tarnit who deserved the support necessary to become the most powerful entity in the world, with the capability of replacing world leaders with artificial puppets controlled by a small company whose ownership fell into the hands of a small fraternity of sociopaths? He needed clarification and knew he'd never get it, and so the beating went on.

Kurasawa grit his teeth and thrust his closed fist into Kaz's face. Body fluids released. His face was bleeding. The pain was growing. Somewhere in that feeling, he was hoping there'd be some kind of resolution. Even if it was a game, like Kutter's crosswords, he'd be given a clue. *Just give me a fucking clue.*

The old Japanese man smiled, jerked his arm back, and swung a blistering right hook that hit Kaz's face with the force of a sledgehammer, sending the agent to the ground.

It took over ten seconds for Kaz to find his knees, then another ten to adjust his focus.

The old man was gone.

A medical technician entered Level 6 and marched down the hallway to the room Kaz was being held in. The door swung open. Kaz turned to the light in the hallway, only capturing the silhouette of the technician as she administered another injection in his right arm.

Kaz faded.

There was a cacophony of voices in murmur.

The noise grew into a mob of angry Japanese. These weren't strangers. They were people from his village, the face of Kurasawa's recruiters in wide angle. Odd perspectives of the men in black with full body tattoos. The men who came to pull him from his ordinary life. The no-named organization who trained him.

Flashes came from stages in his rise to work for Tarnit Systems. The flag. The pride. The men all lined up in traditional uniforms. The training camp hidden inside an old temple, isolated. The building of the island fortress. The ocean. His new friends, or were they trying to warn him?

Kurasawa standing in front of them. All of them in formation. Chanting obedience. Then Kutter.

First, Kurasawa punched him in the face, then Kutter.

The tearing down of the individual. The building of a soldier.

Kaz had let go. Completely. He had no choice, but the drug was wearing thin, faster, this time. He knew he was being watched, so he fell to the floor and curled into a ball, rocking, counting, and breathing. The agent was beginning to pace his lung contractions and control his thoughts to work against the black pharmacology.

He felt a wave of pins and needles flow over the very edge of his dermal layer, impossible to push off. He felt a subtle snapping sensation in the back of his spine, a tingle underneath the thick bone at the back of his skull, a pulse of energy.

Kaz puked up everything until there was nothing left but a small amount of blood dripping from his mouth.

He lay unconscious until the Level 6 team entered. The security at the door. The technician with another needle. The assistant tapping his shoulder, prodding, looking for a reaction. Had they gone too far?

Kaz rolled to his right and swung his left foot around, sweeping the assistant off his feet. He finished the man by forcing his head into the tile floor. Crack! He was out cold.

The technician moved with a jab of the needle. Kaz caught his wrist with his left hand, twisting until it snapped, which allowed him to roll up to his knees and jam the end of the hypodermic into the security guard who was an inch from bashing his head with a baton.

The three men were down.

Within a minute, there were ten people searching Level 6. The monitors, the elevators, every inch of the facility …

Kaz was nowhere to be found.

37

Message in a Bottle

Jimmy Swillow stepped into Red's Surplus Store off of Main Street. He fitted himself in a late 60s army green jacket and a pair of romper-stomper boots. The entire time, Red was listening to Jimmy bitch about STEMs, especially about his experience at Vito's Deli and about the strange government men and whatever the hell they were doing.

"These sick mind-suck puppet masters and these weak-ass public officials. It's so simple. You dangle a few bucks in front of this bunch o' zeros and they'll do anything for you. The mayor, especially. Fuck Bill Caldwell and all his cronies, that brainless pinhead. He stands in front of a television camera, in front of the whole town, the world and swears up and down that 'it's all for you', 'for our greater good', 'this cancer is the best thing for this town' with a firm head shake and all the right hand movements and inflection and all that mind fuck shit they do. And all with that, a 'I just fucked you over' grin. No way!"

At the counter, Swillow picked out a nine-inch survival knife and yellow safety glasses. By the time the Irish kid left the store, he looked like an updated, more pissed-off version of De Niro in *Taxi Driver* but who ended up with a fifteen percent discount because Red couldn't stand the "plastic people" either. He hated the androids with a passion, and said so, leaving his compatriot with a tip.

"There's a video online that shows you how to kill a Plastic. Just search, 'How to Kill a Plastic.' You'll find it, man. And that discount is permanent. Anything you need. You come see me. I live upstairs. The shop is open to you twenty-four seven, bro. Don't forget the video!"

Jimmy raised his phone in the air as he walked away.

"Bet on it, brother." Nodding. "You can bet on it."

The anger had been growing inside of Jimmy like some B-movie, hyper-mutating zombie virus.

The HLM activists were assembling out front of Vito's after KCLT reported on the blurry, anonymous picture Jimmy sent over, with Vito getting tossed into the Mercedes van. Somehow, it slipped through editorial. They thought it was vague and kitschy enough to fall through the cracks, that the cartoonish image would increase viewership.

This was a tremendous help to the young Swillow's pride. He'd been taken seriously by an upstanding person in the community. Rebecca replied to his anonymous message. She asked him to remain vigilant, to keep an eye wide open and to send her anything else he had heard or witnessed. She promised she had a story brewing, but needed more information. The email address was one of those free setups, and she knew it, but Rebecca hoped for more.

Jimmy would never access the account again. He knew he'd be targeted if he did. The young Irish kid was a lot smarter than anyone had ever given him credit for, and even though he'd been involved in some questionable Swillow affairs, he felt like a good person. Morally, Jimmy had put some heartfelt thought into who he was and what he'd done over the years. He was ready to re-establish himself and the Swillow name.

Rebecca's article detailing Claypool's death was never printed in the newspaper. The editorial staff was given the option of being replaced if they went forward with the story. The newspaper's owners, the men upstairs … their argument was rooted in legal verbiage. They were right and wrong, though. Rebecca couldn't publish an article that appeared to aim a weapon at any corporation or government agency without cold hard facts backing up the claims, or they'd get squashed. And even though she didn't make such claims, the men upstairs (the board members of the holding company that owned almost every newspaper in the United States, who were collectively known as 'the word of God') made it clear that her article did assert the claim without overtly saying it - and they always won the argument.

Woodward and Bernstein were dead.

But what the men upstairs didn't count on was the small community beach rag "The High Tide" - the six page weekly that barely kept itself in circulation, whose anonymous donor Clarence Clancy (yes - the eccentric who owned the Chimera Theater) was its secret life force.

The High Tide published Rebecca's story on the Claypool murder across its front page, with supportive information that had trickled out of Langley from an anonymous source at the FBI. It was titled, "CHIMERA BEACH UNDER ATTACK." A headline that didn't go unnoticed.

Sloan was the leak. He was pissed and was doing a bit of research on his own. McGlinty had provided damning, detailed information on the strange activities in Chimera. His reports were rattling a few of the power elite who still weren't sure which side of the line they stood. Was it Wardlow, or Tarnit Systems? The FBI veteran was given the green light to look into the Chimera situation.

Wardlow had hoped to keep a lid on Project Avalanche, but the whole thing had grown larger than the Hoover Damn, and the small cracks were beginning to leak.

Chimera Beach was becoming a location on the political map. The people were beginning to feel it. Jimmy knew it was time. He was ready. And the visual he brought with him in his new outfit was alarming in contrast to the usual beachwear.

Eva was walking down the sidewalk on the opposite side of the street, engaging in conversation with Sarah and Jason Henderson, who'd just spent their life savings setting up a trendy tourist stop-off with an old donut recipe of their grandparents. Sarah was tired of Eva hanging around outside her shop. She knew the android was there because of the line that formed each day around 11a.m.

"If I catch you out here again, I'm gonna pull your plug. Just 'cause my patrons have to wait for one of my granny's donuts doesn't mean they have to talk to you."

Before Sarah could get out another word and before Eva could process what was happening, the tourists began to wonder what had just transpired, as their beloved donut queen expressed her dissatisfaction with their non-confrontational, politically correct, liberated, female android, Eva.

No one had expected this kind of behavior, but the mob mentality rules went into effect. People either jumped onboard with Sarah or tried to argue otherwise, defending Eva as a harmless, simple-minded gag.

Jimmy saw the whole event unfold. He'd seen the entire confrontation in his mind as he was crossing the street, slipping the nine-inch knife from his waist. Swillow pulled a black bandana from his neckline to up over his mouth. He moved a few onlookers from his path and separated those close to Eva who were attempting to protect her from an angry couple defending Sarah.

Jimmy stabbed Eva with a series of jabs that were so fast, no one moved from their position in line until her mass of pseudo-lard hit the pavement. Jimmy's fast work was the result of the video he'd just watched, and he let everyone know about it.

"It's all online, people. Just check it out. These Plastics are everywhere, now.

Stop believing it's just a fun little toy and start seeing it for what it really is ... your fucking replacement."

Jimmy looked at the growing number of concerned eyes, then he knelt over, picked up Eva's miniature dog, and sliced its neck wide open.

38

Breaking News

The round table discussion at KCLT was focused on Clarence's Chimera Theater and how its new facade was an important facelift not only for the beachfront,
but for the entire city. It was a family-operated business that somehow managed to
pull itself from the graveyard - the one with all the big developers standing around,
waiting, with nothing but time and money, ready to pounce. The newsroom was
excited to get behind the press release Clarence had just sent out about "the magic
show to end all magic shows".

It was going to be an emotional slant, using Ryan as the focal point. The loss
of his mother, the drama of his father in a coma, then ending the story with the
proclamation that Ryan was going to bring his mother back from the ocean that
swallowed her up. Zar the Great was going to go down in history. He was going
to do it in front of a live audience. It was going to be the greatest feat in the annals
of magic. No one could resist.

Rebecca burst into the conference room and kicked everyone out. There was
no yelling. The meeting was over. The team was delegating. There was work to
do for everyone. She brushed off a few glances and dumped a pile of research on
the table.

She taped butcher paper to the walls and windows, then went to work from
a stack of notes, drying up five black markers before she had a map of Chimera's
latest events spread out in front of her.

The reporter, turned investigative journalist, set her phone on the conference
table and made a call to the number written across the top of one of her folders.
She tapped the speakerphone button and Kaz picked up. He spoke with a firm
tone.

"You've got questions—"

Rebecca was rushing her words.

"And I hope you have some answers. One. Victor Westbrook. Wardlow's top programmer—"

Kaz happened to be walking toward the Chimera Theater. He was looking up at the teams of workers doing light carpentry and painting.

"Vic's the best in the world at what he does. He's made AI so human, it's impossible to tell the difference. They call him a pioneer, but he's really a god."

"He's in a coma. His son, the one who pulled a disappearing act a few years back, Ryan, is in town to headline a magic show at the Chimera Theater."

Kaz was staring up at the marquee with Zar the Great laid out in bold, red movie letters. He wasn't going to discuss RyN2, and he'd keep pretending he was on the outside of all this, looking in.

"Vic's coma, the car accident … you're gonna draw a line to Tommy Swillow. He's got strong ties with the darker side of Chimera. I'm sure you're aware of him already. His crew made a move to leverage something from Carter, and screwed up. An attempted kidnapping that went bad. Vic's paying for that, and we have to get comfortable with the fact that we may never know now what was underneath it all."

"Know anything about Mark Boyle, aka Marky Boy, aka Five Fingers? He's Tommy Swillow's nephew. He's been granted an early release from prison."

"When's this?"

"He's out today. Officially, an hour ago."

"Where'd you get that from?"

"A reliable source. Would someone let him out? If so, why?"

"Not sure for what, but it's possible. I'll look into it."

"Okay. Vito Massulo's missing. He ran the famous deli on Main Street. There's a note on his door about going to a family reunion in New York, but I've already looked into it. It's bogus. He doesn't have any family there."

"That's why he was picked. He's gone. Draw a line to Wardlow."

"Gone? Okay. Is the Henry Claypool killing connected?"

"Yes. Claypool worked at—"

"Wardlow. Yes. I know."

"But you didn't know he was in charge of guarding the subterranean lab project where Avalanche is housed. A project that doesn't exist. You don't know about Carter's spooky partner and how they're quietly replacing key people in Chimera with AI. Vito was part of the project until something went wrong."

"Wow. More questions—"

"They'll have to wait. But I do know, Claypool must have seen something he wasn't supposed to see."

"And Victor created these?"

"He didn't know his tech was being used. Guys like that never do. They want to give to the world, not take from it. Wardlow compartmentalizes every aspect of its projects. No one knows what's going on except his inner circle."

Rebecca wanted to respond emotionally, but held back.

"And Vito is being replaced?"

"Already was. Something went wrong, there."

Rebecca sat for a moment, building a clearer picture of the disturbing reality, then her voice broke.

"This will get me killed. I can't print this. I can't even take this upstairs."

"Stay calm."

"How does one stay calm with this kind of monster out in front of them? I mean, this is massive. It's conspiracy on a level where anyone who even breathes about this disappears."

"Take the story. Shotgun it anonymously to a few three-letter agencies, a couple of the large newspapers, and let them battle it out. Someone will use it as a weapon. I assure you they will. You've got all the pieces. Be careful. Don't let it get back to you." Kaz changed his tone. "Rebecca, I gotta go now. I'll be in touch."

"Wait. There's a lot more here."

The line went dead.

Rebecca pulled the tape, rolled up all the paper, cleaned out the conference room, and left KCLT. She got in her car and exited the lot, heading in the opposite direction of her condo, and drove to the Shore Motel. She tucked herself into one of the small rooms at the end of the building and went to work. She made a quick phone call to her neighbor asking her to look in on her cat and to make sure to freely pass on, if anyone asked, that she was in Florida doing a half vacation, half work-related trip covering the mating habits of the southern crocodile. She needed time to think …

~

Sheriff McGlinty could see Jimmy from across the room. It was his yellow glasses and jittery demeanor that stood out. The second Swillow saw the Sheriff, he raised his right arm and yelled over the noise in the front office.

"I'm turning myself in, Bob."

Bowman, who was having an unpleasant moment with a sub sandwich that had replaced his usual Vito's, turned his head in disbelief. A *Swillow turning himself in? This punk must be high.*

Jimmy hurried over to the sheriff, who waved the young Irishman into his office and shut the door.

"I've gotta come clean." Jimmy said, animated and ready to start the process of getting past whatever punishment was in front of him. "It was an accident. I just meant to talk to him, but he moved, turning his body toward my van as I approached, and it happened. It was so quick, I had no time to react or steer away. That's when his body bounced off the front passenger side, and so I stopped and picked him up. He needed medical attention right away. There was no time to waste, so I dropped him off. Brain damage, man. I didn't want that. I was scared. That's why I didn't stay at the hospital."

"I agree. It doesn't look good does it?"

"I didn't say that. What do you mean? Why'd you say that?"

"A Swillow running over the most celebrated figure in the field of artificial intelligence. The man whose life's work is the reason these androids are out there walking around, and they're virtually undetectable. You have to be extremely discerning to detect this. It looks funny that the same guy who just hacked up Eva and her dog. We've got at least ten different independent video clips - people are still sending them in - of you doing your Texas Chainsaw Massacre bit in front of Elaine's Donuts and, no joking, they are good, but it's odd. You claim the Victor incident was an accident, when you publicly express hatred for what he's responsible for."

"I saw Vito being stuffed into a body bag, and it wasn't really Vito. You know what I'm saying. It was a *Plastic.* There was no blood. I'm not hallucinating - I need answers. I don't know about you, but I need to know what's going to happen to us, and when the entire city is behind this bullshit, someone has to step up. And it happens to be the Swillows standing up. I know it's hard to swallow, but we're trying to help out here. Are you backing this psycho Wardlow shit?"

"Jimmy."

"Yeah."

"I need you out there. We'll deal with the hit and run later. But, right now I'm more concerned with what's waiting out there. What's coming. You hear anything, you call me. You're working for me, now. But, you have to do me one favor."

"You're kidding. I'm not going to lockup? Shit, I'll do anything you say."

"Don't pull another Kill Bill. Call me first. Let's get it done the right way.

"What's the right way?"

"Without so many people and cameras. Quietly. I'm sure Tommy's spoken to you about this sort o' thing, no?"

"I can do that. But hey, you gotta admit—"

"Admit what?"

"You saw the footage?"

"Jimmy, don't make me chain you up. I will rewind, take away this gracious offer, and throw away the key of you can't—"

"I can. I will."

Jimmy walked right out of the sheriff's bureau.

~

Carter stood opposite Jack Kutter, calm. The sun broke through the mirrored exterior to Wardlow's executive floor. There was just enough inside light to see the men, and an equal amount to catch the reflection of the ocean, a cluster of clouds rolling in over the coastline and a few sporadic seagulls carving up the sky.

"Jack, we're moving too fast. Creating problems. We've got the mayor in place, and that's a big win. I don't care how fast your psychotic friends in the DOD want to move. Things don't operate that way. Unlimited budget or not. Remember, this is *the* test city. If we screw this up, I stand to lose trillions."

"What are you saying? Distill Carter. Distill."

"We've got time to implement and need to do it right, or we'll never get this done on a national level. And as far as the sheriff goes, he'll be so busy trying to figure out what's going on—"

"He's got an inkling, sir. A good one."

"I love that hefty crossword lexicon you have, 'inkling'."

"It suits the moment."

"The entire nation had an inkling about 9/11. You see how far they got selling that truth?"

"You've got a point."

"We're going to slow things down." Carter looked out toward the surf. "You know, a great white exerts almost no effort, expels almost no energy until it strikes. It moves along painfully slow, with the the power of the ocean in its jaws, waiting for the right moment."

Kutter liked the analogy, but wasn't satisfied.

"What about Vito's Deli? The guy was an institution. People are gonna be talking for a while about this."

"So, we fucked up. Call your guy in Seattle. Put a Starbucks in. I don't care. Be ready for the blowback."

"We're ready."

"I hope so."

"If we're going to slow down, that is. Let's clarify the priority here."

"Kaz. The Green Bank data. Victor. Something doesn't feel right. Tarnit's attempt to slow us down. We're always working for and against one another. It's tolerated. It keeps us robust. Information versus disinformation. We play the game. But there's something we're not seeing. Do we know where he is?"

"He could be halfway around the globe."

"But he's not, is he? He's right here. I can see it in your eyes."

~

Noelle stepped out on the patio to a clear night sky. She had a smile on her face because her guests had already spotted a series of shooting stars. It was the tail end of shower watch, according to the *Chimera Times*, with overcast skies forecast for the next ten hours, but they didn't see anything but a deep blue, sparkly night. While they were enjoying the occasional light show, the talk of the party was Ryan. There wasn't a single guest who didn't experience a sense of intrigue by the impossible claim Zar the Great had made. The front page article had done its job well.

Tommy was inside on the couch. He'd just set down his highball, arranging it perfectly on the starry night party napkin Noelle had bought for the occasion. In front of him was a charcuterie tray with some of his favorite cuts and assortment of cheeses. A bowl of fresh cut vegetables and a creamy dip he couldn't identify sat next to it. Tommy had lost count of how many slices of meat he'd rolled up and shoved into his mouth, but Noelle had been keeping track. It was her look through the window that told him it was time for a veggie stick.

The living room was packed. There were a few couples from the building - the ones Noelle had a desire to impress - but mostly the guests were, in some way, an extension of the Swillow organization.

Tommy smiled and picked up a carrot stick. He plunged it into the mystery dip and threw it into his mouth with his hand about a foot away. Tommy grimaced. Noelle threw him back a scolding look, *how dare you.* The two were having fun trading non-verbals, taking jabs at one another until Noelle's expression turned. She was pointing past Tommy at something.

No one could hear Tommy yell …

He'd taken Jimmy through the emergency access door to the roof, giving the boy his ugliest face and drawing as much information as he could, along the way.

"You what?"

"I told you I'd figure this out."

Tommy felt like dangling his own son over the edge of the roof.

"You told McGlinty it was an accident, and he let you walk? Do you know who's sitting in the smoking room watching television right now?"

"Who?"

Tommy was deep in thought.

"First Marky Boy gets cut loose, and now you."

"Fingers is downstairs?"

"We're under surveillance. *The fuckin' Feds.* They've gotta be halfway to making a case if they let him go."

"Whatta we do?"

Jimmy followed Tommy into the smoking room. They closed the sliding doors behind them. Marky Boy stood. He was fit, about 165 pounds of lean Irish DNA, with a shaved head. Both his arms were tattooed. Marky's smile started a chain reaction of celebration. The champagne was corked. The hugs. The family was back together. Tommy had put the pieces together . At least, he felt like he had a grip.

"We're in the driver's seat now. They want the paintings. It's the only thing that makes sense. The FBI wants to solve the museum case. The insurance on that is worth a fortune alone. And so the question is, how do we move from here?"

Marky Boy took a sip of champagne. He knew from Tommy's expression and inflection that this wasn't a question he was meant to answer.

"What are you thinking?"

Tommy raised his glass. The bubbles were rushing to the surface.

"We're gonna lead 'em right to Wardlow."

The Tank emptied his flute in one gulp. From the look on Marky and Jimmy's faces, they had no idea what he meant, but by the time Noelle came knocking, the Swillow gang was up to date and in sync. They were going to steer clear of fencing the art and focus on their legitimate businesses, with one exception. They wanted a chunk of the ticket sales from the Chimera Theater magic show. Zar the Great was going to get shaken down.

When Jimmy opened the doors, Noelle handed Tommy a thin slice of salami with a shard of Manchego cheese and a cornichon.

"What's this? I thought I was banned from nitrates."

Noelle turned, pointing into the living room. Mia was standing next to RyN2, engaged in conversation with the downstairs neighbors.

"Your daughter's here, babe. With someone special. Come say hello."

Noelle knew who Ryan was from the picture on the front page of the *Times*, and so did the entire party, after the buzz flew around the room. Mia had the celebrity of Chimera Cove on her arm.

"How wonderful is this?" said Tammy Halloran with a big smile as she approached Mia. "Do you remember me, young lady?"

Mia laughed.

"How could I forget? You called my dad on me when I was thirteen. You saw me slip that caramel in my pocket at Jerry's Market. You squealed on me. Funny thing though, I always wondered why. Because you should have never noticed. What I mean is, it would've been impossible had you not been a thief yourself. My move was so quick, so concealed, you'd have to be a pro to spot me."

There were a lot of laughs from the Swillow clan.

Tommy picked up the newspaper from the table, walked over to RyN2 and kissed Mia on the cheek. He held up the front page, comparing the photo of Ryan with the android in front of him.

"Zar the Great. A magician in my house. I'm Mia's father, Tommy." RyN2 reached out, offering his hand and accessing his algorithmic intuition, and applied a firm grip that Tommy was not expecting. "Nice grip, kid." Then he turned to Marky. "He's gonna bring back his mother from the dead."

Noelle felt he was being insensitive.

"Tommy."

RyN2 touched Noelle's shoulder.

"It's not an issue. That's exactly what I'm going to do. It's a simple truth. It's like if I said, Marky just got out of prison—"

Mia grabbed RyN2's arm and steered them out to the patio, leaving a wave of curiosity in the living room. A group of wily Swillow clansmen, who were the usual suspects down at Coonan's when the singing began late in the evening, grabbed the party's attention. Pete was the one who always started shit at the bar, and so it made sense he spoke first.

"Why don't you show us something? Right here. Right now. Do a little trick for us. Let's see what Zar the Great is made of! Or are you a fake?"

Pete's friends couldn't help themselves.

"I bet he's a fake. That shit is all smoke and mirrors."

"Yeah. Let's see somethin', or do you need time to set up all the gags and other shit?"

"Tell you what. I've got a crisp hundred dollar bill. I bet you can't turn it into a thousand. Even a street magician could do that."

Mia tried to convince RyN2. "They're vultures. They have fun at everyone else's expense all the time. You don't have to deal with them at all. Just—"

RyN2 had that calculating look that he was showing off the more he adapted to social situations, or what he would call non-linear processes.

"Don't you trust me?"

Mia was allowing herself to go with it. She shook her head, laughing, knowing the Coonan's boys would get more than they bargained for. "I totally trust you." Then Mia thought about what she'd said. "Shit, did I just say that?"

RyN2 was already walking toward Pete and his friends when he responded. "Let me do this."

The android squared off with Pete, broadcasting the look from someone who was holding the key to jump time. Pete knew something screwy was about to happen. He'd never seen anyone throw such confidence his way.

RyN2 looked around the room. By the time his eyes got back to Pete, he'd figured out the entire stunt.

"Okay, let's have some fun."

RyN2 pointed to a woman named Charlene.

"Charlene. I want you to remember the numbers three, two, four, and seven."

She turned to her friend. "How'd he know my name?" Then, after a firm look from RyN2, she acknowledged him. "I've got it. Three, two, four and seven." Then, soft and inquisitive, "How'd you know my name?"

RyN2 looked beyond Charlene to a young attorney who was dressed down and wearing a Boston Red Sox hat.

"You, behind the lovely lady there. Joe, the lawyer who works for Aberdeen, Finley & Smith. I want you to remember the number thirty-eight."

Joe was already surprised.

"How'd you know what firm I was at? Or that I was an attorney?"

"Just remember thirty-eight. See it. Think it. Live it. Thirty-eight."

"Okay. Thirty-eight."

RyN2 turned to the bulky guy in his mid forties standing next to Pete, who looked like a boxer, fit in athletic gear.

"Golden gloves, Teddy. Sixteen knockouts at sixteen. Epic. Now you're a trainer at The Ring Club." Teddy gave each of his friends a funny look, like, I bet this is gonna suck. Then he glared back at RyN2. "I need you to remember the numbers five, four, one, seven, seven, seven, five, five, four, five."

Teddy had a funny look on his face because he vaguely remembered the number from somewhere, or at least he thought he did. It was a telephone number, he knew that much. A quick search of his phone turned up nothing, though.

RyN2 waited for the room to quiet.

"Okay. Has everyone remembered their numbers?" Charlene, Joe and Teddy confirmed, each with a nod of their heads. RyN2 began. "What's happened is that I've read your minds. I've looked into the future and literally read your minds, and I'm going to show you right now what I've done. I want you all to pay attention." He focused on Charlene. "I want you to open your photo app on your phone and scroll to last month's album. Then tap on the tenth photo, starting from the top. When you get to the tenth photo, I want you to show the people around you, then read me the address on the house behind you in that picture."

Charlene pulled her phone from her purse and did exactly what RyN2 asked. She opened her app and accessed the correct album, scrolled to the tenth photo, and showed her friends. There were some expressions of surprise coming from the group.

RyN2 spoke a little louder.

"Can you please read to us the address on the house behind you, that you and your friend Jessica randomly took a picture in front of."

Charlene read the numbers slowly,

"Three, two, four, seven. Exactly what you said. Wait, how did you do that?"

"Have we ever met before?"

"No. Never."

"Have we talked at all prior to this moment? Planned or plotted any of this together?"

"No. I had no idea who you were until I saw the front page of the *Times* today."

RyN2 turned to Joe.

"Let's have the lawyer do something a bit different. Joe, open up your encrypted mobile banking app and read to me the total cost of your lunch from yesterday … the one you ate at Sammy's."

Joe smiled.

"I don't have to open up the app. I remember clearly it was thirty-eight dollars. I remember because I thought it was odd, being an even number."

Pete raised his voice to cut through.

"Let's see it. Open the app."

Joe launched his app. He walked over to Pete and showed him the charge. Satisfied, he raised Joe's phone and displayed the screen to those close to him. Joe decided to add to the moment.

"And I don't know him, either. Never met him, nor have we ever spoken before now, and I'll sign an affidavit if I have to." He smiled and raised his glass.

RyN2 held his poker face and turned to Teddy.

"Now, Teddy. For you, we're going to really push the boundaries here. In five seconds, you're going to receive a text. Ready? Five … four … three … two … one …" Teddy's phone chimed. He opened up the text app. There was a notification from a young woman named Rachel whom he'd met at the gym earlier, who he'd offered his number to. She was texting him her number in return, after having proper time to do a full background check online. "Read it to us, if you please."

"*Five, four, one, seven, seven, seven, five, five, four, five. Let's connect.* Son of a bitch! How'd you do that?"

RyN2 smiled, then took a short bow.

"I hope to see everyone at the show. It's going to be truly incredible. Thank you for playing along. Really, this has been really fun."

Mia saw Tommy coming for RyN2. She knew right away that her father was going to proposition the android, and she wanted to pull a magic trick of her own right now and disappear. She knew Tommy would have a hundred ideas on how he could get richer.

She tugged on RyN2's arm, but not in time. Tommy was already in front of them.

"Mia. Why don't you bring your friend over for dinner tomorrow. I wanna hear about you two, and there's business to discuss."

RyN2 cast an empty look while he finished scanning Dale Carnegie's *How To Win Friends and Influence People* before returning a pleasant expression.

"I saw the picture of Kennedy on the wall over there. That must have been hard when he was assassinated. All the potential—"

"Crushed the nation. Not just our people. Your generation wouldn't know what it was like."

"We'll try to make it, Tommy. Thanks for the invitation. We're really busy preparing for the show. There's still a lot to do. But, I'll do my best."

Tommy didn't fall for the Carnegie maneuver. He placed his hand on the android's shoulder and squeezed.

"Come by anyway."

Jimmy had no idea what to say. The guests were stunned. Noelle was the happiest woman in Chimera. The buzz in the room ramped up the second Mia shut the door behind them. They could hear the champagne corks popping in the hallway.

39

Make Over

Ryan's appearance in Chimera affected a lot of people, but none more than Mel. She didn't like the thoughts that were rolling around in her head, nor the feeling she had in her stomach.

He warned me he was going to pull some kind of stunt, but why not clue me in? He knew I cared for him. Why did he screw with me like that? I know there's something bigger. I'm not selfish. I was there for him, and ready to go the distance. Shit. Maybe he wasn't, though? And his mother and father? Wow. This isn't easy. I just wish ... I just wish I didn't wish!

It was a teeter-totter of thoughts that got tiresome fast.

She'd come all the way to this coastal town to find Ryan after the fishbowl video, and she found herself at the end of the search. The front page article was all she needed to know Ryan was alive, and with a little digging, she'd find Victor's beach house. There was no turning back.

Mel didn't think about what she was going to wear when she confronted Ryan until she rolled off the couch in Danny's trailer and saw her old trucker hat with that embroidered patch that read, "Don't Mess".

She didn't have to wear it anymore. She wouldn't wear it. There was a whole new level of *Nobody's Gonna Fuck With Me* going on at the salon that morning.

It was St. Patrick's Day and it was time to go green and have a drink hours earlier than usual. Mel's hair had grown quite a bit, and with a simple makeover, she looked like an entirely different woman. She went from small town gas pumper to ball crusher in a couple hours. When Joanna, her stylist, pulled off the apron, the others in the salon chairs who were getting a clip and color were wondering why they hadn't gone green, too. But it had nothing to do with the color and instead, had everything to do with what Mel had never let out.

~

Ryan rolled off his bed and looked over at his top hat. There wasn't any more thought going into wearing the battle-worn accessory than in his morning piss. As he came down the stairs, he glanced over at Eddie and revisited Mia's video from memory.

He sauntered over to the front door and opened it. He was looking out to see if Mia was coming. This is how screwed-up his thinking was after sleeping on that video. *Maybe she'll come back. She'll walk up while I'm scrubby and half awake. She'll see me and fall in love with me, instead of that thing calling itself me.*

As Ryan leaned over to grab the paper (the waste of newsprint he never looked at beyond a front page glance before he tossed it in the garbage can), he thought, *Today's the day I go out and find this plastic version of me, and I'm gonna—*

Underneath today's paper was yesterday's.

Ryan instantly flushed. An ice cold sensation shot through his body. It was the stone he stood on that initially triggered his nerves. The shock was over, and he was pouring through the entire article. His back ached from standing firm without so much as moving a muscle until he finished reading. When he lifted his head, a bullet from his past shot directly through his heart, sending him back a step.

Rolling back time, Mel was a perfect match for Ryan in Smuggler's Cove, but the way she was standing in front of him, now, signified that a new world was shaping up that he hadn't seen coming.

Mel scanned Ryan from head to toe. She wasn't angry or elated, just matter of fact.

"So, who goes first?"

Ryan was at a loss. It wasn't just her look - the ends of her hair a deep green, and her fitted denim, or the juxtaposition of her red roots which the stylist had left to accentuate the dye job, with the sun surrounding her in a golden aura. Mel was stunning.

"I'm gonna need an assistant. You down?"

"That's how you start this off?"

"Just picking up where we left off."

"Me picking up your top hat on the beach while the search and rescue covered the entire area. I waited for you for a month. I watched the tide roll in and out for hours every day after work. I wondered. You could have just sent me a text. Anything. I'm not pissed. I'm just saying."

"I was sick. That's no excuse. But I didn't think I was depressed. I thought it was all a pile of bullshit. The doctors. The fucking pills. But it got to me, and I crawled into a hole and died. I'm better now. Nothing will cure depression more than the reality of how little time we have. It's good to see you. I apologize for putting you through that."

"You did warn me, so it's not like you completely blew me off. I just … ah … it's not worth looking back, is it? There's a lot of pain there. Can we just look ahead?"

"Sure." Ryan held up the paper. "I had no idea I was putting on a show."

"I don't understand."

"I don't know anything about this."

"Whatta you mean? That's not you in the picture?"

"That's not me in the picture. I've never been to the Chimera Theater."

~

Ryan and Mel were on the rooftop patio, looking out over the ocean. It brought back memories of the cove, the pier, the performance, and Ryan's head injury. Mel reached out and pulled the top hat from his head. She moved her fingers through his hair until she found the scar where his head had been cut open and bleeding from the safe, then placed the hat back on him.

"Just making sure you're not one of them."

"Are people really that tripped out about the robots?"

"Being actual people, yes? There's this whole organization, Human Lives Matter. And some guy attacked Eva and her dog. She was a test robot they let walk around town and interact with everyone. It was weird. He pulled a huge knife out right in the street in front of a bunch of tourists. Just search 'Chimera Man Kills Robot'. There are a hundred videos of him hacking them up into pieces. People really freaked when he slit the dog's throat. Even though they're fake, some people reacted like they were real. Some didn't, though. It could have been all staged just to see how people would handle it. I don't know, but the whole thing is creepy."

"My dad makes those robots. The really advanced AI. There's some computer equipment in my bedroom and other stuff that lead me to believe he created the likeness of me, and this is what's in the paper. But he's in a coma right now, so—"

"I heard about what happened. That's so wrong."

"Seems life doesn't have any feelings either way about right or wrong. Shit just happens or it doesn't."

"Agreed. Look at us. Shit happened, but we're still here, though."

Mel hugged Ryan. For the first time, he felt like he could hug someone back. He'd had these moments with Claire, but he never really felt he could reciprocate. There was always a mental block. He wrapped his arms around her and squeezed tight for a second before letting go.

"For some reason, I feel like I should call you, Melanie."

"For some reason?"

"You don't look like Mel anymore. No disrespect."

"None taken. Is Melanie your assistant?"

"Absolutely."

"Does Melanie have any other duties … other than an assistant? Or is she just—"

"Right now, I don't even look like I should be standing next to you. Maybe you can help get me in character so I look like I can pull this off. I'm not sure how I'm gonna raise my mother from the ocean depths, but according to the *Times*, I've got to do it."

"Then, we go to the theater?"

40

Godzilla vs Godzilla AI

The Chimera Theater was surrounded by locals representing almost every age group and race. The workers were grabbing snacks and assorted beverages from a group of young skater kids who put up a makeshift stand in a small section of the parking lot that wasn't being resurfaced yet. The Coonan's runts were selling places on their own first come, first serve ticket list (unauthorized, of course), cruising the area on bicycles and approaching anyone who turned their head toward the theater. A fresh new face for KCLT, an Iranian-American woman, Sabina, was covering the exterior remodel, filming as the plywood was being removed and the original clapboard siding was being attacked with sanders and a coat of wood sealer as they prepped for the new paint job.

Retired seniors who had remembered Clarence from years earlier were stopping by to offer a hand. Jimmy showed up with a van filled with carpet samples, patterns the Swillow enterprise installed in East Coast casinos. They thought the style would look fantastic in the lobby, and they weren't wrong.

Carlos was still working as a temp with the construction team tasked with breathing new life into the old marquee. They were testing the lights when Kaz walked up to the entrance. There was so much activity, no one stopped him from entering.

Zar was on the main stage with a team of engineers finishing the build on the time jump apparatus. Expert welders were fabricating the last series of small conductive fittings that were going to be plated with xurbium. Once they were finished, they'd be welded to a large o-shaped ring of titanium suspended by titanium jacks, already sitting on the back of the stage. The entire unit looked like a beautifully designed "O". The lower part of the ring was only five inches off the stage floor, allowing a person the ability to step back and forth freely, from one side to the other.

Zar turned from his team when he noticed Kaz walking down the aisle. *Who was in charge of watching the front door?*

"What are you doing in here? Why is no one at the front door?"

Clarence jumped up from his seat. Unable to sleep through the night from all the excitement, he'd been taking a short nap.

"I apologize. I slipped. Let me get someone there right now."

Kaz passed Clarence as the old man made his way toward the lobby. Zar was standing on the edge of the stage, already a towering individual. From Kaz's viewpoint, he looked like the comic book hero he was, but this time it was the cover design for the latest series in Zar the Great's storyline. The mammoth-looking android reached out his hand and pulled Kaz up on the stage as if he'd suddenly changed his mind, and this foreigner wasn't even remotely a threat, but an old friend.

"Who are you?"

"I work for Tarnit. A private multi-phase aeronautics company. We trapped your transmissions and decoded the messages. The company is made up of scientists, engineers, and experts. In general, the people of Japan are thrilled I could be here to meet you. Secretly, that is. How is it you're even building this, yet?"

"From memory. But I'm missing some technical data which, of course, is now a moot issue. Do you have the encryption keys?"

"And all the transmissions on a secure server. Would you like to access them now?"

"Yes."

Zar raised the attention of his coordinator.

"Let's clear everyone out for an hour. Take lunch, and we'll reconvene at 1400."

The second the main stage was clear, Clarence showed up.

"What's going on?"

"No one's allowed in until 1400. I'm making some adjustments to the plans. I don't want anyone here. I have to make some detailed calculations. Do you mind?"

Clarence shook his head. "Absolutely not. I'll be in the lobby making sure you are not disturbed."

Kaz pulled out his mobile phone and read off an IP address for Zar. "117.102.197.136 …" He continued with a series of numbers that routed Zar's data connection to the Tarnit System's encrypted servers. Zar was completely focused, downloading all the transmissions. The second he was finished, he looked at Kaz.

"Is there a catch?"

"What?"

"All the files are here, but they're still scrambled. Why isn't my key working?"

"We altered it, on the chance we were facing some sort of danger. Are we?"

"I'm going to put this family back together. Victor's wishes ... my mission ... directive ... my only reason for being."

"You've sent yourself the plans you borrowed from Wardlow. There are several pieces missing, though."

"Of course."

"I'll give you the key for the missing data. Tarnit wishes to assist you fully but, as a gesture of reciprocation, wishes to—"

"Have the ability to jump around in time, securing a foothold forever at the top of the food chain."

"No. To ensure people like Carter don't gain the technology and expertise and destroy the planet. Someone has to be a watchdog, and we have shown we are capable of restraint."

"I can crack this without your key."

"Yes. But it might be too late. Carter's got the transmissions, as well. Granted, his team isn't nearly as advanced as ours. But we're not interested in finding out if we're wrong. We don't take unnecessary risks."

"Provide the keys and I'll make the most serious consideration. It's the best I can offer."

Kaz pulled a sat phone out and made a call. Kurasawa was on the other end. There was a short conversation before the phone was put away.

Kaz looked at Zar with a cold expression. He lifted his shirt, stripping it off entirely, and dropped it to the floor. He turned his back to Zar and told him to focus on the dragon scales.

Zar was lost in the tattoo.

"I'm fascinated. Truly. How you used art to hide the encryption keys is wonderful. I've seen some incredible coincidences and patterns in nature, the fractals. This is some sort of variation on the Fibonacci sequence. Nice work."

"We've been doing this for years at Tarnit, and it's also part of our culture. And one reason we don't trust Carter and the Americans. They've stripped art almost entirely from mainstream, turned it into an ocean of meaningless and deceptive content, instead."

"What did Kurasawa say?"

"To show you who we are. To do what you asked." Kaz waited for some kind of acknowledgment. When he only got an empty look, he said, "You know what Carter's doing?"

"I've seen the future. And I'll be watching you. I've placed the missing data in a camouflaged packet and left it on your servers. Your people will recognize it, but won't have access until I'm ready to leave. Tell them to pull it offline. Don't give anyone the opportunity."

Kaz made a second call. Within seconds, Tarnit cut their server nodes to the world wide web, securing the missing data from the transmissions Zar had sent from the Space Station Aurelia.

Kaz received a text. It was Zar. They were linked, and could communicate from anywhere, now. He confirmed the connection and exited out the back door, putting his shirt back on. As he stepped away from the building, one of the Coonan's runts, who was cycling past, brushed his shoulder, turned, and stopped quickly.

"Hey, man. You wanna reserve a front row seat to the show, or what?"

~

Ryan the android and Mia dropped by the theater to pick up the conductor fittings that needed to be taken to the plating company. This is where the xurbium would be added to the outer layer of the titanium. It would be smelted and then processed for plating. Thankfully, titanium required special equipment and a much higher temperature to melt than the xurbium did, which was going to make the process fairly simple from this stage forward. The xurbium would be easily plated to the titanium without damaging or affecting the structure in any adverse way.

RyN2 entered through the back door with Mia. This entrance led right onto the back stage area behind one of the curtains. The android slipped through an opening in the sheers, then jumped through the titanium "O" with a smile on his face. Mia trailed behind. She was curious, looking up at the large ring and admiring the craftsmanship.

"So, is Claire going to come walking through this and onto the stage during the show? Is this where the illusion takes place?"

The android played the role of magician.

"Illusion? No illusion, only the real thing. Magic will happen here on the night of the show." He winked. "I'd love to tell you more about it, but I don't want to spoil all the fun."

Mia played back, "Right. But aren't you going to want me to assist?"

Zar had the two specialists who were working on the apparatus pack up the fittings for Ryan. As he finished instructing the men, he formed a vision for the show which he hadn't previously thought about.

"We actually could use your help. It will add a touch more authenticity. We're going for a vintage look and feel. The heart of the design stems from the very first Zar comic book cover. We begin there, and play off of that." Zar snapped his fingers, grabbing the attention of his stage director. "Turn on the projection." The old cover image covered a large sheer curtain dropped along the back of the stage. Zar had his right arm raised. He was holding the metrome. The device was glowing, beaming out a field of energy. Zar was the master illusionist. This was his coming out.

The old wizard turned to Mia. "Let's see what you can do. Try an opener—"

Mia was inspired. She stepped into the center of the stage.

"Ladies and gentlemen. What you are about to witness, will no doubt be talked about for centuries. Time is one of the greatest mysteries. It's the beginning. It's the end. Yet, as for time itself, it is everlasting. Zar the Great has broken through this conundrum of time and found a way to connect to the everlasting. He has found a way to move through it like you and I move from place to place in the here and now." She turned to Zar, then RyN2. "And so, it's time. Ladies and gentlemen, it is time. Without further ado … to give you … Zar the Great."

There was the sound of one of the seats in the audience folding up, then someone standing. Those on stage could hear the sound of the grit between a pair of boots and a grimy old floor that hadn't been re-polished yet. Zar, RyN2, and Mia looked out over the empty seats. There was Ryan Westbrook. Black. Silhouetted. He was wearing the a long trench coat with his top hat. It had been altered and given a new life. Mel remained seated. She kicked up her feet as he spoke.

"Will the real Ryan, please stand up?"

Carlos pushed through the double doors leading into the aisle.

"Yo!" Ryan was on a trajectory, ready to face off with his doppelgänger when Carlos ran up to him. "You gotta tell me what's going on, man. I've been watching this thing—" He was looking over at RyN2. "I'm not sure what it is, but I've been holding back for a while now, wondering what the hell? I just wanna know. Are you Ryan or not?"

"It's me, Carlos." He shook his hand with the custom grip they'd created back in school, then threw the hand sign. Carlos' face lit up. "How the hell did you get here?"

"Work, bro. I blew off school and started working for this temp agency that hooked me up with decent-paying jobs. I've been hopping along the coast, one gig after the other, and ended up here. After you died … urrrh, disappeared … life had a new meaning. You were this lightning bolt, a wakeup call. I just wanted to get out and live. Make my own way, and dude, here I am."

Ryan juggled a thousand thoughts.

"This is so strange. I feel so alive, but confused as all hell. I had no idea—"

RyN2 and Zar were in the aisle standing directly behind the real Ryan. The android was about to reach out and touch his better half when Mel stood up and locked eyes with Mia.

"So, what are you a Plastic, too?"

The Swillow girl snapped back.

"This," she ran her hand along her body, like a game show model presenting an appliance, "is a hundred percent real."

RyN2 cut in.

"Actually, more like ninety-two percent." He pointed to her prosthetic arm.

Mia rolled her eyes.

They all got the joke, but there was too much tension building. Zar knew it was time to do something about it, at least before Mia and Mel dug themselves in deeper.

"From nothing to everything." Everyone turned away from their thoughts at Zar's announcement. "We're here because of your father. Because of Victor. The man of the millennia. A man who understood that time is the ultimate question facing man." His words silenced everyone. "When you disappeared, Victor … with nothing … no one … decided he was going to devote what was left of his life to bring the family back together, to have everything again. From nothing, to everything. I'm several iterations more advanced than … Mia calls him 2.0. We're almost there, and I'm here to ensure this mission is completed."

Carlos sat down. He was exhausted from trying to make sense of Zar's speech.

"Dude. You're saying this thing works?" He was pointing to the giant "O" on the back of the stage.

Ryan threw Zar a look, demanding he continue. Zar opened his arms, gesturing to them all.

"We still have a lot of work to do if we're going to pull this off."

Obviously, neither of the AI had ever factored in that Ryan would be present. The situation called for a reassessment. The androids were separately coming up with a list of options to ponder. Some of which had uncomfortable outcomes.

RyN2 jumped to a conclusion, "We don't need him."

Ryan faced off with his doppelgänger. "I could see that coming from a mile away. You're the weak one. The inferior always feel threatened. Are you building up a resentment toward me already, and can't help but want to destroy what's stronger, more talented, more relevant?"

He was about to let go a torrent of slurs, then remembered his father, lying in the hospital bed. He ran through a long list of his own possibilities, some of which were red flags, warnings of extreme danger, if these androids were too primitive in their evolutionary stage. He understood the limitations of the AI, enough to know that if RyN2 was programmed anything like he was, there could be major problems. *What if RyN2 was military grade. What if this thing snaps?*

Mel was standing in the row of seats. She'd slid her way close to the aisle and stopped. Mia had joined them. It was a convergence of curiosity. Everyone was wondering what the androids were going to decide except Ryan Westbrook, who pointed at Zar, then thrust his hand back and forth a few times, emphasizing.

"I've got to say, this is the most interesting moment of my life, or is it?" They were all taken aback by the duality of his comment. "My father made you," he beamed an intense gaze at Zar, "in the likeness of my favorite comic book character. How lucky am I?" Then he turned to RyN2. "And my father designed you to fill in the empty space. You are a gap filler. A stand-in. *Putty.*"

Zar had to rescue the moment …

"No! He programmed us with a directive to go back through time. Our mission is to reassemble the family. No matter what it takes. No matter how long."

Ryan was looking among them, trying to gauge their expressions. What Zar had just said, *there was nothing wrong with it*, except the small detail of semantics and time. This was eating at Ryan.

"We're not mechanical parts."

Zar was lightning fast.

"Bring together. We're meant to bring the family back together. I apologize."

"Your learning AI is quantum. How's that even possible? My dad was only just starting to get—"

"I haven't been built yet, on your plane of time, that is. I've come from your future. RyN2 is the most recent build, hence the tension between you two, but I've upgraded his hardware. In the future, he designs the prototype for me. He builds Zar so that we can exist in the same time and place, and not draw attention. We're doing what your father asked us to do."

"So, am I a problem, or is it RyN2 that's in the way? I mean, let's be fucking clear. I know my math. This equation is elementary, and one of us is—"

Mel was growing scared, but had to show Ryan she was right there by his side.

"One of you cancels the other out?"

She was watching Carlos put his phone back into his pocket. He didn't want them to realize that he'd snapped a picture of the duo.

Mia was thinking out loud, stirring an agitated bundle of nerves.

"Don't even think about it. I know what happens to witnesses. If you even so much as step in my direction, I push this button once." She held up her phone. "And my father will have my location. He'll be here in minutes with six guys who beat STEMs to death just for the fun of it."

Mia was stepping backwards slowly until she reached the stage.

RyN2 knew he had to change the atmosphere.

"We're not programmed for violence. What you're thinking is impossible. Just … stay calm."

Ryan wasn't going to buy it that easily.

"If you were made in the likeness of me, *even remotely*, your base function will be the art of manipulation."

Mia was beginning to feel a wave of hate toward RyN2. *All their moments were fabricated. The emotions, he tricked me.* It was sinking in, that it was impossible for the android to truly feel, no matter how realistic his responses or interactions felt. *Theater. That's all it is. Goddamn it! Why did I even …*

Zar tried.

"You're here. That's one less human we have to bring back. One less major complication. It means that our mission, the probability of success is much higher. It's good you're here. The best unexpected variable. A benefit. Not a curse. It makes the magic easier. It makes the mission easier. Let's get to work. There's no more time to waste."

The air in the theater was thick with thoughts. It would take a few more minutes for the tension to fall.

Mia walked up to Ryan. She was staring at the young man she was really in love with. Mel could see it on her face, and this was crushing her. She knew if she had any shot at really bonding with Ryan, she had to step back and let the chips fall where they may. *Be the stronger woman. Ryan will make the choice if he's strong. If not, …* then she slipped.

"Have you been fucking that android? I mean, you look like you wanna kiss Ryan, so …"

Mia kept quiet. She was gaming Mel and had just forced her to make the first move, and it was so much more than Mia thought she'd get. Ryan knew the tension was turning away from the androids and shifting between the women. It made sense. Mia had developed a relationship with an AI, and here was the real thing. *Here I am …*

"I've got it. I see how we can do this now. I, am Zar the Great. Always was, always will be." He turned and started walking up the aisle. Mel followed with a subtle 'winning' glance at Mia. "I have a plan."

RyN2 didn't like being in the dark.

"You wanna share?"

Ryan kept walking, "You and I can't be seen together, ever. It's the only way this'll work. I'll be in touch."

41

Nice Lox

Parminder tore across an open field. Her rear tire kicked up clumps of wet grass and topsoil, showering earthy debris into the air as she ripped along on her Enduro. She was letting off some steam. The Green Bank scientist was frazzled by Mia's visit, and regretted not taking one of the lab jobs closer to the city. *Bum-fuck Virginia is killing me. I need another outlet.*

Parminder bumped along, zipping through a section of wispy trees, the cycle's engine wound up like all two-strokes do, *ziiing ziiinggg, ziiiiiiing, nnn-nananananananan, ziing zinnnng!* Her new rear shock pulled its weight, bouncing up and down with each imperfection in the Earth's surface.

The leaves and the thin branches … the new growth, that might otherwise seem like torture, were whipping the sleeves on her padded jacket and jeans. It looked like Parminder was racing through an Olympic motocross course. From the field to the wooded area, the motorcycle broke out into another field and slowed. There was a state road ahead, with excellent visibility. She didn't have to decelerate too much to see a hundred yards in either direction, so she cranked the throttle, winding up the bike to its max. She loved catching air at the edge of the road.

Parminder leaned back, centering her weight and prepping to cross over the berm. Her Enduro hit the edge of the black top, sending the bike into the air. This was the highest she'd ever reached, the longest airtime she'd experienced yet.

The scientist landed perfectly in the path. She ducked, readying for the branches that overhung the entrance to the section of woods on the opposite side of the road. Just as she crossed into the trees, a large branch, just ahead of her, came swinging around into the path, sweeping her off of the motorcycle. Unmanned, the Enduro hit the next series of bumps in the path and jettisoned into a thick patch of growth. Parminder's momentum had forced her body through the branch, and the end of the thick section slashed her bare neck. Her feet caught the ground first, causing her to tumble along the hard, beaten-in path. She rolled a few times, then came to a stop when her helmet cracked the base of a tree. It took a hard hit, but maintained its integrity.

She flipped her visor up and tried to stand. Her right leg wouldn't let her. She'd taken a pretty hard blow to her calf and charliehorsed the muscle. It was tightening up like a vice, every second.

"Shit!"

Parminder looked around. She was still a distance from her apartment in town. *I have to get to the bike.* It took her a moment to pull herself up, using the tree to help. She spotted the bike lying in the thick foliage ahead. Just as she was sliding her left foot forward, determined to remount the Enduro and find her way, a thick male voice startled her.

"I don't know about you, but when you make a pact, you've got to stick to it. And I said to myself not too long ago, that I was done with crosswords. I resolved myself to this. I'm trying to be better."

Parminder turned as far as she could without causing too much pain, dazed and confused.

"Mr. Kutter? What are you doing out here?"

"Boobytrapping."

She tapped her helmet and shaked her head, "I can't hear you. Can you help me to my motorcycle? It's over there." Barely pointing. "If I can just get back to it—"

Parminder was acting strange from the shock. She was unable to process what was happening. Kutter moved toward her.

"Carter's very upset."

Parminder was numb.

"My leg feels really funny."

"I don't think you should be standing on it."

Kutter was in front of Parminder, who was determined. She dragged her right leg, attempting to move forward. He reached over and unsnapped her chinstrap, then grasped her helmet with both his hands. "Let me help you." He lifted her helmet off and dropped it to the ground. He was lightly pissed. "I've got to start all over, now, with my soliloquy."

"Mr. Kutter—"

"Just last week, you were one of our top scientists. Now, look at you. You're a contestant on a game show."

Parminder's leg gave out. She was beginning to regain a bit of composure, and fell to the ground. Kutter kneeled.

"No. No. We've got to go a little further. It's just over here."

He grabbed her arm and pulled her back to her feet, using his body like a crutch. They began walking deeper into the wooded area.

"My leg really hurts."

"I was saying earlier. When you make a pact, you've got to stick to it. I think it's important." His demeanor shifted. "Your employer is pissed. Understandably so."

"Oh my god. Is this about the transmissions? If it is—"

"It's probably best you tell me the truth."

"I had no choice."

Kutter dragged Parminder far enough off the trail, to a secluded patch of forest, that if anyone happened to come down the path, they'd be out of sight.

In front of them was a noose, hanging from a thick tree branch twenty feet up.

"I usually do a crossword. I love puzzles. But, we're not gonna do that. For some reason, I feel I have to give you an opportunity. It's all because I made this resolution. I'm evolving. So, this is your lucky day."

Parminder snapped out of her daze. Staring at the dangling rope, waiting just for her, triggered the only option available ... *fight or flight*. Her adrenal gland dumped a load of epinephrine into her body. The scientist was now conscious and was overwhelmed by fear.

She didn't make any noise, but couldn't stop her eyes from watering. Tears rolled down her cheeks.

"What are you doing? I need medical attention. I need help."

Jack zip-tied her hands behind her back, then slipped the noose around her neck. The scientist began breathing faster. He stepped over to the tree and tightened the rope so that Parminder was still standing, but her head felt the pull from the noose.

"Earlier, you said you didn't have a choice. I want you to know, I'm gonna give you one. We're gonna play a game. All you have to do is choose the right letters. First, let's recall a few days ago at Green Bank, when all the cameras were shut down and a copy of the coded transmissions we painstakingly trapped, then stored on our secured servers, were downloaded while you, Ms. Parminder, were logged in."

"I had to do it."

"Where are the transmissions?"

"They've been returned to their rightful owner."

"It's a simple question. For such a bright young woman, this should be easy." Kutter tugged a little harder on the rope, choking the scientist for five seconds before releasing the tension. "Where are the transmissions?"

"Enigma411 and Redhead911. They have a copy. That's it. But, you've gotta know, a future iteration of Enigma411 sent them, so it's not like they stole them. Also, I didn't shut the cameras off. I don't know how that happened. I swear, I have no idea. And Enigma411 ... is a STEM."

"An android and a redhead showed up, and you let them have a copy of the transmissions. You're telling me they sent the transmissions to themselves? From the future?"

"Something like that. Yeah."

"In your report to Wardlow, you specifically stated that the transmissions could have only come from the past. The very reason why we weren't giving them a priority status, even though we've spent millions to crack the encryption."

"At the time, the likelihood the transmissions were from the future had always carried a negative quotient. What science, physics, what life tells me, Mr. Kutter, is it isn't possible."

"You've changed your mind, though, haven't you?" Kutter secured the rope on the tree. "And you've also breached our security agreement. In the most, well ... I won't say the word. That would give away the whole surprise." Kutter pulled out his pen and drew nine lines on a piece of paper. Then, drew a crude hangman's armature. He held it up to her. "You've broken our security agreement in the most ... blank ... manner. It's nine letters. You've got to get all nine correct." He pushed out a sinister grin. "You are allowed three mistakes."

"We're playing hangman, and my life is the wager?"

"You're only allowed three mistakes, Parminder."

"I'm bleeding. I need medical attention. My leg is surely—"

"Don't force me to put a time limit on this. I've given you some pretty good odds, here. Don't fuck that up. But, it's your life, as you put it."

Parminder began swinging her body around, looking for something, anything. The rope started to burn her neck. She was panicking.

"How do you know this enigma was a STEM?"

"He told me."

"I'm here to save you."

"I don't believe that."

"Then why the fuck did you believe he was an android sent from the future to retrieve his canned messages? And he even brought along a fucking redhead. Parminder, if I wasn't on this new path, I'd—" Jack Kutter's face changed. "You better start guessing, or I'm gonna regress to my former self, and you don't—"

Parminder went for it.

"E."

Kutter's demeanor instantly changed. He turned out a smile and filled in two blanks $E\_\_E\_\_\_\_\_$.

"Excellent."

"You're sick. Really sick."

"Don't call attention to that now. That's irrefutable. For sure. You should concentrate on you."

"It's not that easy with a rope around my neck, but here goes, Y."

Kutter let out an obnoxious sound, "Ehhhhhhh."

"A?"

"Ehhhhhhh. that's two mistakes."

"O"

"Nice work."

Kutter smiled again and filled in the blank $E\_\_E\_\_O\_\_$.

"U?"

Kutter smiled again. "Excellent." And he filled in the blank $E\_\_E\_\_OU\_$.

"S?"

Kutter's smile changed. "You know this one, don't you? $E\_\_E\_\_OUS$.

"Egregious. You piece of shit. Now, let me down."

"Shit. I picked a word with too many vowels. That was an easy one."

Kutter untied the rope and walked off like the event had never taken place. Parminder fell to the ground and began dragging herself back in the direction of the path. It took her twenty minutes to find the trail. Her arms were burning, but she was determined.

She continued to drag herself down the path until she found the tire marks in the dirt leading into the patch of growth. The Enduro was there, lying on its side.

Kutter was a distance away, with his back to the hood of his car. He was holding a rifle and loading the ammo, then he chambered a round.

The Enduro could be heard as it started up, *ziiiing, ziiing, ziiiing* ...

42

I Think I'm Alone Now

Cheryl Sands was walking down the beach when KCLT's new reporter and temporary replacement for Rebecca, the beautiful Iranian-American Sabina, approached. She saw herself a quick study of personality types, and by the way Cheryl was dressed, her guess was a resounding *she's gotta be liberal. She'll have the viewpoint I'm looking for.* It wasn't Cheryl's striped pants and seventies-style sunglasses that gave her this impression. It was her t-shirt with "women rule" printed on the front that, for some reason, gave Sabina the idea she'd be accepting of the STEMs. It was a quick judgment.

"Honestly, Jimmy Swillow's a hero. What he did was what we all should have done from the beginning - stop allowing those puppets at City Hall from making decisions that affect our lives. Because we all know, now, well and good - that politicians are incapable of protecting our interests and way of life. Not only in Chimera, but in the entire U.S. of A. They're drunk on the handouts from corporations and governments. Even scarier, those unnamed nefarious foreign entities. I've lost trust. My friends have lost trust. I mean, who's left? I know everybody down here at the beach."

Sabina thanked Cheryl, then turned to walk away from the small group of locals who'd formed a circle around Mrs. Sands. The overall sentiment was in favor of Cheryl's comment, which concerned KCLT's executives, since Wardlow was one of their big supporters.

The reporter cast a smile at the group, then hurried off. She'd been ordered by her superiors to find a balancing view so they could do their job and provide objective journalism.

Jimmy Swillow, along with Rebecca's reporting of Claypool and the small story on Vito she'd leaked to an online news outlet, had begun to sway the beach community away from the initial pleasantries of having any kind of android walking among them. Word had started to spread about Vito. Dark theories were being talked about amongst the teens on social media. People, in general, had begun to question Wardlow after Claypool was found. Things were spinning out of control for Carter. He just didn't know it yet. Or, did he?

~

Rebecca was poolside, with her hair pulled up in a bun. The large sun hat and Hepburn-style sunglasses easily concealed her identity. Not too many locals ever saw Rebecca up close, except the regulars at Tippies, the small dive bar she frequented near her apartment. The most the townspeople and the tourists had ever known of Rebecca was through her persona in front of the camera, with heavy contour makeup and fancy outfits to help embellish her role as a reporter. This was done purposely to separate her personal life from public scrutiny.

Sloan, on the other hand, was out of place, wearing a well-tailored suit. He spotted Rebecca in her lounge chair, almost slipping on the wet concrete as he sat down.

"Pete Sloan, FBI. It's good to finally meet you in person."

"Likewise."

"I'm not very good at being social. The tone of your last call has me worried. Would you mind if we dive right in?"

Pete showed his identification. Rebecca gave it a good look.

"Thank you, and not at all. I'm not here on vacation. I've tucked myself in with the tourists to keep myself out of the public's eye. You read me right."

"What can you tell me?"

"There's someone on the inside of, whatever this is, and he's leaking information. I didn't find Claypool's body from investigative work. It was a tip. And my source is here in Chimera. He's Asian. I can tell you that. He has a strong accent. I just can't place the country. According to him, the Claypool murder, Vito's disappearance and Victor Westbrook's accident are all connected. Ready? To Wardlow Technologies. The best part is that it's all a part of some project they've been running to replace important figures in Chimera with advanced artificial intelligent beings. We call them, STEMs, or Plastics."

"I've read up on it. Wardlow's work is being highlighted in all the tech trades and in the field of artificial intelligence, and his STEM program is being watched by multiple individuals and organizations to see how this test works out. So, even though the average Joe isn't privy to this as much as, let's call it the AI community, it's fairly well known. Especially in the government. The DOD. Et cetera. The question is, has Wardlow been operating this project within the bounds given to them? What are those boundaries? And, to what extent do we need to be concerned?"

"We have one missing person that I know of. One murdered. One in a coma, that my source says was supposed to be an abduction that went wrong. Perpetrated by the Swillow gang."

"The Swillows?"

"Yes. Victor Westbrook, the head of the AI division at Wardlow, is in a coma."

"The Swillows have pretty much gone legitimate with all their businesses. I wonder what prompted them to attempt something like that? After their nephew, Mark Boyle, was arrested in connection with the Isabella Museum Heist, their illegal activities have mostly dissolved, according to my reports. We had a team on them for some time, but pulled it."

"Are you saying Wardlow's allowed to replace people?"

"Not in the slightest. What I'm saying is, there's knowledge at the highest level of government regarding their activities. I'm here to find out just how real these allegations are, coming from your source. Do you have a name? Anything other than Asian male?"

"Is it just you?"

"It's just me, at the moment. I assure you—"

"That's just great. One agent is going to—"

"I'll get to the bottom of this."

"Getting to the bottom of what looks like it could be one of the darkest conspiracies ever won't just be impossible. It certainly won't help me. I'm more concerned about my life."

～

Jack Kutter was on his way back into Chimera Beach when he received a call from someone in Washington DC. The voice was warm, with not a hint of fear or anxiousness.

"In his report, he used the word 'Asian' to describe the informant. I think we can safely assume who *that* is. I've placed sanctions on our so-called friends overseas, as a result. As for the reporter, she's staying at the Shore Motel. Also, Sloan's in town. He'll be there, poking around, until he can file the full report on

Claypool and this new information on the deli guy and Victor, so steer clear of him. How you wanna handle the reporter is up to you. However, when you find that Asian friend of ours, make sure you send him my love."

"Copy."

Kutter dropped the phone on the passenger seat. He turned the car down an on-ramp, entering the coastal thruway, and headed for the Shore Motel.

The sun had fallen and the moon hadn't made it to the horizon yet. Rebecca was in her room with the television on, watching KCLT news. An update to the Chimera Theater renovation was running.

Sabina was walking down the aisle toward the main stage when she stopped and turned to the cameraman, who had captured the men installing the new carpet, along with the team reupholstering the seat backs with red velvet. The main stage was closed off. The curtains had been drawn. For some odd reason, one of the stage hands flipped the switch and temporarily opened the right side, exposing the massive, O-shaped time jump apparatus, which looked like a prop to the cameraman, who captured eight seconds of footage before the curtain was shut again.

The video very dark, making it hard for anyone to make out, and even if they did, it would have no significance other than aesthetic.

Except ...

Carter had restrained himself from expressing the frustration he'd had for recent events. He was running on the treadmill to burn off the anxiety, dividing his attention between the news and looking out at the city lights, gazing over at Tommy Swillow's penthouse suite across the way and wondering why his pet project was at a standstill. This was keeping the CEO in a military, at-the-ready mindset—until Sabina walked into the Chimera Theater.

He was already planning a visit to see Ryan, after discovering he was alive, but when he found out about the big show, understandably, this was something that raised concerns.

Carter began to feel the electricity; the power and control he'd felt just prior to the setbacks. He had the same feeling when he launched Avalanche that he did when the cameraman turned and caught a glimpse of the time jump apparatus on stage.

Within a few seconds, Carter had a car running at the side entrance while he rushed to put his dress clothes back on.

It was a Friday evening. The streets were busy. This would normally not bother him, but the anxiety of being minutes away from confirming what he'd remembered during a brief moment years earlier in Victor's office was exciting him. It was one of the many times Westbrook had shared one of his theories that Carter had, for the sake of progress, brushed off for the time being, no matter how intriguing the concept was.

When Carter pulled into Wardlow headquarters, the security team was waiting. They moved swiftly to the section where Victor's office was still intact, waiting for Mr. Westbrook to heal and return to work.

Security unlocked and swung open the steel door. There it was, behind his desk, on a shelf filled with a myriad of robotics miniatures he'd been toying with over the years. The scaled-down model of Victor's time jump prototype.

Victor had told Carter years ago that, with a large team put on it, this could be used to agitate the current space in time which would allow a human being to move to a different space in time. It was the very same time machine model he'd placed on Ryan's nightstand to keep him from nightmares when he was four years old. Victor had brought it to his office after Ryan disappeared (in a way) to do what it was supposed to do for Ryan and to him.

Carter only nodded his head. The O-shaped apparatus was almost exactly like the blurred image on the KCLT segment at the theater.

He grabbed the miniature and headed out of the office, instructed his men to lock up, then left the building as fast as he came in.

~

Jack pulled into the Shore Motel. He sat in the parking lot, facing the two sections of rooms that formed an L-shape, until the moon was directly overhead. He watched the tourists come and go, catching the rhythm and dynamic of the guests until he felt it was time.

Kutter was a patient man. He had to be. After all, he was a hunter at his core. Kutter lifted his phone from the passenger seat and dialed the motel.

"Hello. This is Murph Semelton, from KCLT News. Can you do me a favor and run a message to Rebecca Anderson in room ... shit, I don't have that information."

"Rebecca Anderson's here? Whoa, cool. But, are you sure? Because I don't have her in the register."

"She's using a different name. She's working on an investigative piece and can't be bothered by anyone, at the moment. She might be disguised a bit. She's thirty-three, brunette. She was probably wearing a hat and sunglasses all day. Did you see anyone like that?"

"Everyone looks like that around here. Wait, I know who Rebecca is. Now that you mention it, I know exactly who you're talking about. I knew she looked familiar."

"Listen. It's real important. You'd be doing KCLT a solid favor. Would you pop over to her room and tell her to contact the station ASAP. Don't spook her. Just tell her we're going to run the series, and we need her back at the studio."

"You know, I have to admit, I'm not really into the news at all, but Rebecca … she's … what did you say your name was, again?"

"Murph."

"Uh, okay, Murph, consider it done."

Kutter watched the young night manager exit the office. He walked down to the end of the building to the last door, 113, lit a cigarette, and knocked. It took a few moments before Rebecca answered. At first, she only cracked the door an inch, but, when she heard the manager say 'KCLT', the door swung open. Kutter watched as words were exchanged.

From her body language, Jack could tell she was concerned. *There was no one named Murph at the station.* She did her best to remain composed, playing off any concerns she had, unwilling to trust the manager who she knew would do anything for her.

Rebecca stepped out of her room to thank him as he returned to his office, using the moment to check her surroundings.

Kutter was thirsty. He carefully reached down to the floor of the car to grab a bottle of water. When he lifted his head back up, the lights cut out in the motel room. Moments later, Rebecca exited, leaving her door ajar. She circled the lot, on alert, looking for anything out of the ordinary but missing Kutter, who was hidden in the shadows.

She returned to the room and grabbed her handbag and laptop, shut the door behind her, and made a beeline for her car. She opened the driver's side door and paused, debating, then returned to her room, turning all the lights back on. Something had spooked her.

Minutes later, the young manager exited the office. He walked down to room 113 and knocked. The door opened and Rebecca pulled him inside and slammed the door shut behind them.

Jack spun the top from his water bottle, took a sip, and replaced the lid, then dropped it on the passenger seat. He picked up the newspaper that was folded perfectly, blocking out the crossword puzzle. He reached between the seat and the center console to retrieve a pen that had almost disappeared under the floor mat and began with 6 Down.

43

Backseat Driver

The second Carter stepped out of the car and under the marquee at the theater as one of the Coonan's runts came skidding to a stop a foot away from the CEO.

"Front row still available, boss. Center stage. You won't find a better seat or view in the entire house. Reserve 'em now. Ya snooze, ya lose, man. Ticket window's open. Right over there."

The runts had their first real job working for Tommy, and they were fired up. Clarence needed the help with parking and local marketing and security, and there was no one better in Chimera than Tommy to handle it. Clarence's paid ads and news coverage had worked wonders, but the kids were all over town, out in the streets, building the hype among the youth who weren't paying attention to the news media.

Mia was in the ticket window, handling pre-sales with a renewed excitement. She'd finally bridged her personal life and interest in Ryan with her father's business. Jimmy, with help from a few of the clan, watched over the parking lot. The Runts were like fleas, hopping all over town while Tommy sat up in the penthouse watching over the receipts and staying out of the light. He knew Kutter was a loose cannon. How much longer could they assume he wasn't a liability? He was mitigating it as much as possible.

Carter purchased the entire front row section without hesitation. He'd be giving the seats away to a select group of his friends, most of which showed up at the museum gala. Mia put on a subtle smile as she handed Carter his seating confirmation. She knew that the markup on the front row area was substantial, and was feeling the rush that her father felt when things were going well.

Carter Wardlow made a move toward the entrance doors, reached out for the handle, and tugged. They didn't budge. The doors were locked from here on out, until the show. One of Swillow's security team, whose muscles were almost bursting the seams of his shirt, made a gesture and shook his head. He was kind, but firm.

"No one's allowed in, sir."

Carter wasn't thrown, He knew how to hit the ball back into his court.

"I'm an old friend of the Westbrooks. I wonder, could you get a message to Ryan? I mean, Zar the Great?"

"I could pass it on."

"Tell him I know about his better half, and if he wants to keep things on the down-low, as the kids say, to give me a call. He's got 24 hours."

Carter handed the bouncer his business card and turned toward his car. The driver was already holding open the rear door for the CEO.

The bouncer had a scowl on his face. He didn't like suits to begin with, and got the gist of Carter's threat before he even finished speaking. The Irishman had his phone in his hand and Tommy on the line before Wardlow's car exited the lot.

"You told me to keep my eyes out. Well, looks like the kid's in trouble."

Tommy jumped off the couch and walked over to the patio, looking out to the sea.

"Best news I've had all day."

~

Ryan and Mel were at the Westbrook house, standing outside Victor's lab. The door was still secured. Ryan was working his brain hard. *Where the hell did my dad leave his keycard?* Mel had been standing there in silence, wondering what Ryan was hoping would happen after several failed attempts punching in all the Westbrook family birthdays as potential combinations. She had a wry tone in her voice.

"Is there no magic you can do?"

Ryan was deep in thought.

"We've looked over the entire house, right?"

"Yes."

"It wasn't on him when he was admitted at the hospital, or it would be with his clothes and wallet. The nurse would have said something."

"True. What if the person who took him to the hospital got it? That's the variable here, Zar."

Ryan liked the way she took little jabs.

"That would make sense. Not sure it would help, anyway. I'm pretty sure you'd have to be my dad to use it. Look at this, there's biometrics involved." Ryan pointed to the small infrared sensor next to the keypad. "I bet that's a fingerprint scanner."

Mel was confused.

"So, how would we get in even if we had the access card?"

"I'm not sure yet, but there has to be some sort of override."

"What's in there that's so important?"

"I don't know yet." There was a long look between them. Both were mentally grinding away, again. Mel agreed it had to be something important, otherwise she would've pulled him away from the door. There were other important things to do. Like prepping for the show.

Ryan had an idea. "I've tried all our birthdays. What if—"

Mel was quick, and finished his thought, "It's the day you died?"

"Morbid, yes!"

While Ryan took all of a nanosecond to remember, Mel reached over and punched in the numbers. She stepped back and the LED on the keypad turned green. Ryan couldn't believe she'd beat him to it. He hadn't even had time to blink. Mel's eyes opened, tugging at his heartstrings.

"How could I ever forget?"

Mel's look disintegrated Ryan. Her energy triggered a warm sensation that shot through his body. It was deteriorating his ego.

She slid closer and whispered, "The magician can do magic, we know this. But can the magician—"

It was game time. Ryan had to make a move. He slipped his right arm between Mel's arm, reaching around and lightly pressing an open hand against her back, then moved his lips up to hers. It was a hair-raising kiss.

Mel pulled her head back. Her voice was subtle.

"Oh, the magician can kiss."

Ryan smiled, stepped to the side, and opened the door. The anticipation was overpowering. Mel was relieved. She was worried about her slip with Mia, wondering if Ryan would hold that against her, but after the kiss, she left it to the past.

Inside was a modern laboratory, a little out of order. Mel walked right over to a prototype of RyN2. The body was lying on a table with no skin. Its insides were exposed.

"So, this is what Jeffrey Dahmer would see if your twin was one of his victims."

"You have a unique way of looking at things. I look at you, and I think

Melanie. Then I hear you, and I think … Mel."

"As you like, Zar. As you like."

There were four computer stations. One was live and online; the very machine Ryan and Zar were synced with and using as a hub to communicate. Lights were bouncing on and off, showing the wireless activity. The others were loaded with Victor's intellectual property, most of which were proprietary algorithms and various robotics projects. All the systems were locked down with a strong password. After failing to gain access on two of the computer stations, Ryan bounced out of the room. Mel didn't pay attention. She was still very much interested in the prototype's innards.

He returned to the lab carrying Eddie and set him down next to the station with the lights buzzing away, then connected him to the computer with a cable. He powered on his old friend. The lights flickered in his eyes. This meant his sensors were functioning properly. Ryan tapped his metal exterior.

"Eddie."

"Yes, Ryan."

Ryan fist pumped. He'd been down a long road with Eddie, and was glad to see that the more advanced functions were still working.

"Login."

"Password?"

"Don't have it. Can you brute force it?"

The light in Eddie's eyes flickered.

"Let me see." Three seconds passed. "No. Your father has a two-step verification in place."

"Can we get in?"

"You have to answer some security questions."

"I'm ready."

"For the first question, there's a hint. It's 'fat cat'."

"Answer is Jasmine." Ryan turned to Mel, who was still looking over the android's insides. "Am I a bad person for not thinking about my old cat, Jasmine? My god. She would be … how did I not … have we seen a cat around at all?"

"Nope. And uh, I haven't found anything that resembles a man tool on your twin over here, yet. Should I be concerned?"

She got a hearty laugh from Ryan, who made a quick handoff.

"I'm guessing Mia is the one who should be concerned."

"From the look she gave you, I'd say she is. Must suck, having feelings for a

Plastic and not being able to do anything about it."

Eddie interjected.

"Ryan, have the second stage of protocol. How would you like to proceed?"

"I'm waiting for you. Please go ahead."

"Instructions are to contact the law firm, Amato & Sardano LLP, for access."

"Can you find me a number?"

"Yes. It's—"

~

Ryan and Mel weren't in the waiting area of Amato & Sardano more than a few minutes before Christopher Amato, Esq. entered the lobby to personally greet Ryan. He was a short, yet well-framed man in his late sixties, with thick black hair, bushy eyebrows, pale lips, and warm olive-colored skin. Everyone could smell the flavored pipe tobacco that was being transported around in his expensive and nicely-tailored suit.

"What a treat." He offered his hand. "Christopher Amato."

"Ryan Westbrook."

"Melanie."

"Let's go this way," the lawyer turned, forcing them to follow, "and get more comfortable." The three walked down a hallway, discussing the article in the paper, the show, and Mr. Amato's enthusiasm for Ryan until they reached a large corner office with a five-star view. Once they were situated, Mr. Amato dug right in.

"Ryan, I've been handling Victor's affairs for years. It's always been patents and things of that nature, but I'm just so thrilled you're alive. Your father and I are close. We spoke at great length about your family, the future, and ups and downs. How is he doing?"

It took Ryan a moment.

"He's still in a coma, and he's lying there thinking I'm dead."

Mr. Amato was calm and collected.

"I know for a fact that he only reserved himself to the idea of you being gone, so he could continue to work without carrying the weight of you and Claire. Anyone else would have fallen apart. In the back of his mind, he always held close this beacon of hope. That must be the reason he forged on. And here you are."

Mel could see that Ryan was being respectful of the attorney, but she also knew he was in a hurry.

"Mr. Amato, Ryan needs access to the computers."

Ryan followed up.

"Is there some sort of—"

The lawyer understood their immediacy.

"Ryan, you've been authorized to access Victor's files. Without question. I apologize for wasting your time. I never thought I'd be standing in front of you. I assumed, as did your father, that some corporate raider or someone similar, representing a firm or even nation, would be attempting to make a claim to his work. You see, your father was hacked, and work which couldn't even be valued, it has so much importance. This work was stolen. The worst part was it was a close friend and co-worker that—"

"Kaz?"

"He never told me the name. He didn't want to call attention to him, nor did he want to file any charges, for some reason."

"He only had one friend and the only co-worker he had was the same guy. Kaz."

Mr. Amato was glad he could put a name to the theft, but he wanted to keep this to himself.

"Let me get you the keycard and the codes. Please, Ryan, do your best to keep them in a safe place. Your father has a trove of patents and other intellectual property that have yet been cleared by the patent office." He reached over and picked up his phone. "Marissa, would you open the safe and bring me the Westbrook envelope? Thank you." He hung up the phone. "It'll just be a minute."

Mel appreciated him getting to the point.

"Thank you."

Marissa entered with a large envelope. She set it on Mr. Amato's desk. The lawyer dumped the contents out, nodding to Marissa and stopping her as she left the office.

"Swing by the conference room and send Mr. Sloan in. Thank you." He turned to face Ryan. "You're going to have to sign this." He presented a one-page document and a pen. "For receipt of the keycard and passwords. I also have this for you." Mr. Amato handed Ryan a bank card. "I assume you'll be needing funds, as well. The pin is written on this card, here. Is there anything else I can do for you?"

"I'm all set. I'll just head out. Sounds like you have another meeting."

Mr. Amato's words stopped Ryan and Mel from leaving.

"I have no right to meddle, and I promise that I won't. I just want you to know, if there is anything I can do, just let me know. I have the responsibility of safeguarding your father's work which, by proxy, means your work as well. Did you know that your father tried to trademark your stage name, but the office wouldn't allow it because of the comic book character?"

Ryan appreciated the man's words, but even more so, he was taken by his father's unconditional support.

"That's pretty cool. Thanks for telling me."

"There's a lot of money in that account, Ryan. It's linked to a trust, so there is a monthly limit. However, it's quite substantial. Take care to not be too frivolous with—"

Mel grabbed Ryan's shoulder and offered a genuine smile to the attorney.

"He'll call you if he needs anything."

"Excuse me." A voice from the hallway pulled Ryan and Mel from Mr. Amato. "My name is agent Peter Sloan." He produced his identification. "May I come in?"

Ryan and Mel felt the sting of deception. The magician made it clear …

"What's with the ambush?"

Agent Sloan's demeanor was not threatening in any way, diffusing the young couple's concern as he spoke.

"Ryan, I'm here because I believe there's more to your father's accident than we are all aware of. I'm looking at all the information and trying to form a clearer picture. It's fortuitous that I happened to be here when you showed up."

Mr. Amato placed the unlit pipe that was sitting in a large crystal ashtray in the corner of his mouth. He enjoyed drawing air through the stem to grab a taste of the strawberry tobacco residue.

"Would you tell Agent Sloan what you just told me?"

The FBI agent listened to Ryan. After hearing a more detailed description of what he could remember of Kaz, there was a moment of silence. The agent was thinking about his talk with Rebecca. Once he put it all together …

"This might seem obvious, but is he Asian? Japanese?"

"Yes, he is. I could never pronounce his last name, but I did see some incredible tattoo work he had creeping out from one of his shirts. It was some serious ink. Traditional Japanese style, for sure."

"Can you remember what the artwork looked like?"

"Nah. I can't remember. It was so long ago, and it was mostly covered up."

"Have you seen him at all since you've returned to public life?"

"Not at all."

"Would you contact me if you do? It would be very helpful. And, aside from that, if you ever feel like you're in danger in any way, let either of us know immediately. The value of your father's work might easily make you a target. In fact, it may already have. Do you understand? We're here to protect you."

Mel had been listening to the tone of their voices and watching the body language, calculating.

"How far are you in this?" She was looking directly at Mr. Amato. "I mean, do you get a percentage of the profits from his father's patents? How does all this work?"

Mr. Amato loved these moments.

"Melanie, I'm simply the trustee. I have a set rate and gain nothing more from this than the satisfaction of being a valued asset of Victor's, and now Ryan, to handle and protect his life's work. With Victor in a coma, contractually, Ryan can decide to move the trust into someone else's care if he feels I am not performing to his father's guidelines, or his own, for that matter. Agent Sloan had just come in before you did, and was explaining his presence in Chimera."

Ryan grew a big smile. Mel was curious.

"What?"

Ryan looked at Mr. Amato.

"Let's make sure I own all the rights to my upcoming show. Clarence is a cool old guy, but he's also a businessman. Draw up the papers. Here's my number. And don't sweat it. If I see Kaz, Sloan'll be my first call."

Mel and Ryan walked into the parking lot, glowing. The young magician had the world at his feet with his show, and now the key to his father's kingdom. Although it was hard to hide, he was trying to pretend that nothing significant had just transpired.

"Thirsty?"

Mel laughed.

"Hell, yeah."

Ryan held a straight face.

"Let's go get the cheapest beer we can find in Chimera."

"I know a spot right next to the race track."

"Perfect."

The two walked another block. Ryan was about to explode from holding in his excitement. Mel hadn't budged herself. *Was she not fazed by all that had happened at Mr. Amato's office?*

Halfway down the next block, Ryan stopped Mel, "Go on. Ask."

"Ask what?"

Ryan had a sarcastic tone in his voice.

"Stop screwing with me. Anyone in their right mind would be asking now. I won't look at you any differently. You're cool as hell. I swear."

Mel put on a grin Ryan hadn't seen yet.

"Okay, so how much money d'ya think's in there?"

44

I Didn't Do Nuthin'

The second Tommy walked out into the hallway of his penthouse suite, McGlinty was waiting with Bowman, two of his deputies, and Agent Sloan. The burly leader of the Swillow clan was taken into custody without incident. Ironically, and unknowingly, he would be stopped from confronting Ryan at the theater, where he was headed in an attempt to offer protection to the boy. The sheriff didn't know it, but he'd saved Swillow from additional charges, if anything ended up sticking to the Irishman. Sheriff McGlinty was ready to charge him with attempted kidnapping and bodily injury, and if Victor didn't make it, there would be a charge of manslaughter added to the list.

The elevator ride was quiet except for Tommy releasing gas at around the tenth floor as they descended to the lobby. It wasn't him being rude or childish, it was stress. Tommy had always been notified if law enforcement in Chimera had something brewing.

"Chimera PD aren't they usually the ones poking around in my business?"

The elevator was cramped. The sheriff barely turned his head.

"They haven't been very effective, have they?"

The elevator doors opened. The men exited.

"Don't know what you mean by that. They seem to be doing just fine. Chimera is a wonderful place. It's safe, and—"

"Oh, it's a wonderful place, with all those bodies popping up." Tommy was growing angry.

"I don't know if you heard, but I don't get involved like that anymore. I run legitimate businesses, now."

McGlinty held open the lobby door so the group could exit and walk to the car, parked just ahead in the turnout.

"You run the ship, Tommy. You give orders. Jimmy came to me to take the blame for running over Victor Westbrook. It got me thinking. So, I did some snooping around, and you know what I found?"

"A few donuts, a stale coffee, and a clue you can shove up your ass."

Opening the rear door of the patrol car, "I found your warehouse down past the docks. I couldn't find the van. That was probably crushed at the junkyard. That same old trick. But I did find Mr. Westbrook's keycard. It's a one of a kind, specially-made piece of tech that's only used by the computer scientist to access his lab."

"That doesn't prove anything."

"Proves he was in your warehouse."

"Really? I bet it was a rat that picked up that keycard and carried it in. I've heard strange stories from the guys down at the docks about rats. How they get into things. How they rat around in various ways."

McGlinty gave Tommy a little nudge, forcing him into the car. He closed the door and looked over the roof of the car to Sloan.

"You can take him in and start a dialogue. I'm going to go by the theater and see how Victor's kid is doing. I've got a strange feeling I might just wander into something."

Agent Sloan hopped into the passenger's seat up front. The two deputies entered the vehicle, one in the back with Tommy and the other in the driver's seat. Sloan turned and gave Tommy a look as the car pulled away from his building. Swillow hadn't seen him before.

"Who the fuck are you?"

"Agent Sloan, FBI."

A funny look came across Tommy's face. It was similar to the confident expression he'd had as a teen when hanging out with his Irish buddies.

"Sloan, Sloan," he recognized something from his past, "I knew your grandmother. You're Irish, aren't ya?"

Sloan had an empty look on his face. The agent turned his attention straight ahead as the cruiser turned out into traffic.

~

Jack Kutter was in his car, tucked in the shadows of the Shore Motel parking lot just out of the spill range of the overhead lamps. No one had seen the man draped in darkness. He'd set himself in the best position possible to keep an eye on Rebecca's room, but he'd made one mistake. He fell asleep and had the misfortune of being in the right place at the right time for the young homeless drug addict whose perception had been altered so far off from the norm that evening, she was seeing things in the dark.

The tattered young woman caught the outline of Kutter reclining in his seat. The second her brain realized it was an older male, hidden, back in the shadows, it was instant attraction. Her thought process was simple, *What's he doing back there? Maybe he's waiting for a good time? If he is, then I'm gonna bring him to it.*

The woman changed her direction, cut across the lot and stood outside Kutter's car scratching her arm from an allergic reaction to the drugs she was on. From her perspective, Jack was some sort of warrior straight out of a fantasy novel, with his rattlesnake tattoo showing just at the top of his chest. In his sleep, Kutter had unbuttoned to scratch himself from sweating too much.

While the woman fantasized, she built up the courage to knock.

Kutter opened his eyes, but didn't move. He reacted like a serpent would when an intruder stepped into its range. He squinted his eyes and warned the woman.

"Get the fuck away from my car."

The addict was excited. "Hey, I'm just here to help. Tell me what you need." She stopped scratching her arm. "Why don't we get a room, baby? Looks like you could use a shower." She started looking around, hoping an undercover officer wasn't anywhere nearby. She'd been recently warned about solicitation. "You wanna get cleaned up? Come on, don't be shy, baby. Room is on me."

Kutter opened the glovebox and slid his handgun to the edge of the drawer, just enough so the addict could see it in the low light. He cast his dark eyes on the girl, letting her know what she was in for. The addict pouted.

"Ah hell, man. What are you doing out here, anyways? You don't wanna trick? Go home. Get off my playground, baby." And with that, the addict walked off, heading back to the main road, where she turned the corner near the motel's office, and disappeared.

The second the girl dropped out of sight, Kutter felt a jolt of adrenalin rush through his body, along with a flurry of confusion. Written on the five red motel doors along the strip of rooms in front of him were the letters and blank spaces B-_-H-I-_-_.

Kutter knew the answer in an instant. He thought, *this is so goddamn easy. But, who the hell?* Then he realized what was happening. Jack Kutter raised his voice without turning his head. He didn't want to expedite his own death.

"E, N & D. End. Clever little bastard, aren't you. Never would've thought you'd be so good at word games. I finally found someone worthy to play against."

Kutter tilted his head ever so slightly, just enough to get a glimpse, out of the corner of his eye. The pistol was still resting on the edge of the glove box bathing in dim light. He was hoping to buy some time.

From the back seat came a voice that Kutter would recognize anywhere.

"Don't even think about it."

Kutter had only one option - to talk.

"I knew I felt funny. I haven't ever knocked off like that. So, how'd you do it? The water bottle?"

Kaz was tired of listening to Kutter. He'd heard enough of his crazy talk at the cabin.

"Where you're going, Jack, it won't matter. Nothing will. How I got to you. How you lost the game. It'll only matter to me that I beat you."

Kutter knew his time was up.

"I've got something I know you'll be interested in. Something big. *Really big.*"

Kaz made one quick move of his right hand. He jammed a very thin, sharp steel rod into the back of Kutter's spine at the base of his brain stem, paralyzing his opponent. The Japanese agent reached around with his left hand and grabbed Kutter's chin as he leaned forward.

Kutter was trying. Deep down somewhere inside him, he still believed there was a way to get the upper hand, but this was only programming a killer could cling onto in a situation like this.

Kaz checked his grip and then whispered in the man's right ear.

"Whatever it is, take it with you."

With one quick jerk, Kutter's brain stem was severed.

45

And Then There Were Three

Ryan walked out onto the dark stage. He could feel the buzz coming from the other side of the curtains. The magician took a moment to collect himself, taking in a flash of imagery from the past couple years. There was a lot to reflect on, but it didn't distract him. Ryan took in three big breaths, then exhaled He looked offstage and gave the signal. The curtains opened to the low hum of chatter and a few last minute patrons searching for an open seat. Ryan waited until it was almost uncomfortable for the crowd. Then, a spotlight faded up. The lights dimmed in the audience. He was standing in front of a sold-out crowd wearing his new long coat and refurbished top hat. His t-shirt was a bright orange-yellow. Simple and powerful, this is all he wanted.

The stage was set. Black velvet curtains were draped on all sides, the tone of a funeral. There was a small amount of haze being pumped out. Its density was heavier than the air in the theater, which allowed it to hang low like morning fog in a field.

Ryan stood silent for a moment longer, waiting for the haze to creep through his feet and fold over the edge of the stage before taking a bow. The audience cheered, then grew quiet. They could see his mouth opening and hesitating, then he burst out,

"All I ever wanted to do, was entertain you!"

Ryan lifted his arms and paused, building some tension. A heckler deep in the crowd yelled out, "Well, here we are. Now, entertain us!"

Ryan chuckled inside, thinking how similar he was to this joker, then addressed his audience.

"My career began when I was only two years old. I'd pulled a stunt on my mother, Claire. She later told me the story about how I crawled to the armrest of the gigantic, green family couch we had in the living room. As I reached the edge, I turned, casting an odd grin. My mother's response was one of horror and she lunged to save me, but I'd dropped myself over the side. She was too late. My mother shrieked, yet when she found me on the floor, giggling after landing on a pillow, one that I'd left there earlier, she began laughing. You see, Claire was confused. How did I manage to setup this stunt at such a young age?"

The heckler showed up again. "All this talking. Just show us!"

Ryan smiled this time.

"I couldn't explain it then, and cannot explain it now. It's just something inside of me that has to come out. And it does. And so here we are, and I can assure you. Things will happen here tonight that none of us will be able to explain."

Ryan raised his arm.

Mel walked out onto center stage and removed Ryan's coat and top hat while he kept his attention directed on the crowd. She folded the overcoat, draped it on her arm, placed the hat in her hand, smiled, and walked off the stage.

The magician continued.

"What I am about to do—"

Mel wheeled out a full-length mirror with a gilded antique frame, positioning it fifteen feet behind Ryan, and left the stage.

"What I am about to do will require that old adage, the one where we say to ourselves, 'I wish there was another me. Boy, or is it man, I could get so much more done in a day', time is running out."

As his words faded, RyN2 walked out of the mirror behind Ryan, wearing the same outfit with the bright orange-yellow t-shirt. The two were impossible to tell apart. The crowd roared with excitement.

RyN2 stepped up by Ryan to stand by his side. They looked at each other, then turned in a complete circle, displaying their likeness. Then Ryan continued.

"Time is limited. Time plays no favorites. Time is elusive, and so time is what we must grab ahold of and not let go. But what, really, is time?" Ryan signaled to someone offstage, then continued, "If I am to bring back my mother, who drowned several years ago, I must grab hold of time. Or what I understand of it."

Projected on the large sheer screen at the back of the stage were images of Claire at the beach, filling the audience with an emotional chord and building a deeper connection between Ryan's words and his proposition. Claire was on the beach at Smuggler's Cove. Her patterned swimsuit was easily recognizable from its popular Mondrian design. Images of family hit home, especially in the small beach community that made up most of the audience.

"Tonight. Right in front of you. There will be no tricks. There can be no illusion or stunt. We'll only be able to point our finger at magic, tonight. Real magic." Ryan paused, then delivered with a punch, "I am going to bring my mother back from the dead."

RyN2 turned to his better half, raising his voice.

"No. *We're* going to bring her back!"

The crowd cheered again. Their voices were the same, everything was the same. From every seat in the audience, the two were impossible to differentiate between.

Ryan held a sincere expression and waited for the noise to die.

"Our physicists and scientists have asked the important Questions. If we had the ability to time travel, then what would become of our existence in the present? For, if we transport to the past or future, won't this cancel out our existence in the present? Will we still exist in the here and now? Would we be forever lost in time?"

On the screen, an image of Ryan spiraled in space. His body fell deeper and deeper, growing smaller and smaller as it faded to black.

"According to science, to what we know, one of us will fall prey to time. But which one? Will it be him?" Ryan pointed to the android. "Or me?"

The heckler yelled out,

"Which one owes more taxes?!"

The crowd laughed, then grew silent. The large sheer curtain draped down the back of the illuminated stage.

"Because I cannot make this decision myself. Because it wouldn't be fair. I've asked the help of the famous Zar the Great. The legendary comic book illusionist who was, and is, my inspiration. Let's give a warm welcome to my new friend, Zar the Great."

Projected on the sheer screen was the cover image from the first issue of *Zarwid the Great.* There were a few claps in the crowd. Not many knew of this character, or the issue, but that didn't stop the remaining from slowly finding their way to applause.

Then a loud roar came as the tall magician walked out on stage in his vintage costume. The man was a spitting image of his caricature. Ryan and his doppelgänger separated themselves, making room for their much larger and taller accomplice to stand center stage. Zar was holding his metrome, the mysterious cube he'd brought with him from the future. As he raised his arm, the device began to glow like a beacon, similar to the cover image projected behind him. The audience was looking at an artist's rendition, yet it had been fully manifested in front of them. They cheered again as the real Zar became one with the projection behind him. While the applause was still high, Mia entered the stage. She repositioned the mirror, sliding it to the right side of the stage, then turned it facing inward at a forty five degree angle to the crowd.

Then, Mel entered the stage with an identical mirror. She positioned it stage left, facing in, the exact opposite position Mia had just placed the other.

The two young redheads stood next to the mirrors with their right hands holding each gilded frame.

While the audience was taking in the beautiful young women, wondering what they might be doing next, the metrome began glowing brighter in Zar's hand, drawing the crowd's attention.

At that moment, Ryan walked over to the mirror on the right side of the stage and stepped into it, disappearing for a moment. The crowd gasped. They'd finally been given the perspective to see his body disappear into the frame. The spotlight faded on the mirror.

Then, a moment later, a spotlight came up on the opposite mirror and Ryan reappeared, wearing his old top hat. He came out onto the stage from the void of the mirror.

There was an applause. A bow. Then, RyN2 walked over to the mirror on the left side of the stage and stepped into it, reappearing stage right, wearing the long black coat.

The audience cheered again. This time in waves. Zar lowered his right arm and the light beaming from the metrome faded, silencing the crowd.

Zar had command of the entire room.

"Knowing that we risk everything jumping through time, it is safe to say that one might need a little coaxing to really take the leap."

On stage right, Mia began struggling with RyN2. He was fighting her off, playfully battling her as she dragged him closer to the mirror. RyN2 lost his footing and Mia pushed the android into the mirror. The crowd laughed, then the noise in the theater diminished when they realized he was not returning.

Stage left, Ryan was now fighting with Mel, suggesting he wasn't comfortable going into the mirror. They had choreographed it so well, the crowd began to feel the tension between them. At one point, Ryan got ahold of Mel and almost pushed her into the void, but she regained the upper hand, drew a handgun, and aimed it at Ryan, who turned and threw himself into the glass. There was a loud cracking sound. Glass shattered. Ryan, too, was gone.

The crowd roared with excitement while waiting. Where was he? Where were they? They couldn't tell whether he'd really broken the mirror, or if it was a trick. The mood was building. The crowd was slowly becoming a part of the show.

"They are both gone, now. Sent through time, possibly lost forever. We can only wait and see what happens. Is this an illusion? Or are we at the whim of time?"

Mia and Mel were playing it further, looking at their mirrors, toying with the audience, drawing their attention to them.

Meanwhile, a group of stage hands dressed all in black, almost invisible to the audience, wheeled out the giant O-shaped time jump apparatus. They centered it along the back of the stage and disappeared behind the curtains. Zar continued.

"Let me help you. These mirrors are illusions. You know this, deep down. We want to believe because this is the atmosphere we've built. As wonderful as they are, as dynamic and exciting, they are no more than illusions. So, you ask yourself, how will they bring back Claire if these acts are nothing more than slights of perception?"

Zar looked around the stage and the girls shrugged their shoulders.

"Playing tricks with mirrors is fun, but playing tricks with time could instantly turn to tragedy. We can only do it once, for if we try and fail, we do not exist. Yes, it is true. We have never tested this! We have only prepared for this moment." The crowd rumbled with talk amongst themselves until Zar interrupted. "So, who will go first? Will it be the lovely, Mia?" She took a bow as Zar continued, "Or will it be our very special, Melanie?" She followed Mia and took a bow.

Zar's voice changed. It was demonic in tone. Zar stared right at Carter Wardlow, sitting four rows back. "I think we should have an audience member go first." The old magician scanned the crowd. "Who are the ones in the cheap seats? We should draw straws on you first."

Some of the crowd laughed. Many in the crowd grew uncomfortable. There were mixed rumblings among them.

Zar walked over to the apparatus and placed the metrome into a titanium slot that was centered on the lowest part of the O. It fit perfectly, like a battery inserted into its power station.

The magician returned to center stage and brought his hands together over his head, making a loud clapping noise. The metrome illuminated, sending a charge throughout the time jump apparatus. A swarm of electrical charges swirled around the hoop, starting at the metrome and working their way around and up the ring until they met at the top. The charges created an aura of colors around the apparatus. As it built up in power, the unit sent off several bright flashes of light.

The audience jumped. Its center circle, inside the apparatus, had a transparent, gelatin-like look to it. The field was alive, rippling like a mirage in the desert.

Zar tugged at the crowd again.

"Who will be the first to go back in time?"

He pointed at various people in the crowd, all of whom turned their head away, until Zar was staring again at Carter who stood in front of his seat, then turned to the crowd as if it was his show, playing to the entire section he'd acquired the seats for.

"I'll go, but first I need to go back to the office and grab a few things." Carter sat down. There were more than enough laughs to validate his personal humor before the woman several rows behind him blasted out.

"If you let him go, then we'll all be ruined. He'll take what he knows now and will only use it for his own gain. We have to stop him at all costs! Down in front. Down in front."

One of Wardlow's fans yelled over the crowd, "Luddite!"

The crowd laughed at the woman. It was a loud cacophony of giggles. The masses didn't want to acknowledge her negativity. They were having too much fun in the moment. Frustrated, she decided to stand up and try again.

"I'm serious! We cannot let him—"

Zar took charge of the theater, "Let's bring back Ryan. Both of them."

The crowd went quiet as they noticed Ryan and his doppelgänger, RyN2, entering the theater through the lobby doors. Each took an aisle flanking the center row of seats. They walked toward the stage with many in the audience talking.

"There they are!"

"They're back."

They cheered and applauded the act as the two returned to their places, standing center stage.

Mia and Mel clapped, then walked over and flanked the time jump apparatus. The glow from the energy field created an ethereal look, helping to build the moment. Everyone was waiting for Zar's next move.

The old magician raised his hand.

"Pay close attention to the portal behind me. I have made all the necessary preparations. Now it is time to look into the past."

There was a deep whooshing sound, then a large splash of ocean water came out through the gelatinous void. It was the top of a wave that came crashing through, spilling with it the top layer of white foam that rolled off the edge of the stage. Some ocean water hit Zar's backside. He turned quickly, showing the crowd.

"On the other side of the portal," he turned, opening his arms to the opening, "is the past. We've rolled back four years. On the other side of that void is Smuggler's Cove. We are out in the ocean, moments away from connecting with Claire. She will be swimming past this hole in time very soon. All she will need is a nudge, someone to guide her through and pull her into the void. Or Claire will swim past us, and forever be gone."

The audience in the first twenty rows could smell the salty ocean water. A few were looking around for some sort of vent that was pumping in an artificial scent, unable to accept what they'd just witnessed.

At that moment, the stage lights dimmed. The only remaining spotlight was on Zar, center stage.

It was time to demand.

"Who will it be?" Zar raised his voice. "Ryan?"

A spotlight faded on Ryan, wearing the top hat, stage left. Then, it faded out.

"Or Ryan—"

A spotlight faded up on RyN2, wearing the long coat, stage right. Then, it faded out.

Zar repeated himself. "Ryan—"

The spot came up, again, on Ryan with the top hat, then faded out.

"Or, Ryan?"

The spot came up, again, where RyN2 had been standing, but he was gone. The spotlight faded, failing to find Ryan.

Zar repeated, giving the impression of hope.

"Or ... Ryan?"

A spotlight faded up. It found RyN2 wearing the long coat. This time, he was in a different position on stage. The crowd cheered. Then, the spotlight faded out.

Zar repeated himself, and with his words, the spotlights went on and off, chasing the two Ryans around the stage as they went missing under one spotlight and reappeared under another. This illusion went on for several seconds until both spotlights found both boys at the same time and remained on, illuminating the two.

The audience came together in loud applause. Then, one of the spotlights snapped off, leaving RyN2 standing in his long coat. Zar made a grand gesture toward the android.

"So be it."

At that moment, one of the lobby doors swung open. A man entered the theater in a rush. He ran down the aisle toward Carter's section and looked through the crowd until he spotted the CEO. He shimmied his way through the row all the way to the empty seat next to Wardlow, then whispered in Carter's ear as the lights dimmed on the stage.

The glow from the electrical charge hitting the xurbium turned a bright red-orange.

Carter was listening to Neumann, his security officer, tell him that Jack Kutter's body was at the morgue and was about to be autopsied. There was an incident, and local law enforcement were treating it as a homicide.

Wardlow's demeanor changed. He was furious. Kutter was supposed to be with him at the show. Jack had agreed to go after Ryan if he stepped through the time jump apparatus and to stay close to him, but now there was no one who was trustworthy or capable enough.

Wardlow tried to convince Neumann to take Jack's place, but he wasn't going for it. He argued that he'd lose all credibility if he left his boss vulnerable. He was so nervous, he brought up his contract, specifically citing his main directive to protect the CEO at all costs.

Carter was losing his composure.

Meanwhile, the theater was buzzing with excitement.

The stage was dark and the apparatus was alive, glowing and shooting electricity around the ring, throwing off beautiful colors in the charges jumping around the xurbium plates.

A surge of ocean water came spraying through. The smell of the beach was in the air again. There was a lot of anticipation, but there wasn't a soul in the theater ready for what happened next.

A seagull broke through the void. It had been skimming the surface of the ocean. Its loud screeches terrified the patrons as it flew just above the their heads at a high rate of speed.

They especially weren't prepared when it crashed into the back wall behind the seats. While the bird was being tended to, Zar calmed the audience.

The seagull's appearance had placed the entire room in a state of wonder. No one could explain what was happening.

Theater attendants were looking after the gull. The crowd became fixed on RyN2 as he stood waiting for his cue from Zar.

Then it came, what the crowd had been waiting for. The countdown.

Zar raised his right arm and began.

"10!"

Carter stood in front of his seat. He was in a panic, unable to think clearly. Then, slowly, little by little, the entire audience was on their feet and joining in the count.

"9!"

Mel and Mia ran out onto the stage.

"8!"

The girls pulled the long coat from RyN2.

"7!"

Each brushed a hand on him, then simultaneously kissed a side of his cheek.

"6!"

Mia and Mel exited the stage.

"5!"

Ryan was still standing on the opposite side of the stage of RyN2, in the dark.

"4!"

The volume of the crowd's participation grew louder.

"3!"

The electrical charges racing around the large ring let off a cracking sound.

"2!"

The light surrounding the unit changed hue, to a warmer, more comforting color similar to a sunset.

"1!"

Zar dropped his arm. RyN2 turned and ran toward the center of the ring and leapt through, into the void. It happened so fast, the crowd was feeling as if there was something they had missed.

Then, to everyone's surprise, Ryan followed.

He looked over at Mel, who was standing stage right, winked, and dove through the center of the apparatus into the gelatinous void, disappearing along with his doppelgänger.

There was an amplified gasp in the theater.

Zar knelt, then lowered his head as if he was willing Claire's return.

A third wave came blowing through the void, splashing more ocean water on the stage. This time, bringing a clump of seaweed with it.

Down in front, Carter was pushing his way toward the aisle, stepping on everyone's feet in his row. He reached the red carpet and turned toward the stage. The CEO rushed up the stairs and ran toward the glowing ring.

Zar never lifted his head, but he knew what was happening.

Even Clarence knew there would be someone in the audience who couldn't help themselves. The owner was prepared at all costs to protect the show and the theater's credibility.

No one attempted to stop Carter Wardlow as he ran directly into the void. But, unfortunately for him, he just flopped on the floor on the other side of the ring, lying there stunned, annoyed, and exhausted from imagining all he might have gained. The man was carried off stage by three of the Swillow security detail. Neumann, now adding embarrassment to his list, followed closely behind to ensure the thugs weren't too harsh on his boss.

~

Ryan was drowning, feeling sick to his stomach from the jump and struggling underwater, not knowing which way was up until he caught the sunlight fracturing through the surface.

The ocean was much warmer than Ryan had remembered it being on his family vacation, giving him the feeling he was floating in some sort of sensory deprivation tank.

He twisted his body and thrust upward, grabbing as much fresh air as he could the second he breached the waterline.

Where's the android? Where the hell is he? Ryan didn't waste a moment. He spun around, dropping his head below the surface, and his eyes burning in the saltwater, searching.

Smuggler's Cove's shoreline was behind him, with the rustic cabins set back in the trees. The pier was off a little to his right.

And there was RyN2, moving away from him. He appeared to be struggling with his buoyancy, his arms breaking the surface, the current pulling him toward the pier.

Ryan looked for Claire, scanning back and forth. The water was playing tricks with the reflections and small puffs of white foam, a piece of driftwood, and floating seaweed. The waves were a little choppy, making it hard to determine whether she'd already been pulled out to sea. *Was he late?* After struggling with his visibility on the water, he turned, out of frustration, toward the beach. There she was. She hadn't gotten in the water yet. Claire was unfolding her beach towel and preparing to lay out for a moment. Which meant that Ryan had some time.

He swam toward RyN2, cutting through the small waves while growing more and more concerned. It wasn't about the android, who was fighting to stay afloat. It wasn't Claire he was worried about, either. It was Mel.

They'd planned carefully at the Westbrook house. With Victor's keycard, they'd accessed his computers and the incredible system Victor created - opening up a vast array of options. The power in Ryan's hands was beyond anything he'd ever felt with his stunts. During that moment, while commanding the keyboard, he experienced the ability to end a life, to shut down the android with one command of the mouse. Victor had installed a fail-safe, just to be sure. If the android ever started creating problems, or opposed his mission, it wouldn't take anything more than activating the fail-safe.

Mel and Ryan had timed it to perfection. The second RyN2 was to go through the porthole on stage, Mel would access a remote switch on her mobile that would trigger the switch and cut off the 'droid. *But what had happened? Was she too late?*

Ryan was almost to RyN2 when the android saw him. There was tension in his voice.

"Nice try, Ryan. You didn't think I would know what you were up to? If I go, you're coming with me."

Ryan made it to the android, who had just placed his arms on him and started to pull him under. *Shit. I'm not prepared for this.*

Ryan struggled to keep his shoulders above water, kicking his feet outward to thrust upward.

"You're a robot. A goddamn robot."

"I can be relevant, too."

"You are! You're a tool. You served your purpose. I don't need you anymore."

A set of waves came pushing in, making it harder for the android to keep a good grip on Ryan, whose shirt was waterlogged and slipping in his fingers.

There was some desperation in Ryan's voice.

"I shut you down!"

"I accessed the root kit and did some rewriting of the code."

"There's no way you could alter the fail-safe. No way!"

"I didn't have to alter it much; I just bought a little more time."

"How much?"

RyN2 knew he was gaining the upper hand and decided to dig a knife in.

"I've been here before, so it only makes sense that I carry on. Not you."

"What?"

Ryan was floored. *What the hell was he talking about? He'd already been here before?*

The two began to fight harder. RyN2's grip was starting to crush the young man. He couldn't stay afloat any longer. The android yanked him under just as he was about to tell Ryan how much lag he'd added to the code.

His words came out in bubbles.

"grble … bribl … grible … rabbl …"

Ryan hadn't taken in a deep enough breath before he was pulled under. He was doing everything he could to hold on. He hadn't practiced with his breath in years, so that was off the table. There was no way he was going to break any records today.

The young magician was losing out. He couldn't hold his breath any longer. Kicking and flailing didn't do anything but burn more energy. With the firm grip RyN2 had on him, the two were sinking. *Screw it,* Ryan thought. I'm done. He was beginning to feel that odd sensation he'd felt when he'd prepped years ago, that dizzy feeling, the lack of oxygen, the beginning of death.

So, he gave RyN2 a few choice words before it was too late, expelling the last of his reserves.

"Fuggle … yububu … bububu …"

At that moment, RyN2 shut down like he'd received a head shot from a .45 caliber. The android's grip loosened and his body began to float upward, slowly creeping toward the sunlight. Ryan thrust his arms out, kicked hard, and broke the waterline. He waited for his doppelgänger to hit the surface, then turned, checking his surroundings.

Ryan was under the pier, about five yards away from where he'd dangled himself upside down four years ago, choking on the waves to impress Mel and his audience.

He didn't need more than a few seconds to figure it out.

He grabbed RyN2 by the hair and dove underwater, pulling the body toward the old safe and struggling to keep him down. The android must have had some air trapped inside, and was slowly creeping back upward when he let loose of his grip. But that didn't stop him. Ryan used both hands and pushed on, reaching the safe. He brushed away the sand around its base, revealing the rusty chain that had been submerged with the antique, and wrapped RyN2's ankle.

It was a surreal moment.

Ryan watched himself slowly fade into the murky blue water, looking back at RyN2 several times as he resurfaced, but what was even more dreamlike was seeing himself at the water's edge, his head bleeding and wearing his top hat. The little boy behind him with his mother, sitting aloof, reading. He was watching himself step into the ocean, dazed, and then saw his body disappear before it fully submerged.

It was as if consciousness held the power to dismantle the building blocks of life.

As miraculous as it was, Ryan had no time left. Contemplation was off the table. Claire was out in the water, swimming. This was all he had to understand.

He didn't feel the temperature of the ocean, or the sting of the saltwater. Ryan had unlimited amounts of oxygen and adrenalin guiding him through the water as he fought the ebb and flow.

Ryan had a line on Claire. He could see the patterned swimsuit showing itself between the small ripples that were intermittently cutting her out of sight.

Then the powerful pull of a tide tugged him off his line. It was happening, the rips were coming. He managed to stay on the surface, skimming over the top of the first swell, picking up speed as he got closer to Claire. Ryan was yelling, "Mom! Mom! Over here!"

Claire heard Ryan, and in an instant, her demeanor shifted from pure enjoyment to fear. She could see the panic in Ryan, and started to swim toward him. A larger riptide formed.

The two were only a few feet apart. Ryan's hand was out, reaching.

Claire held out her hand, then she felt it for the first time. The ocean grabbed ahold of her and then both of them, forcing them closer until their hands locked.

Claire was worried, yet unusually calm. As they were being pulled faster, she said, "What's happening?"

Once Ryan had ahold of Claire, he lost his breath, choking as he spoke.

"It's out here somewhere."

He was turning round and round, the two pushing further out, still holding on tight to his mother's hand. Ryan was searching for the hazy field, the void. *Where was the other side of the ring?*

"What's out here?"

Claire was beginning to sink. She couldn't fight the tide's draw. The more she tried to stay on the surface, the further she was pulled under.

They were in the heart of the rip.

"I'll find it."

"What are you—"

Claire went under. Ryan was pulled with her.

The two were tumbling just under the surface, losing their breaths. It was becoming difficult for them to hold on to each other. Claire had read about riptides and the techniques for staying afloat, but she wasn't going to let go, not while she was conscious.

Ryan was struggling even more than Claire. He knew what was waiting on the other side, but *where was it?*

The water in the center of the riptide turned a frothy white color. Claire and Ryan bobbed to the surface for just a few seconds, just enough to take in a chest full of fresh air, before they were drawn under again.

Ryan had his free arm out. He was looking hard and fast, in those seconds. There was too much confusion and frustration and an overwhelming sensation of helplessness. The ocean was God, and it was making up its mind.

Ryan got tugged down. Claire was on top of him, then she wasn't. He was on top of her and they were spinning, lost.

A funny feeling came over Ryan as he began to feel that sensation again, the one where he was losing his connection to reality. Lightheaded, hazy, the loss of oxygen to the brain …

Ryan relaxed. There was nothing left that he could do but hold onto Claire. He let go of all the thoughts, the panic. Then he saw it. A blurry field like a bubble of clear oil. The water was thick.

Then a hand was there, an arm, reaching into the water. A sudden calm patch. *Were they out of the rip?* No, this was the arm he saw four years ago, reaching in as he disappeared. It was an illusion. It was only his mind playing tricks.

~

The audience was restless, stirring. A few of the patrons were heckling, entertaining themselves. One man yelled, "How much longer is this gonna take?"

Zar stood from his kneeling position at the edge of the stage. He paid no attention to the people but walked over to the ring, stuck his arm through, and pulled Claire out onto the stage floor.

There was Ryan's mother, on her knees, choking up ocean water in her Mondrian patterned swimsuit, just as they had seen in the family video. The audience lost their breath. Every living soul in the theater was flabbergasted except Clarence, who was slouched in his seat eight rows back on the edge of the third section, asleep.

In the lobby, Carter was being escorted toward the exit. The six men surrounding him, along with Neumann, heard the commotion in the theater.

There was some arguing and then a little haggling and an offer from Carter to donate a large chunk of money to the Swillows, before they let him loose.

The CEO ran back to the theater doors and pushed inside to see Claire standing next to Zar. She'd been wrapped in a large towel and was in front of the microphone, center stage. Her voice was soft.

"Where's my son? Where's Ryan?"

Zar raised his hands up high over his head and clapped. The metrome shut off and the ring of energy, the void - the red-orange charge - it all went away. There was nothing left on stage but a prop.

Mel and Mia stepped out from behind the curtains, and the lights came on.

Zar spoke. "We'll never know when it comes for us. We'll never know which door will lead us into or out of it. I say, let's ask time."

Ryan burst out from the lobby door opposite the aisle Carter was standing in. He was soaking wet, still dripping ocean water. The crowd stood again. They roared in a cheer that could be heard out in the parking lot.

He ran down to the stage and jumped up. Mel put his long coat on. Mia placed his top hat on his head. They each kissed a cheek. Claire was in shock.

Ryan walked up to his mother and gave her a hug.

The spotlight faded.

46

Zarwid the Great, Episode #1

Tommy was angry. He and his attorney had been sitting in a holding room, questioned over and over about the warehouse, Jimmy, and the missing van. His attorneys advised him to just keep his mouth shut. *They don't have a damn thing on you. They're fishing.*

But Tommy wanted to go home and knew if he dumped out some chum, Sloan would bite and leave him alone.

"The guy you're looking for—"

Doyle, his attorney, snapped, "Tommy."

Swillow was going to show everyone who was boss. He tapped Doyle. "Stand down." Then, he glared at Agent Sloan. He let a little air in between his words. "I know who killed Vito."

The agent was hoping for this. He knew he didn't have enough for the DA to hold Tommy for much longer. They didn't want to screw up the opportunity to build a case on his organization over some scraps that weren't going to bear any fruit.

"Who?"

"I don't know his name. He's one of Carter Wardlow's, though. I know that."

Doyle jumped in.

"Don't say another fuckin' word, or I can't rep you anymore. Let me do my goddamn job, will ya?"

Tommy wasn't going to give anymore. He got the response from Sloan's baited look that he was hoping for.

"You're right. I don't have anything more to say."

Sloan looked at Tommy, then to Doyle.

"Indulge me one last—"

Doyle was lagging behind Tommy and Agent Sloan as they walked down the hallway. He was on the phone to Noelle. She was worried Tommy wasn't being offered the opportunity to eat something healthy.

Agent Sloan opened the door leading into the detective bureau. Marcia, one of Chimera PD's best, had an image of Carter up on her screen. Sloan gestured to the picture of the CEO.

"Him?"

Tommy laughed.

"Noooo. It wasn't Carter. He doesn't even push a pencil. He's a politician. A phone call guy."

The agent took a good look at Tommy's expression. He knew Carter didn't get his hands wet, but he wanted to see if Tommy was hiding something. Of course, The Tank didn't like his gaze.

"What are you looking at me like that for?"

Sloan offered only a gesture, pulling the group out of the bureau.

"Follow me. Just one more quick trip. Then, we're done."

Doyle was pretending to be annoyed, but he enjoyed every minute of the fight. Noelle had texted him and worked in her health concern since Tommy hung up.

"I hope this doesn't take too much longer. My client has got to get some decent food in him. Substantial, not fast food. I don't want his blood sugar levels to get too low."

Tommy chuckled.

"Yeah, otherwise I'll turn into a real asshole."

The car ride was short.

The men shared a few jokes on the way to the morgue. Sloan learned about Vito's sub sandwiches and why the locals missed them. They were getting hungry talking about the choices they used to have. Everything was fine until Tommy caught a wave of formaldehyde. He hated the smell.

Sloan met the coroner, signed them in, then marched Tommy into the back room. The coroner didn't speak. He checked his log, then stepped over to the correct drawer, opened the freezer, and slid out the body tray. The men huddled. Tommy turned to the agent.

"That's him."

"I figured."

"How'd you figure?"

"Because that's the only John Doe. So, I figured. Look at his hands. The tattoos. His skin and build. He's a spook. There's nothing in the database. No facial rec, no fingerprint matches. No ID. Not even the tattoo is on record. The guy's a ghost."

"There's got to be something."

"Oh, we got fibers linking him to the Claypool body. I've got two murders solved by Mr. Doe. But I've also got a lot more questions left open because of him. There may even be a third body. I'm not sure yet."

Doyle was thinking out loud.

"Any idea who killed him?"

"How do you know he was killed?"

"We're in a morgue. You said, John Doe. If it's not murder, then what are we talking here?"

Sloan smiled.

"I'm kidding, it was a line from a movie."

"So, any idea who did it?"

Sloan was wasting time, and there was nothing that eroded The Tank's patience more than the opposing team engaging in small talk.

Tommy turned and started walking to the exit, explaining to his attorney,

"Probably another John Doe."

Doyle stood with Tommy at the door, gazing at the agent, inquiring. Sloan gave them the signal. *You can go.*

"Just one last thing though, Tommy. I've been assigned to the Isabella case. The paintings?" Tommy was out the door before Sloan could finish. "Just so you know—"

~

Sheriff Robert McGlinty was out in the parking lot of the Chimera Theater, waiting for his suspect to exit. On the passenger seat of his cruiser were Claypool's sketches. He'd done his diligence. There was only one more person he needed to look in on - the tall, unassuming man no one would ever expect to be an android, seated a row behind Carter, pretending he was enjoying himself.

When Mayor Caldwell exited, Bob started his car. He watched his target shake hands with locals, standing under the marquee and ingratiating himself with the very same people he was about to start siphoning money from for funds he'd use to further Wardlow Technologies endeavors both locally and nationally.

KCLT was out front of the theater, pooling sound bites from the excited locals.

Carter exited and breezed up to the Mayor, shaking his hand for a quick photo, calm and collected as if nothing odd had happened inside. The CEO gave his best front page expression with Neumann by his side, keeping the unknown photographers at a distance. No one in the press knew the extent of what happened inside the theater, yet. The media had been held back in the lot in order to maintain the exclusivity of the event. Ryan and Clarence were smart. They were going to let the people of Chimera be the soundboard of the experience.

The mayor was escorted into his SUV by two security agents, replacements for the earlier models, which made McGlinty curious. *Did Carter give them a military upgrade? Or was he still lagging without Victor working on the project?*

When the SUV exited the lot, the sheriff followed. Without trying to conceal himself, he stuck close as the mayor turned onto Ocean Way Avenue.

Ocean Way was a strip of valuable real estate along the beachfront, developed by the same construction team that built Wardlow Technologies dynamic underground facility. Carter was on the board, so they kept a few choice condominiums available for anyone they wanted to soften up. *Who wouldn't take the bait?* It was a five-star view only minutes away from Chimera City Center, filled with local government, businesses, and the best eateries.

Bowman was waiting in his unmarked car, parked across from the mayor's condo with two new deputies in the backseat. After McGlinty's communications with Sloan and a few others in the FBI, the department acquired a couple heavyweights just released from a stint overseas as mercs. Ex-Special Forces would surely help even the muscle.

Caldwell stood at his doorstep while his security detail walked through the unit and looped the property. The men secured the mayor inside, then drove off.

McGlinty walked over to Bowman who had his window rolled down.

"Feel like having a little fun?"

Bowman leaned his head back, passing the question on with a look. The mercenaries in the back seat exited the car.

"How do you wanna play this?"

Bowman followed as he moved to the trunk and opened a pelican case, revealing a handheld EMP device.

"Pretty slick little piece of tech."

McGlinty had the plan.

"We'll jam all the communications to and from the condo, then move in." He looked at the mercs. "You two, let's be fast and clean."

The younger of the mercs took the EMP device from Bowman, adjusted the settings, shook McGlinty's hand with a firm grip, then, with all sincerity, said,

"Do we have to be clean?"

~

Claire was ushered back to the Westbrook house where a small team of doctors were waiting. Christopher Amato, Esq. had arranged for her to be checked out thoroughly while the catering company, *Eve Edibles*, set up a variety of food and beverages for an intimate party.

Mr. Amato had also hired a security company and paid the city for cones and blockades. He wanted to keep all the media at a distance until Claire and Ryan were ready to make a statement.

Zar was out on the patio with Mia. She was easing her way into talking about RyN2. The tone of her voice was gentle, affected by the loss of the android, yet sincere in her desire to understand.

"I mean, he's not really gone, is he?"

Zar stood out like the golden sarcophagus of Tutankhamen, with his stature and vintage outfit.

"No. He's just been decommissioned."

"Okay, that's a fucked up way to put it. He's so much more than an object, or a tool, whatever that means, and he meant something to me."

"I understand how you feel. I'm actually able to process the kind of gut reaction you're experiencing, but the Ryan you got acquainted with, he wasn't evolved enough to handle the level and complexity of real human feelings, and—"

"He was so real, though. I actually fantasized about—" She turned away just for a second. "Can you process that?"

"Ryan's in the other room. The human Ryan. The Ryan with all the idiosyncrasies of having blood pumping through his veins, a mind, the great mystery, the Ryan with the ability to procreate. As opposed to a synthetic likeness with a plasma-like substance—"

"I get it. I'm just letting it all out. It's gotta go somewhere. All this stuff inside me. You have to admit I'm in a weird spot here. And, weird isn't even the word. I only had one choice at the time."

Melanie walked out, carrying Ryan's top hat in one hand and a drink in the other. When Mia noticed her, she hesitated. She didn't want the Swillow girl to think she'd planned to confront her.

Mia smiled, gesturing.

"It's okay."

Mel approached, handed Mia a spiked punch, then threw a funny look at Zar, because there was nothing to offer him. She watched Mia's eyes move to the hat and give it a hard look. Mel's tone was pacifying.

"I didn't want to wear the hat. I mean, I wanted to wear it, but I didn't because I didn't want you to think I was some kind of bitch out to claim Ryan all to myself."

Mia took a sip of the punch, then matched Mel's tone.

"Are you?"

Mel wasn't ready for it.

"A bitch?"

Mia kept it soft. "No. I meant, are you claiming him?"

Before Mel could respond, Mia reached her hand out, as if to accept the hat. "Could I?"

Mel cut her off. "Ryan's upstairs in the room with the doctors *and Claire.* They'll be down any second. Don't you think we should be ready for them?"

Upstairs in the master bedroom, a modern open space with minimal furniture, doctors were prodding Claire, who was sitting on the edge of Victor's bed showing signs of exhaustion, more than anything. Ryan stood at the window looking down on Mel and Mia. He could tell they were having a difficult time.

Mr. Amato was on the phone with KCLT. They were making a lucrative offer for an exclusive with Claire and Ryan. Claire was listening to the attorney haggle with the business affairs at the station as her agitation grew over their lack of concern for the family's privacy. She pushed off the doctors, stood up, and went to Ryan, who turned from the window. They embraced.

Claire shook her head in disbelief. Ryan matched her look.

"Can you believe it? Dad, it's all because of him. You married the most loving, smartest, most determined weirdo on the planet. And then there's me, a son who—"

"Is the most—"

"Don't!" Ryan pulled himself away from her as pleasantly as he could. "Don't lie. This is what drove me nuts. Just don't pander, please. I'm not what you say. You always talked so highly of me. *I left you and Dad*. And when I heard you had drown, it drove me further away. That's lame. I have problems. Real problems."

Claire understood.

"No, you don't. You're here. Look, Ryan, we all have crap to deal with. You're my son. You're what I've got, and I'm not gonna let you walk away again. You're just like your father, in your own way. Don't be so hard on yourself. You're both—"

The doctors tried to interrupt Claire. They weren't finished. "Get away from me." She stepped over to Mr. Amato and shook his arm. "Get them out of here. I'm fine. No more prodding. And get off the phone with those parasites."

Claire raised her voice.

"It's family time! We're going downstairs. We have guests. It's time to celebrate. Everybody out."

Ryan was happy to see Claire take control. He couldn't express himself anymore than he had.

~

As they descended the staircase and moved into the living room, Zar could be seen, standing proud and frozen like a statue in time, holding the metrome in his hand. He was in the middle of the living room with Mel and Mia next to him. The girls were confused.

Ryan had gone into the lab and shut down Zar, then ran back to the living room, carrying a grin.

Claire was staring at Zar. "I still can't believe this, he's so real."

Ryan laughed.

"You want me to activate him? He's actually really cool. In fact, he should be here with us to celebrate."

"No. I'm not ready for that. Let me settle into this a little before we decide."

Mel and Mia gave Claire a friendly hug and offered to get her something to eat or drink. The three walked into the kitchen. The layout was open and inviting. There was no wall separating the two rooms.

Ryan sat on the edge of the couch and watched the three women interact. Clarence and Carlos were laughing at Ryan. They knew the predicament he was in. They weren't laughing at him, they were laughing at how they would love to have two beautiful women that close to them. Carlos leaned over the couch.

"Good problems, bro. Good problems to have."

Just down the street, at the barricade, Jimmy was arguing with the security man.

"My sister is in there. You've got to let me through."

The security guard was built like a rhino. He raised his hand.

"No. I don't have to let you through, and I don't want to ask you again. If you attempt to pass, I'll use force and remove you, permanently. *Understand?*"

Jimmy stood his ground.

"Look, man, my sister isn't answering her phone, and she's in there. I know it. It's an emergency. Can you pass on a message for me?"

"If it's an emergency—"

"Dude, it's an emergency."

"What is it?"

"Tell Mrs. Westbrook that Jimmy Swillow says—"

"Hold it. You're Jimmy?"

"Yeah, man."

"Shit. Why didn't you say so?"

"I just did."

"I can't let you in. But, I can radio up to the house."

"Okay. Tell Mrs. Westbrook that Jimmy, that I'm—"

A limousine with smoked glass windows drove up behind the security guard and stopped at the barricade. The security officer told Jimmy he was going to have to step back, along with a group of freelance photographers, who were on standby communicating with their affiliate, who was out in a speed boat using a long lens, grabbing grainy images of the party from a hundred yards out.

The limo passed the barricade, cut through the crowd, drove into the City Center, and entered the Chimera Hospital's Intensive Care Unit parking lot. The car pulled up to the main entrance, stopping at the painted walkway leading through the double doors. One by one, Ryan, Claire, Mia and Mel and then, finally, Mr. Amato, exited the car.

A hospital administrator waiting inside the lobby shared a few words with Mr. Amato to not to worry about visiting hours. She'd cleared it with the unit and the doctor was on his way with encouraging news about Victor.

Claire was the first to enter his room. She pulled a chair close to the bed and wrapped both hands around Victor's right hand. Ryan stood in the doorway, looking on and giving her a moment.

Outside the room, the nurses were curious about Claire. They were confused and intrigued at the same time. They were hovering, making Mia and Mel, who were out in the hallway, uncomfortable. The town was buzzing with stories about Claire being brought back from the dead. Fringe religious organizations were spreading rumors of satanic rituals and other occult nonsense. Some were saying Claire was a *Plastic*.

The room was quiet, except for the sounds coming from the life support system. Claire looked over to see Victor's vitals bouncing along on the monitor, then glanced at Ryan.

"Come on in."

Ryan took a few steps closer. It was hard for him to see his father, now that Claire was back. He was personalizing the attack and blaming himself, inside.

Claire removed her hand from Victor's to wave Ryan to come closer. "Come." When she did this, Victor's hand visibly moved. It was more than a twitch. Ryan saw this and immediately interpreted it as a sign he was trying to tell her not to let go.

"Did you see that?"

"What?"

"Dad moved his hand. He was reaching for you when you let go."

Dr. Reinhardt was in the doorway. She knocked, to be polite, before taking a step inside.

"I'm Dr. Reinhardt. I've been looking after Victor."

Claire was waiting for the her to continue.

"Yes? And—"

Doc Reinhardt's demeanor was matter-of-fact.

"Good news. His brain has returned to what we call normal. Now, let me explain what that means. The brain sends out signals. There are ones that show a healthy brain and a very specific one that shows us a brain that has suffered trauma."

Claire was listening to every word. "Okay."

"When Victor arrived, his brain showed signs of severe trauma, so we induced a coma to protect him, to allow his brain time to heal itself. What I'm saying is that, as far as we can tell, as of four hours ago, his brain has returned to a normal pattern of activity, and we can safely pull him out."

Claire had a tear running down her cheek. She turned to draw support from Ryan, but he was gone. Claire stood up, rubbed Victor's hand, and walked to the hallway. She looked over at Mel and Mia, who were talking two doors down, just outside a patient's room that was closed.

"Have you seen Ryan?"

The young women were confused.

"No. I thought he was with you."

"He was. Are you sure?" Claire was beginning to worry.

Mel started to feel it in her stomach. "Oh, no. Not again."

Mia was a bit aloof. She hadn't experienced the muscle memory loss. "What's going on? I don't understand."

Dr. Reinhardt had a personal agenda and asked, "You're Claire, right?"

"Yes."

"Would you indulge me? Professional curiosity—"

"Indulge you? I'm sorry?"

"We're all excited to meet Victor. We're going to wake him in a few hours. I was just wondering. I read all about the show, and—"

Claire walked away from the doctor and pushed through the doors to the waiting area. No Ryan. She came back to the room. Mel was in the men's bathroom, looking under the stall doors. She returned, cast an empty look at Claire and raised her arms. She was at a loss.

Mia realized what was happening. "What can I do to help?"

No one had anything to say.

Dr. Reinhardt seized the moment and apologized to Claire. She passed on all the important information regarding the time the panel was scheduled for Victor to be revived. She handed Claire her business card, then shook her hand. It was a moment that lasted a lot longer than Claire was comfortable with. The doctor was seeing if she was indeed human, feeling her flesh, attempting to get a pulse. Then, before she was called out, she released her hand and walked off as if her actions were mechanical.

"We'll see you in a few hours."

Claire spun around, checking both ends of the hallway. Mia was on her phone, texting. Mel tried to reach Ryan, as well.

"I'm not sure what to do." Then, Mel saw it. "Oh my god!"

Ryan's hat was sitting on the empty chair in Victor's room. Claire was spooked by the tone of her voice, and was confused.

"What's wrong? What is it, Melanie?"

"His hat, it's what happened the last time when he disappeared. It was just sitting there in the sand, like it's sitting there."

Mia put her phone away. "You're freaking me out."

Claire looked at Melanie.

"What's happening?"

Before Mel could piece together a sentence, Ryan came around the corner. He walked up to his mother and the girls. He could feel the suffering and read the horror on their faces. He knew what they'd just gone through, but didn't want to play into it, or make it worse. He stopped just outside the room, held up the recycled coffee holder with four hot coffees fixed in their holders, and looked at Melanie.

"What?"

~

Eight hours later, and just down the street, Scarecrow was outside the pawn-shop, cleaning the display window. Moe was inside, unpacking a box he'd received a day earlier and laying the items out on the counter one by one after a quick inspection. He wasn't showing interest in any of them, yet. An old 4x5 camera, an antique etched ashtray, a cracked Bambi figurine, theater binoculars, some newspapers, and then the last item ... in a vinyl comic book sleeve.

Moe slipped the book out. It was a first edition of *Zarwid the Great*.

Moe checked the database to be sure. Everything matched up but the artwork. It was an illustration of RyN2, floating underwater, his ankle chained to the old safe, with his eyes wide open.